SHATTERED
Secrets
BETWEEN
Us

THE WILLOW GROVE SERIES
ANGELA VAN LIEMPT

First paperback edition October 2025

Cover design by Gigi of Gigi Creatives at https://www.instagram.com/heygigicreatives/

Chapter heading illustrations, and skull tattoo art by Whitney Law of New Ink Book Services https://www.instagram.com/newinkbookservices/

Character art of Frankie & Rhett by Anastasia of https://www.instagram.com/mirolu bova_art/?hl=en

Editing by Kayla Ramoutar

Formatting by Angela van Liempt

ISBN 978-1-0694701-1-9 (Paperback)

ISBN 978-1-0694701-0-2 (E-book)

ISBN 978-1-0694701-2-6 (Hardcover)

Published by Dawn Publishing

www.dawn-publishing.com

INTENDED FOR MATURE AUDIENCES

This book is an adult romantic suspense and contains mature themes and content that could be triggering for some readers. For more information, please visit:

https://www.dawn-publishing.com/romanticsuspense

For readers who understand it's never just a book... And for Roman who patiently listened to me talk endlessly about this one.

Prologue - Rhett

Boston. The end of Everett Morrigan

The boat had arrived on schedule and unloaded, departing a few minutes after midnight as planned. I never missed a detail. My father had trained me too well for errors. But this time, I wasn't running a job, I was ending the version of myself I hated.

Months of lies, betrayal, and deceit came down to an elaborate takedown of a network I'd helped build. If it worked, I was out. But if it didn't, I'd go down with them.

Fluorescent lights buzzed overhead as I moved through the warehouse, casting shadows over crates of engine parts, concealing guns beneath counterfeit money. This was the same place I'd walked in on one of my father's prospects arguing with a new dockworker just over a year ago. The new dockworker was Finn Roscoe, a cop, deep undercover, caught in his own personal hell the moment he found his brother tangled in the case he was investigating.

My family's business.

I was done with people falling in line because of my last name. Done carrying the weight of a legacy with blood on my hands, like

1

it was the only thing that made me matter. And I had promised my sister that her son wouldn't have to grow up believing this life was worth inheriting. Roscoe offered me a way out. I became his informant, and I fucking hated it.

My breaths fogged in the air, steady and focused as I texted Roscoe on my burner.

All set.

He'd better not betray my trust, not now, not after I'd held up my end of the deal.

The heavy metal door creaked open, shutting with a dull thud, and slow footsteps echoed off the walls. Teams were positioned somewhere nearby, but it was too soon for them to breach the door. I stood in silence, waiting with my gun drawn. Faint red lights glowed from the cameras hidden among the stacked crates as I slid between them.

No one should be here yet.

A man stopped, brushing snow off his jacket. "Where are you, Everett? It's just me." His eyes, glossy with dilated pupils, widened as I approached, and he flipped his ball cap backward.

"You're high. Get the fuck out of here, Miles," I said, scanning over his shoulder. Roscoe's brother wasn't part of the plan.

"I'm the reason Finn's here, I won't let him risk his life for mine."

I snatched the hat off his head, flipping it around so the visor hung over his eyes. "Turn around and go home, I won't ask again."

"This isn't just business anymore, he's my brother—"

"Who's gonna bury you if you stay, is that what you want?" I moved closer, staring down at his face. He looked younger than twenty-four, a fucking college dropout, throwing his life away. He'd gotten in too deep, working both sides, and if one didn't kill him, the other sure as fuck would. I checked my phone, but Roscoe hadn't responded. "They know. If you stay, you're dead, and I can't let that happen." I grabbed Miles by the back of his neck, forcing him to leave, but he resisted, breaking free.

"They threatened to go after my sister, I had to tell them... How did they know about her?"

Engines rumbled and silenced. Doors slammed.

They were here.

This time, I dragged him by his jacket toward the back door, throwing it open with my elbow. Snow blew inside the warehouse as I shoved him outside. "Fucking go, man. Get out of here!"

"What about Finn? I can't leave—"

"You can, and you *will*."

Thunderous footsteps entered the front of the building, followed by a loud crash. I needed to close the deal, recording everything on surveillance before Roscoe could get his teams in here. Shielding Miles, I blocked the doorway with my back to him, but he rushed inside, darting past me. I grabbed his jacket, holding him back as two groups of armed men strode into the warehouse. The double doors swung open behind them like a dare to leave. Lines of suspicion and betrayal etched onto the faces of my father's loyal partners as they glared at me.

"Stay behind me." My gaze locked on Jake Noble, a boss's son, as I spoke to Miles through clenched teeth.

"It's all here, let's get this done," I said.

"You were supposed to be alone." Jake stalked closer to me, aiming his gun at Miles. "Why isn't he dead yet?" He called over his shoulder, not dropping the gun and I stepped aside, taking Miles with me. Jake couldn't be much older than Miles, but he was unpredictable, killing for fucked-up satisfaction.

Miles lunged forward, and the mechanical clicks of guns bounced off the steel walls. My instincts begged me to move, but I stepped between him and the barrels like I was chasing a death wish as he shouted. "What about you, Jake? Do they know you're a fucking liar?"

"Morrigan, take care of him." My father's enforcer ordered someone I didn't recognize to pry open a crate, turning his attention back on me. "Tonight." He raised his eyebrows as he stared at me.

I nodded as Miles paced behind me, but I didn't let my guard down or turn my back on the outnumbered threats surrounding us. If the deal fell apart, we'd both be dead.

Jake gave orders and trucks backed up near the doors, snow whipping sideways under the harsh glare of floodlights.

Standing beside me, Miles turned his hat around again and crossed his arms as men trained their guns on us. Each crew worked fast and methodical in silence, uneasy allies for this one big score as they emptied the crates of weapons and cash. Miles fidgeted next to me and his jaw opened, like he was going to say something.

"Not one word," I said, and he snapped his mouth shut.

"You can't kill me," he whispered.

Keeping him alive required him to follow orders. I grabbed him by the throat, bringing my face inches from his ear, and pointed my gun at him. "Don't move, don't speak, or we both die, got it?"

His pulse raced underneath my fingertips, and I eased my grip on him as his eyes met mine. He swallowed, his voice rasping as he spoke. "Got it."

Letting him go, I kept him behind my back with a hand on his arm as my phone vibrated inside my coat pocket. They were coming.

Shadows shifted outside. One of the men opened a crate and fumbled with a sealed package. As it hit the floor, gunshots exploded, and I yanked Miles to the ground. Chaos tore through the warehouse as police shouted and bullets sprayed against metal. The exit sign at the back of the building was a beacon, and I scrambled to my feet. "The door!"

Miles bolted for the door, but Jake stormed toward him, baring his teeth with eyes blazing. He raised his gun and fired as I took aim at him, pulling the trigger. The shot ripped through the noise of gunfire, slamming into Jake's shoulder. He staggered but didn't fall, and his eyes darted wildly from Miles to me, smiling as Miles jerked back with a choked gasp. He fought for air as blood soaked through his jeans.

More gunfire erupted, police barked orders, and Finn Roscoe sprinted toward me as I knelt beside Miles, bunching his sweater up and applying pressure to his gaping stomach wounds. "Stay with me, kid." But I'd been around long enough to know it was too late. I couldn't save him. No one could anymore.

Finn yelled orders on his radio. "Gunshot wound, code three..."

I held Miles's hand as his breathing rattled, and he gestured for me to lean closer. "The picture."

Slumping to his brother's side, Finn picked him up, holding Miles against him. "No, fucking hell, don't die..." He laid him down and hovered over him, pressing down on his bleeding wounds.

Jake charged toward us, pointing his gun at Finn, and I jumped up. A high-pitched ringing filled my ears as I focused on my target. Every sense in my body narrowed on the threat in front of me and the weight of the gun in my hand. I leveled my aim. My fingers squeezed the trigger. Once. Twice. This time, the fucker landed hard in a dead pile on the floor.

The ringing faded and sirens blared, growing louder.

"He's still breathing." Finn looked up at me. Blood coated his hands and clothes, but a flicker of hope lingered in his expression.

Crouching next to him, I couldn't say the words I knew to be true.

He's not surviving this.

I covered them both, scanning the warehouse as teams of police and SWAT secured the building, arresting the living and calling in a coroner for the dead. Medics arrived on the scene, loading Miles's lifeless body onto a stretcher.

Police followed me to my car, but Finn cut them off, vouching for me. "He gave us this case, he's under agreement. He's taking me to the hospital." Blood smeared pink in the snow as he dragged a shaky hand across the front of the car, clearing my windshield.

"You want to write me up, go for it. My brother's dying, I don't give a fuck what happens to me right now." Finn climbed into the passenger seat, not waiting for permission, and one of the officers hesitated, but gave me a nod.

I tailed the ambulance over frozen streets, sliding on the edge of control around turns. Sitting in the passenger seat, Finn's knee bounced, and he clenched his fists before scrubbing his palms against his jeans as though he could get rid of the blood or panic, or both. "What the fuck was Miles doing there?"

"I don't know."

"They knew he was working both sides, didn't they?"

"Yup," I said. There was nothing I could do to make this better. It was over, and I already had my escape out of Boston planned.

Finn's knee stopped moving, and he looked at me. "Is that all you've got to say? If he dies..."

"I tried to get him to leave, man. I fucking tried. We didn't get him out in time, he refused to give it up."

This world doesn't care who it takes. My father used Miles like he did me, like he does everyone.

I parked on a side street near Mass General, and we got out, breaking into a run as snow blended with the blood on my skin.

My mother had raised me, but she'd given me the Morrigan family name at birth, my father's last name. He had taken me in when Mom died. I was seventeen and desperate to belong, easy to ma-

7

nipulate. I'd fallen for his lies, and he'd convinced me that his way was the only way. It had taken years to learn the truth the hard way. Nash Morrigan was nothing more than a calculated businessman, operating on the edge of the law, and a cold-blooded killer.

The longer I stayed under his control, the more I risked becoming a man I despised. This life never made family or built loyalty. This world tore families apart, shattering lives.

Miles's sister was a trauma nurse working in Boston, and his roommate for the past couple of years. I didn't know her name, and until now, I'd never seen her. Of all nights to work, her shift had fallen on tonight.

I stood hidden off to the side as Finn rushed to her side. Between hyperventilating sobs, a raw, desperate scream escaped her as she clutched her brother's dead body on the stretcher. His blood soaked into her scrubs, staining her hands, matching Finn's. Matching my own.

I never wanted to witness that pain again.

Slipping away before she could ever lay eyes on me, I rushed toward the exit.

"Everett, wait!" Roscoe called. His footsteps thudded behind me, but I didn't turn around. I was running toward freedom on my own terms.

I burst through the doors into a blizzard, stepping in thick snow. A car sped by, sending slush over my jeans, and sirens wailed as I cut across Blossom toward my car.

Finn reached for the driver's side door as I sat in the seat. "Stay, testify—"

"It's over, Detective Roscoe. I'm done, no more wires, no more fucking police."

"They killed my brother, it's not fucking over." Finn wiped a bloody hand down his face, leaving streaks on his skin.

I started the car, and the wipers cleared snow from the windshield. I couldn't afford to let myself feel the hell he was going through. "You've got a family who needs you more than you need me. Let me go, you owe me that."

I'd given them more than enough evidence to put my father in jail. The question was for how long.

Finn's eyes watered, and he pressed his fingers to them. Dropping his hands, he gave me a hard look. "It should be me dead in there, not him."

"It almost was." I kept my voice calm and even. The need to put my plan into action, distancing myself from this city, consumed me.

As Finn hovered by the open door, snow lashed his face. "They'll kill you."

"They'll have to find me first."

"Right," Finn said. "Well, you know where to find me. You can trust me, that'll never change."

I trusted no one, and *that* would never change. Flashing red and blue lights neared the hospital. I threw the car in drive and gripped the door. "Go back home. Get away from this shit before it ruins your entire family." Slamming the door shut, I sped away, leaving him standing on the side of the road. I had one more piece of business to take care of.

I headed northbound, merging onto Route 1. Coated with snow, the Tobin Bridge looked like bones. Snow blew across the road, making it nearly impossible to see, as I made my way across the bridge to Chelsea. The car fishtailed, but I regained control and drove to the storage unit I'd been renting under a fake name for the past year.

Swiping the keycard, I drove into the facility and parked. I made my way to the last unit at the end, tugging my hat low over my eyes. The lights flickered on as I unlocked the rusted door and pulled it open. Shoving old furniture aside, I found the safe and spun the combination lock until it clicked open.

I unzipped the first duffel bag stashed with two guns hidden among my clothes, untouched. Stacks of cash lined the second bag, held together with rubber bands, a phone, a set of keys to a truck I'd bought with cash, and a passport and documents with my new name.

My mom's last name with a version of my own. *Rhett Marshall.* My mother was too good for the world she'd gotten dragged into. She'd fallen for my father's charm and lies, never knowing he already had a wife and daughter tucked away. She'd known what his life was before I ever did and kept me from him, warning me to stay away, but his world had intrigued me. He'd turned her into a monthly expense check. I might have her name on paper, but I'd have to pull a miracle out of my ass to earn it.

Using a bottle of water and a rag, I cleaned the blood from my hands and changed out of my blood-soaked clothes and jacket, shoving them into a garbage bag to throw away later. Survival meant leaving town when necessary and adapting. I stepped outside, locking the door behind me, and hurried back to the car. Taking shortcuts through alleys and side streets, I headed into a twenty-four-hour parking garage. I entered my code and drove to a secluded space near the back on the lower level, parking next to my truck. Throwing the bags in the backseat of the cab, I drove out of the garage onto the street. The truck had better traction, allowing me to speed toward I-93 South onto Mass Pike, leaving the city in my rearview mirror.

Using the burner phone, I dialed Vivian's number. My sister was the one person I trusted, and I had to warn her. If she hadn't been there after I moved in with my father, I would've chased the money and power, ending up in the same tragedy as Miles. The only difference was that Miles belonged to a family who would never be the same. His death would gouge a hole out of their lives, while mine would leave nothing more than a ripple.

Somehow, men like me kept going, and good men like Miles became victims of their shitty choices. He paid for the mess we'd created with his life, and in our world, that was the expected cost of loyalty. *Family.*

Vivian hesitated before speaking. "Who is this?"

"It's me."

"Jesus, Everett, maybe not wait hours to call me after all hell breaks loose, fuck! They raided Dad's house and arrested him. Where are you?"

"I'm leaving, Viv."

A long silence hung over the line before she replied. "You killed Noble's son, didn't you?"

I didn't answer her. Didn't have to. She already knew what I'd done.

"For how long?" she said.

"Not sure yet, they'll kill me if I stay. It's safer for you and Zach if I'm gone—"

"He left me in charge. He thinks I'm going to run an illegal shipyard. I'm a lawyer, I've got my own clients to take care of." A faint clink of ice in a glass and an exhale came through the line. "He wants me to represent him—of course he does, it's what I do, what I've always done. Come to his fucking rescue."

"So do it. Just don't do it well. You hold more cards than you think, Viv."

"How will I contact you?"

"I'll be in touch." Snow battered the dark highway as I drove, making it impossible to see the lane markings. I'd push myself and drive as far south as I could through the night.

"I know how it works." Her voice muffled, like she spoke over the rim of a glass.

"Don't drink too much, stay sharp—"

"I'm a decade older than you, I know what I'm doing."

"You've got all the information you need to run that place legit. You still have the password for my computer at work?"

"Of course I do, Ev... What am I calling you now?"

"Rhett," I said But I didn't share my last name. Maybe Vivian would figure it out, but I couldn't bring myself to say it.

"Did the line drop?" Vivian asked.

"I'm still here. Listen, don't tell anyone I called. Do not trust anyone, Viv. As far as you and Zach are concerned, I'm a traitor, a rat, and you want nothing to do with me, got it?"

"Promise me you'll take care of yourself and come back, I'll need you around when he gets out looking for someone to blame."

I didn't make promises I couldn't keep.

"Promise. I'll call again in a couple of days," I said. "Take care of yourself too."

"You know I will."

I ended the call and stuffed the phone in my pocket. My sister and nephew were all I had. I never let myself get too close to a woman; it was safer that way, easier. Being alone meant there was no one to hurt or lose, but it sure as hell wasn't a life I wanted. I was the asshole who wanted more, I just didn't believe I deserved it.

ONE

Frankie

TWO YEARS LATER

Death had intrigued me growing up. Not the dying part, the *surviving* part. Willow Grove Hospital was nothing compared to the trauma cases I'd seen working in Boston, but when EMTs brought in a guy who'd had a dirt bike accident, it triggered memories of my brother's dirt bike crashes. My frantic ten-year-old self had run *toward* the blood-gushing wounds and broken bones instead of running away; I was hardwired to *fix* when everything fell apart. Twenty years later, at four in the morning during my ER night shift, I strolled into the break room with an extra-large coffee, and the only thing I wanted to fix was my growling stomach.

Rummaging in the fridge, I unwrapped my ham and cheese sandwich and plopped down on the worn leather chair in the corner, scrolling through my phone. I bit into the dry, slightly stale bread, but it barely registered as I closed the open apps, leaving behind the image of me and my two brothers' smiling faces. Lena, the woman who'd had my back since college and hopefully my future sister-in-law, had taken the photo a month before my younger brother, Miles, died. That was the last time we had all been together. She'd left a corporate world behind and had just bought a local dive bar, but it needed a ton of work and a new name. Miles had insisted she name it after a damn *bird*... something that stood for loyalty and friendship. His words still lingered in my mind every time I walked through the door.

Magpies mate for life, they're the ride or die of the bird world.

After two years, the Magpie Bar was the town's most popular hangout, and I still had that picture set as my wallpaper.

My career had taken me from a trauma nurse working at Mass General to my hometown emergency room. I've held people's hands as they died, even after we'd done everything we could to save them. I'd witnessed death tear families apart, but nothing prepared me for its knock at my own family's door. Grief's ripple effect was like a tsunami of pain, sadness, and anger, forever on rinse and repeat.

Miles had gotten himself into bad shit, *terrible* shit, and it got him shot and killed. I had tried to watch over him, make sure he was getting clean like he'd promised. Hell, I'd lived with him, but failed to fix him. And there was more to it than the hollow, *wrong place at the wrong time, he was a drug dealer*, story that investigators, including my older brother, Finn, had told us. If I could get my hands on the sealed police report they refused to release, maybe I could find out his murderer's name, and why they'd *really* targeted my brother.

Shaking my depressing thoughts away, I shoved the last bite of the sandwich into my mouth, downing the rest of the coffee as I stood. With the elastic band from around my wrist, I pulled my dark hair into a semblance of a bun on top of my head, catching a glimpse of the dark circles under my eyes in the mirror behind the door. Picking up too many overtime shifts was kicking my ass. "Jesus, I need sleep."

"Code Blue. Code Blue. Emergency Room." The robotic voice blared over the intercom.

Nothing cleared my mind more than the sudden focus of a code blue. I shoved the staff room door open, running toward the ER.

Snatching a pair of gloves from the supply cart, I rushed into the trauma bay, where a team worked on a boy who couldn't be over seventeen. He lay motionless on the gurney with his eyes rolled back in his head. Blood covered his face, soaked into his shirt, and his chest wasn't moving. His skin was cold under my touch as I secured a mask over his mouth and squeezed the Ambu bag.

I glimpsed his wristband. His name was Meyer Young, and he had just turned sixteen.

As he always did, Logan silently mouthed the words to "Pink Pony Club" with each chest compression, using the song's rhythm to guide his pace. Determination hardened his features as a grim expression settled on his face.

My favorite coworker and friend, Zoey—*Dr. Harper*—an absolute force of nature, furrowed her brows in concentration as she took charge, calling out orders. Each team member yelled confirmations through every command, all with the same goal. Save this boy's life.

Adrenaline surged through me as time unraveled, slipping away, but I couldn't stop to think about this kid dying and what that would mean for his family. Tilting his head, I held the mask over his mouth and nose, squeezing the bag in a timed dance with Logan's compressions, but the rise in his chest was minimal. "His breathing is too shallow." I locked eyes with Dr. Harper as she moved around the dying young man.

"We intubate," Dr. Harper said. "Where's RT? Call them again."

"Someone get me an RSI kit and scope." I counted six seconds and squeezed the bag in a steady repetition, desperate to get air into the boy's lungs.

Logan's hands pressed down repeatedly with good compressions, as another nurse stated, "No pulse."

"Charge the defibrillator to 200, ready to shock," Dr. Harper demanded.

The team stepped back, removing their hands from the kid, and I inhaled sharply, letting the aroma of antiseptic fill my nostrils to replace the indescribable scent of blood, sweat, and looming death.

Electric shock vibrated through him, and his chest jolted slightly. The monitor beeped with a faint flicker, growing steadier as we surrounded him again, desperate to stabilize him.

Dr. Harper held her fingers over his carotid. "We got a pulse." The slow, jagged lines of his heart rate sliced the monitor screen, and she reached for the ET tube.

"Come on, kid, you've got this," I whispered near his ear as I handed the video laryngoscope to Dr. Harper and took off the mask. Opening his mouth, I moved fast, tilting his head back as the doctor examined his airway with the scope.

"Clear his mouth, Frankie." Her stoic expression masked all emotion as she surveyed the boy. "These kids think they're invincible, driving like Andretti on a racetrack."

I used suction to clear the blood from his airway. "Ready."

Dr. Harper inserted the scope into his mouth, and I handed her the tube. Guiding it in place with steady hands, she removed the scope. "Inflate the cuff," she ordered, and I inflated the balloon at the end of the tube.

As soon as she confirmed the tube's placement was good, I put the mask back over his mouth and resumed squeezing the airbag. But this time, his chest rose and fell deeper, and color flooded his pale cheeks. I leaned close as the whirring of the ventilator filled the room. "Keep fighting your way back, you've got this."

Stepping back, the doctor stretched her neck from side to side. "Keep ventilation going." She rounded the gurney, assessing him as she gave med orders to the nurse in charge of his IV.

Twenty minutes later, the on-call respiratory therapist arrived, and a staff member wheeled the boy with a new lease on life to the ICU, followed by his sobbing parents. I tossed my gloves in the biohazard bin on my way toward the nurse's station and slid into the bathroom to wash my hands. The sudden weight of exhaustion consumed my body, but I clung to the lingering adrenaline, splashing cold water on my face. The kid's recovery would be painful, but he survived.

He gets another chance.

I found a quiet satisfaction when the chaos of saving a life gave way to the knowing we'd pulled it off together. A sense of control took over like a drug I couldn't get enough of.

One nurse sat charting while another entered the med room as I approached the nurses' station. Zoey Harper smoothed her dark, textured hair behind her ears and drank from a paper cup, leaving a maroon smudge on the rim. She plopped down in a wheeled chair, tapping the cup and glanced up at me. The fluorescent lights humming above the curved desk somehow made her features even more striking than they already were, accentuating the freckles on her dark skin. "Hey, good work tonight."

"You too, it felt good to use those skills again. I don't get the opportunity much anymore."

"Weren't you supposed to move back to Boston?" she asked, taking another sip of coffee.

I was getting caffeine envy watching her devour it.

"I wasn't supposed to stay here for two years, but here I am." Grabbing the notebook from my pocket, I looked up a patient's chart on the computer as I sat beside her. "I don't think I can leave for a while, not with Dad and Finn—" A yawn broke free and my eyes watered as I stared at the screen.

"Still not sleeping?"

"Not really."

"You know what your problem is, Frankie?"

"I don't have that kind of time, Zo."

"You lack balance. Stop trying to fix everyone's shit and let them do whatever they want. You can support your dad and brother without sacrificing yourself. That's why you can't sleep. Me? I sleep like a baby."

"You take melatonin, it doesn't work for me. I've got plenty of balance."

Rising from her chair, she angled the cup toward me. "You work too much and don't get out enough."

"I get out—"

"Not like you did in Boston, and your back deck doesn't count." Zoey tossed her cup in the garbage and chatted with a social worker, directing them to a patient's room.

I'd had a social life of concerts, restaurants, and bars in Boston. Some nights I'd meet friends after work, something I never did anymore... but that was before Miles died. That was before everything changed. With an exhale, I typed away, finishing up the charting I'd meant to do earlier.

Zoey walked around to the front of the desk, hovering in front of me as she checked her watch. "Why don't you come out with me and Kai this Friday? A friend of his will be there, and he asked if we knew anyone. Naturally, I thought of you."

I stifled another yawn. "*Naturally*."

"He's cute, nice, has a job." Her pager beeped, and she glanced down at it attached to her pocket. "I wouldn't set you up with an asshole, give me some credit, please. Just give it a chance, one date. Let me help you cure this dry spell you're stuck in." Zoey reached over the desk and grabbed the phone, cradling the handset against her ear as she dialed, speaking briefly before hanging up. "X-rays are ready for your lady in room five. If nothing is broken, I'll discharge her before shift end."

"Where are you going Friday night?"

Am I actually considering this?

"The Magpie, where else? It'll be fun. And Lena said she'll take a few hours off and hang out."

"Lena says she'll take it off, but she can't be at the Magpie and not work. Won't happen, not with how busy it's gotten lately." Summer was one thing with her newly built patio, but October in Massachusetts meant hockey season, and Lena had installed two large TVs, bringing in more customers.

"She needs to hire more help."

"I think she just did," I said. "A friend of Finn's or something."

"He's back to work?"

"Three days a week in a desk job he complains about every time I see him, but yeah. I think he should just quit and work with Lena

21

full time. He's happier when he's there, but you know Finn, he doesn't know how *not* to be a police officer."

The call bell rang; my patient in room five demanded more pain medication at precisely six o'clock, informing me it was ten minutes to the hour. With a promise to be there soon, I logged out of the computer and tucked the notebook back in my scrubs pocket.

Sitting back in the chair, I rubbed my eyes. Fuck, I was tired. Too tired to make plans for Friday night with a man I'd never met.

Zoey walked away from the desk, and I called after her. "You know what, I'm not interested. Friday. I'm just gonna pick up that shift instead."

Logan sauntered up to the nurse's station, cleaning his round-framed glasses. Placing them back on his face, his forehead creased, and he tilted his head to the side as he studied me. "Who aren't we interested in this week? And your patient in room five has requested pain pills at promptly six o'clock." He tapped his watch.

"On my way." I stood, retrieving my access card clipped to my chest pocket for the med room.

"Think about it," Zoey called over her shoulder as she rushed down the hallway.

Logan followed me, and we took turns accessing the medication system. His lips turned into his pouty deadpan, amused expression. "You should just go for it. He can't be worse than the last guy you went out with."

"The one who wore a suit and tie to the movies? He wasn't terrible, just not for me." I left the room with a blister pack of medication in hand, letting the door lock shut behind us.

"He sounded like the... *gentile* type, sweet. Nothing like the soulless prick who shall remain nameless." Logan scribbled on a piece of paper before clicking the top of the pen and stuffing it into his shirt pocket.

The emotional wreckage of leaving my college boyfriend—the prick who shall remain nameless—four years ago, had faded into a distant, bitter memory. Sharing a hometown made it difficult not to run into him, and I stopped worrying about it. I'd moved on and embraced single life, dabbled in online dating, getting satisfaction from a career I loved.

"I like my life the way it is without awkward first dates and small talk with someone I don't know."

"So, skip them. The next man who lights a fire in you, just dive headfirst," Logan teased, sauntering away in the opposite direction.

A smile spread across my face. Skip first dates and awkward bullshit. He might be on to something. I tucked loose strands of hair back into the elastic band and made my way toward room five, stopping for a cup of water to bring with me.

An overhead light brightened the room as I entered, and the woman pressed the button to raise the head of the bed. A man shifted in the chair underneath the window. Outside remained as dark as midnight, without a hint of daylight.

"Hi, Ms. Lane, how are you making out?" I asked.

"Well. It is about time." She pressed her lips together and smoothed her silver hair as I logged onto the bedside computer and checked the medication against her wristband. Her eyes darted from the wall clock to the man across from the bed. "Five minutes after six, I told you to step out and let them know the time."

"Thank you for your patience," I said sweetly as I handed her two pills. Maybe a little *too* sweetly.

Rotating the pills between her fingers, she lifted the glasses hanging from a silver chain around her neck and slid them on her face. She examined each pill as she answered my questions, and I assessed her, taking her vitals. I offered her the cup of water, but she refused. "I am not yet ready," she said.

"Take your time." I stood next to her, holding the cup.

Tension settled in the room as the man rose from the chair. He wasn't much taller than me but had the solid frame of a linebacker. He picked lint from his sport coat as he approached, and I caught sight of a gold ring with a red stone on his pinky finger, along with a matching watch clinging to his wrist. Grimacing at his phone in the other hand, he glanced at me. "We were told she can get out of here soon?"

The woman flashed me a quick smile, her mouth switching back into a frown as she reached for the cup of water, closing her eyes with each sip.

I focused my attention on her. "The doctor will be in soon with your X-ray results—"

"She lives alone and had a fall," her son said. "Now, I can't leave town until I know my mother's able to go back home safely." He smiled, but his eyes held a flat expression.

I spoke slowly, choosing my words. "We want the same thing, sir. Like I said, the doctor will be in with an update very soon." My phone rang, lighting up the front pocket of my scrub shirt with a phone call. I had forgotten to leave it in my purse after my break, and the ringer was on.

"You can get that." He glared at me. "Don't mind us."

Embarrassed at my lack of professionalism, I snatched it from my pocket to turn it off as the call ended, and he leaned in, his eyes narrowed with suspicion. "Nice picture. One of those two your boyfriend or something?"

"Or something." I stuck my phone back in my pocket. "Can I get you anything else, Ms. Lane?"

She rested her head on the pillow. "That will be all. I am sure I will be out of this dreadful place soon enough, and my son can be rid of me again."

Her son watched me with an unnerving intensity, and sweat pricked the back of my neck. I straightened my back and looked him in the eye, addressing his mother. "Ring if you need assistance, Ms. Lane."

I walked toward the door, but footsteps echoed on the tiled floor behind me, and a hand touched my arm. I bristled, stepping into the hallway.

The man put his hands up with a smirk on his face. "Sorry to startle you." He rubbed his chin. "I don't make it this way often, unless my mother needs me. I just want to thank you for taking good care of her... I didn't catch your name?"

"I didn't give it." My time as a trauma nurse in the city had desensitized me to most of the rudeness I'd encountered. Being yelled at, shoved, or told to fuck off hadn't forced me out of nursing, not when everything else gave me so much... *purpose*. But this man's curiosity made me uneasy on a primal level.

He pointed at my name tag. "Frankie. Short for something?"

I flipped the ID card around, grateful only first names were on it. "Nope. Have yourself a good day." I spun on my heels and walked away, leaving him standing in the doorway. I could feel him watching me, but I didn't turn around.

This shift couldn't end soon enough.

Two

Frankie

F inishing my shift, I grabbed my backpack and purse from the break room and slung them both over my shoulder. I took the service elevator down to the first floor and shoved the heavy door open to step outside. Frost covered the cars in the parking lot, and a gust of wind sent my ponytail whipping against my face. At least I'd be awake for the drive home. I approached my bright yellow Jeep and opened the driver's side door, tossing my bag onto the back seat. Rust crept along the hinges, and I ran my fingers over the orange crust. I'd bought it secondhand when I moved back, but two years of neglected maintenance was coming back to bite me.

I climbed into the driver's seat and shut the door, shivering. The engine squealed when I started it, blasting cool air through the vents that gradually warmed as I sat against the cold leather. An ache pulsed at the back of my head, moving along my temples, and I rubbed my tired eyes and pulled the tight elastic from my hair.

The heat melted a path through the frost on the windshield, lulling me into my thoughts. That kid could be taken off the ventilator soon if he showed improvement. Maybe one day he would be someone who made an impact on the world. Unlike my last patient's son. The X-rays were clear, and Zoey had discharged Alice Lane. I should've asked that man *his* name.

With a deep breath, I blinked a few times and stretched my neck from side to side, pulling my phone from my pocket. Lena had been the missed call from earlier, and I dialed her number. If she needed me that early, it must have been important.

Her voice picked up through Bluetooth as I pulled away from the parking lot. "Did your mom get hold of you?"

"No, why?" No hello or how are you, not unusual for Lena, but concern laced her tone.

"Your dad was at the bar last night—"

"Jesus Christ, what'd he do?" The throbbing in my head radiated toward the back of my neck. The part of my dad that *functioned* within his alcoholism had faded over the past few months.

28

"He didn't go home last night. Your mom called this morning, and Finn went looking for him." She yawned loudly. "Last I heard, she went to work, but he's worried about her."

"Did he go see her or at least call?" My mind whirled with ways to fix the situation, and Finn wasn't the solution. He was done with our father, tired of helping and getting nowhere. I could time the cycle. Dad would be good for days, sometimes weeks, until the grief and blame landslide hit and he spiraled, landing at the bottom of a forty-ounce bottle.

Silence filled the car.

"Lena, still there?"

"I'm putting on make-up, the phone's perched on the bathroom counter. Heading into the bar for a delivery. I tried calling her, but she's not answering, neither is your dad. Finn just left for work, he said he's on it—"

"He's not on it, he's over it." I rubbed my face with one hand and gripped the wheel with the other as the car veered toward the shoulder. I needed to stop by Mom's shop, make sure she was okay, find my father, and get some sleep before my night shift.

"Frankie, you can't fix this, but I thought you should know in case he shows up on your doorstep. I think you should turn your phone off and go home to bed. I'll call her again later."

"No, I'll go see her on my way home, thanks for letting me know."

"If you need anything, I'm here, okay? And your brother is trying, he doesn't want this all on you."

29

My brother had given up trying... but Lena was the one Finn always listened to. "You lectured him, didn't you."

Lena's smile radiated through the phone. "I did no such thing."

"Tell him to back off for now and focus on work," I said. "I'll handle this one, he can get the next."

"You're a better woman than I am. My patience is hanging on by a thread and it isn't even my problem."

"Mine's gone too, I just hide it better." I yawned and the pulse thumping in my head settled into my temples.

Jesus, Dad.

The call ended, and a constant rattling from the engine interrupted the quiet in the Jeep. I needed to bring it to a mechanic. The stairs on my back deck needed repair, along with a leaky tap in the kitchen sink, and perhaps an extensive repair on my personal life. Moving back home to Willow Grove had been a good decision; my family needed me, I was close to my friends, and the small-town pace was slower. But coming back home was supposed to be healing and ease stress...

My brother is dead, I don't know who killed him, and my family is falling apart.

I called my father, but his voicemail picked up. Thumping over a pothole, I passed by Java Brew, a local coffee shop near the hospital, but the drive-thru line reached the road. I parked and headed inside to get the largest black coffee I could get my hands on. Sleep was out of the question, and caffeine was essential if I wanted to calm the storm between my parents.

I placed my order, unable to resist adding a blueberry cream cheese Danish, and moved aside in the crowded line. My phone vibrated inside my jacket pocket. It fell from my grasp, sliding across the floor, where it collided with a rather large work boot.

The man wearing the boots grabbed a coffee and a brown paper bag off the counter and bent down to pick up my phone. A plaid flannel shirt peeked from underneath his jacket as he rose. Lifting his head, his piercing gaze regarded me with quiet curiosity, and I tucked my wild strands of hair behind my ears. I glanced down at the bloodstain on my scrubs, impossible to hide.

He scanned the coffee shop, his solid frame moving easily through the people waiting for their orders as he approached me. "Is this yours?" he asked, holding my phone toward me.

"Thanks." My fingers brushed against his rough skin as I took my phone and wiped off the screen, searching for scratches.

The man towered over me, but his closeness didn't come across as imposing. He had a ruggedness about him, rough around the edges, but without the casual nonchalance most men from Willow Grove carried. I'd bet my next paycheck he wasn't from here.

Light filtering through the window illuminated his hazel eyes as he swept them over me. "Is it broken?"

"Not the first time it's survived a fall." I held it up. "The case might be bulletproof too, who knows."

He curled the top of the bag in his fingers as he drank his coffee, the line between his brows deepening for a moment.

"On your way to work?" he finally said.

"Just finishing." My ID dangled over the zipper, and I tucked it inside my jacket, out of habit more than anything else. This guy had a cautious ease about him, not at all creepy. "Are you on *your* way to work?"

"Sort of."

"Well, either you are or you're not, there's no sort of." My back straightened, and I folded my arms across my chest.

"Frankie?" A familiar woman called from behind the counter. She wiped her hands on a towel and smiled as she handed me an extra-large coffee and my Danish in a brown bag.

A growl rumbled from my empty stomach as I stepped outside and opened the bag, hurrying to my Jeep. "Raspberry? *Shit*."

The man from inside glanced around the open door of his truck as I passed by and peered inside his paper bag. "Did you order blueberry?"

"How'd you know?"

"This must be yours. I haven't touched it if you want to switch."

"You ordered a raspberry Danish?"

"They're the best." A hesitant smile cracked his face, a flicker of warmth in his eyes as he got out of the truck and stood in front of it.

He was not a typical attractive man. He was... different, beautiful with a sexy edge of mystery.

"I completely disagree. Blueberry all the way, it's sweeter." I placed my cup on the hood of my Jeep and rolled up the bag, making no attempt to walk toward him. He was still a stranger, and I wasn't an idiot. "You can have your sour raspberry back."

He sauntered toward me, and we traded our paper bags as though it were an illicit exchange. Unrolling the bag, he took the raspberry pastry out and took a bite. "Perfect," he said with a nod as he walked back to his truck.

"You're welcome." I grabbed my steaming coffee and slid behind the wheel, a grin spreading across my face. The engine screamed as I started it, and I turned up the radio to drown out the high-pitched whine, cursing under my breath.

He backed out of his parking spot and waved as he drove away.

I didn't even ask him his name. He who loves raspberry Danishes, who I'll probably never see again. Him.

I pulled out of the parking lot, and someone gave me the finger when I cut them off. I mouthed the words "I'm sorry" and sped through town toward my mom's flower shop, answering my phone when it rang.

"You're going to see Mom?" Finn's tone remained calm as he spoke to me, like he would to an unhinged criminal. "Dad won't answer his fucking phone."

"Hello to you too. I'm almost at the shop."

"We can't keep doing this, Frankie."

"You think I don't know that? He needs help and he won't listen to anyone. I'll talk to Mom."

"Text me once you're home safe, okay? I'm at work until four, and I'll be at the Magpie with Lena after. Stop in on your way to work tonight and we'll talk then."

"Maybe, sure, if I have time." Sleep might not happen for me today.

Chatter filled the car through the phone, and Finn's muffled voice responded to whoever was talking. "I got to go," he said to me.

"Talk later."

"Ten-four."

The line went dead, and I tried my dad's number again, but switched the music back on when it went to voicemail.

I had hoped returning home after Miles's death would be a way for me to help my parents and Finn pick up the shattered pieces, but with every step forward, I took ten more back. I refused to lose control.

The perfect solution existed, and if it didn't, there would be another way out of this. Dad needed someone in his corner; Finn had his own demons he never talked about. I would have to be strong enough for all of us. Responsibility weighed on my shoulders, and I steadied myself with a deep breath.

THREE

Frankie

Nestled downtown among boutiques, restaurants, and the one art gallery in Willow Grove, my mother's flower shop thrived. Nora Roscoe was a familiar name to the locals. Her reputation for exquisite interior design and overseeing restorations of landmark buildings had funded her early retirement dream of opening a flower shop.

I hadn't been able to refuse Mom's suggestion of calling her store *The Francesca Rose*. The pressure of being named after a gorgeous apricot flower, symbolizing endurance, success and loyalty, was enough. But every time I walked up the cobblestone steps, the elegant silver lettering on the sign over the shop seemed to mock me with its unattainable perfection.

As I parked alongside the curb, coffee spilled through the lid down my lap, blending with the dried bloodstain. Blotting the wet spot with a napkin, I got out of the Jeep. I couldn't wait to strip off my scrubs and shower.

I opened the paned glass door, welcomed by the soft hooting of an owl. Mom's woodland soundtrack instead of door chimes changed with the seasons. Entering the store felt like a game of birdcall roulette. A rush of cinnamon, spices, and orange filled the room, and wisps of steam curled from a diffuser on a table at the bottom of the narrow staircase. The accent wall was new. Black wallpaper with a peach and yellow rose pattern covered the wall leading up the stairs.

"Frankie?" Mom called from upstairs.

"Down here." Taking the lid off my cup, I drank the rest of my coffee.

Mom carried rings of vines and wire down the stairs. "I'm pissed off at your father."

"Lena filled me in—"

"He's been out all night, hasn't called, texted, no idea where in the hell he is." She stormed past me toward a large table covered in branches, dried flowers, scissors, and a half-made wreath.

I followed her to the table. "He's around, I'm sure he's fine."

"It isn't *fine*, Francesca." Brushing her feathered bangs aside, she shot me her brown-eyed glare, the same one Finn gave me way too often. Miles and I had inherited our father's blue eyes and dark hair. The thought of him sent a wave of grief rocking through me, and I swallowed a lump in my throat before it consumed me.

I sidled up to the counter and settled on a stool as I placed my cup on the counter. "He's struggling—"

"And I'm not? You don't see me drowning my problems in alcohol and running away." She cut vines with quick snips of the scissors, her fingers dangerously close to the blade. I hopped off the stool and pried them from her hand.

"I'm stopping by the Magpie tonight to talk to Finn, you don't have to do this alone. I'll take care of Dad today, maybe he went out to the cabin—he's done that before, right?"

My parents had owned a cabin in the woods since my brothers and I were kids. Less than an hour away, it had been Dad's idea for some quality family time, but my last visit was years ago during a summer break in college. Life had gotten busy, and with Miles gone, the thought of dredging up nostalgic memories in that cabin was unbearable.

"He insulated the well for winter, so for all I care, he can go live out there until he straightens himself out," Mom said. She sorted through dried roses, selecting a few still clinging to their yellow hue. "His car is still in the driveway, he's not far. Unless he's in a ditch somewhere..." Her face paled as she glanced at me. "Jesus, you think he's hurt?"

"I just left the hospital, he's not there." The tension headache returned, throbbing in my neck as I stifled a yawn.

Placing a hand on my cheek, she smiled, tears glistening in her eyes. "I love your dad, but if he doesn't get his shit together, I'm going to kick his ass, hear me?"

"Loud and clear, let him survive this fuck-up today and we'll take it from there, okay?"

She patted my face. "This isn't for you to fix, Francesca." Snatching the scissors from me, she resumed cutting branches and twisting them around the wire. "When you do locate the asshole, tell him we need to talk. For real this time." She paused her agonizing snipping for a moment and swept a glance over me. "Go home and shower, there are stains on your scrubs and I don't even want to know what they are."

"I love you, Mom."

She nestled a small pumpkin among dried roses and ferns, smiling as she admired her work. "Love you too."

The owl's mournful hoot echoed again, and I faced the door as the man from the hospital strolled in. He offered a hand to my mother and my stomach clenched, flinching as she shook his hand and introduced herself.

"I'm Nora, nice to meet you," she said. I waited for him to return the greeting, but he only nodded in response and asked about a flower arrangement.

Mom excused herself and headed to the fridges out back for the flowers he requested, and his gaze fell on me. "Frankie, right? I just dropped my mother at home and wanted to bring her some flowers before I left town. Thanks for taking such good care of her." He browsed through the shop with his hands in his coat pockets.

I folded my arms across my chest. "I'm sorry, I didn't catch *your* name."

"I didn't give it," he said. His tight smile did nothing to lessen the eerie stillness in his eyes.

My skin crawled, and my senses heightened. I curled my fingers around my phone inside my pocket as the man sent every warning bell in my body screaming.

Get a grip, he didn't say or do anything derogatory, and he's leaving town.

My mom returned with a bouquet of gold and red flowers in a vase shaped like a pumpkin. "Will this work for her?"

"Perfect, thank you for your time." He paid for the flowers, making small talk with my mother about the flower shop's name, inquiring about the family behind the business.

She didn't hesitate, and the knot in my stomach moved into my chest as she told him our last name.

Roscoe.

Carrying the vase, he turned to leave. "Have a good day, Francesca." He sauntered out the door and walked past the windows, out of sight.

"His mom just got out of the hospital, had some sort of spell. You were her nurse?" Returning to her wreath, Mom plucked up a flower and inhaled it. "Even dried, Francesca roses still smell like tea."

"I was." I stared at the door in a weary daze. What about him made me so uneasy?

"You clearly made an impact on her. He's headed back to Boston, and he's worried about leaving her alone."

"Boston?"

My mother held up the finished wreath. "Missing city life?" Her linen pants swished as she hung the wreath on the wall, tucking it among the others.

"Sometimes, I guess. I miss a lot of things." I slid the cardboard sleeve off my coffee cup and folded it, smaller and smaller, until it fit in the palm of my hand. My mind drifted to the night Miles died. Finn had shown up during a busy twelve-hour shift, panicked. Miles was in the ER. Finn had begged me to stay away, but nothing could've kept me from running to see him. I refused to accept it was too late, not for Miles.

Death had won, stealing my baby brother forever. Tears burned behind my eyes, and I blinked hard, forcing them away.

Mom's voice shook me back into the shop. "For what it's worth, I'm happy you came back. Didn't expect you to stay as long as you did, but I'm glad you're here."

Stuffing the folded cardboard into the cup, I threw it into the garbage can behind the counter. "Yeah, well. It hasn't been all bad." I pulled my hair off to the side, stretching to relieve the stiffness in my back. "I'm going home to shower and change, but I'll call you when I find Dad."

Tying the knit belt of her sweater around her waist, Mom tilted her head to the side, furrowing her brows. "Next time you're off, go do something fun, hang out with Lena and Zoey, get dressed up and go on a date—"

"I've got too much to do. There are boxes in the spare room to unpack and repairs to take care of—"

"There's more to life than work, Francesca. When was the last time you had sex?"

"Jesus, Mom." I spun my keys around my finger, gripping them in my palm. "That's my cue."

I moved to hug her, and she stepped back, waving a hand over me. "Not with those germ-infested scrubs."

"Next time I'll throw on a hazmat suit before I come see you." I leaned against the door, pushing it ajar, and the owl sounded again. "Seriously? Can't you get regular, sweet-sounding door chimes? What's next? Seagulls?"

"I like them, they make me laugh, and if I don't laugh, I'll cry." Mom's smile dropped to a frown. "I don't want him home until he's himself again, tell him I said so. You're the one he goes to first."

"He might never be himself again," I muttered, stepping outside. "Talk later." I missed my dad, the steady man who tinkered in the garage, showing me random car things to look out for and fix before they became a bigger issue.

Leaning against the cool brick of the building, I scanned the street for the man from the hospital, but he was gone. I approached my Jeep and unlocked it, peering into the back window at the cluttered backseat before getting in. Leaving Mom behind at *The Francesca Rose*, I headed onto the quiet wooded road toward my townhouse on the outskirts of town.

FOUR

Frankie

Drifting onto the shoulder of the tree-lined road, I gave the wheel a sharp turn and straightened out as I checked my phone. Still no answer from Dad. The rest of the drive passed by in a blur as I navigated on exhausted autopilot until I rounded the last bend, where the familiar row of townhouses came into view.

Secluded but convenient, my townhouse backed onto a quiet stretch of forest with a river flowing through the trees. This place had been one of the few available, rent was more affordable than in town, and after I'd spent two weeks living back home with my parents, I'd acted on impulse before reason and signed a lease. I hadn't expected to renew the lease, but the third year was approaching, and I had no plans to leave.

Using the remote clipped to my visor, the garage door rolled open. I parked and grabbed my bags from the backseat, pressing the button on the wall as I entered my house through the door leading into the kitchen.

"You're home."

I recoiled, my heart pounding, as my father stood at the counter, his back to me. "Jesus, Dad, how did you get in here?"

"Your patio door was unlocked. That's a problem." With a shaky hand, he dumped spoonfuls of sugar into a mug of coffee but didn't turn around as I dropped my purse and backpack on a chair, hanging my jacket on the back of it.

"That's not the only problem." I sent Mom and Finn a quick message to ease their minds.

Turning to face me, he ran a hand through his disheveled hair and over his uneven stubble, the gray hair in his beard longer than the rest. He gulped his coffee and made a disgusted face. "I didn't make it strong enough."

Relief that he was okay and the need to hug him battled with the urge to yell at him for being an ass. "Mom's angry and worried about you, so is Finn."

"I know."

"If you know, why not let her know you're safe?"

43

"She doesn't deserve me like this."

"You don't deserve yourself like this." I approached him as he stared into his cup. "You can't keep doing this, let us help. I've got a ton of resources, so does Finn—"

"I had a bad couple of days. If I could drive, I'd go out to the cabin for a while. I'll shake it off and go home." He made his way to the patio doors, unsteady on his feet. He wiped fingerprints off the glass with his sleeve, and slid the door open, stepping onto the back deck.

I filled a mug with coffee and joined him outside. Sitting on the cushioned chair, he placed the mug on the table. "You need to be more careful living alone here surrounded by nothing but trees. It looks like someone moved in next door." He shook his head. "Lock the damn door, Francesca."

"I don't need a lecture from you." Sitting in the chair next to him, goosebumps covered my bare arms, and I leaned forward, turning on the small propane space heater. *Real* birds chirped, not Mom's fake owls, and the river's current echoed through the trees. The sun reflected off the few red and gold leaves still clinging to the branches. I inhaled the crisp fall air, the calm reminding me why I didn't want to leave this place.

"We need to have a conversation about you going to rehab or AA," I said.

"Been to rehab, doesn't work. I've got it under control, I tried to tell your mother. She won't listen." Dad stretched out his legs, holding the mug with both hands. A large dark stain covered the front of his shirt, and he smelled like he hadn't showered in a week.

How had it gotten this bad? Miles's death had sent him down a dark road, and I couldn't fault him for that, but retiring from the police force might have been the worst decision my father had made. His drinking spun out of control not long after and kept spinning two years later.

To prevent him from taking off again, I kept my voice calm as I spoke. "Mom listens, she's just tired of your bullshit."

His head jerked in my direction. The lines etched on his forehead and around his eyes creased deeper as he looked at me. "I lost my son. You can't understand the hell—"

"No I can't, but I lost my brother. I loved him too." I fought back tears, breathing deeply to regain control. For two years, I had requested access to my brother's police report, only to be denied. And my father never admitted it, but I knew he'd seen that file before he retired from the force. "Maybe if you tell me what was in Miles's police report, I'll have a better understanding of all the hell."

He scrunched his face, shaking his head. "There's nothing you don't already know, why bring that up?"

"Someone murdered him and got away with it. If we knew who hurt him and why, and that someone was still looking for him... I just think it could give us closure." My forced confidence masked the apprehension in my voice.

"Your therapist tell you that?" He huffed as he sat back in the chair, rubbing his hands over his face. "It's an open and shut case, I've been over this. He was involved in a bad drug deal, shot and killed, end of story."

"If it's so simple, let me see it then. You and Finn are both cops, can't you just get it somehow?" Moving closer to the heater, I rubbed the chill from my arms. "It's not end of story for me. Whoever did this to him needs to pay—"

He released a deep sigh. "I wanted to believe he'd come back to us, do the right thing. I didn't raise a criminal. But he chose his life, got involved with the wrong people and it got him killed, okay? Nothing we can do about it now. You saw the toxicology report, he was high, he died. *End of story.*"

"You're right," I whispered. "Nothing we do will bring him back. But we're still here, and we need you. *I* need you."

"Fuck." A laugh escaped him, and he shook his head, rubbing his eyes. "I'm gonna land on my feet, just needed a place to rest for a bit and thought you would understand."

"Says the man who can barely stand up right now," I mumbled, drinking the rest of my coffee. He didn't get it, what if I never got my dad back? "When was the last time you ate something, real food?"

He shrugged, his glassy gaze staring toward the trees.

I rose from my chair, stretching. "I'm going to change and make breakfast."

"Over-easy with toast?" he said between slurps of coffee.

"I'll get right on it." I wanted to smack him and scream at him to bring back the father he used to be. The one who wasn't a shell of a human, barely existing. But I remained silent, retreating inside, and walked upstairs to the bathroom.

Stripping off my filthy scrubs, I dropped them into the over-flowing hamper and stepped into the hot shower. I scrubbed every inch of myself, turned off the tap, and dried off. Darting from the ensuite bathroom to my bedroom, I yanked on a pair of sweatpants and a T-shirt, and aggressively combed through my wet, tangled hair. As I set the hairbrush on my dresser, I glanced at my reflection in the mirror.

My eyes were unique and expressive, and the one feature I loved about myself. But for the first time, I noticed something different in them. I traced my fingers along the sides of my face and leaned closer to the mirror. A tiredness that no amount of sleep could fix stared back at me. And my eyes hadn't changed. They were just older, softer... if not a little broken.

I'll be thirty next week.

My twenties had been goals and accomplishments, overshad-owed with incredible loss, leading me right back to where I'd started. And I'd convinced myself love wasn't on my radar, but if I was being honest, I *yearned* for it. But I refused to settle for anything less than a real, can't-live-without-each-other love. Anything less would break my heart into a thousand pieces, and not worth the heartache.

I'll be waiting a while for a love like that.

I laughed to myself at the fantasy I'd conjured up in my mind and turned away from the mirror.

"Frankie? You fall asleep up there?" Dad called from down-stairs.

"I'm coming." I headed downstairs to the kitchen and made breakfast. My father's head lolled to the side and his eyes drooped shut as I carried two plates of eggs and toast outside.

I dropped the plate onto the table in front of him with a clang. "Eat something," I ordered, sitting beside him.

His eyes flew open, and he bolted upright. "I just need sleep—"

"Food first, and you can crash on my couch."

He stuck his fork into the eggs, dipping his toast in the runny yolk. "Still haven't set up the spare bedroom yet, have you? Need help?"

"No, but you do." The anger inside me surged, boiling over. I'd gotten nowhere with him this morning.

"Fucking Christ, I heard you the first time."

His words stung, and my jaw tightened as I struggled to hold myself together. "Right now, I'm the only one with a shred of patience to deal with you, don't be an asshole."

Chewing his food, he glanced at me, his eyes half-mast. "I deserve that."

"Yeah, you do."

"I'm sorry, honey. I'll do better."

"Good. I mean, I don't believe you, but good." I pulled the crust off a piece of toast and popped it in my mouth, but it was no blueberry cream cheese Danish. Where did the attractive man from the coffee shop *sort of* work? I wouldn't mind running into him again, we had pastries in common if nothing else. Thinking of him eased the frustration with my father.

My father stood, abandoning his plate on the table as he stumbled inside. He knocked a chair over and almost fell bending down to pick it back up, but I didn't help him. I grabbed our plates and placed them in the sink as a wave of exhaustion consumed the hurt threatening to slam me on my ass.

Dad ambled into the living room and collapsed on the plush couch. "It's freezing in here." He folded his arms across his chest with his eyes closed, resting his feet on the armrest.

I turned on the propane fireplace, and flames danced behind the glass. Pulling a blanket off the loveseat, I draped it over him. "I'll drop you off at home on my way to work later."

"If she'll have me back."

"Do better, Dad. Please."

He drifted off to sleep, unresponsive and snoring.

The familiar cycle of guilt sank into my chest like walls folding in on me. My dad, Jared Roscoe, the tough guy with shoulders big enough to carry the weight of the world, the man who I used to turn to when I had my heart broken and betrayed, was no longer my safe place to fall. I hardly recognized him anymore, and it hurt.

I handled those wretched, aching feelings the best way I knew how. I chased them away, packing them down until they went numb, dusted myself off and kept going. At least I was aware of what I was doing, healthy or not.

Hauling my tired body upstairs, I stopped in the hallway at the entrance to the spare bedroom. My keyboard piano sat on its stand in the back corner, gathering dust. I'd taken lessons until I left for college and had always dreamed of having a house with my own upright piano. I missed the peace my fingers over the keys gave my mind, but I never played anymore. No reason. No excuses. I just hadn't made the time.

The closet overflowed with boxes, and plastic containers stacked against the wall. Near the window, folded blankets lay in a pile on the daybed. In the center of the floor, a paint can and brushes rested on a plastic tarp.

Mystical Lake blue.

I had planned to sort through the boxes and paint the room, but dealing with Miles's belongings would be like reopening a wound I wasn't ready to face. Leaving the room, I walked down the hallway to my bright bedroom. I yanked the drapes closed, watching as a car turned onto the street. It slowed to a crawl, passing by the row of townhouses as if it was searching for something. Glare from the sun reflected off the windshield, hiding whoever was inside.

There was no reason to feel unsettled. Cars passed through my neighborhood all the time. They could be a delivery driver searching for an address, or someone lost, checking directions. But worry tightened my chest, and I couldn't tear myself away from the window. I gripped the edges of the curtains, watching through the gap between them. The car gained speed, driving away.

I'm overtired and paranoid.

Collapsing into bed, I tugged the thick duvet over myself and closed my eyes, sinking into the mattress. The unnerving encounter with the man from the hospital plagued my mind as I begged for sleep to take me.

I shifted my thoughts to the raspberry Danish man from the coffee shop instead. He had an unassuming sexiness that lingered with me. I should've asked his name. The tension melted from my body as I recalled the details of his face, strong jawline, his hazel eyes, his mouth... and sleep finally pulled me under.

FIVE

Frankie

The parking lot was full when I arrived at the Magpie Bar, and although it was only six thirty, darkness had already settled in. Curved lights lit up the weathered brick that made up the top half of the building, casting shadows over the matte black wooden siding on the bottom half that Lena had painted. A glow from inside spilled through the windows onto the pavement, and the double doors in the center swung open and closed as people came and went.

I parked near the patio that stretched along the side of the building and stepped out of my Jeep into the crisp evening air. Smoke from a food truck drifted toward me, teasing my appetite with the smell of deep-fried deliciousness. I should've eaten more than a container of ramen noodles for dinner. The chill bit at my cheeks as I hurried toward the front doors, balancing a tray of coffees. I had less than an hour before my shift to talk to Finn, nowhere near enough time to come up with a solution to help Dad, if one existed at all.

Several men chatted near the entrance on the vacant patio, discussing tonight's hockey game. Pendant lamps attached to the front entrance gave enough light to confirm one of them was Clay Preston, my early twenties mistake. He was the first man I'd ever loved. We'd shared an apartment near UConn, where he immersed himself in business, landing a position with an elite finance firm before graduation, and I studied nursing.

Clay appeared polished, sophisticated, and could persuade situations to his advantage, including me. But he was a lying, cheating asshole, and I left him. I just... *left*. No drama, no fight, no apology worth listening to. I was too proud to admit my heartbreak, and Miles had taken me in, no questions asked. We'd shared an apartment in Boston, and I threw myself into long shifts at Mass General, chasing every nursing certification I could.

I kept my focus on the doors as I walked up the stone stairs past him. His expensive suit and too-perfect smile did nothing to hide the arrogance, but seeing him again evoked no feelings at all, not even anger.

I shifted the tray, freeing my hand to open the door, and he locked eyes with me.

Okay, maybe I still held on to some anger.

Fuck. I didn't have the energy for him.

"Is one of those for me?" Clay asked. The smart-ass smirk on his face complemented his gelled hair. Wrinkles creased along the bottom of his suit jacket as he removed his hands from his pockets. "Haven't seen you in a while, how's life?"

"Just great, excuse me." I reached for the brass door handle, but he beat me to it.

"Allow me."

As I rushed by him, exuding too much confidence, the coffee sloshed against the plastic lids, spilling from the openings down the sides and over my hand. Wiping it off on my jacket, I moved through a boisterous group near the fireplace toward the bar area, lit up with diagonal strings of lights stretching from exposed beams along the ceiling. Billiard balls clattered, and laughter erupted from the pool room off to the left. Light bulbs inside bell jars hung from copper fixtures, casting a glow in the room. My mother had helped Lena with the renovation design, but Lena's steampunk modern style came through in the bar's details.

Light from the Magpie Bar sign attached to the brick wall cast a vibrant blue across Lena's chin-length blond waves. Her height gave her a natural command of the room as she stood behind the bar, pouring drinks beside a coworker. She waved to me over the growing crowd beneath a big-screen TV showing sports announcers.

Propping the tray on the varnished bar, I leaned forward and grabbed a handful of napkins to wipe up the spilled coffee.

"You're saving me right now." Lena picked up a cup. "The coffeemaker shit the bed, and I won't make it till two o'clock without this."

"No problem. Who's the other coffee for?"

"Out back with Finn." Lena took someone's order, turning her attention back on me. "I saw Clay found you."

"I didn't know he was looking for me."

"He's been asking about you, but I told him you weren't interested. He's become a bigger douchebag since we were in college."

"I didn't think that was possible." I tightened the elastic holding my hair in place, and opened the lid on one of the three cups left, sipping the hot, bittersweet coffee. "What's he doing back in town? I haven't seen him in months."

"Catching up with friends." Lena tossed up air quotes, raising her voice over the growing noise.

"I'm surprised he still has them around here."

Reaching across the bar, she tucked my loose hair back in the elastic. "If he gives you trouble, let me know."

"He won't, don't worry." I scanned the bar and recognized the regular Magpie staff, but there were a couple of people who appeared to be new. I tapped the two remaining coffees. "Who's the other coffee for?"

"A friend of Finn's is helping with renos and bartending for a few months. Get your ass back there and sit for a bit before your shift." She held the swing gate open, closing it as I walked through toward the back. "By the way, we're celebrating your 30th birthday here—"

"Lena, no..."

She put a hand up. "I'll keep it small, but we're doing this. It'll be fun! You better still be off on that Friday night. Do not pick up a shift, Frankie."

The conversation with Zoey came to mind. Maybe a night out would be fun, especially on my birthday. "I'm off, I promise I won't pick up." With the tray in my hands, I headed for the door leading out back, calling over my shoulder. "I'll only do this if you actually step away from behind the bar and join us."

"Already have it set, hence the new guy out back."

"We're saying words like hence now?"

"I went from brilliant finance woman to bar owner, I'm clinging to hence."

"And I've never seen you happier," I said, shoving the door open with my hip.

"Best decision I ever made, well unless you count your brother." Tilting a tall glass with the Magpie logo to the side, Lena filled it with dark amber liquid from a beer tap, leaving a perfect head of foam, and slid it toward a waiting hand.

Lena was the one good thing to come out of my relationship with Clay Preston. I'd met her through him, and we'd bonded in college. But all it had taken was one visit from Finn, and they'd been drawn to each other like moths to a massive flame, going strong for six years.

The door swung shut as I left her behind, and the back room opened to a microbrewery where Lena and Finn had studied the process of making the Magpie's signature brews. Tools lay scattered on a folding table, and planks of wood had been placed against the back wall next to a small cooler room. But the quiet conversation drifting from the office caught my attention.

I stepped over a tangle of power cords, making my way closer as Finn's urgent voice carried down the narrow hallway. Straightening my back, I walked into the office. "I've got coffee..."

The man sitting across from Finn, with his ankle casually resting on his knee, glanced up at me.

It was *him*. Raspberry cream cheese Danish man.

And he smiled at me, his piercing, deep-set gaze holding onto me, leaving me breathless. My heart raced, wild and unexpected. Why did this man have such an effect on me? I'd never felt so flustered around a man before, not like this.

Say something.

"So you're the other coffee."

"Is there a Danish to go with it?" he asked, his eyes unwavering, never leaving mine.

"Had I known, there might've been."

"Raspberry?"

I grimaced. "Bad choice, but I guess, if it has to be."

Finn rose from behind the desk and took the tray, handing a coffee to... *him*. "You met already?" Taking the lid off the cup, he sat back down and glanced between the man and me.

"If you count the coffee shop this morning with a pastry mix-up, sure. But no, we haven't met, not really," I said. "How do *you* know each other?"

"He's working for Lena, renos, bartending, whatever she needs done." Finn shot the man a quick glance, but I knew my brother well enough to feel the sudden shift rattled with tension. "This is my sister, Francesca."

As the man stood, I caught sight of the tattoos winding down his arms beyond the sleeves of his T-shirt. One on his left forearm held my focus. It was a shadowy figure with hollow eyes and a finger pressed to his lips. The long, razor-sharp nails demanded silence. I wanted to reach out and trace the lines inked into his skin. I wanted to know his story and where he'd come from.

I lifted my head, and our eyes met. His expression held a dark, magnetic, brooding intensity that was impossible to look away from.

"I'm Rhett," he said.

Finn observed us, his knee bouncing under the table as he drank his coffee. Why was he so nervous?

"Frankie." I extended my hand toward him, and he slowly took it, not in a handshake, but in a silent acknowledgement. And maybe my mother was right, and it had been too long since I'd had sex, but I hesitated. The warmth radiating from this stranger's skin against mine made it difficult to let go. "Do you have a last name?" I released him from my grasp.

"Marshall." Taking the other coffee from the tray, he nodded at Finn. "I'll go finish the trim on those cabinets." He held the cup toward me, his eyes softening. "Thanks for the coffee."

"You're welcome."

As Rhett left the office, I sat in his chair. His body heat lingered, and perspiration gathered at the back of my neck. Unzipping my jacket, I leaned against the chair. The man had a name, and my body reacted to him, betraying my good sense. "How do you know him exactly?"

"Through mutual friends years ago," Finn said. "He's not your type."

"How would you know what my type is?"

The chair creaked as Finn shifted in his seat. "It's not that guy, trust me. You got Dad back home. How'd it go with him?"

Right, real life.

"I fed him, made him take a shower, and clean himself up. Dropped him off a brand-new man. I just hope he stays sober for more than a few hours," I said. Finn fidgeted with papers on his desk. I had to leave soon, and he wasn't paying attention. I sat up, placing my cup on his desk, and clasped my hands together. "He refuses to get help or talk to anyone. I'm trying, Finn, but he's struggling."

He rustled the papers and handed me a business card for a detox center. "I got him in the first of next month, thirty days, dry out, before the holidays—"

"Dad won't do that, it's not going to work. And if by some miracle he actually says yes, what? Release him at the worst time of year for people grieving? He'll be right back where he started. We need a better plan."

"All right, what have *you* got? You can't keep picking him up when he falls on his ass and think it's gonna be okay, Frankie, Jesus. How long will you put up with his bullshit?"

Anger burned on my cheeks as I glared at him. "Until I'm sure he won't fall apart."

Finn toyed with the black ring on his index finger. *Miles's ring.* His brown eyes glazed over as he stared at it. "She'll leave him. If he doesn't stop, Mom's gone."

"I won't let that happen." I placed my hand on his arm, and he broke his stare to look at me. "Look, just take care of the bar with Lena, and let me figure this one out."

With a quick squeeze of my fingers, he pulled his hand away, dragging it down his face. "I'm back at work, stuck behind a desk. It sucks."

"It'll get better," I said.

"I stayed away too long." A worried frown creased his face, his mouth moving as he gnawed on his cheek.

"You needed the time—"

"Not this much, I don't know who I am anymore," he muttered, shoving his chair back and standing. "I should get back out there and help Lena." He looked at me, and a hint of sadness marred his composed expression. "You don't work next weekend, right? Wanna go to the range with me?"

"Sure." I'd been going to the range since Miles had died. Finn had been insistent on teaching me to handle a gun, but I thought he just missed having Miles with him. I'd started going to appease him, but after almost two years, I found it, strangely, a way to relax. "Next Saturday works, I'll be off at seven thirty, let me sleep for a bit and I can meet you in the afternoon."

"I'll see you before then anyway," he said as I got up from the chair.

"Stop worrying, Finn. We'll get through this."

"It's not that easy."

"I know."

I trailed Finn out of the office, drawn toward the sharp scraping of wood at the back of the room.

Rhett hovered over a cabinet door, his arms in constant motion as he worked with tools, carving the edge. He stopped and glanced up at me, pushing his safety glasses onto his forehead with a nod.

Unable to stop myself, I smiled at him on my way through the door to the bar. He was a friend of Finn's, working for his girlfriend, *my* friend. How bad could this guy be?

Lena mixed a Bloody Mary, pouring vodka and tomato juice in a tall glass rimmed with salt, impaling olives and a slice of lime through a toothpick. I shot her my best *I need to talk to you* look, and she bent close to hear me.

"Why didn't you tell me your new hire is hot?"

"Okay Ms-don't-set-me-up-with-anyone." She laughed, handing the Bloody Mary to a woman wearing a ball cap. "He's only been here for a couple of weeks, but he's cool. I officially give my approval."

I glanced at my phone. "Shit, I've got to go. I don't need setting up, I'm just making a point, that's all."

Lena wiped her hands on a towel and leaned across the bar as I rushed through the swing gate. "He's also your new neighbor as of a few days ago, I'm surprised you haven't noticed yet."

"My what?"

That man lives next door to me?

"You're welcome," Lena said with a mischievous smile. She tended to another group of people at the bar alongside Finn, who waved as I headed for the door.

It had been nice having no one living next door. Our decks were so close, separated by nothing but lattice and vines. I'd gotten used to sitting outside without feeling watched.

From the pool room, Clay loosened his tie, holding a cue as he watched me leave, his eyes burning into my back. I ignored him and stepped outside, taking a deep breath before rushing to my Jeep. A twelve-hour shift stood between me and any further thoughts about my new neighbor.

Six

Rhett

M usic pumped through the speakers at the Magpie. A handful of people sat around the bar, with a couple laughing in the poolroom. I recognized the man from two nights ago, the one in a suit and tie who Lena told to fuck off when he asked about Frankie. I wiped sticky beer off the bar's surface, watching him as he moved behind the woman he was with. He leaned over her with a cue stick, rubbing chalk on the end like it owed him something.

He looked around the bar, grinning at whoever was watching, and took the shot, striking the cue ball, pocketing none of the balls.

"The table's warped." The man grabbed his glass off a round table, downing the beer as he made a disgusted face. As the woman lined up the next shot, he slapped her ass, spilling beer on the floor.

Disrespectful prick.

I reached for the swinging door, ready to escort him out, but Lena grabbed my arm. "Just leave it."

"He's a fucking asshole."

"You have no idea." Finn rolled a dolly stacked with two kegs through the door. "We should ban him from coming in here. Rhett, can you hook up the IPA and I'll get the Lager?"

Lena sat on a stool behind the bar and opened the inventory book. "As much as I'd love to keep him out of here, he hasn't done anything to warrant *banning* him. He's not usually in town, not this long anyway."

"He treated my sister like shit. That warrants it," Finn said.

I rolled the first keg into place. "I have no problem asking him to leave, no banning required." A hissing sound escaped as I hooked the tap to the CO_2. "What'd he do to her?"

Running into Finn's sister was inevitable the longer I stayed in Willow Grove, and after two weeks, the unavoidable had happened. Finn had one rule. He promised to help me lie low until my father's release from prison, but I had to keep my mouth shut about... *every fucking thing*. And stay away from Frankie. Make that two rules.

But I sure as hell hadn't expected how meeting the woman I'd once witnessed at her worst would make me *feel*. She'd looked at me with genuine interest and unexpected warmth, like I was worth knowing, not just a hunted nobody on the run. And living on the run was getting fucking lonely. No woman had ever intrigued me like Frankie in that coffee shop. She seemed oblivious to the way her blue eyes captivated with an alluring confidence, holding onto something dark. I wanted to know her, and that never ended well for anyone who got close to me. Francesca Roscoe didn't know how our pasts linked, or who I was, and she never would.

Lena got up and filled a glass, angling it under the tap until the beer ran clear of foam. "Clay lied to her, cheated on her, he tried to control her... that was what, Finn? Four years ago since she broke up with him?"

"Something like that." Finn connected the other keg to the tap and wiped his hands on a towel. "Lena said you found a place and moved in already, you should've told me you were looking, there's a few apartments downtown."

"I needed something furnished with a short lease."

With Lena's help, I found an inexpensive townhouse distant enough from town that I could make a quick getaway if I needed to. Without the steady flow of shipments and profits from the bar I managed in Boston for my father, the big money had dried up, and my stash was running low. But Lena had neglected to tell me until after I signed a lease that I'd moved in next door to the one woman I was supposed to avoid, and her brother was about to give me the Roscoe glare.

"He moved in next door to Frankie." Lena regarded me with a raised eyebrow and a smile. "It's perfect for him."

A grimace twisted Finn's face as he pushed his cheek against his teeth with his fingers, his eyes narrowed in thought. I'd kept in touch with Finn over the past two years, on my terms. But I'd given him the number of my burner months ago, and he called when he discovered my father was about to be released from jail. Not a day had gone by since I'd been in town that Finn didn't look at me with regret. I should never have kept in touch with him.

Leaning against the bar, I folded my arms across my chest, not giving him the satisfaction of looking away first. "It's better than staying in that shitty hotel, I don't even see her, man."

Lena sighed, moving between us. She grabbed Finn's face and kissed him. "What is with you lately? He's not Clay fucking Preston." She nodded toward the obnoxious laughter echoing from the poolroom.

Finn spun his keys, gripping them in his hand as he gave Lena another quick kiss, turning his attention back to me. "It's not like you'll be in town for long."

"That's the plan," I said. "Nothing's changed."

"Who says?" Lena held her phone, changing the music. "I thought you guys were friends. Rhett, you're going to fall balls-deep in love with this town of ours and never want to leave." She flashed a smile and headed over to a table of women waving to her near the fireplace.

"I'm late for work." Finn grabbed his jacket from the back of a stool, shoving his arms in. He lowered his voice. "Cover the tattoo, if anyone recognizes that, it's over."

I rolled my sleeves down. "Any more rules I'm forgetting? Jesus Christ."

"Yeah, a big fucking rule. Not Frankie, Stay away from her. I owe you, and I want to help, it's what Miles would've wanted. But he died because of this shit. My sister is off limits."

"She'll never know, I wouldn't let anything happen to her."

"You can't control everything, not anymore." Finn zipped his jacket, nodding toward Lena across the room. "That goes for her too." About to leave, he hesitated, turning back to face me. "Thanks for helping her out."

"That's why you're paying me," I said.

Finn had told Lena I was a carpenter by trade and an experienced bartender. He paid me in cash, and I didn't know how he got around it with her, but staying out of their business worked for both of us. For the past two weeks, I'd built cabinets during the day, and helped behind the bar most nights, keeping my mouth shut.

Frankie's asshole ex-boyfriend stumbled out of the bar with the woman's arms wrapped around his waist, and I cleaned up around the pool table before heading into the back room to finish the cabinet doors for Lena. As I worked, the constant buzz of the saw couldn't drown out my thoughts.

My father, by blood only, had been questioning Vivian and her ability to run the family business in his absence. With his release coming, he was making moves, and she had started to crack under the pressure. I would've stayed buried on the West Coast until death found me if not for my loyalty to her and her son. My sister had never been the anxious type, or one to panic, but a month ago, she'd begged me for the number of my latest burner, and her messages hadn't stopped since. Our father would lose his mind when he realized how far down the family business had fallen. His network had lost trust, the family had dispersed, and allies with the Nobles had backed away. It hadn't helped that I'd killed one of their own without consequences. Either Vivian packed up and disappeared with her son, or I returned to Boston and cleaned up the mess I had helped create. She needed me by her side to prove the Morrigan family still had power, but the Nobles wanted me dead.

We'd narrowed it down to a three-month window. I'd given her a plan to import more metals and navigation equipment, helping her rebuild the business from the inside. My father had paid for me to get a college degree, grooming me to know how to move stuff, making it look clean, even if it wasn't, and I'd been damn good at it. Too good, and now I needed another way out.

Nash Morrigan had been right. There was no way out.

A searing pain shot up my forearm like glass slicing my skin, and I flinched, yanking my arm back as I dropped the chisel. Blood pulsed from a deep wound, dripping onto the floor. I wrapped a rag around my arm and applied pressure.

"Hey, Rhett, Sandy is coming in tonight after all—what the fuck happened?" With a gasp, Lena rushed over, her eyes wide as she stared at the chisel lying on the floor, blood coating the blade.

"It slipped. You have a first aid kit, or duct tape?"

How the hell did I slice my arm open with a damn chisel?

Her head snapped up. "Duct tape? Let me see." She forced me to unwrap the rag and gagged, speaking through shallow breaths. "That looks bad, you need to get it looked at. I'll drive you to the hospital—"

"I'll drive myself." I pulled the rag tighter, tucking the edges into the sides to secure it as blood soaked through the fabric and ran down my hand.

Lena handed me a clean bar towel and helped me wrap it around my arm, absorbing the blood. "Are you sure you can drive?"

"More than sure." Grabbing my keys, I headed for the back door. Walking through the bar with blood on my hands didn't seem appropriate. "Back in a bit."

"There's no rush, Sandy is coming in to work the bar tonight." She put on rubber gloves and grabbed a stack of paper towels and a spray bottle of cleaning solution. "Looks like a crime scene." She turned her head and gagged again.

"There's not enough blood for that," I mumbled as I headed for the back door, feeling Lena's eyes on my back.

SEVEN

Frankie

I hurried to Bay 1 for an incoming trauma. An early snowfall always brought in car accidents, and this afternoon would be a busy one in our little town of Willow Grove.

I grabbed a lab kit for bloodwork and pulled on a pair of disposable gloves as paramedics rolled in a woman strapped to a backboard on a gurney. Darla, a day-shift nurse on the verge of retirement, walked up to the woman first with a vitals cart, and handed me a bag of saline. Her composure in stressful situations made her one of my favorite nurses to work with.

"I'm dying," the woman gasped between sobs. Tears mixed with blood from a gash along the side of her ashen face.

Darla took her vitals and patted the woman's arm. "We're here to take care of you,"

I flushed her IV line and hung the bag of saline, disposing of the empty one. "What happened?" I asked, opening the supplies to draw her blood.

The paramedic rattled off words like an announcer. "Her name is Bonnie, MVC, a truck hit the driver's side, she was the only passenger, abdominal pain, tachy, BP dropping."

Dr. Harper hurried to the bedside, and the two EMTs moved out of the way.

"Her BP is 88 over 50," Darla said.

"I'm going to take some bloodwork, Bonnie, okay? You'll feel a poke." I fastened the tourniquet around her upper arm as she nodded, fear filling her eyes. Wanting to be as efficient as possible, I shut out the chaos surrounding me and focused. I felt along her arm, and a whisper of a vein bounced underneath my touch. I cleaned her skin with an alcohol wipe and anchored the vein as I inserted the needle. Blood flashed back into the tube, filling it, and I gently gave each one a shake.

Grasping my hand, Bonnie lifted her head to get closer to me. "It hurts so bad... in my stomach."

"Can I lift your shirt?" I asked.

She blinked her eyes, and I peeled up her torn shirt, gently pressing the faint bruising along the left side of her distended abdomen. Her hand shot up to her shoulder. Instinct and experience suggested a ruptured spleen, but I needed a clearer image for the doctor to confirm, second-guessing myself.

"Right *there*, I'm gonna die, I can't breathe. I've got kids at home." Her voice cracked as she spoke.

"Can I have the ultrasound machine?" As my words came out, Darla handed it to me with a knowing smile. "This will be cold," I said. Quickly applying gel to her skin, I dragged the probe back and forth over her abdomen, focusing on that upper left side. A dark area among the shades of gray stood out, and Dr. Harper moved next to me, watching the screen. "She's bleeding," I said.

"Ruptured spleen, let's move, prep her for the OR." Dr. Harper called out orders as I wiped the gel with a towel.

Darla and I helped the team move her to the operating room. The OR nurses and anesthesiologist were waiting to greet the patient, and we transferred her over as soon as the doors opened.

Walking back down the hallway next to Darla, I stopped to pump sanitizer onto my hands from a dispenser on the wall. "Looking forward to being free of this place?"

"You'd think so, but I'll miss all this, it's become part of me now." She glanced at me with a wisdom I couldn't comprehend. "It goes faster than you think, Frankie. Learn from your mistakes, ask questions when you're unsure, and don't be afraid of therapy to process the worst days."

"I should get that tattooed on my body, so I never forget it."

"That's a tad extreme." She stepped into the bathroom as I approached the nurse's station in the ER. The mention of tattoos brought Rhett to my mind, and the designs inked on his arms. Zoey waved me over to where she sat at a computer, dragging my attention away from my mystery neighbor, who I hadn't seen since the Magpie. I braced myself for whatever was coming next.

"Wanna put those skills to use and stitch up a wound?" she asked.

"Sure." I'd been trained and certified to suture simple lacerations, but it had been months since I'd closed a wound. There was something satisfying about bringing the skin back together to stop the bleeding. I loved being part of the healing process.

Logging out of the computer, she stood and headed toward a bay closed off with curtains. "Let me take a quick look at this guy, but it sounds like it's within your scope. Grab a suture kit, meet me in Bay 2."

I scrubbed my hands and headed toward Bay 2 with gloves and supplies. Moving the curtains aside, I stepped inside the small, enclosed space. A man sat on the gurney with his head angled down as Zoey finished examining him, her voice melodic as she talked. I recognized him before he looked up, and my pulse skipped.

Zoey shifted to the foot of the bed, offering a clear view of the blood-soaked towel Rhett clutched against his arm. "Mr. Marshall, Frankie's going to suture that gash and have you on your way." She turned on the bedside computer, typing frantically. "It's not as deep as I thought. Simple sutures will do it, five at most. Order's in, you can give the lidocaine too, I'll hang around to make sure you have no issues, but he's all yours."

All mine... if only.

Snapping my mind out of the gutter, I turned my attention back to him. Splattered blood in varying shades of red had smudged into his jeans and work boots.

"Hey," he said. The harsh beam from the mounted exam light shone in his eyes, making them appear more green than hazel. "Had a minor incident."

"I see that."

"You two know each other?" Zoey gave me an amused glance.

I cleaned a side table with disinfecting wipes and lowered it next to the bed. "He's a friend of Finn's."

"I'm her neighbor," he said at the same time.

I washed my hands in the bedside sink and set up the suture kit before donning a mask and gloves.

"You moved into the vacant place *right* next door to her?" Zoey asked.

"I did." His focus remained on my every move as I laid an absorbent pad on the table and reached for his hand.

"Can you place your arm across the table?" I asked.

"Whatever you want." A smile graced his full lips as he pulled the towel away, exposing a profusely bleeding laceration.

Sitting on the stool, I wheeled close to him. His cologne mixed with something masculine and enticing, even through my mask, and I concentrated on his wound. With gauze soaked in saline, I gently cleaned and irrigated the gash. Sweat beaded at the back of my neck. His unwavering attention made me... *nervous*. Not in a creepy way, but in a way that made my heart race.

Jesus, Frankie, you're at work and he's a patient. Focus.

I picked up another sterile gauze with my forceps to dry it, stopping as he flinched. "Are you okay?"

"Keep going," he said.

Zoey turned off the computer beside me as chatter erupted from the nurses' station, and someone peered between the curtains into the room. "I'm sorry to interrupt, Dr. Harper, you got a minute?"

"Give me ten minutes—"

They glanced between me and Zoey. "We don't have ten minutes."

"Go ahead," I said as I held a small syringe of lidocaine toward Rhett's forearm. "I'm good, I'll call if I need you."

"Thanks, Frankie." She bolted from the room, shutting the curtain behind her.

Rhett reached across the table and touched my hand holding the needle. "What's that for?"

"Sorry, I should've told you what I was doing. It's just going to freeze—"

"Are you sticking it right in the middle?" He pulled his hand back.

"Just at the edge." Still holding the needle close, my eyes locked on his and heat rushed to my cheeks. "For someone who doesn't like needles, you've got a lot of ink."

"That's different."

"More painful?"

He didn't break eye contact. "It goes numb after a while."

"This will numb your skin so I can put that cut back together."

He frowned, tilting his arm back and forth as blood trickled over his skin, falling to the pad. "I should've just used duct tape."

"Yeah, that's not happening. Put your arm back down."

"You're bossy," he teased. "I don't respond well to orders."

"Neither do I..." I softened my tone as I continued, "*Please,* put your arm back down."

"You make it hard to say no."

"Good." I smiled underneath the mask. Flirting with this man came way too naturally, and I reminded myself again that I was a professional at work, and he was a patient, nothing more.

"How long will this take?"

I pursed my lips to keep myself from laughing, grateful for the fabric covering my mouth. "At this rate, we'll be here all night. But if you do as you're told, fifteen minutes?"

He held his arm still. "I'll do as I'm told for fifteen minutes."

"It'll sting a little." I angled the needle to inject the lidocaine.

"Go for it." He winced as I stuck him with the needle, giving it a minute to numb.

A comfortable silence filled the space between us as the seconds ticked by, surprising me. For a dark, brooding man, he made me feel at ease in his presence without trying.

"I'm just going to poke you a little to make sure it's numb." I touched the reddened skin near the bleeding gash with the tip of the needle. "Feel that?"

"Nope," he said.

"Perfect, let's do this." I clamped the pre-threaded curved needle in the holder and adjusted my grip. My eyes darted up at him. "Ready?"

"Just do it, Frankie." As he said my name, his face was close to mine, and I couldn't look up at him.

Piercing the needle through, I created the first stitch. "You know, if you wanted to see me again so bad, you could've just asked. This really wasn't necessary."

"Fuck, I wish I'd known that before I sliced myself with the chisel."

"And like you said, we're neighbors, so it's not like you don't know where to find me." I didn't break my gaze from my work, focusing on each careful suture through his skin, but felt his eyes on me, and heat coursed through my body.

"I'll remember that."

The lesion had cut along the tattoo of the cloaked figure. "This will leave a scar on your tattoo."

"I don't care," he said.

"Does it mean something?" Poking the needle through his skin on the opposite edge, I secured each stitch. "I don't have any, but don't they usually have some sort of symbolic meaning for people?" I had overstepped the nurse-patient boundary and stopped myself, shaking my head. "I'm sorry, it's not my business." The wound closed in a straight line, and I admired my work.

"Regret." His gaze dropped to his forearm. "You impress me, Frankie."

"That's the nicest thing you've said to me in the short time we've known each other." I cleaned around the sutures and placed a bandage over the wound, debating if I should push him on the tattoo, but curiosity won, blurring those lines again. "Regret? Your tattoo?"

"It's just one of those I wish I never got."

I ran my gloved fingers along his arm. "You could always have it removed, or covered with a new one, but that would mean more needles."

"Good point." A sexy smirk crossed his face, making his eyes crinkle.

Why does he have to be so damn attractive?

"Keep that clean and dry for the next day or two, wash with soap and water, change the bandage—"

"I've got it from here." He stood, rolling down his shirt sleeve. "Thanks."

"You're welcome."

Cleaning up the tray, I dropped the needles into the sharps container and discarded the rest in the trash can. The metal of the curtain rings clanged as I washed my hands, and I glanced over my shoulder. Rhett lingered between the curtains, waiting as if he was going to say something, but stopped himself. The space he took up in front of me was getting really comfortable, really fast. I'd dated, been in a long relationship, dated again, but nothing had ever felt like *this*. Except I couldn't put what *this* felt like into words. It was raw chemistry, instant attraction, sexual tension.

It had been a while, that was my problem. I wasn't thinking clearly with too much going on in my head.

"Have a good rest of your shift, Frankie."

"I'll do my best," I said, following him out of the room.

Rhett walked away, and I turned in the other direction, running into Logan in the hall. "There's a delivery for you."

"What delivery?"

"See for yourself. Who is that tall hotness?" he gestured as Rhett left our line of sight.

"My new neighbor."

"Will he be attending your birthday gathering next week?"

"No, we just met."

"But he lives right next door? Spill that tea, Frankie."

"There won't be tea to spill." There never could be. Not with a man like *him*.

A bouquet of pale orange roses lay on the nurses' station counter. The unique mesh wrapping and '*The Francesca Rose*' logo revealed where they'd come from, but their sender remained a mystery.

"These are for you," Logan handed them to me in a grand gesture.

Another nurse, Nancy, who was new to the unit, approached, and Darla sat at the computer behind the desk.

Darla took her glasses off. "You got a secret admirer?"

"Doubtful." I inhaled the powdery sweetness and plucked the small card from an envelope.

The three of them stared at me wide-eyed. "Well," Logan said, "don't leave us in suspense, read it out loud."

I glanced down at the note. "I'm not reading it out loud."

Francesca, thank you for taking such wonderful care of my mother. Best.

Unease sank into my gut, sending a chill through my body as I held the card. That man bought flowers from my mother's shop and sent them to my work? What the *fuck*? Who was that guy?

"That look on your face implies the opposite of romance." Logan scowled as he tried to look over my shoulder and read the card, but I held it against my chest.

"Definitely not romance, just a thankful patient from yesterday." I forced a smile through the sudden wave of panic that hit me. My eyes swept past the hallway, but he wasn't among the few people sitting in the waiting room, or in any of the bays.

"Party's over, isn't it? No admirer, nothing exciting." Nancy shook her head, pulling a notepad and pen from her scrub pocket as she walked away.

Either this man had an odd fascination with me, or my instincts were wrong. I trusted my instincts, they'd never steered me wrong, and these flowers, *Francesca* roses, carried a warning.

Zoey rushed down the hallway toward us at the nurse's station, her lips quivering and tears streaming down her face. She gestured toward Logan and me, her words hushed. "On-call room."

This wasn't good.

We hurried after her into the room and closed the door. Zoey flicked on the light and sank onto the cot in the corner, her shoulders rising with a shaky breath.

"Jesus, Zo, what happened?" I knew this meant terrible news.

"The kid died, didn't he?" Logan crossed his arms as his eyes darted from Zoey to me.

Zoey's face crumpled. "We did everything we could, but... Meyer's gone." She fell apart, burying her face in her hands as she cried.

Shock numbed my body as I sat beside her. The kid from a few nights ago, the one we saved... *Dead.*

I rubbed her back. My eyes blurred with tears, and a heavy ache settled in my chest. Logan paced with a hand over his mouth, barely holding back his own tears.

I'd been trained to repair wounds, stop bleeding, keep a heart beating or lungs breathing, but no training prepared me for the weight of loss when death won. That part I carried with me, not knowing how to let go.

Eight

Frankie

I stood in front of the fridge with the door hanging open, the cool air on my face. The bare shelves offered no promise of satisfying my hunger. The motor clicked on, shaking me from my blank stare, and I shut the door, leaning against it. I had skipped the grocery store at the end of my shift and rushed home instead. I'd just taken a shower, but a persistent chill had settled into my bones.

Shivering, I grabbed a sweater draped on the back of a dining room chair and pulled it over my head as I turned up the heat.

Unwelcome sadness crept in, threatening to unravel me. The weight of losing a patient, a young man who'd had his life ahead of him and lost his second chance, pressed against my chest so hard I thought I'd collapse.

His name was Meyer, reminding me of Miles. I hadn't been able to save him either.

Rain lashed against the glass doors, and I switched the porch light on, sliding the door open. Blinking rain from my eyes, I craned my head to peer through the lattice and tangled vines between us, but Rhett's place was dark and still. Not that it mattered if he was home, but as good as I'd gotten at being alone, nights like this made my body ache with loneliness.

I shut the door and toasted a bagel, coating it with a thick layer of cream cheese, and sat on a stool at my island counter. The roses lay in front of me, still wrapped in paper. I brushed my fingertips over the soft petals. They'd die without a vase of water, but I didn't feel like I deserved them, not after tonight, and not if they were a gift from a stalker.

Now I'm being overly dramatic.

If they hadn't come from Mom's shop, I'd throw them away. I bit into my bagel and held the card up, rereading the man's message. He hadn't left a name. His mother was Alice Lane, but an online search hadn't turned up anyone resembling her son. She must've remarried or kept her maiden name. Maybe he was harmless, but his behavior during our two encounters had set off an internal dark feeling I couldn't shake.

My phone vibrated against the counter, and two messages from Lena lit up the screen in quick succession. I read them and closed my eyes in defeat. Dad had spent the past few hours at the pub, getting drunk, and now refused to go home. Finn was working late, unable to get away, and Mom wasn't responding. He'd lasted a matter of days before needing me to step in.

I called Lena, and she picked up immediately, launching into a conversation without saying hello. "I know this is the shittiest timing—I talked to Logan—I am so fucking sorry about that kid, but I wanted your permission before I let Rhett step in with your dad, because that won't end well."

"I'm on my way," I said between the last bites of my bagel. I couldn't let myself think about the kid anymore, or I'd fall apart. The last time I broke down and cried, really let go and cried, was the night Miles had died. I never wanted to shatter like that again, not if I could help it.

"I know the drill, I didn't give him much and stopped serving him an hour ago, but he's got a dealer among the guys he's trying to hustle. He seemed fine, Frankie, I didn't worry until he joined a pool game playing for money..." A loud clatter drowned her out as she talked.

"I'll be there soon." I fumbled with my keys and headed into the garage, sticking my feet into a pair of sneakers.

"I'm sorry about your patient, I hate doing this to you. Finn can be here in an hour, just let me tell Rhett to drag your dad to his truck and get him home—"

"Please don't involve Rhett, this is my problem." The phone slid from its perch between my cheek and shoulder as I tossed my purse in the passenger seat. I started my Jeep, letting the call pick up over Bluetooth. "Lena?"

"Still here. I'll let him know you're coming." The background noise hushed over the line. "When was the last time you had a day off?"

The garage door creaked open, and the engine faltered as I turned the key in the ignition, finally coming to life. I'd planned to take my Jeep to a mechanic on my next day off, and that had been... "Too long ago. I picked up shifts, but I'm off this weekend."

"Do me a favor and give yourself a damn break."

I waited for the garage door to shut before leaving my driveway and heading onto the main road, my wipers at full speed in the pouring rain. "I'm going to the range with Finn on Saturday. Hey, try to keep Dad from getting his ass kicked until I get there?"

"I'll do my best," Lena said before hanging up.

Entering the Magpie, I searched for my father, but my gaze landed on Rhett as he worked behind the bar. His bandaged arm peeked from beneath his rolled-up shirtsleeves, and from where I stood, I couldn't tell if blood had soaked through the gauze, but I made a mental note to check before I left. I moved closer to the large, curved doorway, leading to an open room with the pool table, and Rhett glanced up from pouring beers with a sudden alertness sharpening his expression.

Cheers erupted from the room as I entered, in time to see my father stumble, using the edge of the pool table to stop himself from falling.

A man in a ball cap chalked his cue and glared at my father. "You're down five hundred, Roscoe, I'm taking this one."

Frustration drowned the ache of heartbreaking loss from earlier. "You're into this for five hundred bucks?" I stood beside my father. Nothing mattered to him anymore. Not me, Finn, my mother... *Life.*

His glazed-over stare surveyed me as he held a square of chalk over the end of his cue, trying to connect but missing with each swipe. "What're you doing here, Francesca?"

"Taking you home."

"Looks like your daughter's calling the shots." Another man laughed, shaking his head as he lifted a beer bottle to his lips. Sweat stains the size of plates lined under his arms.

"Love ya, honey, but I'm not leaving till I finish this game." Dad slurred his words. "Two balls left."

"I'm about to end it now." The man with the hat gestured to his intended pocket, lining up the shot. "Eight in that corner."

My father moved in front of me around the table, unsteady on his feet as he held the cue like a damn weapon.

"Fuck," the man said, missing the shot. "You're up, Roscoe, no way you can get those two balls in. Next round's on me, boys."

"Dad—" I reached for him as he stepped backward and fell, landing on the floor, still clutching his pool cue. I linked my arms under his and hoisted him up, but his weight was too much for me. I could move people larger than him across a stretcher with a slide sheet, but in his drunken state, my father was dead weight. "For fuck's sake, Dad, work with me here!"

"He can't play, he forfeits." The man stared at him with a pitying expression.

Bolting upright, I left my dad on the floor and wandered around the pool table. He deserved to lose five hundred dollars, but the arrogance of the two men as they laughed and slapped each other on the back after the horrible day I'd had infuriated me.

Rhett stepped into the room, and my father craned his neck as he helped him up. Shoving a chair behind my father, Rhett shifted his position closer to me. He observed the men in the room, hinting at his readiness for a fight. A few people left their seats at the bar and strolled over, glancing from the televisions to the pool table.

I won't let them make fools of us.

I picked up the cue from the floor and chalked its tip. "He's not forfeiting shit. Let me step in for him."

Rhett's curious gaze fixed on me as the man removed his ball cap and scratched his head, placing it back on. "Yeah, right—"

"Why not? Are you worried I'll beat you?" Miles had taught me how to play pool. We'd made it a habit to try out a new billiards hall in Boston at least once a week. I could play this game and walk out of here with at least a shred of dignity for myself and my dad.

Three other men who'd been watching from a table against the window put their hands up, laughing as they drank their beers. "Let her do it, no way she'll get both those shots," one of them said. Sudden recognition hit me; the three of them used to work with Dad a long time ago. My father had become a joke to them.

Their eyes suddenly averted as a presence loomed behind me. Rhett stayed in the room, keeping enough distance to give me space, but his proximity gave me a sense of security I didn't realize I needed.

Hiding a deep breath, I approached the table, leaning over as I inched the end of the cue close to the cue ball. "Eleven-ball side pocket."

A gruff laugh escaped someone, but I ignored him, refusing to break concentration. Pulling my hand back, I drove the cue forward, striking the cue ball. It hit the red-striped ball with a sharp clang, sending it rolling into the side pocket. My neck beaded with perspiration, and I fought the urge to rub a hand along it, chalking the end of my cue again.

"That's my girl." Dad clapped, nearly slipping off the chair, and I narrowed my eyes at him as anger ignited.

Shut up, Dad.

"Lucky shot, no way you'll get the eight in, you'll scratch the cue ball, and it's all mine." The man stepped closer to the table, poised for his turn.

"This is all *mine.*" I stretched my neck from side to side as I walked around the table. I positioned myself next to the cue ball and visualized the paths the ball could take depending on where I hit it.

Fuck, what did I get myself into tonight?

Rhett leaned against the wall, watching me with raised brows, not saying a word.

With the eight-ball too close to the corner, and the cue ball tucked near the side pocket, this would be *impossible.*

If Miles were standing next to me, he'd tell me to focus and trust my aim, like we'd done in countless billiards halls. His voice echoed in my mind. "And let the cue ball do the rolling," he'd said.

"You gotta call it, Roscoe." The man leaned over the table with a smirk.

"She's got this, Joe." Dad leaned forward, his elbows sliding off his knees, but Rhett stepped toward him, his eyes on me.

"She definitely does not *got* anything," Joe retorted.

If I struck the cue ball on the left, and it had a slight spin to the right, I could pocket the eight-ball. "Um... bottom right."

One of the staff brought in a tray of beers as laughter broke out again, but I flexed my trembling fingers, steadying them like I was getting ready to suture a wound or start an IV.

Come on, go in, go in, please fucking go in that damn pocket.

I bent forward and dragged the cue back, hitting the left side of the cue ball. It skimmed over the felt along the side, connecting with the eight-ball. I held my breath as it rolled a little too slowly, but the ball dropped into the pocket, and I released the air from my lungs with a huge exhale.

"Give my father his money." I placed the pool cue on the rack and snatched my dad's jacket as Rhett helped him to a standing position. "Let's go, Dad."

"Hell no, it's time to celebrate." He tripped over his own feet and grabbed the back of the chair.

"It's time to call it a night." Rhett's calm voice resonated in my chest, suppressing my anger as he guided my father out of the room toward the bar where Lena waited.

Nine

Rhett

I helped Frankie's dad walk to the bar, keeping my grip light on his arm, while allowing him to maintain as much dignity as possible.

The way Frankie stepped in, *owning* that table, was impossible to ignore. The woman was sexy as fuck, and every time I was near her, something inside me loosened, a part I'd buried for good damn reason.

Off limits.

Her dad sat on the bar stool and looked at me. "You know this new guy, Francesca? Who does he think he is?" He spoke slowly, but still slurred his words, and Frankie let out a frustrated sigh.

Lena reached across the bar, placing her hand on Roscoe's. "Jared, I love you. But this new guy is someone you need to listen to. Let Frankie take you home, I won't ask again."

He patted Lena's cheek with the gentleness of a father, but he shifted on the stool and swayed as he tried to stand, dropping his hand to the bar. Frankie moved to his side, bracing her arm around him, but he shook her away. "I don't need your help, I can stand on my own."

I brought my hand close to her father's back, not letting him see. "Where are you parked?"

Her pale cheeks reddened as she averted her eyes. "You don't have to do this, I've got it from here."

Embarrassment was all over her; I needed to reassure her I wasn't judging. Her father clearly had problems, but he'd also lost his son two years ago. The image of Frankie holding Miles, covered in his blood, flashed through my mind. I could be on the run until the day I died and would never regret killing the man who had shot her brother. "Just tell me where you're parked and I'll get him into the car."

"You're going to bust a stitch," she said, brushing her fingers along my bandaged forearm. A spot of blood had soaked through the gauze.

"I don't care about that right now, let me help you."

She faced her father as he gripped the edge of the bar. "You got your money back, let's go."

As Lena poured a round of beers, she darted her eyes from me to Frankie. "Rhett's going with you, I've got the bar."

"Lena—"

"Frankie." Placing the glasses on a tray, Lena bent close to her. "Let the man help? I trust him."

None of you should trust me, I don't deserve your trust.

But, fuck, I wanted it.

Approaching the door, Jared tripped. I caught him before he hit the floor, and he gave me a sharp look. I lowered my voice as I spoke. "I just want to get you to Frankie's Jeep. She might be a pool genius, but she won't be able to hold you up, and I don't think you want to make a scene for yourself or her."

"Who the hell are you?" Jared huffed. He had the same look in his eyes as Frankie, he just wore the darkness with more practice.

"Rhett Marshall, sir."

He patted my chest. "Don't hurt my daughter." He burst through the door and stumbled out as Frankie came running up beside me.

"It's not too late to turn around and walk away," Frankie said.

"Not a chance." I let the door shut behind us and stood near her father as he held the railing, taking the two stairs to the ground.

Straightening his jacket, he fastened the buttons unevenly and crossed the parking lot, swaying with each step. "Where's the taxi?"

"The taxi is Frankie's Jeep." I walked slightly behind him as her ex, Clay Preston, emerged from a sedan. That asshole had her once and fucked it up. Given the chance and a different life, I'd treat her so well, she'd forget he ever existed.

Approaching the vehicle, I noted a barcode and a small rental company logo sticker on the windshield. He didn't strike me as the type to settle for a basic rental car instead of a flashy luxury vehicle.

He headed toward the Magpie's front doors and called out. "You need to take control of your father before he hurts someone."

"You need to fuck off and mind your business," she said, unlocking her Jeep.

I need to restrain myself from breaking his nose and ruining his face.

A juvenile urge to reach into my pocket for the utility knife and slash his tires came over me, but I picked up my pace toward Frankie's Jeep. Her dad shuffled off balance, fumbling with the door handle, and I caught up, yanking the door open.

"Jesus, Dad. Really?" Frankie rubbed her temples and let her hands fall to her sides. "I thought after the other day, maybe, just maybe you listened to me."

"I always listen to you, honey." Jared tumbled onto the back seat, and I extended my hand. He hesitated, but took it, hauling himself up. He pulled his legs inside, and I shut the door.

Frankie opened the driver's side door. "I'm so sorry about all this."

Rounding the front of the Jeep, I got in the passenger seat and closed the door. "Never be sorry for shit like this, it isn't your fault."

"What are you doing?" Her beautiful mouth dropped open, and her eyes widened.

"Coming with you. Just drop me off at the bar when we're done." Dragging the seatbelt across my chest, I clipped it in place as she started the engine, watching me. I leaned forward and pointed to the check-engine light on her dash. "Something wrong?"

"*Something*... Look, I can take care of this, I've *been* taking care of this, all of it, I just..."

It hadn't taken me long to figure out she'd mastered the skill of keeping her shit together, at least for the world to see. Frankie had walls up around her, and I doubted she ever let anyone close enough to see behind them. "I have no doubt you can take care of this and pretty much anything else, doesn't mean you should have to, especially not alone."

Her father mumbled under his breath, and the smell of alcohol filled the Jeep. I glanced over my shoulder at the same time as Frankie, and she was *right there*. Our faces were so close I could kiss her perfect lips, but I wasn't about to cross that uninvited line. And she was off limits.

"You okay back there sir?" I said instead.

"Just fine." He rolled the window down a crack and leaned against it.

Not moving, her eyes met mine as she spoke. "Are you going to be sick, Dad?"

"Don't worry about me, honey. Where are you taking me?"

She pulled out of the parking lot, glancing in the rearview mirror. "Home."

"I'll need coffee if I'm going home to your mother. She sees me like this, she'll throw me a blanket for the front step, it's fucking cold."

"That's nicer than I'd be," Frankie said, accelerating through a yellow light.

"You could just leave me here on the side of the road, it doesn't make one bit of difference." Jared tried to prop himself up on his elbow, missed, and hit his forehead on the door. Not two minutes later, he was snoring.

Frankie took a deep breath as her eyes flickered from the road to the rearview mirror, avoiding mine. "It makes a difference to me," she whispered. Her hand fell from the steering wheel to turn up the heat. "Do you mind? I'm freezing."

"Do whatever you want, I'm good." I rested my hands on my knees as hers slipped back onto the wheel. All I could think of was how her hands would feel on me, wanting more than I should.

"Whatever I want…" she muttered, her dark hair falling over her shoulder as she stole a glance at me.

She could ask me for anything, and I'd find a way to get it. "Have something in mind?"

"Not something you can help me with, I'm afraid."

"Try me," I said as she drove onto a neighborhood street.

Hesitating, her gaze drifted from the rearview mirror and back on the road. "After you left the hospital today, we lost a patient. He was only sixteen."

"I'm sorry, Frankie, I didn't realize." I draped my arm on the center console, wanting to reach for her hand.

"No, you couldn't have. It happens, you know? It's part of what I do, life. It's just been a rough day, and if I really could have whatever I wanted, it would be to not feel like this again." Her eyes met mine for a second, and she switched off the wipers as the rain subsided.

"If there's anything I can do, I'll do it."

"I guess you sort of are coming with me, as sad as this is."

She slowed down as we approached a two-story house on the corner, and a light flickered on above the garage when she pulled into the driveway. She killed the engine, tilting her head toward me. "This is it, the house I grew up in." She opened the door, triggering the overhead light.

Her father's head slumped against the window, and I carefully opened the back door, raising a hand against his shoulder to keep him from falling out.

Jared's eyes flew open, and he grabbed my arm. "What are you doing?"

I spoke calmly. "Just helping you inside."

Frankie held the doorframe as she stood next to me. "Think you can stand and walk into the house, Dad?"

Releasing my arm, her father swung his legs to the ground and stepped outside. "Yes, Francesca, I can stand and walk, I'm a little drunk, not helpless."

The front door opened, and a woman stepped onto the porch—without a doubt, Frankie's mom. She wore an unmistakable *I want to kill you* expression that Finn had perfected. "Do you know I almost packed a suitcase for your sorry ass?"

Frankie trailed her father as he trudged along the walkway toward the stairs, and I hung back, careful not to intrude, but ready to step in if he fell.

Jared's posture slumped, and he clutched his chest as he pleaded with the woman. "Nora, you said it better than I could. My ass is sorry, please let me in so I can go to bed."

With a dramatic spin, Frankie pursed her lips and rolled her eyes in a silent, exasperated sigh. Even pissed off, she was stunning in a way that made it impossible to look away.

"I can't keep this up, Jared, you're breaking me here." Nora's gaze followed Frankie as she walked toward the porch steps. "And it's not fair to her."

"Don't worry about me, just get in the house." Frankie linked an arm with her father's, coaxing him up the front steps, but he struggled, and I moved closer. "Mom, this is Rhett, he works at the Magpie with Lena and helped me get Dad home; Rhett, my mom, Nora."

As I climbed the stairs, her mother offered her hand, and I shook it. "Good to meet you," I said.

"Likewise." She sized me up, but her stern expression softened. "Thanks for helping Frankie, I apologize for my husband's current state."

"No apology needed, please."

The door hung open as Jared shuffled his boots off in the entryway and sat on the bottom step of a staircase leading to the second floor. "Go home, Francesca."

Nora closed the door behind me. The entryway was grand, reminding me of my father's estate. But with the four of us gathered inside, and despite the family dysfunction, it lacked the emptiness his place always had. Frankie's home had warmth beyond the fireplace blazing in the living room.

"Need me to stay?" Frankie asked her mom.

"I'll deal with him from here." She pulled Frankie into a hug like she wanted to shield her from the world, and I had a flashback of my own mother. I'd never stop missing her.

I didn't belong here. "I'll wait in the Jeep, Frankie."

Her father stood, his voice carrying over mine. "No one is *dealing* with me, *I* deal with me." He reached for the railing and missed, losing his footing on the stairs. Frankie rushed beside him, extending her hand, but Jared brushed it away. Nora wiped tears off her cheeks, and Frankie's eyes watered as she glanced up at the ceiling, turning away. Jared kept talking, but his words trailed off in a jumbled mess. "Why is it so dark in this house…"

"Dad, please," Frankie whispered.

Fuck it, I'm not going anywhere until he's okay. I hope she can forgive me for this.

I took a step forward. "I'm dealing with you so they don't have to. I need you up those stairs without breaking your neck."

Her father stood, and he wavered against the railing, rubbing his face. He placed a foot on the next step. "Fuck, I'm an asshole."

I climbed the stairs next to him. "Take your time."

"I don't fall."

"Good," I said. "I won't have to catch you." I walked with him up the stairs, staying one step behind him.

As we approached the landing at the top, he looked at me. Desperate weariness in his eyes regarded me with defeat. "Make sure she's not too mad?"

"Sure."

Frankie would get as angry as she needed to, and nothing I could do would stop that.

He wobbled down the hallway into a bedroom, and I headed back downstairs. Frankie's mom rushed past me and gave my arm a squeeze. "Thanks," she said.

Frankie stormed outside, leaving a gust of cold air sweeping through the doorway. I followed her to the Jeep as she searched her pockets, swearing. "Where are my keys, I just had them."

Silver glinted on the pavement underneath the light, and I bent down, retrieving her keys. "You just dropped them, that's all."

Clearing her throat, she licked her lips before speaking, and under any other circumstances, I'd find it hot as hell, but all I felt was worry. "Thank you for your help tonight," she said. "I'm sorry again for dragging you into this, I can take you back."

I dared to close the gap between us and stand in front of her, holding up the keys. "I'm in no hurry to leave you." Her fingers grazed mine as she took them, and I wanted to grab her and pull her toward me.

She claimed my other hand, and I let her take control. Lifting my jacket sleeve, she eyed the bandage. "You need to take care of that so it doesn't get infected."

"Frankie..." I struggled to find the right words. I'd been out of practice dealing with feelings and comforting people I cared about.

Did I care *about her already?*

Tilting her head, she readjusted my sleeve. "Let's go, I'm cold."

We got in the Jeep and left her parents' house, heading back to the Magpie. She drove in silence, with her attention fixed on the road. I didn't know her well, but the tension between us was new. "How are you?" I asked.

The traffic light swayed in the wind as she came to a stop at the red light. "I'm fine."

"Fine is an overused word, how are you really?" I stretched my back against the seat, cracking my knuckles to relieve the relentless tension.

Gripping the wheel with one hand, she slapped her leg. "It's a word describing what I am right now. You asked, and I told you, what more do you want?"

I should shut my mouth and leave her alone, not get involved and stay away, like I'd promised Finn. But I couldn't stand to see her hurting, lost in her own thoughts. "I don't want anything. I just know what it feels like to tell people you're fine when you're not."

"What's a better word to use, since you're the expert at not being *fine?*"

"Anything, if it's the truth. You don't have to tell me, it's none of my business, but I know you're not fine, and if you need to talk,

I won't be far." I didn't take my eyes off her as she maneuvered into the parking spot near my truck.

She looked directly at me, her expression unreadable. "Please take care of those stitches before you get infected. I'm sticking with fine."

"Fair enough." I got out of the Jeep and leaned down to face her. "Get yourself home safe." I shut the door and hurried into the bar as a message from my sister pinged on my phone.

Do you know a Frankie Roscoe?

TEN

Frankie

F inn arrived and set up in the lane next to me at the shooting range. Shoving my ear protection to the side, I yelled over the gunfire echoing around me, "I didn't think you were coming."

"Got caught up at the Magpie." He stood beside me, squinting through his safety glasses at my target paper fifteen feet down the firing lane. A rare smile crossed his too-serious face. "Nice, Frankie."

"I'm improving," I said.

"I knew you'd be great." He moved back to his lane and pressed buttons on a control screen, setting his target distance. Loading the magazine, he stretched his neck from side to side, transitioning from my pain-in-the ass older brother to police officer. With an expert stance I couldn't match, his shoulders relaxed as he extended his arms and took a few shots in rapid succession.

When Finn first brought me here, the sound of guns exploding off the walls had unnerved me. But now, as I readied myself for another round, I breathed through the thundering sound vibrating in my chest, chasing all my dark thoughts away, easing my mind. With each shot, the gun kicked a little too high, and I locked my arms, tightening my grip.

Without moving my body, I glanced at Finn. He quickly put the safety on his gun. Pulling back the slide, he snapped it back in place before setting it down, releasing his finger from the trigger. We had an unspoken, choreographed routine at the range. He was always in the lane next to me, taking breaks to coach me when I faltered.

He gestured through the bulletproof partition for me to angle my gun down, and entered my lane, standing beside me again, shoving the ear protection off one ear. "Put that foot forward." He tapped my left knee. "Soften your knees and lock your elbows."

I followed his instructions, not breaking my concentration on the target as he adjusted my thumb supporting my trigger hand. "Like this?"

"Lean forward a bit more." He did the motions beside me, and I mirrored him. "Take back control, Frankie, don't let the gun

SHATTERED SECRETS BETWEEN US

control you, try again." He stepped back, replacing the earmuff with a nod.

I took a deep breath, inhaling the sharp metallic smell of fire-crackers. Adjusting my stance, I relaxed my knees a little and fired at the target, joining the muffled gunshots surrounding me like I was part of a symphony of drums. The weight of the gun felt lighter in my grip as the slide locked open and a click replaced my next shot. Removing my finger from the trigger, I lowered the gun, fumbling with the magazine release as I held it pointed down toward the target. I set it down and pressed the button, rolling in the target.

Most of the bullet holes clustered at the top of the target, but two shots landed closer to the center than I'd ever gotten before. "Would you look at that," I said, unable to stop the grin from spreading across my face.

Joining me in my lane, Finn laughed. "Not bad, not bad at all." He gave me a quick one-armed squeeze. "Want to go again?"

"Hell yeah I do."

My thoughts returned with a vengeance as I set up another round. This place helped me escape the pain of losing a patient, even for a little while. In the days after the boy had died, his family had posted an emotional obituary online—he'd loved his sister, considered the family dog his best friend, and had a talent for drawing. I'd attended his funeral with a few colleagues yesterday. His family sat in a row, clinging to one another, devastated beyond comprehension. Meyer Young's lifetime of potential fuckups, suc-cesses, partners and love ahead of him had been cut short, and I didn't want to accept that we'd *saved* him only to lose him.

One resounding, undeniable message plagued me: life could be brutally unfair, and we were powerless to stop it.

Tears burned my eyes, and I shut them, adjusting my safety goggles to keep them from fogging. I couldn't risk falling apart, or I might never put myself back together, and my family needed me. Mom had an early birthday dinner planned for me tomorrow with a hidden agenda to get us together and confront my dad. Whatever intervention she had in mind wouldn't work.

But no matter how much I smothered myself with work and family drama, I couldn't get Rhett out of my damn head. The rain and night shifts had kept me off my deck for the past couple of days, but one evening, music with saxophones and drums had drifted from a speaker next door. He listened to music. Good music. Somehow, the steady sound coming from his place helped ease my loneliness. I'd even dusted off my piano keyboard and sat with my fingers resting on the keys. I didn't play a single note, but for the first time in a long time, I wanted to.

We were strangers who hardly knew each other. *Fine* had perfectly described my feelings—not elated, but grief hadn't dragged me under yet.

I am fine.

I secured a new sheet of target paper to the cardboard, sending it downrange under the clinical fluorescent lights that reminded me of the hospital. This place didn't offer *comfort*, but it demanded precision and control, similar to the expectations during a busy shift, even when doubt consumed me.

An hour later, Finn and I walked toward the doors together, chatting like we used to when we were kids. The excitement in his voice was refreshing. "Thanks for coming. Did you get to sleep at all this morning?"

"I got enough, but this was good, Finn. We should do this every couple of weeks like we used to." Dark clouds hid the setting sun as a heavy downpour battered the pavement. The past week had become a never-ending rainstorm. I tucked my ponytail underneath my hood and slung my purse over my shoulder.

"You want to come to the Magpie for a drink? There's a game on tonight." Finn said with his hand on the door handle.

"I just want to go home and relax with a glass of wine." *And try to sit on the deck with my space heater, listening to the river... and maybe a little jazz.* Rain tapped the glass on the door as the wind blew sideways. "Is Rhett working?"

Finn exhaled, releasing the door. "I'm not sure, Lena takes care of scheduling staff." He rubbed the back of his neck. "He won't be in town long, just remember that."

"What do you have against him? Seriously, how do you know each other?"

"I told you—"

"You told me what you want me to know, but there's more. I know you. It's like your time in Boston never happened, but it was your whole life for years until Miles died... I don't get it."

He bit his cheek, as he did when frustrated or nervous, and peered through the glass. "I left that life behind, and you should too. Just move on."

"That life took our brother from us. I'll never be able to forget it, not until whoever killed him is in jail."

He just shook his head and opened the door. "Let's get out of here."

Wind and icy rain pelted my face as I followed him outside, running across the parking lot to my Jeep. I needed him to be there for Mom's intervention birthday dinner. The rain drenched my pants and streamed down my face.

I approached his car as he got in, and he rolled down the window. "You're getting soaked, what's wrong?" The stern expression returned, settling over his features like a mask. My brother held onto more darkness than I realized.

"I need you at dinner tomorrow night."

"Lena would kick my ass if I didn't go, we'll be there."

Bending down, I gripped the door frame. "Thank you."

I took a step back as Finn rolled up the window, stopping halfway. "I wouldn't miss dinner, I'll never bail on you. But Dad's got to want to get better, or nothing we do will work." He nodded toward my Jeep. "Go home, I'll see you tomorrow."

Tugging my hood tighter, I raced to my Jeep and followed him out of the parking lot, waving as I drove in the opposite direction toward home. Addiction was a brutal road to navigate. We'd lived through it with Miles and failed. My dad used to listen to me.

If I could make him understand the damage his self-destructive behavior was having on all of us, maybe he'd accept help.

Bright headlights glared in my rearview mirror, and I sped up as a vehicle tailgated me. I turned off the main road, but the car matched my pace, staying too close to my bumper. I glared in my rearview mirror. "Back off, asshole."

I glanced from my mirror to the rain-streaked windshield and increased the wiper speed. I pressed the button on the dash, silencing the music. The sounds of drumming rain and my shallow breathing filled the Jeep. Between the torrential rain, the fog creeping into the darkness, and blinding headlights, I couldn't make out the color or type of vehicle.

Who the hell would want to follow me? The man from the hospital?

But he'd gone home, his mother hadn't been back in the ER, and he'd sent me flowers *thanking* me. The relentless car stayed on my ass, but I was more determined to lose it. The last thing I wanted was for my pursuer to know where I lived. Approaching a subdivision, I tapped my brakes, taking a sharp turn onto the first street. With my eyes glued to the rearview mirror, I slowed down. The car trailed behind me.

Who are you?

I pulled into a driveway, grabbing my phone to call 911, and waited. The battery warning lit up on my dash.

"Do not break down on me now."

Tires screeched on the wet pavement as the car did a U-turn and sped out of the subdivision. A wave of fear tightened in my chest, and I frantically hit the lock button on my car doors, letting the clicking sound reassure me I was safe inside the Jeep. Without a description of the car, my call to emergency services would take resources away from someone who might need immediate help. I could mention what happened to Finn tomorrow instead, maybe even file a police report.

Lights came on inside the house, and I backed out of the driveway, turning around. I sped up, leaving the neighborhood behind, and headed for home through the downpour, checking my mirror for anyone driving behind me.

Eleven

Frankie

The seatbelt pressed into my chest as I leaned forward, squinting through the windshield. I cranked on the defrost to clear the windows, cursing the warning lights on my dash. The drive home had turned into a race against my dying vehicle.

The Jeep stuttered erratically, and my fingers ached, white-knuckled on the steering wheel as I fought to keep control.

A burning rubber smell overwhelmed me, and the lights dimmed as the Jeep lurched forward, slowing down.

"No, don't do this to me, come on... a few more minutes and I'm home. *Fuck*."

Cranking the sluggish wheel, I veered as far off the road as I could, stopping at an angle along the shoulder. The headlights flickered to a glow and died, plunging me into darkness. There were no streetlights until I got closer to my neighborhood. The wipers froze mid-swipe, yielding to the rain cascading over the window, and my breaths fogged as a chill surrounded me.

"Perfect, just great, and it's my own damn fault for not getting it fixed."

Saturday night at the Magpie would be busy as hell; I couldn't bother Lena, relying on my father had proved impossible, Mom would come to my rescue, but she'd come back home with me to talk about Dad and my lack of a sex life, and I didn't have the energy for that.

If I walked fast, I could make it home in twenty minutes. A little rain wouldn't hurt me, and it was cold, but not freezing. Unless that relentless asshole returned and found me walking on the side of the road, alone and vulnerable.

I messaged Finn. *How busy are you right now?*

The Jeep shook from a gust of wind, and rain pelted the roof as I sat waiting for him to respond. Sitting alone. In my broken-down Jeep on the desolate road, close to home, but not quite close enough. I dialed Finn's number, but it went straight to voice-mail, and I hung up, staring at my phone. Two minutes... four...

I searched for a tow company number, but the signal faltered, and I couldn't launch a browser on my cell phone. The condensation forming on the glass triggered a wave of claustrophobia I didn't realize I had.

Looks like a good night to take up jogging.

I grabbed my purse, draping it over my head so it hung across my body. Swearing to myself, I stepped out of the Jeep, slamming the door shut. The wind stole my breath, sending chills through me. I zipped my jacket up to my chin, securing my hood over my head, and locked the doors. Before stuffing my phone in my pocket, I checked it one last time. I could do this. As I walked along the side of the road, the darkening sky cast shadows through the trees, and rain hammered the cement, filling the potholes with water.

Loose strands of hair escaped my hood, and the rain plastered them to my face. Clenching my numb hands inside my pockets, I trudged forward. I could withstand just about anything for twenty minutes, and when I arrived home, I'd arrange a tow and take a bath so hot it turned my skin red.

The rumble of an engine resonated from behind me as headlights beamed closer. My racing heart pounded in my ears. I could run or face the oncoming vehicle and hope it wasn't someone who wanted to do horrible things to me. Willow Grove had always felt safe, but no one had ever stalked me before tonight.

Rain spotted my phone screen as I started to call Finn again, but a familiar truck slowed down, pulling over behind me.

I shielded my eyes from the battering rain as the driver's door opened, and the figure standing in the rain was unmistakably... *Him*.

"Get in, Frankie." Rhett's voice carried over the sweeping wind and rain across the road.

I refused to let him see the rush of sweet relief the sight of him brought me. "Do you always order people around like that?" I walked toward him as he crossed the front of the truck, opening the passenger door.

"Old habit, get in... *please*."

Shivering, I peered up from underneath my hood. Rhett was friends with my brother, and no one worked for Finn or his girl-friend unless he trusted them. I scrambled onto the seat, and he shut the door, his broad frame a shadowed figure as he ran back to the driver's side.

"Are you okay?" His damp hair clung to his forehead, and his jaw feathered as he turned up the heat, angling the vents toward me.

"I'm *fine*." I glanced at him, hiding an amused smile as he gave me a quick side-eyed look. "My Jeep died, no warning, everything just shut off and smelled like burning death." I shifted in my seat to peek through the rear cab window, but darkness obscured the road behind us.

"Burning death isn't good," he said.

I turned toward him, and our faces were inches apart. A slow smile curved his lips as he draped one arm over the steering wheel and rested the other on his leg.

From the time we met, Rhett's subtle charm had disarmed me, and it took me a moment to find my words. I recalled the familiar childhood memories of my father tinkering with old cars in the garage, explaining engine parts and how they worked, while I spun around on a stool until I was dizzy. "I think it's the alternator, I need a tow."

He didn't take his eyes off me, and heat coursed through my body, easing the chills. "Okay. But if you're meeting a tow truck tonight, I'm coming with you—"

"No, I'm done tonight." I straightened my back, facing forward. "I'll deal with it tomorrow."

"I can help."

"Don't you have work?" I asked. His charm extended to showing up whenever I needed someone, but I'd never allow myself to rely on him for anything.

"I'm off tonight and tomorrow." His hand flexed as he gripped the steering wheel, eyeing the side mirror before merging onto the road.

"But you worked today?" I tugged my hood down, unzipping my jacket, and wiped the wet hair off my face. "I'm dripping all over your seat."

He darted a glance my way with raised eyebrows, and I immediately regretted my word choice. "You can do whatever you want," he said.

"So you keep saying... Anything?" I caught a glimpse of myself in the side mirror and wiped mascara from under my eyes before looking back at him. I was terrible at asking for exactly what I wanted from anyone. It had been my downfall in relationships, and I often ended up settling for less than I knew I deserved. And here was this man pushing me to do whatever I wanted. Part of me wanted to invite him home, surrender to the sexual tension between us, and get it out of my system.

"Sounds like you have something in mind." He flicked a switch, increasing the wiper speed across the windshield.

"Are you on your way home next door to me?"

"That is where I live, so yes." He scanned the dark road toward our neighborhood like he was expecting something. "I never see you though."

"I don't see you either, there are never lights on. When did you move in? Lena never told me that detail." I glanced from him to my side mirror, searching for that creepy car as he drove. "When did you come to town and start working for Lena and Finn?"

He regarded me with the same inquisitive expression he often wore, and maybe I shouldn't, but I liked the interest it implied. "You ask a lot of questions, Frankie."

"It's two questions," I pointed out. "I just like to know something about the person who lives beside me. There's not a lot of space between the units."

"Don't worry, I won't cause problems for you." He rounded the turn, and lights came into view. "Maybe I should throw some questions at you."

"Go for it, I've got nothing to hide. Can you say the same?" I wanted to know what life he had guarded behind his mysterious demeanor.

"That depends on what you want to know," he said. "Can I expect loud parties through the walls? A jealous boyfriend?"

I rummaged for the keys I'd shoved in my purse. "I haven't partied in way too long, and unless you count the stalker following me tonight, no jealous boyfriend either, it's just me."

"Someone was following you?" His smile disappeared, and his body tensed as he shifted in his seat. "Did you see who it was?"

I couldn't tell if he was angry or panicked, but his concern was palpable. "I tried. It was too dark, and the rain made it impossible. It looked like a sedan, but I can't be sure. I drove into a subdivision and the car took off." The man who'd sent me flowers had supposedly left town, but one other person came to mind—Clay. He'd lingered in Willow Grove longer than usual, and we had a history, but that didn't make him a *stalker*. "A man from my past has been a Magpie regular these days, but it doesn't make much sense why he'd want to follow me or scare me. I just don't know who else it could be."

"Clay Preston?"

Of course Rhett would know about him. It wouldn't have taken long before Lena filled him in. "That's the guy, but please stay out of it, I don't even know if it's him, I'm making assumptions that are probably wrong. It could just be someone being an asshole for no other reason than boredom." But I didn't believe that, not for a second.

He ran a hand over his stubbled face as he pulled onto our street. "Did you call the police or Finn?"

"They can't do anything if I don't have details to give them, I'll tell Finn about it tomorrow and take it from there I guess." I clutched my house keys between my fingers and my purse on my lap. I couldn't wait to get out of my damp jeans. "You can park in your driveway, I'll just walk over."

"Doesn't work that way with me, Frankie. I need to know you get in safe." Streetlights reflected on the wet pavement as Rhett parked in my driveway. He looked over his shoulder behind us, his gaze intense. "If you need to go anywhere or want anything tonight—"

"Are we back to the *whatever I want* thing?" I asked, trying to ease the tension. His worry made my fear resurface, but I refused to feel on edge in my own home.

"If that's what it takes for you to stay in tonight and lock your doors."

"Jesus, Rhett. Way to terrify a woman. I'm sure it'll be okay, stop worrying."

"Can't help it." He exhaled, and his lips parted to speak, but he smiled instead, shaking his head. "Did you think of something you want?"

"You're serious?"

"Usually," he said.

"Anything I want." Still sitting in his truck, I drummed my fingers against my lips, and his gaze dropped to my mouth. I felt in control, like he'd given me a secret invitation to a party I desperately wanted to attend.

The truth lingered on the tip of my tongue. *I want to know you, all of you.* But I refused to say those words and settled on telling him a different truth. "I want to take a hot bath and drink a tumbler full of wine instead of using a proper glass." The light activated as I grasped the handle and opened the door.

"I've got it," he said, sprinting out of the truck to my side before I could step out.

Standing in the rain, he held my door as I climbed out of the truck. "Thanks for the ride."

"It was nothing." He walked me to my front porch and waited until I was inside to turn away. I glanced out my living room window as his truck left my driveway and disappeared into his garage next door.

He was definitely not *nothing*.

Twelve

Rhett

Frankie was home safe for now. But someone had gotten to her, and I needed to know who they were and what the fuck they wanted. And if it had been her asshole ex-boyfriend, staying out of it wouldn't be possible. She wore a tough exterior but had a softness underneath that I wanted to crawl into, letting her consume me, forgetting everything else. Off limits or not, right or wrong—and I was so fucking wrong for her—none of that mattered when I was with her. All it would take was for her to let me in, and I'd be there, not questioning, not doubting. Any attraction Frankie had toward me would be gone if she knew the secrets I carried and the things I'd done, but if anyone hurt her, there'd be no warning. My instincts would win, and whatever good judgment I had left would disappear, giving way to the man I used to be.

I stepped out of the truck, tightening a C-clamp on the track above a roller after the garage door closed. The house was dark, and nothing appeared out of place as I locked the deadbolts behind me, but I still pulled my gun from my waistband and searched each room. I was alone, separated from Frankie by a wall too soundproof to hear if anyone broke into her place.

I put the gun in the lockbox beside my bed and called my sister.

"Hello?" Vivian spoke slowly, hesitating.

"It's me."

"An actual phone call this time, something must be up."

Faint music played in the background, drowned out by the hum of voices. "Are you somewhere you can talk?" I asked.

"I will be." A door slammed as she yelled at someone. "*Bitch.*" Metal clanged, and silence filled the line.

"Viv?"

"I'm at Dad's club, I locked myself in the bathroom to talk to you. When are you coming back? I went to see good old Daddy, and he isn't saying much, not even to me. He'll be out on parole in the next few weeks. He still trusts me, Rhett, but when he sees the *legit* agreements I just made, he'll lose it. We need to make a move soon if this is going to work."

"We will." I needed to know how she knew Frankie's name. "What did you find out? Who's asking questions?"

"I don't have much, trusting our usual people has been an *issue* as you can imagine."

"That's why we've got to work together, Viv. I need to know who told you about Frankie."

"All I know is Bran Noble's mom lives in a town an hour away from here, there's something about a flower store and that name was mentioned. He's been home since she got out of the hospital, but all of a sudden, he's obsessed with what happened in that warehouse two years ago..." Banging at the door sounded over the line, followed by Vivian's muffled yells. "*Two minutes!* I've got to go, but if they find you, you need to get your ass back here, at least we still have loyal guys willing to take a bullet to protect us. I've got someone keeping me informed. He's... *good.*"

"Who?" I asked. Selling my father out to the cops had shut down most of the *illegal* side of the business. But I'd gained the trust of a few high-stakes players who were on their way out if Nash Morrigan stayed. My sister shouldn't trust any of them.

"I can't tell you, but I need you to just trust that I know what I'm doing," she said. "I'm getting good at this shit, I promise. Who is Frankie Roscoe anyway, I don't remember him."

"*Her.* Don't mention her to anyone, and don't trust anyone. Take care of yourself and Zach. Keep quiet and stick to the plan."

Vivian exhaled over the phone before she spoke. "Money's moving. You were right, those contacts are good, but they're only good because they believe you're coming back. If you don't? Dad will steam-roll over everything and I'll be fucked, along with my son."

I was strategic at bringing in money to the yard. Even from a distance, I had coached Vivian to find the demand and supply it. Ship parts, fuel, dockage, and ample laydown. "You're doing great, Viv. I need you to hang in there just a bit longer—"

"How much longer? We're running out of time."

"Not long."

More noise erupted over the phone. "I'm hanging up now, but I'm counting on you Rhett."

"I know," I said as the line went dead.

With a towel around my waist, I raked a hand through my hair, catching sight of the wet, pink-tinged gauze clinging to my forearm. The gash had sliced through the ink on my skin, cutting across the tattoo. I'd thought about blacking it out with more ink, but something always stopped me. I had the fucked-up belief that covering it would sever ties to the only family I'd known since my mother died. The family that had broken more than it had ever held together.

Silence and loyalty were the two rules my father valued above anything else, and he expected his made family to protect both with their lives. Break them, and he'd break us. He had men who'd become so loyal, they'd die protecting him and his rules.

Turning the light off so I didn't have to stare at myself in the mirror for another second, I got dressed and headed downstairs. I lingered near the living room window, peering at the quiet street and Frankie's empty driveway. The rain had stopped, but the stillness didn't feel right. I had to let Finn know what happened. We'd have to monitor everyone who came into the Magpie, and if she'd let me, I'd drive Frankie to and from work. Whoever followed her had to be chasing the name. Someone had found out she was a Roscoe and was putting together pieces Finn and I had done everything to keep hidden. I wouldn't let her get dragged into any of it.

I grabbed one of the few tumblers I had in the kitchen cabinet and poured whiskey over ice cubes. As I swirled the drink in the glass, I thought of Frankie, her tumbler of wine, and the hot bath she'd mentioned.

I turned on my speaker and played jazz music, keeping the volume low. A porch light came on next door, illuminating the back deck, and I slid the glass door open. What was she doing over there? Stepping outside into the cold night, I shook water off a steel-framed chair and took a seat, stretching my legs out in front of me. The chair hadn't collapsed from my weight yet, but I shifted, testing it out before I leaned back.

The first drink of whiskey burned, giving me clarity for a moment. As the heat settled in my chest, I let the stress ease, just a little. The river's current harmonized with the saxophone, calming me, like nothing I'd had in any city. Willow Grove would never have been a town I'd choose, but the longer I stayed, the more I didn't hate it.

Vines wound through the gaps in the lattice separating our back decks. They were thick enough to obscure most of the view, but Frankie was outside. She crossed her legs, wearing pink pajama pants with fuzzy socks on her feet. The ice clinked against the glass as I took another sip, averting my eyes toward the forest with a smile. She was next to me... *safe*.

Thirteen

Rhett

Frankie uncrossed her legs and sat up, but the lattice and vines hid her face. "Rhett?" She spoke softly, hesitating.

"Frankie."

"Is that *jazz* I hear?"

"Coltrane... you don't like it?"

"It's not that, I guess I didn't take you for a jazz guy." The chair scraped against the wood, and she peeked around the barrier. "That came out wrong, it's nice, I like it."

I stood with my glass in hand and rested my elbows on the railing. "Did you get your tumbler of wine?"

She ducked out of view, reappearing with a glass full of red wine. "The tumbler. Took a bath first."

"Necessities," I said, trying not to imagine her naked in the bathtub... It wasn't working.

"Indeed."

She tilted her head back, and the porch light reflected off her dark hair. I didn't look away as her lips curved on the rim of the glass. I wanted to touch her, taste her, and have her hands on me. She made drinking a glass—a *tumbler*—of wine look sexy as fuck.

"I'm just missing one thing," she said.

"Company?"

"Close. A blueberry cream cheese Danish."

"Raspberry's so much better." A frigid breeze whipped through the trees, and she brushed hair off her face, hugging herself. "I'll take you to get one if you want, crank the heat in the truck. Aren't you freezing?"

"I'm set up over here, how about the company instead?"

"I'll come to you." I paused, wanting to be close to her. "If that's okay?"

Her eyes met mine across the twenty feet between our decks. "Bring your drink."

For someone off limits, the lines were blurred as hell. I walked down the stairs and crossed the yard to her place. The bottom step on her deck had rotted on one side, and I stepped over it to the next one. "Need help with that?" I said, reaching the top step.

"Did Lena clear you to use tools again?" Folding her arms across her chest, she raised her eyebrows over her blue eyes, and her cheeks flushed as she looked up at me. "I'm really not incapable of taking care of stuff, I just work a lot. I'll get to it."

"No judgment, just an observation." I sipped my drink, not breaking our eye contact. "And I absolutely can use tools again."

"Have a seat." She stepped inside and came back out holding a sweater, and when she pulled it over her head, the shirt underneath hiked up, exposing the smooth skin of her stomach.

I swallowed a gulp of whiskey and sat in the chair closest to the door, setting my glass on a table. As she settled in the chair next to me, a soft scent of vanilla mixed with something mysterious surrounded me. She smelled so good that I wanted to bury myself in her.

Heat radiated from a small space heater, and she bent her knees against her chest as she drank her wine.

"I'm doing it wrong over there," I said. "No heat, and my chairs are just metal slats." I patted the arms of the chair and sank deeper into the cushions.

"I like it out here, away from life for a bit, you know?"

"Escaping *fine*?" I couldn't help but try and break through the walls she'd tried so hard to hide behind; I could feel her resistance as she averted her eyes. Someone had scared her tonight, and I was being an asshole. "Forget I said that—"

"You're not wrong."

I carefully weighed my words, navigating that push and pull between us. "Still haven't come up with a better word?"

"*Frustrated,*" she breathed. "There's a word."

I raised my glass toward her. "That's better, you're onto something."

"Thank god." Placing her hand on her chest, she let her head fall back against the chair. Her laughter captivated me more than my jazz music. "I wasn't sure I'd be able to function until I found the perfect word to describe how I feel." She smiled, catching her bottom lip with her teeth like she wanted to hide it.

"Happy to help."

"I'm not saying you *helped*. Despite what you might think, I'm well aware of how I feel about things happening in my life, I just don't want to share it with people I don't know."

"Fair enough." I shifted in my chair, leaning closer. "Did you call a tow truck?"

"Another observation?"

"Call it whatever you want," I said. "I don't want you picking up your Jeep alone."

The glow from her phone cast light on her face as she unlocked the screen, emphasizing her soft jawline. "Not yet. I talked to Finn, and he just messaged me with someone who might help tomorrow."

"I'll help tomorrow. Send me a message in the morning, I'll see if I can boost it for you, and if not, I'll get someone to tow it."

She tapped her glass, gazing at me with her bright eyes demanding my attention, as if she saw me in a way no one else could. "Okay, deal. But I don't have your number."

"What's yours?" I asked, typing it into my contacts as she rattled it off, texting her so she'd have mine. *It's me.*

Her fingers scrolled over her phone, and she glanced at me. "Hi, me."

My phone buzzed with an incoming message.

Blueberry is better and I like your taste in music.

This woman had me smiling more over the past week than I had in years, and if I didn't push her away soon, I'd never be able to.

She set her phone on the table and mirrored my position, leaning toward me. "How do you know Finn and Lena?"

I felt the invisible line blowing up as I treaded over it. How much could I say to her without lying? I didn't want to lie to her. I wanted... *needed* her to trust me.

"I met Finn through mutual friends four years ago. He introduced me to Lena when I came to town for the job he offered at the Magpie." I stared into my glass, swirling the amber liquid, unable to look at her. "How long have you lived here?"

"Willow Grove? I grew up here, left. Came back two years ago, just didn't plan on staying so long."

I met her gaze again. "What was your plan?"

"I guess if I'm being honest, I didn't have one." Cupping the glass in both hands, she took a slow sip. "Still don't."

"Me neither," I said honestly, without thinking. "You like being a nurse? Not sure how to ask that... it seems like a tough job, especially when you lose someone."

"Yeah, it is sometimes, but I love it. I love that my experience, my hands, working as a team, can save someone's life, help them somehow when they're at their worst." She lowered her glass to her lap, and a wry smile touched her lips. "That probably doesn't make a lot of sense. Not sure how to answer that."

"I'd say you fucking nailed it."

She laughed again, and it lightened the dark parts of me, catching me off guard. "What about you?" she asked. "Are you a bartender? Carpenter? A little bit of everything?"

"You could say that." I tipped my glass, savoring the last of the whiskey, weighing my words. "I went to Mass Maritime. Studied shipping, trade, worked in a shipyard for a while. That kind of thing."

"What part of Boston are you from?"

"Charlestown area," I said.

"I lived with my brother in Allston for a couple of years." She put her glass down and pulled her sleeves over her hands.

I waited, unsure if she'd say anymore about Miles. He'd briefly mentioned that he shared an apartment with his sister, once letting it slip that she worked at the hospital, but I knew better than to ask questions. His protectiveness of her had always been clear.

With a quick breath, she faced me. "I had a younger brother, Miles, but he died two years ago."

Every part of me wanted to reach for her and hold on to her until the heartbreak left her face, but I restrained myself. "I'm sorry, Frankie. That must be hell."

"It was... *is* hell." She tilted her head down, dabbing at her eyes with her sleeve.

I'd gotten used to being alone, without attachments or expectations, and built my life around keeping everyone at a distance. Talking to Frankie stirred something in me, making me *feel*. Part of me knew I had to leave her, but a bigger part was terrified of losing this woman who wasn't mine to begin with.

"You got a girlfriend or wife... any kids or people you love over there?" She peered through the barrier to my place. Shaking her head, she grabbed her empty glass and traced the rim with her fingers. "I'm totally interrogating you, not my intention."

"No girlfriend, wife, kids, just me."

"Got it, just you and your jazz music."

"My mom used to be a singer in a jazz band. She would take me with her when she had a gig if I promised to stay quiet, didn't cause a scene. Fuck, I was just a kid, but being in those bars so close to that music..." I sat up, resting my elbows on my knees and clasped my hands together. "She died when I was seventeen."

"Jesus, Rhett, that's so sad." Frankie inched her chair closer, and her hand slipped into mine, bridging the gap separating us. "I'm sorry."

My fingers tightened around hers like her hand belonged there. "Thanks."

"Do you have a dad, siblings?"

"Sort of," I said.

"Like you sort of have a job."

I laughed, rubbing my unshaven face. "I have a sister in Boston with the same asshole father, but yeah, I've got one, I just don't like talking about him. And it's only sort of a job because I just started it a few weeks ago. I'm at the Magpie more than I'm not, but it's only for a few months."

"Are you not planning on staying in town?" she asked, taking her hand from mine.

Time to put a line down between us.

"No, Frankie. I'm not staying."

Sadness flickered in her expression again. Being near me would only put her at risk, and as soon as I found out who knew her name and took care of that problem, I'd have to go back to Boston and face the hell waiting for me. Frankie's brother had died because of that fucked-up world, and I refused to let her ever become a part of it.

"Well, you're here now. I appreciate your help tonight." She got up from the chair. "Before you go, let me see how that cut is healing." Crouching in front of me, she shoved my sleeve up and eyed the bloody gauze. "That bandage needs to be changed, come inside."

"I'll take care of it myself." I stood, towering over her, but she ignored me and opened the patio doors.

I knew when to let a woman take control. Picking at the tape, I followed her into the kitchen. "I'll just throw this one out and stick a new one on."

Frankie pointed at a stool. "Do me a favor and just sit down for five minutes." She went down the hall to the bathroom and returned holding a first-aid kit and placed a towel on the counter. Taking a seat on a stool, she pointed to the one next to her. "I said sit, Rhett. Let me do this."

"Is that an order?" I taunted as I sat beside her.

"If that's what it takes." She furrowed her brows in concentration, turning my forearm to the side as she examined the threads protruding from my skin.

"What do you think?" I asked.

"I think you need to take better care of it, but so far, so good." She ripped open a gauze pack and poured a stream of clear fluid over the dried blood. Sticking her hand in a glove, she dabbed at the red-tinged drips along my arm with balled-up gauze.

Our foreheads nearly touched, and my good sense lost sight of how to make space between us. Every nerve in my body wanted her closer. Her leg brushed against mine, and electricity lit me up like a live wire, but she didn't move away. I forced myself to stay still and let her focus on cleaning my tied-up gash.

She applied some sort of cream with a cautious, strategic touch, and covered everything with a new bandage. "Much better, please let me know if it gets gross again and I'll fix it."

I gathered the dirty bandages before she could. "Is your trash can under the sink?"

"You got it, our places must be the same layout."

"Basically," I said. When I opened the lid of the garbage, a bouquet of flowers lay on top. They were wilted and faded, but not dead, and given someone had followed her tonight, I needed to know where they'd come from. "Do these have a story?"

"It's a bit weird, but I let it go until tonight. I threw them out when I got home, just in case it's the same person." The unmistakable fear from earlier returned to her wide eyes. "Remember the morning you and I met in the coffee shop?" She bit her lip and released it.

"How could I not, Frankie?" I would never forget that morning. She stood against the wall, and I'd recognized her serious expression immediately—like she had the weight of the world on her shoulders. Her phone had slid across the floor, and I wasn't letting anyone else but me touch it. I'd needed to meet the woman from the hospital the night everything had fallen apart. Somehow, I wanted to know she was okay.

"A man was in the hospital with his mom," she continued. My heart raced as she talked. "I was her nurse, and I got a call. I usually don't keep my phone on me when I'm working, but when I pulled it out of my pocket to silence it, he asked me about this." Unlocking her phone, she spun it around on the counter to face me.

The kitchen light reflected on the screen, and I picked it up. The photo showed Frankie, Finn, and Miles together.

A muscle twitched along my jawline as anger worked its way through me. If anyone laid one finger on Frankie, my days of running would end with me in jail, like my father. "What exactly did he say?"

"He just asked if one of them was my boyfriend or something, and I just told him *or something* and put my phone away."

Bran Noble would've recognized Miles in that picture, connecting Frankie. He would make her his latest target until someone paid for killing his son. I'd have to tell her the truth, all of it. "Did you get his name?"

"He wouldn't tell me." She hesitated, rubbing her temples. "But he got mine from my ID and asked my last name."

"Did you give him your last name?"

"Jesus, no, I'm not an idiot."

I exhaled. "I never meant—"

"I know." She softened, dropping her hands. "But I went to Mom's shop after I met you, and he charmed her into it, so there's that. The flowers... they're Francesca roses."

"You're named after a rose?" I asked.

She scrunched her face and bit her lip. "Hard to believe, I know."

"No, I was thinking it makes perfect sense." Frankie was a woman who commanded a second glance simply by existing. "What else did your mom tell you?"

"Right." Frankie blinked slowly before continuing. "Not much, just that the man ordered the flowers over the phone on behalf of his mother, Alice Lane." My hand clenched into a fist and then relaxed. She approached me and tilted her head, her eyes meeting mine. "Rhett. Do you know something I don't?"

Noble's mother lives in Willow Grove. Fuck these damn secrets.

"I just want to figure out if trash flowers guy has anything to do with whoever tailed you tonight."

"You look worried about trash flowers guy."

"The more we talk about it, the more I worry about *you*." The muscle in my jaw spasmed again; I had to portray myself as calm as I could not to panic her.

"It's not even about the flowers, it's how he made me feel. He was too inquisitive, like he wanted something... It was weird. I don't know how else to put it, but when he told me he was leaving town, I thought that was the end of him."

"If he made you feel bad in any way, that's a problem." I ran a hand over my jaw, forcing it to relax. "Was there a note on the trash flowers?"

"Yeah, I kept it, but there's nothing alarming, it just, I don't know, it creeped me out." She rummaged through her purse, dangling behind the chair, and handed a rectangular card to me.

'Francesca, thank you for taking such wonderful care of my mother. Best.'

Staring at the note between my fingers, I pressed my lips together, reminding myself to breathe. "I won't be letting this go, Frankie. You have my number, if you need me, call. I'll be there, doesn't matter when. Promise me."

She stepped back, gripping the back of the chair. "I get that you're Finn's friend, and I'm his sister, but I don't need saving, Rhett. Whatever deal you've got with him doesn't include looking out for me. I'll just report this whole situation to the police in the morning."

She thought I wanted to help because I was *friends* with her brother? I might not be able to tell her the truth about who I was, but I sure as hell refused to let her think Finn had anything to do with my motivation for being near her.

Abandoning my need to keep her safe, I approached where she stood. She didn't flinch, studying me with curiosity. "It's okay, I get it," she said. "I love my brother, but he's got this overprotective, annoying..." With a hand on her hip, she rubbed her forehead, squeezing her eyes shut for a moment.

I gently touched her chin, tilting it upward to look at me, brushing my thumb along her soft skin. She froze, watching me carefully. "I'm not here because I think you need saving. When I say call if you need anything, it has nothing to do with Finn, and everything to do with me needing you to be more than *fine*."

She didn't move or look away. "Glad we got that sorted."

I imagined wrapping an arm around her waist, pulling her close, tasting her wine-stained lips, and feeling her skin against mine. Staying longer would tempt me to do exactly that, but with Frankie, I wanted to do the right thing. I dropped my hand, taking a step back. "Lock your doors and message tomorrow. I'll take care of your Jeep."

She slid the patio doors open, and I stepped outside. "Good night, Rhett."

"Good night, lock the doors." I hurried down the stairs as the door clicked and she pulled the blinds shut.

If Frankie was off limits, I was in trouble. I called Finn, leaving a message when his voicemail answered. "Call me when you get this, we got a problem."

Fourteen

Frankie

Sitting around the dinner table at my parents' house wasn't usually a spectacle, but the dull cake server on the counter could slice through the tension tonight.

"What is this, an intervention? We're supposed to be celebrating our daughter's birthday." My dad took his plate to the counter, dropping it into the sink. "I told you I'll do better, stop worrying.

Is it that hard to trust me?" Swearing under his breath, he left the kitchen, shutting the door behind him as he went into the garage.

Finn shoved a forkful of green beans into his mouth and glared at me. "Told you this was a bad idea."

"Finn, stop." Holding a butter knife toward him, Lena raised her eyebrows. "This is what families do, support each other."

Mom rose from the table and excused herself, placing a hand on Lena's shoulder as she passed behind her and headed for the bathroom.

Dinner together had crashed and burned like a dumpster fire. "I'll go talk to him." Rising from the table, I followed my father into the garage.

Dad stood in the open garage doorway, leaning against the frame. He held a cigarette between his fingers at his side, and smoke billowed around him. "If you're here to lecture me for smoking, I don't want to hear it."

"I'm not." I wandered through the garage and stood opposite him, far enough away to avoid breathing in the smoke.

"I know I fucked up."

"You can change it," I said. "We're not trying to make your life miserable—"

"You're just trying to help, I heard you, I always hear you." As he bent down and took a drag from his cigarette, I noticed his hair had thinned. He adjusted his pants, tightening his belt another notch.

My father was wasting away, and it made me ache with worry for what the future would hold. "There's no shame in getting help, will you go?"

"Rehab? No. But I'll cut back."

"You can't just cut back, Dad. You're an alcoholic, you have to quit."

"It's not like I drink a lot every day." He squinted as wisps of smoke curled near his eyes. "I'll admit I use it to cope in a very bad way, but I don't have a problem, Frankie. I can stop, and I will."

"Is that a promise?"

Dropping the cigarette on the pavement, he crushed it with his boot. "Sure. It's a promise, honey."

"Better clean that up or the lecture will come from Mom, and it'll be worse than anything I can give."

He bent down to pick it up, stuffing it in an empty beer bottle. "She's going to leave me, isn't she?"

"I don't know, maybe." Taking the bottle from him, I collected a few others scattered on the floor and lined them in a box. I closed the flaps and stacked the box on top of an accumulated pile. I turned to him; he looked so old, so tired. "I'll be honest, Dad, I would. I love you, but you're losing your grip on everything. Look at these"—I gestured to the boxes— "*really* look. A social drink, sure. Hell, I do it, same with Mom and Finn, but you've become dependent on it to get through the day. And don't get me started on your constantly taking off where no one can find you. I'm sick to death of picking your ass up in a bar because no one else will anymore." I shook my head, noticing the dimness in his gaze. I couldn't get through to him.

A spark flashed in him like he wanted to say something, but he pressed his lips together and turned away. "I got you something," he said, clearing his throat.

"Did you not hear a word I *just* said?" He would never listen to me. He'd lost a child, and he was well on his way to losing another one. "I don't want anything from you."

"You'll want this, Frankie." He unlocked a filing cabinet beside the workbench and pulled out a file folder full of papers. "Miles's file."

I took a staggering step toward him. His file? I snatched the folder from him before he could pull it away. He watched me intently as he allowed me to take it. "Where'd you get this? How?"

He laughed wryly, a sound I wasn't used to. "I still got friends, despite what you all think of me. They're copies, but it's mostly there."

My fingers trembled as I flipped through the pages. Black lines covered some of the information, but I finally had my brother's file in my hands. Turning to the autopsy report, the one document I was familiar with, I froze. I'd spent countless hours analyzing his toxicology report and his cause of death, detailing the drugs in his system and gunshot wounds. I snapped the folder shut as an ache throbbed in my chest, wiping tears as they slid over my cheeks. I couldn't break down, not here. No matter how much it hurt, I had to hold myself together. "Does Finn know you have this?"

"Nope, it's up to you if you tell him. He might be pissed if he knows I gave it to you, but I don't care. You have a right to see it.

He's not wrong though, there's nothing in there you don't already know."

I threw my arms around him, choking back a sob against his shoulder, and his arms wrapped around me. "Shhh, it's going to be all right, honey. I didn't want to make you cry, I love you too much for that." He patted the back of my head, and I sniffed my runny nose, pulling away from him.

I fought back the yearning to collapse in a crying mess on the floor, wiping at my eyes with the sleeve of my shirt. "I have to hide this." I hurried toward Finn's parked car near the garage. Of course he'd locked the doors. No one would think to look too closely, and it wasn't raining. I shoved the folder underneath the car and rushed back inside the garage. "Easy enough."

My dad pressed a button on the wall, and the garage door closed. "Come on, your mother's got cake. She needs you to blow out a candle, make a wish, you know the drill. And I need to smooth things over with her."

We entered the kitchen, and I shut the door behind us. While loading plates into the dishwasher, Finn darted a worried glance at me as Lena rushed to my side, hugging me tightly. "You okay?" she whispered.

I nodded as my mother set a decorated cake, topped with a closed flower candle, on the table. "Okay, you guys, come here, we're singing happy birthday with smiles on our faces, got it?" She eyed Finn and my father.

I gave her a quick hug. "My birthday isn't until next week, it's fine, I don't need—"

"I don't want to hear it, we love you, and we're doing this." She struck a match and lit a stick in the center of the flower. As the flame touched each candle, the petals fell away one by one.

"Where the hell did you get that?" My father laughed. And it was a genuine belly laugh I hadn't heard from him since before Miles died… It felt like a lifetime ago.

Lena started her off-key version of *Happy Birthday*, and my family reluctantly joined in as my mom glared at them.

As soon as they were done, Finn hugged me. "Happy Birthday, Frankie."

"Make a wish, blow those suckers out." Lena gave me a squeeze. "I know what I'd be wishing for if I were you."

"Love thy neighbor or however the saying goes," my mother said with a mischievous grin as she arched her brows.

I glared at Lena. "Really?"

"Relax, Frankie," Mom said. "She simply informed me of her cute bartender's living arrangements next door to my daughter. I've got to find out the gossip somehow. *That* is all."

Finn looked from Mom to me but stayed quiet. "That *is* all," I said.

We'd never been big on birthdays, especially not for the past two years, but my mother had a thing for wishing on candles. I hovered over the flames as my mind raced through memories, stopping at one persistent thought.

Let love find me, real can't-live-without-each-other love.

I blew the candles out in one breath.

My father added another log to the brick fireplace. He'd only had four beers since dinner, but he'd gotten quieter over the past hour. I knew his subdued behavior was a calculated effort to avoid our negative attention again, and it worked. No one brought up his drinking, sticking to conversations about business at the Magpie with Lena, Finn's frustration over his new position, and my shifts at the hospital.

Finn fidgeted in his seat, chewing his cheek like he did when he was nervous or worried. He'd come with me to the police station earlier to report the car that had followed me without overreacting, keeping his promise by not saying anything tonight. But with no solid information, they only told me to call if anything else happened and sent me on my way.

"Rhett Marshall?" Dad replaced the screen in front of the fireplace and sat in the closest chair. Hearing Rhett's name snapped my attention back to the conversation.

"He's not from here, but I hope he sticks around." Lena crossed her legs, picking lint off her cashmere sweater. "It's been a month, and he's almost finished work out back, can tend bar, and customers don't start shit when he's around." She flashed a smile at me, but I didn't react. "I'd take his company any day over some of the stuffy men in suits I used to work with. I like him. He's got a presence."

I'd been getting rather comfortable in Rhett's *presence*. I traced my chin, remembering his fingertips on my skin. If he had kissed me, I wouldn't have stopped him, but he'd held back, guarding himself. Practical logic told me to keep my distance from a man like him, but reason disappeared any time I was near him.

He had driven me back to my Jeep this morning and waited for the tow truck with me. The mechanic wasn't open on Sundays, but I planned to be without my vehicle for a few days, arranging a ride to and from the shifts I'd picked up to pay for repairs. If that car returned, I refused to be stranded and vulnerable again, and I'd make sure I got a license plate and every detail down to the number of scratches on the damn bumper before it drove away.

Mom leaned back in her chair with her mug of coffee, talking to Finn, and he toyed with the silver watch around his wrist. That watch had belonged to Miles. We'd scattered his belongings among all of us, like pieces of him left behind. I needed to open the plastic bin in my spare room that I'd taken from our apartment two years ago.

"Why don't you work with Lena again instead? It worked well, Finn, you were more content." Mom always encouraged him to leave law enforcement completely.

The aftermath of Miles's death had forced Finn on medical leave from the State Police, recently resigning to accept a position in our local department. He'd quit therapy, stopped taking his anti-depressants and anxiety medication... and he had stopped talking about our brother, falling more silent than he'd ever been. His misery was obvious to everyone who knew him, and as the tension crept back into the room, I braced myself for the pushback, sitting upright and rubbing my hands on my jeans.

As if on cue, Finn rose from his seat and glanced at his watch. "I've got work in the morning and have to drive Frankie home, I think we should head out." He strolled past Lena and stopped. His shoulders relaxed as he glanced down at her. "Unless you need more time?"

Lena's brows knitted together as she stood and laced her fingers with his, pulling his hand behind her back. She was the only person who could calm my brother with a look or a touch, and I was grateful that she had what it took to put up with him, to love him despite himself.

Releasing Finn's hand, she hugged my mother. "Thanks, Nora." She met my father's gaze. "Jared, let me know if you need anything, okay? We're here, right, Finn?"

"Yeah." Finn spun his keys in his hand, gripping them in his palm. "Yeah, of course, Dad, I told you, I arranged—"

Dad sighed, patting Finn's back as he walked past. "Good night, you guys." He embraced me with his hand on the back of my head and kissed my forehead. "Happy early Birthday, honey."

"Thanks," I muttered as he let me go.

Wrapping her arms around herself, Mom walked next to me, stepping outside. "Smells like snow's coming," she said. "It's hard to believe two years have gone by. Hey, have you opened that box of his?"

"Um, no, not yet." Carrying a wrapped piece of cake on a plate, I picked up my pace toward the back door, concealed in the darkness. "Let me put this in the back seat."

Finn opened Lena's door, talking with Dad as she got in the car, and I opened the back door, reaching down to grab the file folder at the same time. Setting the cake down on the back seat, I stuck the folder on the floor underneath my purse.

Mom leaned against the car, looking up at the night sky. "It's beautiful up there."

The endless rain had passed, and a billion stars paved the sky like glitter, but my mind raced with unsettled thoughts. Nothing had changed with my father, Finn still struggled with silent battles, not letting anyone help him, and people still died regardless of what we did to save them, but at the same time, *everything* had changed.

Dad made his way toward the front door, and my mother gave me a quick hug as Finn got in the driver's side, starting the car.

Walking away, Mom spun around with her hands on her hips. "Frankie, did you know Clay's in town? He came in to pick up flowers to bring to someone in the hospital."

I held the door frame, mid-sit. "Who did he see at the hospital?"

"A friend of his father's he said." She dropped her hands and narrowed her brown eyes at me, confused. "Was he ever friends with Miles?"

Miles hated Clay.

"*Never*, why?"

Finn rolled the window down. "Everything good?"

Ignoring him, I stood, gripping the open door. "What did Clay say about Miles?"

"Nothing really, just talked about Boston and that he missed him. I didn't think Clay lived in Boston?" Mom's words caught, and she wiped her eyes.

"He didn't."

"That's what I thought, maybe I misheard. Anyway, I'm going inside, it's freezing." She pulled her sweater tightly around her and rushed inside with a wave.

"Drive safe," Dad said, shutting the door behind them.

Finn drove away from our parents' house, and I kept the folder hidden at my feet as Lena turned to face me. "Are you sure you don't want to pack a bag and come stay with us? Just until we know who your stalker is."

"*Stalker* might be pushing it," I said. "But after that conversation, I'm wondering if it's just Clay trying to assert himself or something."

"You think? He did get obsessive for a bit until you moved to Boston, and he wasn't at the Magpie last night."

The quaint neighborhood faded in the distance as Finn veered onto the wooded road toward my place. "I'll talk to him—"

"If anyone talks to him, it'll be me." Resting my elbow on the door handle, I glared out the window, but it was too dark to see anything except my reflection. I had my brows pinched together tightly enough that lines creased my forehead and around my eyes. My brother had it in his stubborn head that I couldn't handle myself, but I could take care of Clay. Finn's controlling and overprotective nature had annoyed me since before my memory allowed, but he was the only brother I had, and I loved him. I ran my fingers over the file folder. Miles had told me to back off and let him live his life more than once, his words crushing me. Had he thought of me the way I thought of Finn?

"I'll keep an eye on the asshole," Lena said, adjusting the car's dials, blasting heat through the vents. "He's constantly in the bar. I never noticed what car he's driving, but I'll find out."

"It's a rental." Finn glanced at me through the rearview mirror.

"You're observant," I said.

"Rhett noticed and mentioned it today."

"Rhett's off tonight, he'll be right next door if you need him." Lena suppressed a chuckle. "Do you see much of your new neighbor? Not a doubt in my mind he'd have plenty of whatever you need over there."

"Jesus, Lena. He seems nice, helped me with my Jeep—"

"I told you I had someone lined up," Finn said.

"I didn't need them." I met Finn's eyes in the mirror again, and he diverted them back to the road.

"He's leaving town in a few weeks." He placed a hand on Lena's leg, relaxing his shoulders against the seat. "Frankie doesn't need the chaos, trust me."

"But he's here now." Lena glared at Finn. "She's capable of deciding what she needs without her brother telling her how it should be, don't you think?"

His eyes darted back in the mirror at me. "I don't want you to get hurt."

"I won't." I let my head fall back against the seat as we passed streetlights illuminating the subdivision I'd used to escape my pursuer last night. "What's your deal with Rhett anyway, I thought you were friends."

Finn exhaled, tapping the steering wheel with his thumbs. "I trust him, I do. But he doesn't stick around anywhere. There's no stability with him, and you need that Frankie."

"She needs to forget about work for a bit and let go of all the bullshit." Lena entwined her fingers with Finn's. "You could stand to do the same by the way."

"I'll let go with you anytime, love," he said, glancing at Lena and taking me off guard with his openness.

Hidden in the darkness the back seat offered, I caught myself smiling in the window's reflection. Lena was good for my brother, and if he ever fucked it up with her, I'd have to kick his ass.

Finn pulled up close to the garage, dropping me off at home. Stepping out of the car with my purse and the lopsided piece of cake, I snuck the folder in my coat and zipped it up. Headlights shone through the living room window as I entered the house. Finn waited in the driveway for me to close the door. I'd forgotten to leave a light on, and when he disappeared from the driveway, darkness consumed the living room.

A shiver crept through me, raising goosebumps over my skin. I never left my place this cold. Did I have to add fixing my heat to a growing list of repairs? The blinds clattered against the patio doors. Frigid air blew into the room, and I stepped back, banging my heel on the wall. "*Fuck,* that hurt."

I strained to see, feeling for the light switch, and dropped the plate. As it crashed to the floor, I flipped the light on.

The blinds flapped in the wind, caught between a gap in the open patio door. I lost the ability to breathe for a moment as I spun around, holding my breath. Someone had been inside my house.

Are they still here?

I might've forgotten to lock the door, but I hadn't left it *open*. Unzipping my jacket, I set Miles's folder on the cabinet and rummaged for my phone in my pocket, but it wasn't there. Where had I left my phone? I snatched a frying pan from the drying rack and moved toward the patio doors. A strong cologne lingered around me, triggering a memory of familiarity that I couldn't place.

A dull ache throbbed in my head as I shoved the blinds aside and hit the switch, turning the outside light on. Tree branches swayed, casting shadows, but the backyard was vacant. I slid the patio door closed, locking it, and paced through the kitchen toward the door for the garage. Inhaling, I followed the distinct cologne, but it faded with every step away from the deck. With the frying pan positioned to strike, I swung the door open and switched on the light. No one was there.

Of all the times for my Jeep to be in the shop, now had to be that time.

Still holding the pan, I rushed into the living room and found my purse on the chair. I retrieved my phone and brought up the keypad ready to call for help, but the dark void at the top of the staircase held my attention. There were no signs of life upstairs or on the main level.

It had to be the stalker from last night—just great, I'd given the word stalker power over me. I hesitated to call out, in case someone remained inside, waiting for the perfect opportunity to attack. I'd never wanted a gun in my house, especially not since Miles's death, but at that moment I'd give anything to have the weight of a gun in my hand instead of a damn frying pan. My fingers trembled as I hovered over the numbers to call for help, but it vibrated with an incoming message from *Him*. The name I'd given the contact for Rhett.

Are you home?

Yes

A crash echoed from upstairs, and I bolted for the front door, typing another message.

I think someone's inside.

I threw the deadbolt and opened the door, charging from the house, and slammed into Rhett.

Fifteen

Frankie

Steadying me with his hands on my arms, Rhett glanced behind me, his gaze falling to my face. "Are you okay?"

"I heard something upstairs, the door was open..." I took a breath. "I was calling 911 when you messaged."

He moved fast, pulling a gun from his waist and reaching behind him for my hand.

"Do you always have a gun in your pants?" I said, letting him hold my hand. His warmth radiated on my skin, and I squeezed tighter, letting the relief sink into my chest.

"That's a loaded question, Frankie." His fingers tightened around mine as he pushed through the front door, releasing his grip on me. "Lock the door and stay." He headed through the living room, holding the gun with the same expertise as Finn.

The mystery surrounding him tightened into knots, and I followed him. "Are you a cop?"

"No." The muscle in his jaw twitched. "I thought I told you to stay back there."

"You ordered me to stay like a *dog*. I'm calling the police."

He stopped, pressing a finger to his lips to silence me like the man on his tattoo, and continued up the stairs. I didn't possess the ability to let him handle this on his own, so I stayed close to him.

He whispered over his shoulder. "For fuck's sake, if anything happens to you... *get back*."

"You're not leaving me alone down there." My voice trembled, and he reached an arm behind him, shielding me between his broad frame and the wall. My shallow breaths filled the space as my chest pressed against the warmth of his back.

"I'll leave you alone here instead, better?" Angling his gun down, he faced me.

"Much better," I breathed.

His intense eyes swept over my face. "Please, Francesca, keep your feet planted in this spot for two damn minutes."

With a grunt, he left me standing against the wall and moved through each room, turning lights on, yanking the shower curtain aside, and flinging closet doors open. Unable to keep my feet *planted*, I followed him into the spare bedroom, where a stack of books had fallen. The closet door hung closed at an angle, off its hinges, and an overturned bin lay in front of it.

"That's Miles's stuff!" I shoved past him, but he caught my arm, pinning me against the wall, his grip surprisingly gentle.

His body pressed against mine as he brushed my hair aside, whispering in my ear. "Let me go first."

"I think they're gone." I reached for his arms, and he stilled.

Stepping away from me, he tucked the gun in his waistband and explored the closet, glancing out the window. "Call it in. The police, Finn, call it in." He scanned the room, taking a backpack from a shelf in the closet, and handed it to me. "Pack a bag and come home with me, I'll check downstairs." He strode past me out of the room, and his footsteps reverberated on the stairs.

I called the non-emergency line at the police department and messaged Finn when he didn't answer. Dropping the backpack, I picked up the storage bin and stepped over papers and clothes that lay scattered on the floor. I slid down the wall, sitting beside the plastic container, and picked up a worn Bruins hat Miles used to wear, running my fingers along the faint sweat stains.

An ache behind my eyes moved along my face, settling deep into my jaw as a lump formed in my throat. I breathed through the grief, swallowing hard.

Do not fall apart, not now, not like this.

A few childhood photos had fallen from an album, and I gathered them, tucking the images back inside. A faded photo caught my attention, and I held it between my fingers, reliving the memory. I was glaring at Miles as I blew a giant bubble with my chewing gum. He was making a face, trying to pop it with his fingers. I was sixteen at the time, and he was my annoying thirteen-year-old pain-in-the-ass brother. All I'd wanted was for him to leave me alone. I'd give anything to have him back for even one moment. *Anything.*

The unbearable heartache I'd gotten brilliant at keeping deep in my chest clawed its way through my body, threatening to unleash in a mess of tears. Slowing my breathing, I silently begged for the feeling to subside. I stuck the photos back in the album and reached for a crumpled hoodie at the bottom of the bin. Mom and I had donated most of his clothes, except this one. I wouldn't let her get rid of it.

Tears escaped, rolling down my face as I moved the hood aside, peeking inside the sweater, searching for the tag. The note I'd written in black pen had faded, but I could still read it. "Frankie is cooler than me," I whispered through tears.

I'd never opened the box, and some asshole had broken into my house and touched Miles's things. I couldn't think of a single reason or person who'd break in to dig through that box, certainly not Clay Preston.

I slumped forward, covering my face with Miles's sweater. It didn't smell like him anymore. He was *gone*. Choking sobs built in my chest; I couldn't hold them back anymore, so I let go. I buried my face deeper into his sweater as the tears came hard and fast, cursing myself for falling apart in the middle of a crisis.

"Did you pack a bag—" Rhett walked into the room, tucking his gun in his waistband, and I took a shuddering breath, cutting off my sobs. His brow furrowed with worry as he crouched in front of me.

How could I let him see me so vulnerable and weak?

"The police should be here soon. Finn, too." The fabric muffled my voice, but I didn't lift my head.

Taking the sweater from my hands, Rhett brushed his thumbs under my eyes, wiping tears away. His touch was rough against my skin, but tender and careful. I clung to his arm like a lifeline.

"I should've done more, found a way to help him. Fuck, how'd things get so bad?" I rasped.

"I'm sorry you have to deal with all this, Frankie."

I blinked away tears and faced his intense stare, as if he saw behind the wall I'd hidden behind. The raw emotion etched on his face was unreadable. I hadn't known him long enough to decipher whether it was fear or rage.

Adrenaline flowed between us, and I had to restrain myself from wrapping my arms around him. This man begged me to be near him without saying a word, but I craved even more. I needed to lose myself in him.

Standing, Rhett extended his hand to me, and I let him help me to my feet. The messy room was different now, violated. The paint can and brushes in the corner sat untouched beside my keyboard lying on its side, and a haphazard pile of Miles's stuff. Another one of his favorite hoodies, a trophy from his childhood hockey years, his fucking favorite pair of worn-down sneakers. Things he'd never touch again. Anger burned in my chest. Perhaps Miles's past had returned to haunt me and my family, but no one would make me a victim. I would do whatever it took to claim back my space; scrub everything, paint the bedroom, and install extra deadlocks. I'd give in and buy myself a gun.

My breath caught through tears. "My parents can't know about this, and Finn better not make a big deal out of it."

Rhett picked up my keyboard and ran his fingers along the keys. He glanced at me with a thoughtful look that softened his strong features. "What about you, Frankie? I mean, you spend every spare moment fixing everyone else's problems, taking care of people..." He shook his head. "Who takes care of you?"

"I do." I smoothed my wild hair, twisting it over my shoulder. "I keep going and fix things, adapt, put a goddamn smile on my face when I feel like falling apart. I take care of the people I love, including myself." I stormed out of the room. If I turned around, I might give in to the vulnerability threatening to level me and throw myself into his arms. I couldn't allow myself to fall in case I never got back up.

He followed me downstairs. I opened the patio doors; the hint of lingering cologne in my house sickened me. I knew that smell from somewhere.

"I already checked out there," Rhett said carefully.

I stepped outside and took a deep breath. "I just need some air."

My phone rang from the kitchen table, and Rhett handed it to me, glancing at the screen. "It's your brother." He joined me on the deck as I answered the call, giving Finn a quick rundown on what had happened.

Finn went silent for a moment before speaking. "Put Rhett on the phone."

I held out the phone, keeping my eyes fixed on the trees. "He wants you."

He exhaled through pursed lips, putting the phone to his ear. "Yeah."

If Rhett wasn't a cop, who the hell was he handling himself like that? I plopped down on a chair.

Speaking in one-word answers I couldn't string together to make sense, Rhett hung up, giving me back my phone. "He's on his way, let's go inside. Lock this door." Hovering in the doorway, he scanned the backyard like a vigilante. He glanced at me when I didn't move. "Jesus, Frankie, please come inside with me."

I stood and approached him, stopping in front of him. "After this is done, I want you to talk to me, tell me who you are, how you know my brother, fill me in on what you're not saying." Tears burned my eyes, and I swallowed, refusing to cry again. My emotional dam had burst, and I worried I'd never regain control.

He lifted a hand between us and ran his fingers along my jaw. Electricity jolted along my neck, down my arms, and my breath caught. I held it, not daring to release the air from my lungs. My body responded to his touch before my mind gave it permission, and I cursed myself for allowing my guard to unravel.

"Please," he said. "Let me keep you safe."

"You don't even know who to keep me safe from."

"I'll figure it out."

I would figure this out on my own. I'd file a police report and comb through every single word in that folder. "I have Miles's police file." Moving past him, I went inside. "I know he was murdered, Rhett, targeted for something he was involved in, I've always known that." I pulled a chair out and sat at the table as he locked the patio door.

"How'd you get it?"

"Dad gave it to me tonight. Can I trust you not to tell Finn?" I'd give him a piece of my trust, and maybe he'd give me some of his.

Rhett shrugged off his coat and hung it over the back of the chair, placing his gun on the table as he sat across from me. "You can trust me. I won't tell him." Clasping his hands together, he leaned forward, his profound gaze holding mine. "Did you read it yet?"

"Haven't had the chance." Maintaining eye contact, I gestured to the gun before folding my hands together on the table. "Where'd you learn to carry like that if you're not a cop? Military? Something else I should know about?"

"You ask a lot of questions—"

"And you don't seem to have any answers." I sat back in the chair, extending my legs under the table. As I crossed my ankles, I inadvertently kicked him, but he remained unfazed. Having him across from me gave me an odd sense of safety, despite the gnawing feeling he held onto dark secrets he refused to say.

He slid his hands off the table and rested them on his thighs. Something unreadable shifted in his eyes. "None of the above. I worked for my father."

"In a Boston shipyard?" The nagging feeling intensified, and I wanted to ask Rhett if he'd ever met Miles through Finn, but I couldn't bring myself to do it. I'd always suspected Finn had stayed so long in Boston to pull Miles from whatever trouble he'd gotten himself into.

What would it mean if he did, and why wouldn't he have told me?

"My father taught me how to handle myself," Rhett said.

"And that included a gun."

"It did. I don't have contact with him." He sat still, and a hint of muscle tightened along his jawline. He glanced behind me toward the cabinet. "Is that the file your dad gave you?"

"It is. I'll read it once I'm alone." As the words came out of my mouth, the room's familiar comfort disappeared. I had never feared being home alone, but my thoughts spiraled into a blur of what-ifs and unknowns, terrifying me.

What if my stalker comes back?

"There's one problem with that plan, Frankie." Rhett stood as red and blue lights flashed through the living room window and car doors slammed. A sharp knock at the door made me jump up from my chair, but Rhett didn't flinch as he looked at me. "I'm not leaving you alone tonight."

Sixteen

Frankie

The doorbell rang, followed by another knock at the front door. Boots thudded up the porch steps, and an edge cut through my brother's voice as he called my name.

Rhett stood behind me near the bottom of the stairs. I'd never known a man who gave me space to breathe and be my own woman but carried an unspoken assurance that he'd step in if I needed support.

I'm too comfortable in his presence.

"Here we go," I muttered. I braced myself for my brother's crisis-mode to lock in, disregarding me like I couldn't speak for myself.

Finn rushed inside with two officers on high alert. He passed by me with his sights set on Rhett, giving me a quick pat on the shoulder. The other two officers walked through the house, guns drawn as they moved. One headed upstairs and the other into the kitchen.

A third man, taller than everyone in the room, including Rhett, stepped forward. "Francesca Roscoe, Jared's daughter," he said. His smile was genuine, comforting, and he spoke in a steady, deep voice that could lull a person to sleep. "Having a rough night?"

"I've had worse..." I stopped myself. I had a habit of comparing the bad things that happened to me to something that could've been much worse. But he was right; tonight earned the credit for being a rough fucking night. "Tonight scared me," I admitted.

He exuded an unshakable calm, as though my little break-in was nothing, and he'd seen much worse. His smooth dark skin and neatly shaved head gave him an authoritative appearance in his uniform, but he regarded me with the kind eyes of someone who was an adored family member. "I worked with your father." He extended his hand. "Sergeant Fletcher, call me Sam."

"Call me Frankie." I shook his hand, waiting for him to give me a pitying expression, or a comment about my dad, but he showed me grace and asked questions about what had happened when I'd arrived home earlier.

"The house is clear," one officer announced, returning from his sweep of my place.

"She wouldn't be in here if it wasn't." Rhett's voice revealed no emotion as our eyes met.

He shifted so his back was to me as Finn talked to him in the dining room, and I couldn't make out what they were saying. The folder sat on the cabinet in plain sight, but Finn's attention had shifted from Rhett to instructing the officers how to do their jobs.

As the two men raised their voices, uniting against my brother, Sergeant Fletcher stepped into the kitchen. "Roscoe, you are only here as a family member, not a cop." He turned back to me and asked, "Anything else you can think of that we should know?"

I mentioned Clay, the man from the hospital, and the flowers, and Finn took a step toward me. "I wish you told me after the first time you met that guy, or when he was in Mom's shop. I used to be someone you'd call when you were in trouble."

"It just happened, what could you have done about it? I got flowers from a guy who thanked me for taking care of his mother."

"You left your back door unlocked again, didn't you?" Finn spoke with the same condescending tone he used at work.

His attitude toward me had softened when he was on medical leave, but since he'd been back at work, the bitterness had crept back in, and I was an easy target. He knew I'd let him unleash on me without saying a damn word. Mom and Dad wouldn't tolerate it, and Lena would leave him if he ever talked to her like that.

"I can't remember, maybe," I finally said, through clenched teeth. "But you're probably right, I forgot to lock the patio doors when you picked me up."

I straightened my posture, preparing for Finn's lecture. "You put yourself at risk. Don't let it happen again, Frankie."

"Don't speak to her like that." Warning laced Rhett's words, mirroring the hardened look in his eyes.

Finn's shocked expression met Rhett's scowl, and I waited for them to argue, but Finn backed down, and it was my turn to stare wide-eyed in disbelief.

Static from police radios echoed as the three officers conferred, and tension gripped my neck and shoulders. A suffocating unease surrounded me, like smoke pouring from an unknown source threatening to consume me. I'd never worried about leaving doors or windows open, but my sense of safety had disappeared. I wanted the night to end and everyone to leave so I could lock myself inside.

Fletcher entered the kitchen. "I wish I had more for you, there's not much you don't already know. No forced entry, came and went through the back door." He shot Finn a glare. "This town hasn't seen much crime over the years. I leave my own door unlocked sometimes, don't beat yourself up about that." He exhaled, handing me a business card. "We'll talk to Clay Preston and the man's mother, Alice Lane, but if you think of anything at all, please call."

"Thank you." I took the card from him, and a wave of exhaustion gripped me. "I just wonder why, after two years, someone would want something Miles owned."

A sliver of warmth cracked Finn's tough expression. "They went through everything in the room up there, doesn't mean they were looking for *his* belongings specifically. I'll look into it."

"You absolutely will not," Fletcher eyed him. "Not your case." He walked with the other officers into the living room, instructing them to perform another yard check before leaving.

"Come stay with me and Lena, or call Mom, and I'll give you a lift," Finn said.

"I will lock the doors, but I'm not letting some asshole from Miles's past scare me away."

Rhett and Finn exchanged a look without speaking.

They met through mutual friends in Boston, my ass. They're keeping something from me.

"What's that look?" I moved between them, drawing Rhett's gaze downward.

"Grab a few things and come to my place," he said.

"I work tomorrow. I'm staying."

Sergeant Fletcher rapped his knuckles on the wall, stepping into the dining room. "Sorry to interrupt." He hesitated, observing each of us. "We're heading back to the station, Frankie, will you be all right?"

"I'll be fine." I showed him to the door, stepping outside with him, nodding toward the two officers as they gave a polite wave and got in their patrol car.

Fletcher opened the door of an unmarked SUV. "Anything else happens, or you see that car again, call right away. Understood?"

"Understood." I embraced myself against the chill on the front step. Stepping inside, I locked the door behind me, and stood near the window as they left, slowly driving along my street. I didn't want to be alone, but I didn't want to let fear control me. My mother's words lingered in my mind. Clay had lived in Stamford since he'd graduated college, without ties to Boston or Miles. But what if I was wrong? And what if my brothers had kept more from me than I'd realized? I needed to go through everything in that file.

Seventeen

Frankie

I pulled the living room curtains together and went into the dining room toward Rhett and Finn's hushed voices, but as soon as I approached, their conversation ended. Sitting across from each other, they glanced up, and I slid a chair out, joining them.

Finn shoved his phone in his pocket, oblivious to the file folder resting behind him. "If you won't come with me, I think it's best if you go to Rhett's tonight, at least until—"

"Until what? Until some guy from Miles's past comes to find me? You worked in Boston two years ago, if you have any leads, I'd love to hear them."

Finn had been on duty the night Miles was killed and had been with our brother in his last moments. I knew those memories still haunted him, but if Finn chose silence, he'd carry whatever bothered him to his grave.

The heaviness of the night hung between the three of us, and a sudden yawn escaped me. Shaking myself from my dark thoughts of death and graves to keep myself from crying again, I broke the silence. "I picked up shifts all week for extra cash, I'll barely be at home anyway. I have to work, Finn, I can't just hide away."

"How much do you need, I'll give you the money, drop the shifts this week," Finn said intently. "Maybe go out to the cabin for a few days, take a break."

"I can take care of my own finances," I snapped. He knew me well enough not to suggest that cabin, but I knew *him* well enough that he just wanted to help. I softened my tone, attempting to show my brother how to communicate without being an asshole. "Thank you for offering. I'm not ready to go back there, you know that."

Sliding the chair back, Rhett stood and headed for the front door. "Give me ten minutes to run home and grab a few things; I'll stay here tonight."

"My spare room is a mess, the bed is covered with boxes—" I couldn't let Rhett *sleep* in my house, that would be too close, too comfortable, too much... *No.*

"I'll take the couch," Rhett called as he left, shutting the door behind him.

"It's one night, Frankie, let him." Finn typed on his phone. "I just told Lena, she was asking about you, our place is still an option."

He made no sense—one minute warning me that Rhett had no stability and wasn't good for me, and the next forcing me to spend time with him. I squinted at him. "I thought you didn't trust him."

"I never said that."

"You alluded to it, and now you're just okay if he spends the night in my house?"

"I told you I trust him, but I also stand by what I said, he's not the guy for you." Finn got up and stuck his phone in his back pocket, zipping his jacket.

As I rose from my seat and headed into the kitchen for a glass of wine to ease the tension, Finn pushed the blinds aside and surveyed the backyard.

"I try, Finn, but I don't get you."

"There's nothing to get."

"Not true." I opened a bottle of red and poured it into a stemmed wine glass Lena had given me labeled, *Nurses Don't Cry We Wine*. "Since you've been back at work, you're different, and not in a good way. I know you won't admit it, but Mom was right. You were happier running the bar with Lena, and brewing beer actually made you fucking excited, nothing makes you excited." I took a long sip, savoring the bold sweetness. "And stop talking down to me like I'm the same kid you used to boss around."

Releasing the blinds, Finn leaned against the edge of the counter, watching me.

"Want one?" I asked.

"No, I'm leaving as soon as Rhett gets back." As Finn spoke, the front door opened and shut.

"I'm back." Rhett's deep voice echoed from the entryway.

Finn stayed near the counter, his brows drawn in thought. For a fleeting moment, I glimpsed sadness in his eyes, and the lines around them appeared a little deeper, aging him beyond his thirty-four years. "I know you think I'm a hard-ass, but I'm the way I am because I care about what happens to you, just like I did Miles."

An ache formed in my throat, threatening tears, and I drank from my glass to make the feeling go away as Rhett walked into the kitchen. He glanced from Finn to me and turned to leave. "I can come back."

"You're all good, man." Finn kept his attention on me. "I couldn't save our brother, but I will protect you, and if my method turns me into an asshole sometimes, I don't care."

"That's way too much responsibility to put on yourself, Finn. I'm a grown woman and I'm okay, *really* okay. You can relax whatever anger you're holding onto around me. Let go the way you do at the range, like the way it used to be, that's all I'm saying. You're *suffocating*."

He tapped the counter and stepped back. "I'll check in tomorrow."

Silence. That was Finn's way of handling everything. "Sure," I said, sighing.

Rhett followed Finn out of the kitchen, and I stood there aching for my brother... aching for myself. I couldn't imagine a time when the pain of losing Miles wouldn't sneak up on me and almost grind my heart into pieces. With my glass in hand, I turned away, wiping my eyes as tears fell.

"Hey." Rhett's voice was becoming a familiar comfort, even if I didn't want it to be.

"Hey, back." I sniffled, facing him. "Is he gone?"

"Yeah." Placing a bag on the floor, he leaned against the wall. "There's no sign of anyone out there. Do you need anything?"

"*Air.*" I walked toward the patio doors, but he reached for the handle first, opening the door. A shiver rippled through me, and goosebumps covered my arms when the chilly air brushed my skin, but I followed him outside, breathing the frigid night into my lungs. I sat on the chair, placing my glass on the table and rubbed my bare arms.

Rhett yanked his sweater off and handed it to me. "Take it."

I gave in to the inviting warmth of the fabric, and as I pulled the sweater over my head, his scent wrapped around me. "Thanks."

He sat in the chair next to me, revealing the glint of his gun in the waistband of his jeans as he stretched his legs in front of him.

"Do *you* need anything?" I asked. "A drink?"

"Not tonight." His forearms flexed as he crossed his arms, and he glanced across the small table at me. "Although..."

I drank from my glass. "I'm listening."

"Fuck, a raspberry cream cheese Danish would be great right about now."

"Make it blueberry, and you've got a deal."

"If they were open, Frankie, I'd take you." Resting his head against the back of the chair, he closed his eyes.

"I'm holding you to that promise," I said.

"I'll come through for you."

How did he know exactly what to say to calm me? I drank my wine as the river's current blended into the background, and my exhales misted in front of me. Time either moved fast or stood still around us, but we sat in an easy silence. Rhett's chest rose and fell underneath his crossed arms in a steady rhythm. Sinking into the cushions, I tilted my head back. Stars clustered together, forming constellations in the sky. We were so small compared to whatever existed out there. Maybe Miles was a part of all that beauty in some other universe. My mind wandered, and the urge to break the silence hit me.

"Rhett?"

"Frankie."

I smiled, facing him, but he kept his eyes closed. "I'm not sure what I wanted to say."

"You've got all night to think of it."

The cold had stolen the warmth from his sweater, and another chill ran through me.

I got up and stepped over his outstretched legs, leaning down to switch on the space heater. Making room for me, he shifted in his seat, and the orange glow from the heater reflected in his eyes as I stood over him. He sat up and looked up at me. I wanted to drop in front of him, run my fingers over him, grab his face. *Kiss* him. I wanted his hands on my body.

He stilled when I didn't move back to my seat, his gaze falling to my mouth.

I licked my lips as though subconsciously preparing for him to pull me toward him. "I..." *Want you.*

"You what?" he murmured, and I almost dropped onto his lap. *Almost.*

"I'm cold," I rasped.

His hands found mine, hidden in the sleeves of his sweater, and a rush of heat filled my fingers as he held them. "Better?"

"A little."

"Want to go inside?" he asked.

"Not really."

"Want me to warm you up?"

I craved his arms around me, and his warm body against mine, but the intensity of how much I wanted him terrified me. "Sure." The shivers crawling over my skin and down my legs weren't from the cold this time. Releasing my fingers, he wrapped an arm around my waist, gently coaxing me to sit on his lap, and I gave in, settling against him. With my legs swung over his, he held me close, clasping his fingers together, and I let my head fall to his chest.

His chin rested on my head, moving slightly as he talked. "Is this okay?"

Lifting my head, I cupped his face in my hands, his gaze piercing mine. "You tell me."

"Frankie, being near you is more *okay* than I've been in a very long time; I can't stop thinking about you. But I don't want to be your bad decision. I don't deserve you."

I bristled at his words, ending the moment. "That's a bullshit excuse men give women they don't want."

Lines crossed his forehead as he furrowed his brows. "That's not true—"

"Sure it is." I ran my fingers along his jaw, feeling his rough stubble, and he tilted his face into my hand. "If you want to be with someone, if you really want to deserve their time, their body, their everything... fucking do what it takes to *deserve* them." I dropped my hands to his chest. "Why not be my good decision, *deserve* me."

"I'm not sure that's possible for someone like me whose life is too fucked up to fix. I can't do that to you."

"Why don't you tell me what's too fucked up and let me decide?"

He exhaled, shifting his gaze away from me. "There's nothing to talk about."

How could I have been so foolish to want an emotionally unavailable man, giving him the upper hand, the *control* to break my heart? I bent down and turned off the space heater, pulling out of his embrace. The chilly air replaced his lingering heat as I stood. "I'm going to bed. I'll leave a pillow and blanket on the couch. Good night, Rhett."

Not waiting for him to respond, I headed inside and took his sweater off, dropping it on the table. I snatched Miles's police report and hurried up the stairs. I would never tell Finn, but maybe he was right. Getting close to Rhett would only end up hurting me. How the hell did I let someone I'd just met get under my skin so damn fast, and why didn't I have it in me to just say *fuck it* and let him be a terrible decision for just a little while?

With a glance out my bedroom window at the quiet street, I yanked the blackout drapes closed and flopped onto my unmade bed. A light switched off downstairs, and footsteps moved from the kitchen to the living room. Before Rhett had come back inside, I'd left one of my pillows and a couple of blankets on the couch for him. The man wasn't my type. He was unpredictable, a wanderer—he had nothing to offer someone who needed more... *stability* in their life.

Damn Finn and his truths.

Rhett was the opposite of what I needed... Except for his sexy charm, a dose of excitement that intrigued me when it shouldn't, and the way the man looked at me like I was the only fucking woman in the entire world who meant anything to him. Even though he'd made it clear he didn't want me.

I'm in trouble.

I'd be better off when he left town.

Settling under the covers, I turned the bedside light on and opened the folder. I tucked the toxicology and autopsy reports to the back, unable to reread either for the millionth time, and moved onto the next page. Breathing deeply, I skimmed over the transcribed 911 call; an unknown bystander had made the call. There were pages of case information naming the attending officers, and my brother, the *victim*. I skimmed over Miles's age, birthday, description, and could recite the state he'd been found in without needing the horrific words in front of me.

Multiple gunshot wounds. Blood present. Slumped on the floor.

Tears filled my eyes, blurring the words. I wiped them away and continued reading.

Investigators suspected foul play, ruling his death a homicide, and tucked an image of the gun casings on a bloody cement floor among the pages. My stomach churned, and I had to stop myself from running to the bathroom to throw up whatever remained of my birthday dinner. I searched for pictures of Miles, but a photo of the gun was the only one in the file. Knowing my dad, he would've been through this file, leaving nothing unseen, and if that included pictures of his dying son, it was no wonder why he'd used alcohol to numb his agony.

I read through the pages of statements from officers and medics, stopping when I came to Finn's. He'd arrived and found Miles shot and bleeding on the ground, and like he had told me for the past two years, there were no other details that I didn't already know. The man who'd fired the gun, killing my brother, was unknown among a group of suspected drug dealers.

One sentence on the next page stood out.

An officer operating in an undercover capacity observed an exchange of gunfire, consistent with narcotics activity under an ongoing investigation of a sensitive nature, ending in fatal injuries of the victims.

Others had died that night, and anger flushed my cheeks and ears as I hoped the man who had stolen my brother from us had been one of the *victims*.

I kept reading through standard policy-type verbiage, including the phrase, "confidential informant". Miles had been involved in a large ring of criminal activity and was one of many being investigated by undercover officers and law enforcement.

Flashbacks of Miles on the stretcher overwhelmed me, slamming into my mind. Bolting upright, I breathed through the persistent memories. The blood, so much *blood*. I'd held his limp body in my arms, begging for him to fight, knowing he was already gone. I'd never forget the vacant stare plastered on his gray face, pale lips hanging open, as though his silent scream matched my uncontrollable wails. Losing him had broken me apart, and I'd never be able to fully put myself back together.

I didn't want to accept the irritating truth that the police file gave no more answers, no closure... *nothing*. It had left me with a hollow ache in my stomach that radiated through my chest.

A toilet flushed downstairs, and the pipe creaked in the walls as the tap ran, shutting off abruptly. I curled into a ball, pulling the blankets over my head, and sobbed against my pillow, the tears soaking through the fabric. Grief had dragged me down before, and I'd recovered. I could do it again.

Eighteen

Rhett

I tried to stretch out on Frankie's couch with my feet over the armrest, adjusting the pillow behind my head. It had a soft and sexy smell that my body recognized before my brain caught up. *Her*.

I exhaled hard. I was a fucking asshole. I had wanted to curl my fingers in her hair, grab her and kiss her, but I pushed her away instead, and she shut down. The emotion had left her gorgeous eyes as she put a wall up. I could feel it. I had done a good job of putting the distance between us; her brother would be fucking ecstatic that I was following his rules, but I wasn't sure how long that would last. The one woman who ignited feelings I thought myself incapable of... Untouchable.

My phone vibrated with a message from Finn checking in.

Noble's nowhere in town. His mom is home alone, I've got an address. Anything happening?

Kicking my feet off the couch, I got up and moved the curtains aside. I typed a response.

All quiet. He's got someone working for him here, he has to.

If no one knew I was in Willow Grove, they were using Frankie to get to her brother, and I was getting too damn comfortable in a life that didn't belong to me.

Finn sent another message. *Is Frankie ok?*

His unawareness of his sister's pain infuriated me. If he talked to her and paid attention to the signs, he'd know she was barely hanging on.

Fuck the rules. I typed a response. *I'll make sure she's okay.*

Pressing the button to darken my screen, I ignored his reply as headlights lit up the road. I opened the door and stepped outside, but the vehicle turned into the townhouse a few down from Frankie's.

"What's wrong?" She called from inside.

I went back in and locked the door. "Nothing, just a neighbor driving by." I scanned the street through the living room window.

"Are you sure?" Appearing beside me, she looked out the window. With her dark hair in a wild ponytail and wearing a thin T-shirt and matching shorts, I had a tough time not letting myself stare at every inch of her bare skin.

I'd spent a long time believing life owed me nothing, and that I could never give someone what they needed, but fuck, I wanted her. The need to prove myself to Frankie consumed me, and I sure as hell wasn't leaving town until I knew she was safe.

Deserve me.

Challenge accepted, Francesca Roscoe.

"I thought you were sleeping." The sheer proximity of her body to mine had me struggling. I wanted to reach for her.

"I tried." She folded her arms across her chest, pushing her tits up, and I stuck my gun back in my waistband and ran a hand over my face.

I wanted to be her insomnia cure. Hell, I wanted to be *hers*.

Her stomach rumbled in the quiet room.

"Can I ask you something?" I said.

"Just did." Her lips pursed in a tight line, and she held her chin slightly higher than usual.

I held back a laugh. I hadn't known her long, but I knew when a woman was pissed at me. The night had been a disaster, and despite her anger, she was stuck with me until I found the fucker responsible for scaring her. "Are you hungry? I could've sworn that was your stomach growling."

"Maybe." She spun around and walked away from me toward the kitchen.

The way she moved, with those shorts clinging to her, sent heat through me. I couldn't *not* look.

She stretched her neck from side to side, rubbing it as she gripped the counter, and I leaned against the wall. "Want me to make you something to eat?"

She whipped her head toward me, but I couldn't tell if that expression was her annoyed look, or shock. "*You* want to *cook* for *me.*"

Shock?

"I do, I can. What do you feel like?" I shrugged. "I can't bake, so a blueberry Danish isn't going to happen, but I'm resourceful."

"Well, fuck," she said.

Perhaps I was wrong, and that had been her annoyed look.

Her features softened as she spoke. "It's blueberry Danish or nothing." She gripped her bottom lip with her teeth, and all I could think about was what her lips would taste like on mine.

Fuck, indeed.

"Can I look in your fridge?" I asked.

"Go right ahead." She filled a kettle with water. "I'm making tea, want one?"

I rummaged through her bare refrigerator. "Not for me, thanks."

"Doesn't like tea, got it."

"How about coffee?" I grabbed a carton of eggs, mushrooms that appeared fresh enough, and cheese. "You like omelets? I'll make a middle of the night breakfast."

"I can't remember the last time someone cooked me a morning breakfast. Sounds perfect."

She handed me a knife, a grater, and a cutting board, and I grabbed the frying pan she'd used as a weapon earlier. I cut up mushrooms and grated cheese, adding them to the eggs.

When the kettle let out a shrill whistle, she poured the boiling water into her mug, adding a tea bag before perching on a stool at the counter. "Has anything happened since I went upstairs?"

"No." I looked at her. "But I'm not leaving you on your own, Frankie."

I turned back to the stove and flipped the omelet as she held the mug in her hands, watching me. "You like cooking?"

"I do if I want to eat something half decent."

"Self taught?" Her dark eyebrows arched as she blew on her tea.

"Sort of. My mom worked a lot growing up, she showed me the basics, but I like to eat, so if I want something, I learn how to make it." The tension from earlier had dissolved, but a lingering sense of unease stuck around. I kept alert, listening for vehicles near the house, footsteps, anything out of the ordinary. "Where do you keep your plates?"

"Cabinet to the right of the sink." She sipped her tea. "What was she like? Your mom. Only if you want to tell me, just say none of your business and I'll drop it."

I never talked about my mother with anyone, but Frankie's question wasn't intrusive. A protective gentleness surrounded her as she waited for me to respond, I just wasn't sure how. What did I remember most about my mother?

I turned the burner off and slid each omelet onto a plate. "Mom found good in people when there wasn't any. She pushed me to do better than she ever could, she'd kick my ass if I disrespected anyone—especially women—believed if you took care of people you loved, they'd take care of you, and told me life was too short to fuck with... that last one came when she was diagnosed with cancer."

Frankie reached a hand across the counter and touched my arm, sending warmth along my skin. "I'm sorry she's gone."

"Yeah, well, that's life." I set a plate in front of her, rummaging through her drawers for forks like I lived here. My chest ached, but I forced the grief back down and turned my attention to her. There was a piano upstairs that had sparked my curiosity. "Do you play piano? I noticed a full-size keyboard upstairs."

Frankie took a fork from me, and I sat on the stool next to her with my plate. "I used to." She avoided eye contact as she stuck the fork in the omelet.

"Does it work?"

"It works, I just haven't had time."

I ate a bite of food, and her eyes met mine as I tilted my head toward her. I hadn't noticed before, but they were slightly puffy and reddened, like she'd been crying. Her brother's folder was gone when I'd come inside earlier. She must've read it, but asking her questions would only lead to her questioning me. "Are you good? At the piano I mean."

She held a forkful of eggs above the plate and laughed. "You know what, Rhett? I wasn't too bad, even got to do a radio show in Boston when I was in high school. I think that's when I first thought of moving to the city." With a faraway look, she stared at her suspended eggs without eating them. "I loved playing. I miss having a real piano. My parents sold it after I left for college. I actually dusted off that keyboard for the first time the other night when I heard your jazz."

"But you didn't play, did you."

"I did not. Wasn't ready I guess." She finally took a bite of the omelet, and her eyes widened. "This is good."

"Surprised?"

"A little." She took another bite, glancing at me. "Thanks for staying tonight, I appreciate it. But we can't do this every night, I need to live my life. I'm letting the police do their job. I won't fuck up and forget to lock the doors, I'll be extra careful when I'm alone, I'll get a damn gun if I have to. I'm not the first person to have a break-in."

I drank some of my coffee and set the mug on the counter. "Frankie, this isn't just a break-in. It's someone who knows you and your brother." I picked at the omelet as my mind raced. I'd camp outside to keep her safe if I had to and schedule my shifts for when she was at work. "We'll figure it out."

"There is no we, Rhett." Her eyes hardened, and that familiar defensive look settled over her face as her smile disappeared.

My old life and her present had collided, and if I didn't get rid of the threat, I was a long way from proving to myself that I deserved her.

We ate the rest of our food in silence.

NINETEEN

Rhett

I double-checked the address Finn gave me for Alice Lane, pulling alongside the curb in front of the house next door. With my gun tucked into my jeans, I left my truck and walked past the small house. Tightly drawn curtains covered the windows on the upper floor, and an overgrown cedar blocked the front window. Weeds filled cracks in the empty driveway, with no vehicle or anyone in sight, including her son.

I'd driven Frankie to work and talked to Finn for an hour in the bar, gathering information with his help. Bran Noble had discovered Frankie Roscoe, the sister of a man who'd died working for my father, and an undercover cop. Noble might not recognize Finn, but seeing Miles in that picture would've been enough to send him digging into Willow Grove. Even if he had returned to Boston, Frankie would be under constant watch. Whoever broke into her house had a reason.

I had one advantage if I was going to figure out who Noble had working for him—I was standing on his mother's doorstep and not buried in a hole somewhere. He couldn't have known I was here. But once I handled the Noble connection in Willow Grove, and ended the stalking situation with Frankie, I had business to take care of that would end my days of being on the run.

I dodged a swinging basket hanging over the porch, filled with dead flowers, and rang the doorbell. A car drove by as I waited, not stopping. Judging from the fucking state of his mother's house, I couldn't imagine Bran visited often. The Nobles had earned my father's trust, and he'd given them his loyalty. They fucked up working both sides for their gain, and I'd found out about it. They saw me as the rat who'd killed one of their own, ending our families' decades-long alliance.

Footsteps scuffled, and loud, muffled words came from inside. As the door opened, a woman supporting herself with the help of a cane looked me up and down.

She scowled, putting on the glasses that hung from a silver chain around her neck. "Who might you be?"

"Hi, ma'am," I said, smiling. "Bran wanted me to check on you. He wants you to call someone to come clean up your property before winter and send him the bill." I glanced behind her. A TV loudly announced the potential for snowfall from inside the house. "Can I come in? Five minutes should do it, you're alone?"

"I'm always alone. Bring me my gin and tonic, and you can come in." Holding up three shaky fingers, she continued. "Three cubes of ice and a twist of lime."

"Done," I said, stepping inside. I doubted she would have the information I needed, but provoking her son's suspicion would be enough to satisfy me. I followed her along a narrow hallway to a kitchen barely large enough for the round table and two chairs. The place smelled of heavy perfume and menthol. "Where do you keep the gin?"

Ambling toward the counter, she propped her cane against it and opened a cabinet. Bottles of expensive gin lined up in rows filled the first shelf, a tray of pill bottles, one labeled *take as needed* for sleep sat on the counter, and dirty dishes filled the sink. She offered me a highball glass with a trembling hand, and I grabbed the ice tray from the refrigerator.

"Three—"

"Three cubes, got it." I dropped the ice into the glass as she took her cane and headed into a small living room. I found a bottle of tonic water and poured it into the glass, selecting the freshest lime from a bowl of browning fruit on the table.

All that money and this is how Noble takes care of his mother?

I squeezed the lime, mixing the juice into the drink, and slid the wedge on the rim of the glass. Carrying it into the living room, I handed it to her. "I'll make a call when I leave. Someone will come and clean the place and get your groceries. Bran wants to make sure you're taken care of at home, especially since you got out of the hospital."

"My son does not care about me." She sat in a tattered chair with the cane next to her.

I stood between the kitchen and living room, my eyes darting between the window and door. "Do you have a cell number for him? I just have the house number."

She gulped the drink, downing almost half of it in one breath. "In my book." Reaching beside her, she lifted an address book.

I flipped through the pages, skimming through the last names beginning with N until I found Bran Noble's number and took a picture with my phone. "Perfect, thank you." I set the book on a tray next to her chair. "When will he be back in town?"

"The bastard never comes, sends people like you instead."

"Right, anyone else been here lately?" A van approached the house, slowing down, but turned onto the next street.

I wandered around the room and peeked down the hallway at a dark staircase. Unless she had a dead body upstairs, she was alone.

She mumbled something incoherent, but I caught the last part. "I would love nothing more than to slap that man's face," she said.

Approaching her, I adjusted my jacket, feeling my gun against me. "What man?"

"He always wears a suit with a horrendous tie that's too short and refuses to come inside for fear of getting dirt on him. I used to keep a good, clean home..." She downed the rest of her drink and rubbed her eyes. "Oh dear, I am afraid I have forgotten your name already, how rude."

"You've been hospitable. The man with the suit and bad tie. Is his hair always parted on the side, and he's about this tall?" I held a hand up a couple of inches shorter than myself.

"A daft prick," she said.

I liked this woman. One man came to my mind. *Clay Preston.*

"I better run, but someone will be by soon to help you out, just like I said. Make sure Bran gets the bill."

She raised the glass toward me. "You don't leave until I get another one."

"Wouldn't dream of it." Taking her glass, I mixed another drink—a double—and handed it to her. "Have yourself a good rest of your day and tell your son I say hello."

"Did you say your name is Peter?" she called after me as I headed out the door.

"You remembered." I shut it behind me and hurried to my truck, scanning the street.

As I drove to the Magpie, I called a local landscaping company and a residential care service, arranging for yard work, housecleaning, and someone to pick up groceries, giving them Bran Noble's number. I made it very clear that her son would be responsible for all charges and gave them a spare burner phone number to reach me in case a problem arose.

It was time for me to properly introduce myself to Frankie's ex.

The usual Thursday night crowd had gathered at the Magpie, but it wasn't enough of a distraction to quiet the restless thoughts consuming my mind. Clay Preston hadn't been in the bar for days, and Finn found out he'd returned to Connecticut to meet a business partner. If he was Noble's eyes and ears, he'd be back.

Frankie was avoiding me. She'd arranged transportation for the past two days until her Jeep repairs were done. Lena had given me Frankie's schedule for the week, arranging mine so I could leave by seven each night before she arrived home from work. Lena agreed to keep our arrangement quiet if I promised to keep her friend safe, and I'd never broken a promise. Learning Frankie's routine had been easy... Too easy.

She worked twelve-hour days until Friday and was usually home before eight. The pipes in the walls separating us were loud enough to know she showered after every shift, and the cold never stopped her from sitting outside. There was no way she didn't know I was out there too, but she never said a word. Her deliberate silence, ignoring me, somehow amused me when I had nothing to fucking smile about. I responded with music, playing it *just* loud enough to remind her I was still there, and she wasn't alone.

A notification from Vivian filled my phone screen, and I ducked through the door to the back and made my way to the office. As I'd expected, Frankie hadn't sent a message, but I read my sister's. *Been digging, Noble's got someone in Willow Grove working for him. No name. When are you coming home? Two weeks until D-day, maybe sooner.*

Two weeks was too soon.

Working on it, I replied. My sister trusted someone who was feeding her information, and before I returned to Boston, I needed to know who they were and what I was walking into. I called her, and she picked up on the first ring.

"Working on it?" she said. "We're working on a deal over here and you're still MIA—"

"Who have you been talking to?" I lowered my voice, keeping an eye on the door.

"What are you talking about?"

"You're an intelligent woman, you tell me."

She exhaled into the silence. "I need you to trust me."

"I've always trusted you, I don't want that to change. Who, Viv."

"You won't understand, but he's with us, I swear on your life, on my son's life—"

"Don't you dare fucking do that." I ran a hand over my face. My sister had dragged me back into the shitstorm when she'd asked for my help. My problem was I'd do anything to protect her and Zach. If I couldn't trust her, I had no one, and her son would pay the price if she fucked this up. "We lived through this once, what are you doing? Keep it legit, on the books, don't tell anyone."

"It's okay, I know it sounds messy, but please..."

"Who is he?" I snapped.

Vivian spoke quietly. "Luca Noble. He's on our side... he *loves* me, and I love him."

Bran Noble's *nephew*. Fucking hell.

I hung up as one of Lena's new hires walked out back, lingering by the keg cooler with the door open. I'd paid attention to everyone who'd come and gone at the Magpie but hadn't bothered learning the staff's names yet. The more comfortable I became in Willow Grove, the harder leaving would be. And I had to leave soon before my father came looking for me and found... *Her.*

Shoving my phone in my pocket, I left the office to help haul kegs to the front as Frankie's ex strolled into the bar with a shit-eating grin plastered across his face.

"Whatever you're thinking, don't." Lena helped her staff hook up the kegs, shooting me a glare. "Thanks, Ash," she told them.

Despite myself, I burned the name to memory.

The tall, lanky kid with blue hair is Ash.

Comfort in this town had snuck in against my will.

"I didn't say a word." Wiping spilled beer off the bar, I tracked Clay as he joined a group of guys at a round table near the fireplace. He hung his wool coat on a hook, draping his scarf around his neck.

"You didn't have to, I can read it all over your face." Lena stood beside me behind the bar, staring at the table. "You think it's him, don't you?"

"Give me five minutes?" I dropped the cloth and headed around the bar.

Her height made her nearly eye-level as she glared at me. "Don't break anything, in here or on him. An assault charge isn't a good look for a new employee, and I've worked hard to build this bar's non-violent reputation."

"I just want to introduce myself, being new in town and all," I said as I moved toward his table.

A server carried a tray of beers with the blue Magpie logo on the glasses, placing each one in front of the men at the table. Clay's hands moved as he described the new Benz he'd had his eye on, and I approached, standing next to him. He clutched his scarf, looking up at me. "Can I help you with something?"

"A word, please?"

He laughed. "A *word*? Where?"

"Outside."

Rising from his seat, Clay took a drink of his beer and addressed the table. "Excuse me while I have a word."

He motioned for me to lead the way, but I stepped back. "After you," I said.

A woman walked by with her dog, wearing a winter coat to her ankles, and two younger men stood at the edge of the parking lot smoking, the smell of weed drifting in the air.

Clay spun around in front of me. "You got me outside, what do you want?"

I strode past him toward a gray sedan sitting under a streetlight. I wiped the light dusting of snow off the rental car logo. "This your vehicle?"

"For now. Is that why you dragged me out here? To talk cars?" His dress shoes echoed on the pavement as he walked. He stood next to me, and a car drove past us, parking nearby. A couple got out, holding hands as they entered the bar.

When we were alone, I continued. "I didn't drag you anywhere."

"This is a bit fucked up though, you can see that, right?" Clay paced back and forth, crossing his arms. "You're Lena's bartender, nothing more. Isn't she paying you to work?" A chuckle that sounded more like a grunt escaped him, and he took a step toward me, but I didn't move. The Morrigan in me was about to resurface. "Tell me, Rhett, is it?" he said with disgust. "What is so pressing in your tiny world that you dare to *drag* me away from my company?"

I grabbed both ends of his scarf. As he stumbled back, I crossed the fabric over his throat with a sharp tug. He reached up, his fingers clenching around my hands. "What the fuck is wrong with you?"

"What do you want with Frankie?" I spoke calmly. I knew Clay wouldn't cooperate or give me a name, but he would leave tonight understanding that I'd be watching him.

He thrashed his head from side to side, trying to break free, but I yanked the scarf tighter. "What are you talking about? She's nothing to me!"

"I know what you're doing, and if it continues, it won't end well for you." Releasing my grip, I smoothed out his scarf as he wavered on his feet, cursing me.

"I'm reporting this incident to the cops, I can charge you with assault!"

"But you won't." I walked away from him and headed back inside, leaving him pissed off near his car.

Lena looked up at me. "What did you do?" Her eyes darted to the door as Clay entered. He shot me a furious look before returning to the table.

"Introduced myself."

"I can see that. Did he call the cops?" Lena opened the hinged swing door, letting me behind the bar.

"Nope." I crossed my arms, throwing Clay a small nod and a relaxed smile, but he looked away.

I'd gotten to him. He'd relay the information to Bran Noble, and I'd be ready.

Twenty

Frankie

I slumped in a break room chair, sucking back lukewarm coffee like it was oxygen, and rested my head against the chair. I was exhausted; the extra shifts of the past few days made it easier to avoid Rhett, even if I couldn't get him out of my head. He must be working with Lena, because his schedule conveniently allowed him to be home, outside on his deck every night since the break-in.

He played that sexy music like a damn mating call, leaving me torn between yelling at him or running next door to kiss him.

If Finn wasn't around, someone he knew patrolled my house daily, keeping me under constant surveillance. Their intention was to help me feel safe, but the feeling of being watched was a relentless, suffocating pressure on my chest. I had my Jeep back, and the drive to and from work had been uneventful. No one stalked me, or broke into my house, and no more flowers arrived destined for the trash. I had returned to my normal routine, and it helped me rationalize the situation. But downplaying what had happened only heightened my unease.

Insomnia tormented me more than usual. I locked my windows and doors, but every creak in the house had me on edge. If I admitted my fear, Finn would beg me to stay with our parents, or Rhett would show up at my door. Staying with my parents meant becoming a live-in counselor, constantly on drunk-Dad watch, and I needed to shake Rhett from my system.

No, thank you.

Zoey walked into the room, closing the door behind her. "You look comfortable."

"Looks are deceiving," I said, unmoving. "I've got five precious minutes, and I'm taking them."

She took off her lab coat, draping it across the back of the chair, and sank into the cushioned seat. Pulling at the neck of her scrub shirt, she fanned it away from her neck in quick motions. "I've been running all morning, I can't wait for this day to end so I can go home and shower." She ran her fingers along her curly, textured hair, pinned smooth against her scalp. "Question for you."

"Shoot." I yawned and tossed my empty cup toward the garbage can, missing. I leaned forward, rolling it toward me with my fingers, and took aim again, landing it in the can.

"Have you had sex with the new neighbor yet?"

I sighed and slumped back into my chair. "Not only am I *not* having sex with him, I've hardly even seen him."

"Lena told me he'll be working tomorrow night for your birthday gathering." She arched an eyebrow, observing me. "Did you know she hired a band?"

I sat up. "She what? There's no stage at the Magpie."

"Apparently, your neighbor is helping put something together."

"Neighbor has a name, Rhett. I told Lena, nothing big." With a quick glance at the clock on the wall, I stood, stretching my arms over my head. "He's leaving town soon anyway, this is a temporary stop."

"So make *him* a temporary stop." Zoey's lips curved in a teasing smirk.

The door swung open, and Logan walked in, eating a frosted donut. "Who are we making a temporary stop, stitches guy?"

"Rhett," Zoey said.

"He's here." Logan's mouth twisted to the side as he chewed, and Zoey and I looked at each other.

Rhett was *here*?

I sprang to my feet, making myself lightheaded. "He's what?"

Logan pointed a thumb over his shoulder. "The nurses' station, asking for you. He came bearing treats and they're all swooning, so I'd get my ass out there and claim what is yours for the taking." Pressing his lips together like he was holding back a grin, Logan opened the door for me, sweeping his hand in a grand gesture. "Go, I'll check on your patients."

He trailed me out of the room, cupping his mouth as he whispered, "He's adorable."

"Rhett Marshall is not adorable," I muttered.

I heard his deep voice before I laid eyes on him. Staff beamed at him, hovering over a large box filled with a variety of pastries, muffins, and cookies next to a tray of coffees. I approached, and he lifted his head, stepping closer. Heat fluttered low in my stomach as we locked eyes. His brows knitted together, creating lines on his forehead in the familiar thoughtful expression that had grown on me. So much for staying away from him.

A traitorous smile fought to break through; I couldn't help it. "What are you doing here?"

"Deserving you." He held up a paper bag in one hand and a coffee in the other. "You've been avoiding me."

I took the paper bag from him and peeked inside. "Blueberry cream cheese Danish." Pushing the Danish up the bag to avoid touching it with hospital hands, I bit into it and closed my eyes. "So damn good."

"I owed you."

"You owe me nothing." I took another bite. He'd done a nice thing for me and the staff, and I should've thanked him, but a small part of me questioned his motives. "You can't just randomly show up at my work with treats for everyone."

"Looks like I just did." He leaned against the wall, out of sight from prying eyes. "I'll just keep trying until I get it right. This is yours too." He offered me a coffee.

I closed the gap between us and lowered my voice. "What is this? What are you doing?" His dark, penetrating gaze fell to my mouth. I fought to keep myself still and not look away.

"I told you."

"*Deserving* me? Rhett, I don't have the energy for this. The other night you made it very clear—"

"No, I didn't."

"I'm pretty sure you did. The whole 'I don't deserve you, my life is too fucked up to even try' line told me all I needed to know."

He regarded me, his lips parting and closing. "Has anything else happened? Finn and I have been taking turns watching the house, I saw a patrol car—"

"Nothing's happened, no flower deliveries, stalkers, nothing." I checked my watch and rolled up the rest of my Danish inside the bag for later. "I need to get back to work."

He straightened and shoved his hands in his pockets. Why did he have to look so fucking *good*?

I sipped hesitantly at the steaming coffee. Black with a hint of sugar. He even knew how I liked my coffee. "Thank you," I finally said. "I appreciate the Danish, and coffee has kept me going through a horrible dose of insomnia lately."

"I'm not sleeping either... if you're up tonight, I'll be outside."

No thanks, I'd like to keep my heart intact, and being near you makes me feel... vulnerable.

"Is that an invitation?" I asked instead.

He moved closer, leaning down so his lips brushed my ear. His warm breath sent tingles along my skin. "You don't need one." He stepped back, smiling at me, and I almost melted to the floor.

I held up my coffee to hide my face as I walked away from him. "I have to go."

"Have a good rest of your shift, Frankie."

Without turning back around, I called out. "Thank you, Rhett."

Zoey pumped sanitizer onto her hands with a huge smile on her face. "Girl, you're *not* having sex with that man? I don't care how long he's in town, someone gives you *that* reaction? Have a little fun."

I helped a man with a bedside urinal to end my shift after seven o'clock. Taking my gloves off, I settled him back on the bed and pulled the blanket over him.

"You're Roscoe's kid, aren't you?" he said, pressing the button to raise the head of the bead. "Francesca?"

"I am." I checked his IV site and hung a new bag of saline, bracing myself for a conversation I didn't want to have about my father.

"How is your dad making out these days with everything..." The man winced when I glanced at him. "We've heard some rumblings is all, just hope he's okay."

"He's managing well enough, thanks for asking." I handed him his pills and a cup of water.

Tossing them back, he gulped the water and handed the empty cup to me. "Sticking around town these days, that's good for your family."

He reminded me of what I'd missed about city life; small-town gossip made it difficult to keep anything private for long. "Did you need anything else?"

He sat back against the bed and exhaled. "Nothing you can fix, I'm sorry to say."

I patted his arm, dropping the cup in the garbage. "I hope you get some sleep tonight."

"It's a small world. I haven't seen you since you and your brothers were just kids, and a couple of days ago, I saw Preston's son at the Magpie. He's doing well too, I go way back with the family. Weren't you two an item for a while?"

The tension in my neck radiated into my head at the mention of Clay. I couldn't figure out why he was still in Willow Grove. He seldom returned to our hometown and never stayed long. "That was years ago. I hope you have a good night, try to rest until those test results come back."

He smoothed the wrinkles in the blanket over his legs. "You have yourself a lovely evening. I hope to be well on my way out of here by the morning."

"Fingers crossed, good night."

I hurried out of the room. My feet were killing me, and work had bled from my schedule into picking up shifts on my days off. I looked forward to the next two days of freedom.

I finished charting later than expected, and headed down the elevator, shrugging my jacket on. The wind tossed a scattering of dead leaves across the parking lot, and my breaths misted in the crisp night air. My yellow Jeep stood out against the other cars like a beacon.

Beyond the hospital floodlights, a shadow moved in the driver's seat of a parked SUV, and I hustled toward my Jeep with my keys between my fingers, activating the headlights with a flick of a button. I hopped in and slammed the door shut, pounding the lock button with frantic breaths.

Someone is watching me.

I started the engine, grateful for no warning lights on my dash, and drove through the parking lot, slowing as I passed the SUV.

"Who are you?" I whispered, straining to make out more than the dark shape through the tinted windows. It could be anyone on staff, or a family member picking someone up after a shift. Access to the parking lot required an ID card, unless the parking lot attendant opened the gate.

Don't panic, it's probably nothing.

I turned on my music, cranking the volume. Traffic lessened as I dove away from the central part of town and veered onto my forested road, but headlights tailed me too close. Like they'd done the night my Jeep had broken down.

As I passed sparse neighborhoods, I debated turning onto a quiet street, but the SUV retreated. I could've sworn the vehicle from the other night had been smaller than this one.

I picked up speed, seizing my phone like it could somehow protect me, and the SUV suddenly kept pace, its headlights blinding in the mirror. Gripping the wheel with one hand, I lit up the keypad with the other to call for help. But the vehicle swerved onto a side street, sending up a cloud of dust. Adrenaline thumped in my ears, surging through me, making my breath catch in my throat and sweat bead along my forehead.

I'm okay, no one is after me.

I drove above the speed limit the rest of the way home and parked in the garage. I didn't move until the door lowered, caging me inside. My phone rang as I bolted up the steps into the house, and Finn raised his voice over a hum of chatter in the background.

"Did you make it home all right?" he asked.

"Just got in, why?"

Laughter broke, drowning out his words, and a sudden silence filled the line.

"Finn?"

"Still here, just left the bar. I wanted to check in."

"I'm home, everything's good here." Yanking the elastic from my hair, I trudged up the stairs to the bathroom, stopping at the doorway to the spare room. I still didn't know who'd broken into my house and targeted Miles's stuff, but it was too personal not to mean something. Two days earlier, I had randomly called an old number I still had for Clay. I had no idea what I'd say to him, but it rang without an answer or voicemail, and I had let it go, but his mention of Miles to my mother bothered me. "Has Clay been in?"

Finn hesitated before speaking. "Actually, not since the weekend, what's up?"

"Nothing... curious, that's all."

"Mom got to you didn't she? With the Boston stuff."

"It's just a bad feeling..." I tilted my face in the bathroom mirror, examining dark circles under my eyes against my pale skin. Lack of sleep was kicking my ass. "You didn't tell Mom and Dad about any of this did you? They'll panic and we want him to stop drinking, not go on a binge for days."

"I haven't, and I won't."

"Say you promise," I said.

He sighed. "Jesus, Frankie, what are we, twelve?"

"We are what we are, and I need you to promise me this stays between us."

"Fine, promise. Look, I got to go back out front. Lock your fucking doors, all of them, Rhett is next door—"

"I don't need him." I wasn't sure if I was convincing myself or Finn.

"Right, well if you do, he's there. I'll see ya tomorrow night."

"See ya," I said, ending the call.

I twisted the faucet knobs and ran the hot water for a shower until steam filled the bathroom. This would be the last day I'd spend in my twenties. I should be grateful, many never made it to thirty, including my brother, but uneasiness had clung to me for days in a way I'd never experienced before. I kicked off my scrub pants and tugged my shirt over my head, stepping into the shower. The hot water soothed my aching body as I shampooed my hair and scrubbed the day off my skin.

It was cold out, but I could make tea and sit on the deck with my heater for a bit to unwind. Maybe I'd bring my little piano downstairs and try to remember the notes for the first movement of the song *Moonlight Sonata*, or paint the spare room if insomnia kicked in...

None of my attempts to calm my mind helped. Someone had been in my house, and the only thing they wanted had once belonged to Miles. It all connected to something from two years ago in Boston, and I had to figure it out. I couldn't avoid him anymore; I needed to talk to Rhett.

Twenty-One

Rhett

I walked around Frankie's place, but the neighborhood was quiet with little traffic on the main road. Light streamed from every window in her house. As I crossed her backyard toward my deck, the glow from her dining room glinted on my hammer lying on the ground. I'd fixed the bottom step for her before she got home from work on Monday. I picked it up and waited for a minute for any sign of her before I turned around and went home.

I poured a glass of Irish whiskey and took my phone and a small speaker outside, turning on a jazz playlist. Stretching my legs, I peered through the wooden barrier between our decks. She was home safe, but I'd had enough of her avoiding me. I found *Her* on my phone and typed a message, hitting send before I could talk myself out of it.

The invitation still stands.

Seconds passed before her door slid open and closed. "I thought I didn't need one," she said.

"You don't, I thought you needed a reminder."

Her footsteps echoed on the wooden stairs, and I rose, leaning over the railing. She stopped on the bottom step, her long hair falling forward as she bent down, holding a mug. "You fixed it?"

"The wood doesn't match, I hope that's okay."

"It gives my place character, thank you," she said.

The porch light hit her face as she glanced up at me, and I took her in. She had fire behind her eyes, demanding my attention without trying at all, and I wanted to run my thumb over her lips, feeling their softness before claiming them with mine.

Tucking one hand into the sleeves of her pink sweatshirt, she carried the mug with the other. Her slippers thudded up the stairs to my deck, and our breaths fogged in the air.

She glanced down at the speaker on the table. "It's not as loud tonight."

"I didn't realize it was loud before."

"*Deafening*," she teased. "I thought you were having a party and didn't invite me, but now that I have this open invitation, that shouldn't be a problem?"

"Not at all." I took a drink to distract myself from the overwhelming need to grab her and pull her closer. "I don't have a heater, but you can come in if it's too cold."

Hesitating, she tilted her head. "Sure, actually that'd be better, I want to talk to you."

She wanted to *talk*?

I grabbed the speaker off the table and opened the door. "Did you lock your door when you left?"

Stepping inside, she held up a key. "It's locked. I won't make that mistake again, trust me."

"I trust you." I said, closing my patio door behind us.

Because I did. Trust her.

"That's sort of what I wanted to talk about—Jesus, Rhett, it's not much warmer in here." She scanned the room and walked over to the thermostat on the wall, lifting the cover. "Can we turn up the heat?"

"We've been over this, do whatever you want." I set my glass down and headed into the living room, switching on the propane fireplace. Having her here with me eased the constant worry about her safety. This place was never meant to be home, I'd lost touch with that feeling when my mother died. But Frankie stirred a need for something I thought was dead, and letting her go would be rough.

Unless I didn't have to.

"What are you drinking?" She picked up my glass, her eyes thoughtful as she inhaled.

"Just whiskey, try it."

"It's never *just* whiskey, or *just* wine, or *just* coffee, I think everyone prefers something bold or sweet, or..." Bringing the rim of the glass to her lips, she sipped the whiskey, and her eyes widened. "*Smooth*. That's a nice little burn down the throat." She drank from my glass again.

Fuck, she was sexy as hell.

I stepped toward her. "You can have it."

"No, I'm good." She handed it back to me, and our fingers touched as I took the glass from her hand. I let mine linger before pulling them away. "Thanks for sharing." She wandered into the living room and settled on the plush couch near the fire with her mug, kicking her slippers off to reveal dark-painted toenails. "My feet are sore, and I need to warm up." She bent her knees, propping herself against the armrest. "I like this song, it's soothing, like your whiskey."

I leaned against the wall. "Coltrane and Hartman, both Johns. *My one and only love.*"

"Romantic." Drinking from the mug, she pulled me in with a playful look.

I took the bait and sat next to her on the couch. "What are *you* drinking?"

"Just tea."

"It can't be *just* tea," I said, smiling.

"It's tame, vanilla flavored tea, but it's hot and feels good." Her gaze searched the room. "I love what you've done with the place." Her tone dripped with sarcasm as she reached down, absently rubbing her foot. "It looks like no one lives here, Rhett. You really are leaving, aren't you?"

"I never planned on staying." I'd never planned on *Her*. Leaning forward, I placed my glass on the coffee table. "It was already furnished, I didn't need much." As I shifted closer, her unwavering eyes held mine. "What did you want to talk to me about?" Taking a chance, I gently tugged at her feet, pulling them into my lap. I hated to admit it, but I cared about her. I wanted her to be warm and comfortable. She extended her legs over me, letting me hold her cold feet in my hands.

As I massaged each one, her head fell back against the armrest, lolling to the side so she could look at me. "That feels good, I didn't mean for you—"

"Talk to me." I rubbed along her calves over her worn jeans.

"I want you to tell me more about when you lived in Boston."

My forehead tightened as I looked at her. "You'll need to throw me specific questions, you're good at those." And I had better be damn good at answering without giving away anything.

"I think whoever followed me and broke into my house knew Miles. They were looking for something, I just know it. I don't get why now, why after two years. We don't even know who killed him, it's fucking ridiculous, and there was this SUV tonight... you know that feeling where you're being watched?" Frankie shook her head. "I don't know, maybe I'm losing it."

Releasing my hold on her leg, I gripped the back of the couch. "What happened tonight?"

"Nothing, an SUV spooked me. I'm just on edge."

"Why didn't you call me?"

"I didn't need to, nothing happened." She sat up, closing the space between us. "I hate being terrified in my own home. I'm never scared of the dark, I actually like it, but I can't stand it anymore."

My girl had been next door, scared to be alone but too stubborn to reach out. "I knew you wouldn't call, I should've just shown up at your door."

"I would have." Her gaze dropped to my mouth, and she clasped her fingers together in her lap. "It's hard for me to *need* someone like that."

I had never thought of a woman as property like my father, but I wanted to belong to Frankie. I wanted to be the man she called on her way home from work after a shitty day, or the first person she couldn't wait to share exciting news with. I was ready to go so far over the fucking *off limits* line there'd be no turning back. "Frankie, if you call, I'm going to come, every fucking time."

Her gaze shot back up, locking with mine. A hint of anger flashed across her face. "Until you leave town."

"That's not how I want this to go."

"How *do* you want this to go, because I'm confused as hell, and it's not your fault, I just let myself..." She rubbed her forehead and dropped her hands. "I'm trying to avoid you because all I want to do when I'm around you is... something I shouldn't want to do with a man who isn't sticking around. And maybe I'd kind of like to just say, fuck it and—"

My hands were on her face before she finished speaking, and she gasped. My thumb traced across her bottom lip as her hands found their way to my neck, urging me closer. She looked at me with those searching eyes of hers and dug her fingers into the back of my head. I hovered my mouth over hers. Her warm, shallow breaths touched my lips, and I kissed her. Slowly. Holding back until her lips parted, inviting me in.

Her tongue met mine, the smooth whiskey lingering in her mouth, and she slid her hands down my chest, gripping my shirt. I wrapped an arm around her body, bracing us with my hand on the back of the couch as I let her pull me on top of her. She made space for me between her legs, and I kissed her harder, adjusting her beneath me as my cock hardened. I curled my fingers in her hair at the back of her neck, and a moan escaped her lips, her fingernails dragging up my back underneath my shirt. I wanted to kiss every inch of her, be inside her—I wanted to show her how much I wanted her.

Her breaths came out fast as I kissed along her jaw and neck. My fingers found the waistband of her jeans, brushing over her skin, and she arched her back, pressing against me. I needed this woman like fucking *air*. But she wasn't just any woman, and I couldn't fuck this up.

Her eyes fluttered open as she held my face, and I brushed strands of hair off her forehead. "You okay, baby?"

"Very okay," she rasped. "Baby?" Her mouth moved against my lips as she kissed me.

"Just came out." I slipped my hand beneath her sweater, splaying my fingers over her back. I needed her closer.

She wrapped her legs around me. "Old habit?" She traced her fingers along my jaw, kissing me again.

I playfully tugged her lip with my teeth. "I don't have habits I can't quit."

"I doubt that," she whispered. Her pocket vibrated, lighting up between us.

"You need to get that, or do you want me to keep going," I said, breathing her in.

"Fuck, I want you to keep going, but hold that thought, it might be a problem with my father." She freed her phone from her pocket, her fingers grazing my hard-on.

I pulled away, adjusting myself, and turned off the music as she answered.

"Hello?" She frowned, and her brow furrowed as she sat up. "Who's there? I hear you breathing." Dropping the phone, she eyed the caller ID. "Unknown number. Who was that?"

As I stood, the sexual tension left my body, replaced with rage. "We'll have the number traced."

"Rhett. This is fucked up." She shoved her feet into her slippers and grabbed her mug from the table.

"Where are you going?" As I trailed her to my back door, she whirled around.

"You know, I can handle myself, I know how to shoot a gun, I've had patients yell at me, spit on me... but this is pissing me off. People don't just break into someone's house and follow them for no reason, not in this town. I could smell cologne that night, a man's cologne. I've hardly dated anyone in months, and when I did, it wasn't anyone who showed *stalker* behavior at all, even Clay never did anything like *this*."

"Let me come over there with you tonight, I'll stay on the couch again. Or stay here with me, take my bed. I don't want you to be alone."

She cupped my face, and I wrapped my arms around her waist, locking my fingers behind her back like I could keep her with me. "We never talked about Boston," she said.

Back to that. How could I lie to her? "You never asked the questions."

"Maybe there's a part of me that knows whatever you're running from, or back to, will just end everything before we ever start." Rising on tiptoes, she kissed me before pulling out of my arms. "I should go."

She reached for the handle, and I placed a hand over hers. "You should stay."

With her back against my chest, she relaxed and let go of the door. "You knew Finn when he worked in Boston," she said, and I stilled, holding her close.

"I did."

"Did you ever meet Miles?"

I had followed her brother's rules, hell, I'd agreed with them to keep her safe, just biding my time until my father got out of jail. We both wanted Frankie far away from the past, but she wasn't safe anymore. And those secrets were about to shatter.

I'd done exactly what I'd been avoiding for two years. I let myself care about someone and couldn't shut it off.

"I knew your brother, Frankie."

TWENTY-TWO

Frankie

A suffocating hurt ached in my chest as I spun around, out of his arms. I should have walked out the door a moment ago. I should have asked him about Miles in the beginning, when my instincts had begged me to. Rhett's silence about knowing my brother stung like a betrayal. "You lied to me."

"I never lied to you." He lifted a hand but didn't touch me.

"How did you know my brother? Are you *using* me?" A wave of nausea washed over me, and I shoved past him, steadying myself against the counter.

"What? Fuck no, I'm trying to protect you." The creases in his forehead relaxed as he approached, and he spoke calmly. "Every question you've asked me, everything I've ever said to you, has all been the truth. I will never lie to you."

"You knew Miles and didn't tell me. You saw me crying and vulnerable sitting on the floor with all his stuff and said *nothing*." Anger clawed through the hurt, and I folded my arms across my chest. Better to be angry than to break down. "I should've known better than to trust you." I blinked back tears, my gaze darting between his whiskey glass, my mug, the kitchen sink, finally settling on him, meeting his intense stare with my own.

He watched me but made no attempt to move closer. "I'm sorry, Frankie. I wanted to tell you, but—"

"There is no *but*." I snapped, wiping my eyes. "Does Finn know?" I clamped a hand over my mouth as my lip quivered, desperate to stifle the hurt. Rhett's brows furrowed, as though he was debating on how to break more bad news. But I knew. "Of course Finn knows," I said. "That's why he didn't want me around you. He thinks I'm made of fucking glass and would shatter if I knew the truth. He made you keep this from me?" I wanted to *hate* Rhett for betraying me, for breaking my trust, but he looked so... *lost*. I paced across his kitchen, rubbing my arms and massaging my temples.

I can't believe I let myself catch feelings for this man.

"I've broken a few of your brother's rules," Rhett said, unmoving.

"That list must be a mile long." I pictured Finn pointing to each finger as he dictated rules, and Rhett's careless nods in agreement. "And he approved you moving in next door?"

Rhett perched on the edge of a stool. "He was pretty pissed about that, but Lena found me the place, and Finn wouldn't dare say a word to her. He's let that one go." His gaze dropped to my mouth, lingering on my lips before meeting my eyes again. "Turned out to be one hell of a stroke of luck I sure as fuck don't deserve."

Goddamn him, and the way he looks at me with that fucking smile.

"You think this is funny? The past month, getting to know you... was a lie." My shoulders slumped as I stepped backward, bumping into the counter.

Falling for you.

"I promise you I'm not laughing." He closed the gap between us, and I cursed how my pulse raced and heat rushed through me, my body craving more. His features hardened into unfamiliar seriousness as he placed his hands on either side of me. Perhaps I should've broken free and run for the door, but the burning need to know him and what else he'd kept hidden held me captive. With our faces inches apart, he continued, his smile not returning. "I've been more real the past month with you than I've ever been with anyone. The man you've gotten to know is all me." His fingers brushed my hand, and when I didn't jerk away, he cupped my face.

What kind of hold does he have on me?

His thumb caressed my cheek, and my breath caught in my throat. "You and I weren't supposed to happen—that's *very* against the rules," he said. "But I wouldn't change a thing."

"You said you'll never lie to me. Keeping secrets is lying."

"Not when the secret keeps you safe."

"I've never been unsafe until now." I couldn't steady my shallow breaths, and heat settled in my cheeks. If either of us took half a step closer, our bodies would be touching.

"Frankie, I promise I won't lie to you, but I *will* do whatever it takes to protect you, and that means keeping you far away from my past."

I'd always known my brother would never help or trust a criminal, but I didn't know what to believe anymore.

"Is that why you never stay in one place? *The truth will set you free*... right? I'm going to need to hear yours now, starting with Miles, or else today will be the last time you call me Frankie, baby, or anything at all."

The line between the truth and lies had blurred, mingling with Rhett's intentions; I couldn't tell them apart anymore. His chest rose and fell as our eyes locked in a silent battle.

He took a deep breath and stepped back. "Miles worked for my father. I kept an eye on him for months until Finn showed up." Rhett dragged a hand over his face. "I agreed to help him get his brother out of my fucked-up world for immunity and a way out. That's how I know your brothers, Frankie."

"You're a criminal." Falling for a man living a secret life on the run hadn't been part of my plan.

He leaned against the wall and crossed his arms, creating more distance from me. "My father is a dangerous man. It's fair to say I've done things I can't take back, but I am not him. I'll never become him."

Finn wouldn't have allowed Rhett anywhere near Lena or me if he didn't trust him, but Rhett knew a side of Miles's life I'd never understood. "Who's your father?" I asked.

His throat bobbed as he swallowed. "Nash Morrigan."

"Morrigan Shipyard," I whispered, piecing the past together in my mind. "Miles dropped out of college and got a job there. He hid it for months before I found out." I stepped toward him, but he remained still, watching me intently. "You don't have your father's last name."

"I did. I grew up Everett Morrigan. I wanted out of the life that would've killed me, so I changed it to Rhett Marshall. My mother's last name."

"How long ago was that?" My questions outpaced my mind's ability to process his answers.

His jaw clenched and forearms tightened as he kept his arms folded. "Two years."

"Were you there when Miles died?" Unable to fight it off any longer, I started crying, my tears burning my face as they fell.

Rhett came toward me and raised his hand, as if to wipe my cheeks, but I backed up. He stopped and took a deep breath. "I was there."

"Fuck." I turned away from him. "Did he say anything before he died? Finn said he was unconscious by the time he got to him and when I saw him…" I choked on tears, and then Rhett's hands were on my arms. I reached up, my fingers interlocking with his before I could talk myself out of touching him.

"'The picture,'" Rhett said, his eyes leaving mine as he glanced around the kitchen. "I'll never forget it, but no idea what it means. Do you?"

"No, but he had lots of pictures, you saw them all over the floor." I needed to get home and examine every single photograph in that bin. Details from Miles's file filled my mind. *Confidential informant.* "You were working with the police." It wasn't a question. Gripping the counter with my other hand, I let Rhett steady me. "I want to hate you for keeping this from me."

"I wouldn't blame you if you did."

"I want to hate Finn for not trusting me enough to tell me who you really are."

"He couldn't, I shouldn't have either."

I pulled out of his embrace. "Why did you tell me then?"

"You asked."

"I asked the right questions, and apparently you lack the ability to lie to my face, you mean." A wave of dizziness made my head fuzzy, and I breathed in, exhaling slowly. "Who killed my brother, Rhett?"

His green eyes darkened, holding mine. "That man is dead."

I swallowed past the grief as a sudden flash of relief coursed through me. "How can you be so sure?"

Rhett's shoulders slumped, and he rubbed the back of his neck. He looked like a man who had nothing to lose. "I was the one who killed him the night he shot Miles. I was just too late to save your brother."

I felt the words in my soul, felt the way they shattered the secrets between us into a thousand pieces, leaving an open wound of truth that I wasn't sure I could process. Saving lives was a part of me; taking one was unimaginable.

But something inside me cracked through the anger I'd clung to for the past two years since Miles's death. The question hung heavy on my lips. *Was he the first person you killed?* But the truth wouldn't set us free. The truth would force me to question my deep affection for a man capable of committing such a dark act of violence. Rhett had been gentle and kind with me, showing up when I needed him. This man made me feel alive and safe in a way no one else ever had. And Rhett had done the one thing I'd wanted for the last two years. He'd made the man who killed my brother pay the ultimate price.

"I'm not a cold-blooded murderer, Frankie." His gaze held me as though he could see parts of me I buried even from myself. He held his unwavering stance in front of me like nothing I could do or say would make him leave; if anyone was walking away from whatever this was, it'd be me. "The man from the hospital—"

"Trash flowers guy?" I asked, shaken from my thoughts. I wiped my eyes, clearing the blurry haze.

"His name is Bran Noble, and the man who killed Miles was his son. I think he recognized your brother, maybe both of them, from the picture on your phone."

My shallow breathing sent another bout of dizziness through me. I sat on the nearest stool. "What are you, mafia families or something?" I rubbed the tension in my neck as he got me a glass of water.

He handed me the glass and sat on the stool beside me. "Or something."

"And Finn knows all this and let you work at the bar for his girlfriend? My brother doesn't trust anyone." I sipped more water, not taking my eyes off him. "Why Willow Grove, why now?"

"Finn offered, and I accepted. It's close enough to Boston, and my sister will need help when our father gets out of jail, which is any day now."

"Is he in jail because of you?" I'd overheard enough of Finn and Dad's conversations when they talked work to understand what it meant to be an informant. If Rhett had been the one responsible for his father's imprisonment, he wouldn't be safe when the man got out.

"I'm part of the reason."

"You killed this Noble person's son... So, he has a revenge problem? And that includes me, maybe Finn... and you?"

"Baby, the only thing that matters to me is keeping you safe. I'll take care of his revenge problem."

I had a bigger problem. Hearing this man talk like that stirred something in me, complicating any ounce of good judgment I had left. I'd found myself in a situation that tossed my morals upside down, trapping me between what was right and overwhelming feelings for a man who may or may not be a criminal in the mob. I needed to go home and gather myself, go through Miles's things.

"Want a drink?" Rhett crossed the kitchen and took a tumbler out of the cabinet. He dropped a handful of ice into the glass and poured a generous amount of whiskey. "I bought red wine—"

"No, I don't want a drink. What have you been doing for the last two years? Living alone, like a wanderer who doesn't exist?" I had to know if another woman was out there somewhere expecting his return. "Is there really no one waiting for you to come home to them?"

He narrowed his eyes at me, the amber liquid catching the overhead light as he drank it before setting the glass down on the counter. "You asked me this before, and I'll give you the same answer. Other than my sister and her son, I've got no real family." He gently wiped tears off my cheeks with the back of his fingers. "The only woman I can see myself coming home to is you, but I'm not sure that'll ever be possible."

His words rattled around in my chest. The desire to grab his shirt and bridge the remaining space separating us was an unbearable pressure, a suffocating weight on my chest. Rhett had become the man I could see myself coming home to. But tonight had changed everything. Tilting my head back, I placed my hand on his chest, feeling the steady rhythm of his breathing. "I'm not sure about anything anymore, but I need to go home and figure out what picture Miles was talking about."

"I'll come with you."

Dropping my hand from the warmth of his chest, I walked away from him. "I need to be alone right now." A gust of cold air blew in as I opened the patio door and stepped outside. He followed me down the stairs.

I spun around, yanking wind-blown hair out of my eyes. "Alone means not you, not now."

"I know what it means, but I'm not leaving until I know you're safe inside." He waited as I stormed up my deck steps and unlocked the patio door. I slammed it shut so hard I caught my finger in the door. "Fuck me," I muttered, clutching my throbbing finger in my cold hand as fresh tears stung my eyes.

Anger and hurt consumed me. Finn knew our brother's killer was dead and never told me or our parents, unless Dad had also been aware. Their secrecy had left me blindsided, unprepared for Miles's past resurfacing, and for what? I was involved anyway, and all their secrets had done nothing to keep me safe. I'd keep myself safe.

Twenty-Three

Frankie

I locked the door and rushed upstairs, but as I sat on the floor next to Miles's storage bin, the paint can in the corner begged for my attention. I reached for a paintbrush and ran my fingers over the soft bristles, eyeing the room around me. With a sudden burst of energy and a need to regain control, I draped the plastic sheet over the floor and taped the windows. The flathead screwdriver I'd used to remove the wall plates rested on the daybed, and I grabbed it, kneeling beside the paint can. I dipped the wooden stir-stick into the can of thick blue paint and swirled it.

Connecting my phone to a speaker, I selected a jazz playlist. I moved with the drumbeat as I poured paint on a tray and slid a sponge roller through the calming blue hue. The saxophone's mellow tone helped still my mind as I focused on the careful paint strokes. I broke down the conversation with Rhett into details I could manage, but thinking of him only brought me back to feeling his lips on mine, his arms around me, and how being near him awakened every damn nerve in my body.

Sweat gathered behind my neck, and I opened the window a crack, letting in a rush of cool night air.

The picture.

Miles had been sentimental, hanging onto mementos and printing photos that held meaning for him. He used to tell me the digital ones got lost, buried and forgotten on our phones, and preferred saving the moment in a frame or an album.

I painted on autopilot for two hours. Paint fumes consumed the bedroom, and I shoved the window open wider. The paint job was far from perfect—a few speckles lined the ceiling where my brush had a mind of its own—but the walls had transformed from stark white into a calming shade of blue. I gathered the plastic off the floor and sealed the paint can, carrying all my supplies into the garage where I washed the brushes in the sink. I dried my hands and took a deep breath. I was ready to tackle Miles's bin.

Red taillights crept past our row of townhouses, their light visible through the garage window as I squeezed between my Jeep and the workbench for a better look. I switched the garage light off, my heart pounding against my chest, but the vehicle continued past my house. I regretted not picking up a shift tonight, longing to be at work surrounded by people and not terrified in my own house.

I headed back upstairs and scrubbed my hands in the bathroom before stepping back into my newly painted room. The plastic bin sat in the middle of the floor waiting, but my keyboard distracted me. I plugged it in, taking a seat on the daybed. I'd bought it so I could practice when I went to college, and it had been an escape for a long time. Miles's favorite piece was Beethoven's *Moonlight Sonata*.

I could hear the notes in my mind, and my fingers reacted. I positioned them over the piano, warming up the keys. With careful control, I released my pain, letting it flow through my fingers. My left hand kept a steady, rolling rhythm over the keys while my right hand held onto the melody. I gently placed my foot on the pedal to blend the sounds together.

The desperate ache in my chest dissolved, and the sadness poured from my soul into the music. I abruptly stopped as tears streamed down my face, and took a deep breath, flopping back on the daybed.

I finally made music again, and it felt like beautiful, chaotic emotion. My world stilled. A glimmer of joy cut through the constant sorrow living inside me, and I smiled to myself. I knew the moment would end, and I'd snap back into a reality I couldn't control, but I took pleasure in simply *breathing*.

My phone vibrated next to me. A notification from *Him* popped up on the screen.

Are you okay over there?

Was he spying on me?

I responded to him. *Just fine.*

That's not good.

Fine is good.

His reply came a moment later. *It's late, your lights are on, I worry.*

Those words helped me feel less alone, and I reread his message a few times before responding. *I painted the spare room and made music again.*

I heard. That was you?

Yes

You sounded amazing, Frankie. I really am sorry, please don't hate me.

I wanted to invite him over so we could pick up where we'd left off on his couch, but he'd grown up in a life of crime, raised by criminals. He'd killed at least one person—even if that man deserved to die for what he'd done to my little brother. The practical version of myself took over, and I messaged, *I don't hate you,* instead, because despite everything, I didn't hate Rhett Marshall.

I held my phone to my chest until it vibrated.

Goodnight, Frankie.

Goodnight, Rhett.

I closed the message, and my brothers' smiling faces, frozen in time, greeted me. Emotion tightened my throat. I got up from the daybed and sat on the floor next to the bin, staring into the cluttered mess of mementos, albums, and his clothes.

Miles had never been without stacks of cash and was constantly high, denying it to my face when I'd asked. We'd fallen into a cycle of my accusations and his hurt feelings over my lack of trust, often leading to him storming out of the apartment. Defeated, I'd given up, stopped fighting and let the silence win, keeping peace with him. Miles had checked in, texting me many times a day, until the day he died. I still had his last message.

I hope the full moon doesn't treat you bad on your shift tonight, let's do breakfast when you're off.

I folded Miles's sweater, placing his hat on top of it, and pulled out a photo album. Mom had put the albums together, one for each of us, when we moved out of the house. I turned the pages of photos with captions written underneath each one. Birthdays, hockey pictures, a photo of me carrying a bawling Miles with a bloody knee. Mom had captioned that one, "Francesca saves the day."

Francesca couldn't save the day when it had mattered most. No one could.

What picture did you mean, little brother?

I snapped the album closed and stacked it with the others on the floor, and a photo slipped free, landing face-up. It was an image of Clay with Miles... *smiling* with a blurred background of a pool table behind them. Clay Preston had been making an unwelcome comeback into my life these days, hanging around the Magpie, talking to my mother about Miles. My brother's life was more of a mystery to me than I realized.

Tucking the photo inside the cover of the album, I rummaged through the bin, setting aside ticket stubs and hockey pucks. A Bruins jersey lay at the bottom, its sleeves folded tightly, making it smaller than it should be. I picked it up and set it on my lap, prying the sleeves apart. Something poked through the left sleeve. Digging my hand inside it, I pulled out a frame containing a physical photo of the one on my phone. I eyed the bent metal, and a memory resurfaced, taking me back to a rare moment when we'd sat at the kitchen table in our apartment eating takeout pizza. I could still remember Miles sitting across from me like it was yesterday, his messy dark hair sticking out from underneath his ball cap.

I had propped this picture on the window ledge next to us as he picked off the olives. I had said, "if you're this sentimental at twenty-five, I can't wait to see you at forty-five with a wife and a couple of kids idolizing you."

"The dream. Not gonna happen for me." His typical humor had faded, replaced by a seriousness that had unsettled me. "The three of us in one picture never happens, Frankie," he'd said. "I'll end up breaking it, take it with you and put it on a mantle or something when you get your first house so you'll get to look at my ugly mug every day."

He'd died two weeks later.

I carefully turned the frame over and pressed down on a corner that had lifted, but it remained stuck. I picked at the edge of the frame, and something bulged behind it. Removing the metal clips,

I released the back, lifting it away from the glass. A USB stick was taped to the cardboard.

The picture.

I scrambled to my feet and rushed to my bedroom, throwing on the light. I hadn't used my laptop since college but had stored it in my closet. The computer bag was at the back, behind fancy high-heeled shoes I never had a chance to wear anymore.

I needed to know what secrets Miles had kept on that USB. And I needed Finn to know he could stop hiding the truth from me.

I picked up my phone and dialed his number.

"What's wrong? It's after three. Are you okay?" Finn said on the other end.

"I know the truth about Rhett, but what I don't understand is why I had to hear it from him and not you. Why after two years of my constant *begging* to know who killed Miles, you couldn't find it in yourself to tell me the asshole was dead."

Finn's sigh drifted over the line. "He fucking told you? I knew he'd crack."

With Rhett's confession, I knew who'd been watching me and why. I'd be able to stop him. "I have information the police can use to find the man who's been following me, maybe he was the one who broke in—"

"Stop talking over the phone," Finn hushed. "Don't say anything, just listen. Frankie, you need to keep this to yourself. If anyone knows *his* identity, he's as good as dead."

I'd lived life without Rhett up till now, but the thought of him dead left an emptiness inside my chest. My world had flipped upside down since he'd entered it. Shivers crept through me as I ended the call and opened my laptop. My online search revealed vague details about the Nobles and Morrigans. I discovered that the families' charitable donations were entangled with accusations of money laundering, fraud, and murder investigations.

I'd have to find another way to handle my stalker, without giving away the new piece of surreal information I still hadn't wrapped my mind around.

Rhett was a *Morrigan*.

Twenty-Four

Frankie

With a severe lack of sleep hiding under my eyes from a night spent wrestling with a stubborn USB password until five o'clock in the morning, I'd crashed for an hour on my couch with the fireplace going. I had awoken in a panic when a notification on my phone chimed, but it had been a message from Zoey letting me know when she and Lena would be over. A long, hot shower had given me a dose of energy to drag myself out for a birthday celebration, even though partying was the last thing on my mind. I'd imagined the grace of a new decade would give me a new perspective, but fear and unease clouded turning thirty.

I hadn't given up on the password. If Miles had put the USB where I'd find it by attaching it to a photo of us, the password couldn't be far behind.

Spritzing on some perfume, I checked my reflection one last time in my bedroom's full-length mirror. I'd traded in scrubs for a cute outfit and styled hair. My black jeans were soft and stretchy against my skin, and I rarely wore red, but the new shirt Lena had convinced me to buy fit me well. I turned around and glanced in the mirror. Three sets of ties held the backless, long-sleeved shirt together, but they threatened to unravel at any moment. My shirt falling apart would be a problem at the Magpie tonight.

A knock downstairs jarred me, but a second break-in wouldn't include a warning. I left my bedroom and headed downstairs, expecting to find Lena and Zoey at my front door, but Rhett gave me a wave as he stood on my back deck holding a box.

Turning on the outside light, I opened the door. "I didn't expect to see you until later at the bar."

"I wanted to see you away from a crowd, make sure you were still talking to me."

I moved aside. "Come in."

"That's a good sign." He wore a rugged jacket and jeans, and his subtle cologne mingled with the leather. I wanted to see the hardened son of a mob family and feel repulsed, but I only saw

Rhett, the attentive man. "I wanted to wish you a happy birthday before your big night." He set the box on the table.

"Thanks."

His gaze lingered like a touch as it swept over me, sending heat rushing along my skin. "You are beautiful. I should have said it before now."

"Why didn't you?"

"Wasn't sure I'd get away with it."

"And after last night you thought you'd push your luck?" I asked.

"You let me in, so I thought I'd keep the truth going."

Our banter had fallen back into an effortless rhythm. I'd miss how comfortable I felt in his presence if he left. I'd miss *him*. "What's in the box?"

"Something that made me think of you."

"Should I be scared?" I teased, catching myself. Not only should I be scared, I *should* stay far away from him.

He's dangerously safe.

"Never with me." All traces of a smile left his face as he glanced at me. "Do you have a lighter, matches?"

I handed him a pack of matches my father had left behind. He lifted the lid of the box and took out a plate with a blueberry cream cheese Danish and a candle. "For you," he said, lighting the candle. "Wish for something impossible."

"And you'll make it come true?" I bent forward and looked up at him. "I don't think it works that way."

A hint of a smile tugged at his lips. "Can't hurt to try."

Closing my eyes, I repeated the same wish I'd made at my parents' house and blew out the candle. I broke the Danish in half, but Rhett turned down his share, declaring his love of raspberry, and checked his phone.

"I have to get to the bar." He reached inside his pocket and gave me a small box with a peach ribbon around it. "One more thing."

"You got me a present?" I took the box from him, shamelessly letting my fingers brush against his.

He tucked his phone away. "Open it."

I opened the lid. A delicate silver bracelet was nestled inside with a detailed open rose charm attached. "Rhett, this is gorgeous, but you didn't have to, we barely... I don't know what to say." I ran my fingertips over the rose and slipped it over my wrist. "A Francesca rose."

"Happy birthday." Taking my fingers in his, Rhett tilted my wrist and fastened the clasp. I shook my hand, letting the charm dangle.

The past twenty-four hours had left me emotionally drained, filled with uncertainty and unanswered questions. Rhett was all wrong for me, we'd never last—the chemistry between us was a fire that would end up a pile of ashes, taking me with it. But the impossible truth was how much I wanted him to be mine.

The doorbell rang, and we both looked toward the front door as Lena and Zoey's laughter carried from outside.

"Lena and Zoey are here," I whispered, inches from his face. I tucked my hair behind my ears and stepped away, heading for the front door.

Lena walked in carrying grocery bags as Zoey hugged me. "Where's your blender? I'm making us margaritas before we go out." She strolled into the kitchen, pausing when she saw Rhett. "Any plans to return with coffee and doughnuts again?" Her eyes darted toward me with a mischievous glint. "People have been asking, that's all I'm saying."

"I'll be back." Rhett glanced at me with a smile. "I'm late for work."

Lena carried two bags of takeout from my favorite Mexican restaurant. "I'll warn you, it's busy, and Finn is in a mood."

Finn would be on damage control, panicking because I knew the truth... at least part of it.

"Burrito bowl is Zoey's," Lena said. "Here are your tacos, and this beast of a burrito is mine—I'm starving." She placed our food on the counter, brushing perfect blonde waves off her forehead.

Rhett locked the patio doors. "Have fun, ladies, call if you need a drive to the bar." He surprised me with a kiss on the forehead. "See you later." He strolled out the front door. "Do me a favor and lock the deadbolt behind me."

Rushing toward the door, Lena's jaw dropped open as she wrinkled her nose and mouthed the word "adorable". She threw the deadbolt and headed back into the kitchen as I set the blender on the counter. "Sweet fuck, Francesca, that shirt is perfection. I never see you out of scrubs anymore."

"If the ties would stay together, it would be." I turned around as the bottom knot came loose.

"Come here, sweetie." Lena gestured, taking a step closer. She bent down, untying, and retying each set of strings. "I'll double-knot them so they don't come undone."

"That works." My back straightened as she pulled too tight. "Breathing would be good, Lena."

"Sorry, how's that?" She readjusted them, and I moved, reaching behind me.

"Feels okay now."

Pink liquid danced in the blender as it whirred, splashing at the lid. "Strawberry margaritas?" Careful not to spill anything on her white sweater dress, Zoey prepared two glasses, garnishing each with sliced limes, and mixed another non-alcoholic version for Lena.

"I might need to hire you." Lena perched on a stool and bit into her burrito.

"Thanks, but not my scene." Zoey slid the drinks in front of us, and we raised our glasses, clinking them together. "Cheers, Frankie. We love you."

"I love you too." I took a slow drink, letting the chilled strawberry sweetness blend with the salted rim. The tequila warmed my chest going down, and as I exhaled, the tension in my shoulders eased a little.

"Girl, where'd you get that?" Holding her fork with one hand, Zoey reached across the counter with the other and touched my bracelet. "It's so pretty."

I set my glass on the counter as Lena eyed the bracelet. "It's stunning and totally your style. Is it the self-love birthday gift you get yourself every year?"

"Um, no. I didn't bother with one of those... Rhett gave it to me." Lettuce spilled from my taco as I picked it up.

Pushing her braid off her shoulder, Zoey lifted the glass to her lips. "Tell me you're finally having sex with that fine man."

The memory of Rhett's mouth on mine and along my neck sent a shiver through me. If my phone hadn't interrupted us, would I have had sex with him? Fuck, I might've. "Not exactly."

"How exactly?" Lena swiveled her chair toward me, revealing smooth leather leggings as she crossed her long legs.

"We kissed, that's all." His confession played again in my mind, but I couldn't share the truth with my friends. Not tonight, maybe never. *Rhett killed the man who shot Miles, he grew up in the mob. The man I've fallen for is a criminal, but I don't know how to walk away.* I still hadn't grasped the weight of what he'd told me; I had no idea how I would explain it to them.

"It's just the beginning, my friend," Zoey said. "A new decade, love, passion, and a healthy amount of sexual tension."

"She's good with words." Adjusting the buttons on her shirt, Lena hopped off the stool and gave me a hug. Her blushed cheekbones lifted as she smiled. "I'm driving our asses to the bar, you two drink up."

"Love, passion, sex, sure." Throwing back the rest of my margarita, I finished my tacos and shut the empty container. Zoey refilled my glass before her own, and the two of us cheered to ourselves for simply not having to work, expressing gratitude for our aligned schedules the past few weeks.

As we talked and laughed over the next hour, a pleasant buzz drowned out my worries. Lena cleaned up the kitchen as I slipped into the high-heeled shoes I'd found in my closet—impractical as hell for the chilly fall night—and a long wool coat. I locked the door behind us, and we piled into Lena's hatchback, making our way to the Magpie.

Twenty-Five

Frankie

Warmth and the smell of the fireplace greeted me as I stepped out of the cold and into the Magpie. In the back corner, on a small wooden stage, colored lights and a spotlight highlighted the band as they played a mix of popular and classic songs. Lena sashayed behind the bar and gave Finn a list of drinks for the table. I could feel Rhett's nearness before I saw him. As Finn leaned closer to kiss Lena, I caught sight of Rhett's back. He poured beer from the taps into glasses and set them on the bar for waiting customers, and our eyes met across the crowded room like a scene straight out of a movie.

I wound my way through groups of people toward the bar. A flutter of excitement radiated from low in my belly into my chest, raising goosebumps along my back like fingertips along my skin.

Rhett glared at the two men who moved in front of me, blocking my path. "Hey, pay attention. Give her space."

They glanced behind them, and the taller man shot Rhett a look, but they both took their drinks and got out of my way. Perspiration beaded at the small of my back, and I shrugged my coat off, draping it over my arm. He leaned over the bar, his lips brushing my ear as he spoke. "It's good to see you."

"Miss me already?"

"Always." He stepped back and took another customer's order as Finn and another employee placed a variety of cocktails on a tray. Lena put her arm around me. "I'm done driving. Let's have some fun."

We trailed the girl carrying our drinks to the table, and Finn pulled out chairs as he chatted with my friends who'd arrived. He waited until I greeted them before pulling me to the side.

I shook my head. "I can't do this now—"

"I wasn't starting anything," he said. "Happy Birthday, try not to worry about shit tonight, we'll deal with it tomorrow."

"You sound like Mom." I hung my coat on a hook near the table as he rolled his eyes at me. Before I took my seat, he embraced me in a rare hug.

I sat with my friends, and their laughter and light conversation wrapped around me with a feeling of comfortable normalcy. Colleagues I'd gotten to know since returning home, along with Logan and his partner, Zoey, and Lena, all celebrated with me, sharing funny work stories over drinks. Laughter and clinking glasses filled the bar as Lena presented a sparkler-topped cake. The band played for a while before wrapping up, and a hockey game appeared on the TV screens.

Lena waved Rhett over and introduced him to the few of us left at the table. I stood as he approached, and he placed his hand on my back, igniting warmth through me.

"Let me know if you need anything else." He pulled my chair out, giving me a playful smile, grazing his fingers along my bare back as I sat next to Zoey.

As he strode away, Zoey pressed her lips together and narrowed a teasing gaze at me. "Damn, girl, tell me he's taking you home tonight."

Unable to suppress my smile, I let the ridiculous grin spread across my face. "We flirt a little—"

"Oh please, that's hotter than a little flirting."

A server balanced a tray of shots on his upturned hand, and Logan stood. "One last toast."

Shots made their way around the table, and I held it up to my nose, inhaling a sweet butterscotch aroma. "Thanks for celebrating with me tonight."

"Cheers to thirty, honey," Logan said, and a low hum of cheers repeated as I tipped the glass to my mouth, letting the warm liquid course down my throat.

As the night eventually wound down, and people left, I excused myself and headed to the bathroom. My steps were more confident than steady, and the feeling in my head wasn't quite drunkenness... but *close*. Exiting the stall, I washed my hands and glanced at my flushed cheeks in the mirror.

Time to switch to water.

Clay leaned with his back against the dark brick wall as I made my way along the narrow hallway back to my seat. Despite the alcohol in my system, my back stiffened on alert.

He placed his hand on the wall, blocking me from walking past him. "I thought you'd be here. Happy Birthday." His glassy eyes appeared distant as he tried to focus on me.

"Out of my way."

Stepping back, he raised his hands. He let me pass but followed me back to the table where Lena sat waiting for me. I rushed to join her, almost stumbling as I plopped onto my chair.

Clay's presence near me ignited an anger I hadn't felt for him in years. "What do you want?" I seethed.

"To talk to you." He flipped a chair around, sitting with his chest against the back of it.

"She has nothing to say to you," Lena said from across the table, but he ignored her.

"He's leaving." Shifting in my seat, I glared at him. "If you don't get away from me, I'll have you thrown out, is that what you want?"

Lena shoved her chair back and stood, glancing toward the bar. "I'm on it."

A sarcastic laugh escaped him, but his expression turned serious, and he leaned in. I recoiled from him, but not before I caught a hint of cologne. *The* cologne. He had been in my house.

"Francesca," he slurred, "you think you've got it all figured out."

"I sure as hell have you figured out—"

He shook a finger in my face, and I grabbed it, yanking it down to the table. "You know nothing," he said, rage dripping in his tone. "You've got no fucking clue what's going on right under your nose."

My pulse raced, thumping in my ears before subsiding. "What were you doing in my house?"

"*He's* your intruder?" Lena bent down as she spoke to Clay. "I'm banning you from my bar, asshole." She placed her hands on my shoulders. "Come with me—"

"I'm okay where I am." I kept my eyes on the man I had *loved* at one time. A knot of regret twisted in my stomach.

Lena glared at him. "I'll be right back... are you sure?"

"He won't do anything to me, go." Now that he was here, I had a few questions before Lena had him removed. "Why were you following me? What did Miles have that you wanted bad enough to break into my house?"

He tilted his head to the side, facing me. Stale beer coated his breath as he spoke. "I thought something that should've been destroyed two years ago might still exist, and if you know what's good for you, you *will* let that little incident go." Clay picked up my glass, swirling the melting ice cubes as he scanned the bar. "You know that guy watching us?"

I followed his gaze to where Lena was talking to Rhett behind the bar. Rhett snapped to attention, and his eyes fixed on me above the crowd gathered around them. "What does it matter?"

Clay made a disgusted face. "Are you fucking him?"

"You're such a prick." I snatched my glass from him and set it on the table. Every instinct told me he wanted whatever was on the USB stick. If Miles had hidden it on a photo only his siblings would find, undiscovered for two years, he sure as hell didn't want it in Clay Preston's hands. "Did you work *with* my brother, or does he have information that could bury you?"

Shock crossed his face, and he slammed his hand on the table. Chatter hummed around us at other tables, blending with the sounds of the hockey game. "They know who you are," he muttered.

"Who knows what?" I rose out of my seat, and he stood, holding the back of his chair for balance as he mirrored my stance.

"It doesn't matter, Francesca, it's too late for both of us." Grabbing my drink off the table, he tossed it back with a smirk. He wrapped an arm around me. I stepped back, but his hand slid underneath the bottom tie of my shirt.

"Get the fuck away from me." As I twisted out of his grasp, Rhett cut across the room with Finn on his heels. He had Clay's arms pinned behind his back in one quick motion, freeing me from his hold.

"Are you okay?" he asked, tightening his hold on Clay.

"He's the one who broke in. My stalker. I need to talk to him out back." Shaking with anger and unsteady from the alcohol, I marched toward the bar, passing Lena as she held the door open.

"I've got the bar covered." Lena redirected the patron's attention with a bright smile as Rhett hauled Clay to the back office and the door swung shut behind Finn and me.

"Get your fucking hands off me." Clay angled his head toward me. "I thought you had enough sense to stay out of this, but you knew, didn't you? You're just like your fucking brothers, both of them."

He wouldn't tell me anything if I didn't gain his trust. I placed a hand on Rhett and spoke slowly to mask the alcohol's effects. "Come on, I know you don't hate me, Clay. If there is something I should know, just tell me. We can work together—"

"Fucking *bitch*, you think I'd trust you? You're on your own, I'm getting the hell out of here."

Clay's hatred toward me and my family erased any pity that had crept in, and Finn didn't intervene as Rhett shoved Clay's face against the desk, holding him down. "Apologize."

"For what? Telling the truth?" Clay coughed, his breath fogging a spot on the desk. "She's fucking clueless, man."

Yanking Clay upright, Rhett made him face me. "Tell her you're sorry," he said, remaining composed.

Finn sat in the chair behind the desk, folding his hands behind his head. "I'd do what he says."

Despite the constant tension between them, I had believed Rhett and my brother were friends who had a past I didn't understand. But the way they worked together, and after Rhett's confession last night, a brutal knowing caught me off guard. I didn't know the extent of his past or the crimes he had committed, but Rhett trusted Finn, and the feeling was mutual, or Rhett wouldn't be in Lena's bar.

My brother trusts a man raised by the mob.

"Fuck, *sorry*," Clay said through clenched teeth, jerking out of Rhett's hold. "Get the fuck off me." He glared at Finn. "I'll report you, dirty fucking cop."

Rhett's hands clamped down on Clay's shoulders as he thrust him onto the chair. "Ask your questions, Frankie."

The room tilted slightly, rebalancing, and I braced myself against the wall as a precaution. "You followed me and broke in looking for something, and I need to know why. And why now?" I shook my head to dispel the dizziness. Rhett frowned, his eyes dropping to the empty chair, but I waited, refusing to show any weakness.

Clasping his fingers together on the desk, Finn narrowed his eyes at Clay, his nostrils flaring. "You broke into my sister's house, you sick son of a bitch. I need to know who you're working for, or even better, where we can find him."

Taking a deep breath, I swallowed hard. "Bran Noble. You know him?"

With a sharp turn in his seat, Clay faced me... and so did Finn.

"Answer her," Rhett said. His grip tightened on Clay's shoulders as he tried to get up.

"Rhett Marshall? Is that your name?" Clay looked up at Rhett standing over him. As he shook his head and faced my brother across from him, he hesitated. His eyes widened at Rhett's forearm. "Holy fuck, you're a goddamn Morrigan." He let out a short laugh, then fell silent. "If you have any indication of what a smart decision might be, you'll go back wherever you've been hiding the last two years."

Leaning forward, Rhett placed both hands on the desk. "Where is he?"

"Boston, but you know that," Clay said.

Finn stood and perched on the edge of the desk. "How long have you worked for the Nobles?"

"Come on, Finn, I wouldn't hurt your sister —"

"Already have," I said, forcing myself to stand straight.

"You know what I mean." Clay gripped the desk and looked over his shoulder at me, swaying in his chair before he turned his attention back on Finn. "I don't work for anyone, I'm cutting my losses and leaving town tonight. Frankie isn't at risk, I made sure."

I approached, reaching for the back of an empty chair, but Rhett pulled it forward for me and I sat down. The USB stuck to the photo lingered in my mind, but a nagging feeling warned me to keep quiet. "What did you want from Miles?" I asked him. "And how'd you know to come to me?"

"He trusted you." Clay's eyes flickered from my brother to me. "More than anyone. I thought he might have left something behind that could... assist me in a predicament, but it turns out I was wrong."

The door swung open, and Lena headed toward the office. "His friends are asking about him, what do I tell them?"

"You have friends?" Rhett said.

With her hand on her hip, Lena eyed Finn. "Take care of this *quietly,* please." She pointed at Clay. "You're banned from here, I see you again, I'll call the police. Got it?"

Clay gave her a salute. "Whatever you say."

"Tell his friends to bring a car around back, he'll meet them there." Finn pulled Clay to his feet by the shirt and patted him on the chest. "Don't go too far, we aren't done."

Lena spun on her heels and hurried toward the front of the bar.

"Stay with Frankie," Rhett said, escorting Clay out of the office.

The heavy exterior door slammed shut, leaving me alone with Finn. "I can't believe you never told me who Rhett was, what he did." My mouth felt like sandpaper, and my head throbbed. "I need water."

Finn got up and crossed the small room toward the fridge, returning with a bottle of water. "I couldn't say a word. It's a classified investigation that's technically still open."

"But you trusted him to come here and work for Lena? Does she know who he is?" I unscrewed the cap and gulped it down like I'd run a marathon.

"No, and don't tell her."

"I read Miles's file."

Finn crossed his arms and paced, biting his cheek. "How?" he demanded.

"I can't tell you—"

"Dad," he muttered.

"Relax, you were right. But I do have one question, and I'd appreciate your honesty, no lies."

He stopped pacing. "Shoot."

"If Rhett was a *confidential informant*—"

"Did he tell you that? Rhett should've kept his fucking mouth shut, Frankie. Just you knowing what he did puts you at risk, especially now. Clay is hiding something."

"Let me finish, please. I won't do anything to get you or him in trouble." Finn held his hands up and gestured for me to keep going. "What does that make you? Because the only thing I can think of is that you had to be undercover, but you acted like a bystander. Were you working on that case, investigating our brother?"

"That's more than one question."

I crossed my arms. "I've got time."

He exhaled through pursed lips. "He wasn't involved when I started, but when I saw him working at the shipyard, I lost it. I just wanted to get him out. That's how Rhett found out. He walked into the middle of an argument Miles and I were having and chose to work with me instead of killing me. Is that enough truth for you?"

Standing, I closed the office door and spun around, meeting Finn's curious expression. I didn't want to mention the USB until I tried one more time to unlock it before anyone else. If I couldn't figure out the password, I'd hand it over to Finn. Another day wouldn't make a difference.

"After two years of feeling lost, not knowing if Miles's killer was still out there, this is enough truth for now. And go ahead and judge me for saying this, but I'm glad he did it." Tears welled up, and I blinked back the threatening blur. "Know that I love you, you drive me fucking crazy, but I love you." My hair swished against my back, and my heels clicked on the floor as I moved to open the office door. The cool air in the room sent a rush of shivers down my bare back, and I reached a hand behind me. At least the ties hadn't come undone.

"Frankie." I spun around, placing a hand on the wall to steady myself. "If he hadn't pulled the trigger, killing that man," he said, "I wouldn't be here. So yeah, I trust him, but that doesn't mean he's good for you. Don't get too close or forget where he came from, who he is."

Unable to meet my brother's eyes, I turned for the door and headed back to the bar. One look at my face, and Finn would know it was too late. "I'll be out front with Lena for one more birthday drink before this night is done."

"Drink more water," Finn called from the office, but I didn't answer him.

TWENTY-SIX

Rhett

The sensor light flickered on in the small parking lot behind the bar, and Clay stumbled as I released him. This asshole had been the reason Frankie didn't feel safe in her house or driving to work. He'd had his hands on her when she asked him to let her go. I would never let him near her again.

Straightening up, he adjusted his dress shirt. "I don't care who the hell that tattoo says you are, you have no idea who you're dealing with."

Tension creased my forehead as I ran a hand over my face and exhaled. "I know exactly who I'm dealing with. You're Noble's errand boy. What does he want with Frankie?"

"She'll get dragged into this, just like her junkie brother." He flinched as I stepped toward him, intending to wipe the smirk off his mouth. "Which Morrigan are you? If I didn't know better, I'd bet my life you're related to Nash."

I never thought I resembled my father—my hair was too dark, and my eyes not dark enough—but if Clay had a sliver of intelligence to piece it together, it wouldn't take long for Bran Noble to figure out I was in Willow Grove.

"If you care at all about her and really don't want her involved, tell me where to find him and I'll take care of it myself," I said, keeping emotion out of my voice.

Clay laughed. "I say anything, I'm a dead man." He walked across the pavement, more sober than before, but still listing sideways. "You ever hear the saying, don't bite the hand that feeds, Mr. Marshall, or should I say *Morrigan*?"

"Can't say it's one that resonates."

He waved a finger at me. "Right, you're a rat. I am an untouchable, wealthy man."

"Who does what he's told." I took a step closer, forcing him further from the door into the darkness. He worked for the Nobles, and they were paying him well. He'd do whatever they wanted to save himself. "She's done nothing to you, and you marked her for them." Anger moved through me like gasoline waiting for a match. My jaw tightened, and my fists clenched and released.

"She wasn't *loyal*. I fucked up once, and she left like a coward. I made a good life for myself, I got out of this town, and I won't allow anyone to take that away from me. You can all fuck off."

Cracking my knuckles, I held my fist in my hand. "*You* can fuck off. Stay away from Frankie, stay away from this bar, and if I catch you near either again, you can say goodbye to your good life."

He raked his fingers through his hair. "I don't take orders from you."

I reeled back and slammed my fist into the arrogant fucker's jaw. He tumbled to the pavement, landing with a grunt, swearing as blood dripped down his face and soaked into his designer shirt. Stretching my fingers, I stepped back as headlights shone on us and two men rushed from the car toward him.

Spitting blood, Clay looked up at me as the two men reached under his arms, yanking him to his feet. "And she thinks *I'm* the asshole? You're fucking crazy."

I pinched my thumb and index finger together, leaving an inch between them. "Just a little," I said with a smile as they loaded Clay's drunk ass into the car and drove away.

I walked back inside and locked the back door. As I entered the bar, I surveyed the room, preparing for chaos, but people carried on like nothing had happened. They drank cocktails and beer, cheering as the Bruins scored a goal.

Finn nodded in my direction and got up from where he sat next to Frankie and Lena. Frankie swept her hair to the side, exposing her back, the shirt held together with nothing but flimsy ties. It didn't matter if she wore stained scrubs or dressed up in an outfit clinging to every curve on her body, she always had my complete attention.

A woman leaned on the bar with her elbows propped up on the varnished wood. "Hey there, handsome."

"What can I get you?" I wiped my hands on a towel. My knuckles throbbed, but I wasn't putting ice on them here.

"Vodka cranberry." She dropped her arms, displaying her cleavage, but I averted my eyes to her face as she talked and mixed her drink. "I haven't seen you before, are you new?"

"Enough." I stuck a wedge of lime on the rim of the glass and handed it to her.

With a crooked smile, she gripped the straw and took a sip. "When's your shift done tonight?"

"I'm married," I said. Finn darted me a suspicious look, but I ignored him.

"Too bad." She dipped her finger in her glass and stuck it in her mouth as she walked away.

Frankie and I made eye contact, and she looked away.

"*Married?* The old you would've been all over that." Finn leaned against the counter behind me, his eyes glued to the hockey game.

I stood next to him. "The old me is dead."

"The new you might be too if you're not careful," he said. "What the fuck was that about with Clay? You think they know you're here?"

"If they don't yet, they will." I watched Frankie as she sipped an amber drink on ice with a curled lemon peel. "What's she drinking?"

"Whiskey and amaretto—"

"You made her a Godfather?"

"She wanted something sweet with whiskey, it's the first one that came to mind," Finn said, scanning the bar. He jerked his head toward me. "You were supposed to stay away from her, what happened to *off limits*? If you've got a thing for my sister, that's a problem."

"They know she exists, that's the problem."

Turning away from the crowd, Finn lowered his voice. "I'm looking into Bran Noble's whereabouts."

"That's not good enough, she needs to be monitored around the clock. I can't leave town until I know she's okay, but if Bran is back home, I need to talk to him."

"Talk to him? Fuck, Rhett, there's no talking. I'll keep my family safe."

"Not without my help."

"I know how to do my job."

I rubbed my face. "This isn't a job, it's personal." The memory of Miles's body convulsing as he dropped to the floor flashed in my mind. I'd never witnessed Finn so helpless, and I had been too late to save their brother. If anything happened, we couldn't fail again.

Chairs scraped across the floor as Frankie and Lena stood. Frankie grabbed her coat and purse and walked toward us.

I reached through the door to the back room and grabbed my jacket from a hook. "Lena's got a full crew on tonight, I'll drive them home."

Finn grabbed his keys. "I can—"

"You can't just drop her off and leave. I'm going to the same place."

As she leaned on the bar, Frankie rested her chin on her hand. "I'm about ready to take a cab home and avoid you both." She spoke clearly enough, but her cheeks were flushed, and there was a haze in the way she looked at me. I wasn't leaving her alone tonight, drunk and unprotected.

Embracing her, Lena kissed Frankie's cheek and pulled away. "Go with Rhett, Happy Birthday." Finn gripped the edge of the bar, appearing unimpressed, and Lena slapped his ass. "Would you lighten up?" She pointed to the three other staff serving customers. "I hired more staff for a reason, I'll let them know we're leaving, and they'll close tonight. Let's all get out of here."

Finn wrapped an arm around Lena, pulling her close as she turned to Frankie. "You sure you're okay after tonight?"

"Never better." Frankie struggled with her coat, and I held it up, angling it so she could get her arms in the right sleeves.

"Just... just get her home safe, please," Finn said.

"You have my word, Roscoe."

Turning my back on Finn and Lena, I followed close behind Frankie, shoving the door open for her. Her shoes clicked on the wooden steps as she steadied herself with her hand on the railing.

"Here." I offered my hand, and she grabbed it, linking her arm with mine.

"You'd think I forgot how to walk. I don't wear heels much anymore."

"Me neither," I said, and the sound of her laughter reached inside me. I wanted this woman more than I deserved her.

"Well, you're welcome to these, my feet are done." She released me as we approached my truck, and I opened her door, helping her onto the seat.

Walking around to the driver's side, I scanned the parking lot for anyone watching or vehicles waiting, but except for a few people out for a smoke, it was quiet.

My eyes darted from the rearview mirror to the road as I left the Magpie and drove home, but no one followed us.

"I'm sorry tonight got interrupted." I turned on my jazz playlist, keeping the volume low, but Frankie turned it up. The slow, relaxed melody filled the cab.

"Despite the Clay Preston shitshow—I'll deal with all that when my head is clear—I still had fun, maybe too much." Her coat fell open as she crossed her legs. "Thanks for stepping in with him."

"We'll figure it out." I reached across the armrest and gave her knee a gentle squeeze. As I pulled my hand away, her fingers tightened around mine, and I laced my fingers through hers.

Her head flopped against the seat, tilting to the side, and I could feel her eyes on me. "I saw a beautiful woman flirt with you tonight."

"The only beautiful woman in that bar tonight was you." I checked my side mirror and veered onto our dark forest road.

"You're good, I'll give you that."

"It's true."

Shifting in her seat, she ran her other hand along my arm, dropping it to where our hands met, and toyed with the bracelet I'd given her. "Finn told me he wouldn't be here if not for you."

"Did he?"

"He did." She stared out the front window, her smile fading. "Thank you."

"Frankie, don't thank me." The sadness in her words broke me. "That was the worst night of my life."

"Mine too. But if you ever thought you could tell me about it, I'm ready to hear it, as fucked up as that is."

I brought our joined hands up to my mouth and kissed the back of hers. "It's not fucked up, it's human." I wasn't sure how I'd be able to tell her I'd seen her that night. "I'll talk about it with you, just not tonight. Not on your day."

"Sure, I understand," she said through a yawn.

"You need sleep." I drove onto our street, surveying the neighborhood.

The corners of her eyes crinkled as a playful smile crossed her face. "I'm fine."

"Of course you are." I pulled into her driveway and shut the engine off. Reaching over her legs, I opened the glove compartment and grabbed my gun from a holster I'd attached inside.

"Always prepared."

Tucking it into my waistband, I got out of the truck. "Always. Stay here until I get your door."

She surprised me by waiting instead of bolting from the truck the way I'd expected. I stayed close, steadying her as she maneuvered to her front door and unlocked it. She stepped inside the house. "Are you coming in?" she asked.

"That's the plan."

"Since when do you make plans?"

"Since I met you." I trailed her inside, securing the deadbolt behind me, and walked through the house. "It's quiet."

"I doubt Clay will be back after tonight." She flung her coat over the living room chair, using the back for balance. As she reached down to slip off her shoe, she caught herself before falling.

"Sit down, Frankie." I guided her onto the seat and held her foot in my hands, searching for the clasp on her shoe.

Sinking into the chair, she regarded me with a smile and tilted her foot as she tugged her pants up her leg. "The side."

My hands were too large for the small buckle, but I finally unfastened it, releasing her foot from the shoe, and moved on to the next one. She sat upright with her feet on the floor and leaned forward. "You always know exactly what to do for a woman?"

I stayed crouched in front of her. "Only the ones I pay attention to."

"Happens a lot, I bet." Her fingers traced the tattoo along my forearm. The one I hated and let no one come near. But her? She could touch me wherever she wanted.

"Not as often as you'd think."

"I don't know," she sighed. Her gaze drifted to the ceiling before settling on my face. "You've got a *charm* that screams, I'm gonna pull you in and leave you behind." She spoke slowly, as if trying to enunciate her words, but the lingering effects of the alcohol wouldn't let her.

"Well, Frankie, I could say the same about you."

Her forehead creased as she furrowed her brow. "What do you mean?"

"You've got a charm that *commands*, I'm gonna pull you in and become someone you can't live without."

Her mouth fell open. "I think that's the nicest thing anyone has ever said to me."

I couldn't help but smile. "Good, I think." I stood, and her upward gaze tracked my movements. "I'll get you water," I said. "It'll help."

She reached behind her, shifting in her seat. "I need to change out of this shirt, it's too tight."

Taking my extended hand, she rose to her feet and headed upstairs.

In an impossibly short amount of time, Francesca Roscoe had consumed me in ways I never thought possible. I wanted her to be mine.

Twenty-Seven

Frankie

S tanding with my back to the mirror, I reached behind me, fumbling with the knots on my adorable, pain-in-the-ass new shirt. I lost my footing and stumbled as I glanced over my shoulder. Lena had tied the shirt so well that I battled with both frustration and grudging admiration. Giving up, I dropped my arms to my sides. My drunkenness had turned into a consistent but pleasant buzz that might not be so nice in the morning.

I sat on the edge of the bed. Rhett was downstairs. A different side of him had emerged tonight. He'd handled Clay with a skilled, practiced competence that should've unsettled me, making me question what sort of man I had let into my life. But his controlled strength only made me feel safe, and that scared me more than anything. Men like Rhett Marshall didn't settle in one place. Men like him didn't *stay*. But he was here now. It wouldn't be the worst thing in the world if he freed me from my shirt, if his fingers touched my skin, if his lips were on mine again… I was so tired of treading in shallow water, not doing anything except working and taking care of people.

Being with that man made me feel something other than grief and heartache. I wanted to forget the worry, bury the fear, and lose myself in him. I rose from the bed, bracing myself on my dresser as I looked in the mirror. My red lipstick had long since faded, and I retrieved a tinted lip gloss, pressing my lips together after I applied it. As long as I kept my expectations to nothing more than enjoying the company of an interesting man, I'd be fine.

Before I could change my mind, I left my bedroom and padded downstairs. Sitting in a chair near the fireplace with his legs sprawled in front of him and shoulders relaxed, Rhett looked at home—*comfortable*—in my place, fitting in like he belonged here with me.

He glanced up from his phone as I approached, his eyes lingering on me. "Something wrong?"

"I've got a little problem." I stepped over his outstretched legs to face him, and the tension from earlier returned to his shoulders and jaw.

"What sort of problem?" As he sat upright, his bent knees almost knocked me off balance, but he gripped my legs to keep me from falling.

I turned around, and he released his hold on me. "I'm literally tied into this shirt," I said. "I'd hate to take a pair of scissors to these ties."

"How'd you get into the shirt in the first place?" Warmth radiated from him as he stood, and my breath caught in my throat.

"Lena double-knotted me when the ties wouldn't stay." I let my hands fall to my sides as his fingers brushed my skin, raising goosebumps, and I shivered.

"You cold?" he asked.

"Not at all." This was all *him*.

"Lena triple-knotted you." He worked the tie at the small of my back with steady, unhurried fingers. His touch burned through me, making it impossible not to want more.

The shirt loosened at the bottom.

"Two left." His fingers trailed to the middle of my back, tugging at the next knot, and I reached a hand along my thigh behind me until it found his leg.

The tie at the center of my back released, and he swept my hair to the side, his fingers brushing against my neck. Heat flushed my cheeks. "I like your hands on me." The words fell out before I could stop them, and his hands stilled against me.

"I like having my hands on you, baby," he rasped.

"Careful," I breathed. "Keep calling me that, I might start to like it." Resting my head against his chest, I massaged his leg.

"Is that a promise?" His lips moved against my ear, and my pulse raced.

Promise.

I reached up, tracing the line of his jaw, feeling his rough stubble as I shifted around to face him.

Rhett's intense gaze swept over me like it could start a fire. "There's still one more." He lifted his hands to the back of my neck, undoing the last of the ties, and freed me from the confines of my shirt as it slipped down my shoulders.

This man was going to ruin all others for me.

I wasn't sure if it was the alcohol making me bold, or the way Rhett made me feel desired, reckless... *alive*, but my body responded to his attention and arousal stirred low in my belly. I dared to ask him the question in my mind. "Do you want me?"

He carefully held my chin, his lips meeting mine in a slow, deliberate kiss. Tilting my head up to look at him, his fingers brushed along my neck. "I've wanted you since I met you, but I meant it when I said I won't be your bad decision."

"I know what I want."

"You're not sober enough for me to take what I want."

Encircling my arms around his neck, I pulled him toward me, capturing his mouth with mine. He hesitated, but kissed me back, and I guided his hands around my waist, parting his lips with my tongue. His embrace around me tightened, holding me against his body as his mouth owned mine, like he couldn't get close enough. I ached to feel his skin on mine with nothing between us.

Easing out of his arms, I unbuttoned my pants, stepping out of them as they fell to the floor, and tugged my shirt down my arms. Either by some miracle or subconscious planning, my lacy half-bra I had worn under the backless shirt matched my panties. "I want this, Rhett." I threaded my fingers through the belt loops of his jeans, kissing his neck as I pulled him toward the chair.

As I collapsed onto the cushion, I tugged him down with me, his arms bracing himself over me like a protective cage. His throat bobbed as he swallowed, his face inches from mine. "What do you want exactly?" he asked.

"That's simple. You. I'm sober enough, I promise." I grabbed him over his jeans, but he was already hard underneath my touch.

He knelt between my legs, his gaze intense and piercing. "I'm not having sex with you tonight, Frankie. I'd love nothing more than to take care of you, but only if that's what you want, and only if you promise to keep it about you, not me."

Cupping his face in my hands, I let my assertiveness take control. "I want to forget all the bullshit and feel good tonight. I want you to touch me, kiss me, I want you close to me. You're not a bad decision, the past few weeks have been the most fun I've had in years, and I... I *trust* you."

Trusting him had snuck up on me, but I did. I trusted he wouldn't hurt me.

His hand moved up my arm, and his fingers held the back of my neck, tangling in my hair as he kissed me. I nibbled on his lower lip, teasing him with my tongue. "I want to feel you against me," I whispered, and he broke our connection to yank his shirt over his head, tossing it to the floor.

He grabbed me again, pulling me close, and I ran my fingers over the tattoos spanning his right arm. A saxophone, vintage microphone, flowers, and an abstract design all intertwined... With a gasp, I wrapped my arms around him and dragged my fingernails up his muscular back, feeling the heat of his skin against my body. He shut out the world, igniting every nerve inside me with *need*.

His lips moved along my throat. "What else do you want?"

My breathing turned shallow as I sank back into the plush chair. I reached behind myself but struggled to unhook my bra. "I want you to touch me, all of me... as soon as I get this off."

"Come here," he said. His gaze drifted to my lips, and he kissed me while his fingers traced a path to my lower back, unhooking my bra.

I rubbed the back of his neck as we kissed in an unhurried rhythm, our tongues teasing each other like long-lost lovers. His hands massaged my thighs, moving up to my hips, and I gripped his ass, desperate to bring him closer. "Undress me, Rhett."

"Whatever you want, baby." Reaching behind my neck, he gently fisted my hair. The strands tickled my skin as he tugged me back, his eyes never leaving mine. He released my hair and hooked his fingers under the thin bra straps, sliding them with an agonizing eternity along my arms. My chest rose and fell in shallow breaths as he slipped the lacy bra off, and my nipples hardened as the cool air touched my skin. "You're fucking beautiful."

I tugged at the button on his jeans, but he leaned over me, trailing a path of kisses along my neck, working his way down my chest. He cupped my breasts, teasing my nipples with his thumbs, and a moan escaped me.

"Fucking hell," he groaned, the words hot against my skin as he wrapped an arm around my back, pulling my breast in his mouth.

His tongue traced circles around my nipple before he claimed the other, and I arched myself against him. "Keep going," I muttered.

"Is that an order?" His eyes darkened with sexual intensity as he lifted his gaze from my chest.

"You're damn right it is."

"I'm not good with orders," he said, his voice a murmur against my skin as he kissed down my chest to my stomach, lingering along the lace of my panties.

"Get good with them, baby." I stroked his hair, holding him where I wanted him.

"Keep calling me that, and I might get too good with them." He curled his fingers around my panties and tugged them down. "Lift your ass for me," he commanded, and I slowly did what he asked.

Desire and anticipation pulsed between my thighs as he backed up, sliding the lace fabric down my legs and off my feet. I lay back on the chair naked, loving the way Rhett's eyes drank me in, raking over my body. "What about you? I think you need to be naked too."

"Tonight is for you." His warm hands traveled up my legs, and he took his time as he reached my thighs. "Where do you want my mouth?"

His presence held a comfortable ease, and he made asking for what I wanted feel natural, something I'd never experienced before. "On me, everywhere," I said.

He hovered over me, kissing me with a playful smile. A hint of cologne mixed with lingering soap on his skin, and I breathed him in as he pulled away, moving my legs apart to settle on his knees between them.

With his hands on each side of me, he stopped. "You said *everywhere*, are you sure?"

I smiled at him, licking my lips. "I'm very sure."

The ticklish graze of his stubble accompanied each kiss as he trailed them along my inner thighs, one and then the other. I arched toward him, releasing a whimper, desperate for him to touch me. He slid his hands from my hips to my ass, his grip firm and possessive, guiding me along the chair, closer to the heat of his mouth.

He moved his hands back up my body, and I sat up, kissing him, deep and desperate, wanting this man to *bury* himself inside me. "Want more?" he rasped.

"*So* much more."

Taking my wrists, he lifted my hands over my head, coaxing me back as his other hand moved up the inside of my thigh. He dragged his fingers between my legs, sending a sweet ache through me so intense, I gasped. "You're wet," he rasped. "It's sexy as hell."

I moaned, squirming beneath him. "Please keep going."

He released my wrists, and I gripped the back of the chair, moving against him as he dropped back down, spreading my legs further apart. He brushed his lips against my throbbing center, glancing up at me with sexy, hooded eyes, and arousal rushed between my legs as I arched toward him for more.

Lifting my legs onto his shoulders, he massaged my thighs with his hands while exploring me with his tongue. "You taste amazing," he groaned.

Each slow lick inside me with his warm breaths on my skin made me moan harder. The world around me dissolved. Only Rhett and the euphoria consuming me remained. "Jesus Christ," I cried out as my orgasm built, taking over.

"Not quite, but close," he said. His mouth *devoured* me with hot pressure, licking and sucking. He hit the sweet spots that made me grab the back of his head, holding him against me. "Come for me, Frankie."

"Is that an order?" I panted through my ragged breaths.

"It sure as fuck is." He dipped a finger inside me, curling it forward, keeping his mouth on me, using his tongue to edge me closer.

I shamelessly thrust against him, and he slid another finger deep inside me. With each wave of pleasure, I squeezed my legs around his shoulders and *let go*. "Holy fuck, don't move." My eyes rolled back as I pulsed around his fingers, and he gave me a gentle suck. The grip I had on his head relaxed, and my breathing steadied. "That was..."

He slowly dragged his fingers out of me, leaving a tingling warmth, and guided my legs off his shoulders, caressing them softly. Placing tender kisses along my thighs, he made his way up to my chest as I lifted my head. "Satisfactory, I hope?" he asked, his eyebrows raised as he looked up at me. "Happy Birthday, Frankie."

"Five very gold stars." I wrapped my arms around him and kissed him. "I want you to feel that good too."

"I always feel good when I'm with you." He got up off the floor, adjusting himself, and grabbed a throw from the couch, draping it around my shoulders. "What can I get you?"

"There's nothing you can get me right now that can compete with *that*." I yawned, my eyes heavy and head aching as my orgasm subsided, and the alcohol wore off. I didn't want him to leave, and assertive, newly thirty-year-old me, who was making it a habit of asking for what I wanted, took over. "Stay with me tonight?"

"I'm not going anywhere." He put his shirt back on and bent down, kissing my forehead before walking into the kitchen and running the tap. "Want water?"

"Sure, I'm going upstairs." I stood and gathered my discarded clothes, holding the blanket around my naked body. Unsteady on my feet, I held the railing as I trudged upstairs toward my bedroom. Questions about Rhett and the events from earlier still lingered in my fuzzy mind, but every muscle in my body had relaxed like I'd taken a Rhett-sized miracle drug. An image of a pill bottle with Rhett's face on it popped in my head, *take as needed*. I could live with that prescription.

Leaving the light off, I dropped the blanket and shivered. I pulled a T-shirt over my head and sat on the edge of the bed, slipping into a pair of pajama shorts. The wooden floor in the hallway creaked as Rhett came into my room and placed a glass of water on my bedside table.

He took one look at me and pulled the duvet down. "Get in," he said.

I couldn't think of a smart-ass retort, so I crawled into bed and sank against the mattress as he covered me up. Crouching next to the bed, he kissed me. I held his face, keeping him close. I craved the safety and comfort of his arms around me, and I didn't care what it meant for our undefined relationship. "You're not sleeping on the couch tonight."

"I'm having a hard time saying no to you."

"Good." I scooted back and held the blankets open. "Come here."

He lay next to me, clasping his hands behind his head.

I turned on my side, facing him. A muscle twitched along his strong jawline, and his lashes fluttered as he blinked slowly, staring at the ceiling. In the short time I'd known him, I'd gotten close enough that I could feel his tension when something troubled him.

I rested my head on his chest as he slid his arm around me. "Talk to me, Rhett, what do we do next?"

"I'm working on it. What is it that Clay does for work?"

"He works for some elite financial firm in Connecticut. Why?"

His fingers traced back and forth along my arm. "I want to know what Noble's paying him for."

"He's a liar and a cheat. He wants to be worshiped like he's a fucking king because he rolls with corporate royalty." My chest tightened as I spoke, and the anger I thought I'd long buried resurfaced. "I don't know much about your world, but if Clay's working for a mob guy, I'm not surprised."

Rhett faced me, his expression serious. "He hurt you."

"A long time ago." My eyes drifted shut, and I opened them, yawning. "I'm over it, I just haven't forgotten what it felt like."

He turned on his side and pulled me against him. Heat from his chest warmed me through my shirt; he smelled so *good*, a sensual masculine scent, unmistakably *him*. With our faces inches apart, I ran my fingers through his short hair and along the back of his neck.

"I'll never hurt you," he said.

"I hope not, I won't hurt you either."

"That's the nicest thing anyone's ever said to me." His lips found mine, softer this time, and I kissed him back.

People broke promises all the time, and maybe I'd end up alone, picking up pieces of us that would fade into memories. But I wanted to believe that no matter what happened, I would never regret letting myself feel alive with him.

Twenty-Eight

Rhett

Leaving Frankie wrapped up in blankets, snoring, I headed downstairs on a few hours of sleep, in desperate need of strong coffee. I rummaged through her cabinets, finding coffee and filters, and filled the basket without measuring. Scrolling on my phone, I noted the missed calls from Vivian and pushed the button to start the coffee. I moved instinctively, entering the living room. Pulling back the curtains, I peered outside to scan the neighborhood. An older couple down the street carried bags of groceries inside, and a small red car drove by like any other rainy Saturday morning.

But this wasn't any other day, and I needed to figure out what the hell Clay wanted with Frankie and why.

The Nobles dealt in counterfeit money, drugs, running guns, and shell companies—not so different from what we'd done. We'd worked together. When my father got into trafficking women for his strip clubs, he'd crossed a line I could never come back from. It disgusted me and made it easy to sell him out. I sold them all out.

Clay was a money guy, he'd know how to run cash through the business to make it legit, and he had ties to Willow Grove, a new interest for Bran Noble once he'd seen that picture on Frankie's phone.

Turning away from the window, I glimpsed Frankie's bra tucked next to the chair cushion. I picked it up, holding the lace in my fingers, picturing how it hugged Frankie's curves. I had her naked in my arms, kissing *every* delicious fucking inch of her. Running my hand over my chin, I could still taste her. Somehow, last night, she'd let me get close to her, and for the first time I let myself plan on not letting her go. I craved more of her.

Shaking off the desire to crawl back in bed and hold her, I walked into the kitchen and poured coffee, adding some kind of non-dairy milk Frankie had in her fridge. I sat on a stool at the counter and unlocked my phone, finding my sister's last message. I never forgot a face or a name, but Clay Preston had eluded me, and he didn't remember me either. Someone had kept him a guarded secret, and it hadn't been my family.

I searched for him online. Images and articles from a prestigious financial firm specializing in elite clients came up. They all praised his work ethic and highlighted awards and his successes. He was among the youngest with such accolades.

He was full of shit. Perhaps Clay Preston had been the reason Miles had worked both sides.

I took my coffee onto the back deck and shut the door, dialing Vivian's number. I almost hung up when she didn't answer on the fourth ring.

"It's about time you called me back," she said.

"You know a Clay Preston?" I kept my voice quiet.

She hesitated. "Not personally."

"He's a problem."

"I didn't think you trusted me after I told you about Luca."

"I shouldn't." Sitting in a chair, I gulped down the coffee as rain speckled my shirt. My sister had never given me a single reason not to trust her. "I don't have a lot of options right now."

"It sucks going rogue, it'll kill you. Come back, I can offer you protection here, but not while you're alone in nowhere town."

I glanced through the glass door behind me, but Frankie still hadn't come downstairs. "What the fuck are you doing?" I'd been the one in control, untouchable. Breaking away from my family had thrown me into territory I didn't know how to navigate. I should've stayed away... but I'd never have met Frankie.

Her words caught as she spoke. "You were supposed to come home weeks ago. We need you here. Enough time's passed, Noble won't dare kill you, not now. Not with Dad getting out. They need each other, it's good for business."

"I killed the man's son, Viv." No amount of time could pass to end his hatred. He wouldn't rest until I was dead. "When's release day?"

"Monday," she said.

"Monday?" Two days was nowhere near enough time to get my head back in the game, not with a target on Frankie's back. "And how do you think he'll take to your new boyfriend?"

"Before everything went to hell he would've *welcomed* him. I don't know what he's going to do now. But between Luca's men and ours, we're taking back control, Rhett. That's why I need you, so we can be a united front, and *that's* why Bran Noble won't touch you. Running the business—"

"I was supposed to return to help you and Zach get out of the business, not control it."

"There's too much money involved to let it go," she whispered. "I can do this, *we* can. You've earned it more than me."

"I don't want his fucking money, Viv." I exhaled and drank from my mug. "Is Bran in Boston?"

"Actually..." She sighed. "Don't cut me off and just listen."

I cursed under my breath. My sister was fucking the enemy, and I didn't know what the hell to do, but I needed information fast. "I'm listening."

"I'm attending a charity event this evening, and he's supposed to show up, so he's here. We're keeping an eye on him, and that man you mentioned, Preston? He's on the attending list." She paused. "I told Luca about your woman situation."

This kept getting worse. "Don't go tonight—"

"I'm going. Look," she said, her voice hardening into the sharpness it always had when she refused to take no for an answer, "something is up, I'm your eyes and ears here, and you are *still family*. We've got an ally with the Nobles, most of them hate Bran and want him gone. But no one will take care of it. And I want everything solid before Monday."

"Your ally is related to Bran Noble. You can't trust him." I shut my eyes, pressing my fingers against them as I leaned back in the chair. "You've got a death wish, Viv. Where's Zach in all this?"

"He's good, he's in college, unaware. No one knows Luca and I are together... No one who will cause problems. I'm building a network, just like we talked about."

"The network was supposed to be involved in turning the business straight." I shook my head. "Fuck."

"Can you get here tomorrow or Sunday?"

I'd have to go back, but not until Finn or someone was closely guarding Frankie. "I'll be in touch." I slid the patio door open as water rushed through the pipes in the walls. "Gotta go. Don't give me anymore reason not to trust you, *please*."

"You hurt my feelings saying that, Rhett. You should know better."

"Right." I hung up and stepped inside, carrying my mug to the counter for a refill. The floor above creaked, and light footsteps descended the stairs.

I glanced over my shoulder as Frankie shuffled around the corner into the kitchen. Her oversized sweater fell to the hem of her shorts, and she pulled her hair into a ponytail. She approached and gave me a sweet look with a hint of sexy. The quiet smile she saved just for me played on her lips.

"Good morning—" I said, but before I could turn around, she wrapped her arms around me from behind, placing her hands on my chest with her head against my back.

"Thanks for last night." She spoke softly, and I placed the coffee cup down to take her hands in mine, intertwining our fingers against my chest. I reached my other hand around to grab her ass.

"I should thank *you* for last night." Facing her, I kissed her beautiful mouth. "I'll take care of you anytime you want."

"I'll remember that," she said between kisses, tucking her cold hands underneath my shirt and rubbing my back. She prodded my lips with her tongue, and I kissed her harder.

Tightening my arms around her, I pulled her close, letting my hands roam her body. With a sigh, her hands slid down my back until she was grabbing my ass. The doorbell rang, and she froze, her body tensing. "I'm not expecting anyone."

I moved past her toward the front door and saw Finn standing on the step through the living room window. "Your brother's here."

She opened the door, and Finn hurried inside, shooting daggers at me. "What are you doing here?"

"Not leaving her alone like we talked about," I said.

Frankie shut the door, crossing her arms. "Don't start, Finn. What are *you* doing here?"

"We need to talk." Finn paced, his gaze darting between Frankie and me, and her hands flew to her mouth as her eyes widened.

"Is it Dad—"

"Clay's dead," Finn said.

"What do you mean *dead*?" Panic filled her voice. "Did he get into an accident last night?"

"This wasn't an accident." Finn watched me as I surveyed the road through the window for cops, or worse.

"When are they coming?" I said.

Finn sat heavily in a chair and rubbed his face. "Soon, they've already called Lena in to the bar and last I heard, his friends from last night are at the station."

"What the hell happened to him?" With her fingers on her temples, Frankie shut her eyes and opened them. Dropping her hands, she reached into the cabinet for a mug. "Coffee, I need coffee."

Taking the mug from her hands, I led her to a chair. "Sit, I'll get it."

She plopped down with a thud, pulling her knee to her chest. "Who saw him last? Us? Did you put him in a cab last night?"

I filled the mug with coffee, leaving it black. "His friends picked him up." I placed it in front of her.

285

She flinched as the hot coffee touched her lips. "Did you see him leave?"

"I waited for him to get in the car." I stood next to her as Finn shifted in the chair, bouncing his knee. "What they do to him, Roscoe?" I asked, and he jerked his head toward me. Our eyes locked, and I knew exactly where his mind had gone.

The one thing we'd tried to avoid was unfolding. Our past had returned.

Finn checked his phone and locked it. "Housekeeping found him in a room at the Cross-Trail motel. They slit his throat, and he bled to death."

"Fuck." Frankie slid her mug away.

"What time?" I asked.

He nervously pushed his cheek against the side of his mouth. "The call came in after three."

My jaw clenched as I leaned back against the counter, folding my arms across my chest. If Bran Noble was in Boston, who had he hired to kill Clay? Unless my sister was a liar. She wouldn't do that to me, she couldn't. "Any leads?"

"Not sure." Finn leaned forward in his chair, and his knee stopped bouncing. "I'm assuming you've been here all night?"

"He hasn't left," Frankie said.

Finn glared at me. "Keeping her safe?"

"You're damn right."

"Stop." Frankie's coffee spilled over the cup as she slammed her hand down on the table. She bit her trembling lower lip. "If someone killed Clay... slit his *throat* after he left the bar last night, after he talked about Miles, admitted to breaking into my house, do you think they're done? Is he the one they wanted all along? Maybe whatever Miles had... maybe they think it's gone, or Clay had it and lied..."

Fuck, I was an insensitive shit. She was sitting there listening to us discuss her ex-boyfriend's murder—the asshole she'd given years of herself and *cared* about once—as though we were discussing a grocery list. She'd only landed in the middle of a complicated mess because a man recognized the men on her phone screen.

The chair scraped against the floor as I yanked it out and sat next to her. "I'm sorry this happened to him, and that you're caught up in it."

"Jesus Christ," Finn exhaled. "We don't have time for this."

I focused on Frankie as she blinked, wiping underneath her eyes. "What's next?" she said.

Finn rose from the chair. "Get dressed, Frankie, that's what's next. Police will be here soon, you tell them he talked to you last night, don't say too much, keep it simple—"

"I'll tell them the truth. When I left that office, he was *alive*." Sliding the chair back, she got up, turning away from us. "I'll be down in a few minutes. If there's *anything* else either of you haven't told me, I want to know what it is when I come back." She left Finn and me facing each other as she ran upstairs.

TWENTY-NINE

Rhett

Finn and I sat in silence for a minute at Frankie's table before he finally spoke. "They want to talk to you more than they do her, so do I."

"So talk."

Finn glanced toward the bottom of the stairs as the pipes groaned, and the taps turned on upstairs. "Is your ID good?"

"On paper, the old me is dead. But there's no hiding, not anymore." I stretched my legs out. "I'm not running. Whatever happens to me, happens. But I'll die protecting her."

A rhythmic tapping hit the table as Finn bounced his knee again. "I don't even want to know what you two have going on here. You never should've gotten her involved."

"Me? Fuck, man. This started with Noble in the hospital and that photo—"

"So what does he want? You or me?" He put his head in his hands and spoke to the table. "They've got to know you're here after last night, unless Clay never told them."

"With a knife to his throat, he would've told them what they wanted," I said. Biding my time in Willow Grove after two years had blown up in my face. "Our plan is falling apart, but I will fix this."

Finn looked up and back at me. "You talk to your sister back home?"

"Yeah," I said, "but you don't want to know." Finn would lose his shit when he found out who she'd aligned herself with.

He exhaled sharply, frustrated. "Fuck, I know that look. She's working an angle, isn't she?"

"If you want to call getting in bed with Bran Noble's nephew an angle."

"Oh, Christ. We need to get you out of here—"

Dropping my arms, I sat forward. "I told you, I'm done running. It's over."

Finn observed me for a moment and glanced outside the patio doors. "Then we make sure no one knows she's connected to you."

"It might be too late for that," I said, "but if Noble knew where to find me, I wouldn't be sitting here right now. I'm going to Boston tomorrow."

Finn spread his hands on the table in agitation. "They'll kill you."

"Promise me you'll keep an eye on her until I'm back—"

"She's my sister, Rhett, of course I'll take care of her." He ran a hand over his head. "It's you I'm worried about. And if they find out I'm the cop who put their men in jail, Frankie will be in danger, along with Lena, my parents..."

Frankie rounded the corner, wearing jeans and a black sweater that hugged her body. The ends of her ponytail were wet, and her cheeks flushed. Her eyes carried a distant look I couldn't place, but I wanted to know it. I wanted to know what was going on in her head. She picked up her coffee and stood looking at us as she took a drink. "Full disclosure time."

"What do you want to know?" I asked.

"Not you, me." She held up a small device, a USB stick. "You told me Miles's last words to you were *the picture*, right? Well, I went through everything in that bin and found this taped to the back of a photo."

"When?" Finn stood reaching for it, but she snatched it away from him. "Why didn't you say something?"

Fire burned in her blue eyes, and she set the mug down. We'd kept secrets from her for two years. She was about to blast Finn, and we both probably deserved it. "I'll figure out the password before I hand it over."

"You don't want that kind of heat on you Frankie," he said. "It's withholding evidence."

"No one will know." She held the USB in a death grip. "You both had two fucking years, I'm asking for one day." Taking a quick breath, she swallowed. "He left it for me, it's my decision." Her eyes flickered between Finn and me. "Neither of you will say a word to anyone, not until I hand it over."

I stood and approached her. "Not a word from me. Finn?"

"Have you tried to get into it yet?" he asked.

Frankie turned the device over in her fingers. "Of course I did. It's locked, encrypted or something. I read about it online, but it doesn't matter—I knew Miles, I'll crack it."

"You get one day," Finn said. "When do you work next?" He trailed her into the living room, but she ignored him. "Francesca?" He reached for her arm, but she stepped away, her gaze fixed on the window as a car neared our street. Finn continued, "It's important that you tell me what your schedule is this week, Rhett's going to Boston, and I need to know where you'll be."

Reaching inside the entryway closet, she yanked on a jacket, but it caught on something. "He what?" She spun around, still tugging on its sleeve, but it didn't budge. "You can't leave, that man will know, he'll hurt you or do what he did to Clay... Fuck's sake." Tears filled her eyes as she wrestled with her jacket, and I released the hanger's hold on it.

"Where are you going?" I asked as she shoved her arms in the sleeves, freeing her ponytail from beneath the collar.

She didn't respond to me, turning on Finn again. "I work tomorrow, most of next week. Tell him he can't leave."

Finn's tone softened. "He won't listen to me."

An unmarked car pulled into her driveway. From the window, I could see two cops talking, not getting out right away. I recognized one of them from the night of the break-in, Sergeant Fletcher. I moved between Frankie and the door. "Baby, where are you going?"

"Don't baby me right now, *don't*."

Finn glared at me, his eyes burning with anger. I'd broken his rules, but he'd have to get over it.

"Aren't we supposed to go with them?" she asked. "Isn't that how this works?"

"They won't let me on the case. They'll probably talk to you, us..." Finn opened the door before the two officers could knock.

A woman with bright silver hair scanned the house over Finn's shoulder. Glancing down at herself, she buttoned her black suit jacket, hiding a coffee stain on her white shirt. Staring at me as she walked inside, she introduced herself. "I'm Detective Clark with State Homicide."

Sergeant Fletcher stepped forward, staying behind her. He carried an air of suspicion but kept it under control. He'd been kind to Frankie and knew her family, but I couldn't stop my instinct to position myself subtly in front of her. She gave me a sharp look and moved aside, shaking the detective's hand.

They talked with Finn, asking him questions about the bar and the last time he laid eyes on Clay Preston, before turning their attention to Frankie.

Detective Clark peeked around the corner into the kitchen and upstairs. "Ms. Roscoe, I've been briefed on your brother's case. I'm sorry for your terrible loss." She nodded to Finn.

They suspected Clay's death had a connection to Miles. Frankie's expression shifted from lingering frustration to agonizing heartbreak. It brought back the memory of the night in the ER when she held her dead brother on a stretcher. I moved closer, wanting to wrap a protective arm around her.

"What do you need from us?" Frankie's tone sliced through the small talk.

Sergeant Fletcher cleared his throat. "Is there a place we could sit and talk, Francesca?"

Leaving her jacket on the chair, Frankie led them to the kitchen table. Finn and I glanced at each other as Sergeant Fletcher held out a chair for Frankie before taking a seat next to her.

Detective Clark nodded to us. "Gentlemen, would you like to join us?"

Finn took a seat near the patio doors, and the detective turned her attention to me. "Mr. Marshall?"

She'd done her research. I'd bet my life she knew I was a Morrigan. "Please, you take the chair, I'll stand."

"Suit yourself," she said, taking a seat. Placing a notebook on the table, she held a gold pen over the page and addressed Frankie.

"A witness said you and Mr. Preston had an argument last night around eleven o'clock, can you elaborate?"

Frankie curled her fingers into a fist on the table as she rehashed the conversation with Clay, and how he'd grabbed her. "Rhett and Finn intervened, and we all went out back until Clay's friends picked him up. There's nothing more to tell. He was alive when he left the bar."

As Frankie talked, Detective Clark scribbled in the notepad, tilting her head up to face me. "Mr. *Marshall.*"

"That's right," Frankie interrupted before I could confirm.

Arching her eyebrows, Detective Clark wrote something down, drawing a line underneath the words, but I couldn't make out what they said. She narrowed her authoritative eyes at me. "You were with Mr. Preston outside behind the bar. In fact, friends of the victim saw you punch Mr. Preston in the face. We'll need you to come down to the station to meet with investigators who spent time with them this morning."

Frankie jerked her head toward me, but I didn't meet her hard stare, holding eye contact with the detective. "No problem," I said, unmoving.

This time, Sergeant Fletcher's gruff voice cut through the tension as he directed his question at me. "And where were you between the hours of midnight and three thirty this morning?"

I glanced from him to Frankie. "Here the whole time, just like she said."

Detective Clark regarded me as she spoke to Frankie. "Ms. Roscoe, is it true that you had a history with the victim?" Her gaze broke away from me to Frankie, and Finn let out an annoyed huff as he shifted in his seat.

Jesus Christ, wrap this up.

Frankie was the victim, and they were treating her like she was on trial. Tightening my fingers around my thumb, I cracked the knuckle, attracting attention from Finn and both officers.

Sitting in the chair without fidgeting, Frankie showed no trace of emotion on her face. "Our relationship years ago has no relevance to this."

Sergeant Fletcher clicked a pen. "You'd mentioned last time you have items belonging to your brother, Miles Roscoe, in this house."

Frankie's eyes watered, but not a single tear fell. "Nothing of interest, sentimental stuff. You're not having it."

"I'm sorry, Francesca," Sergeant Fletcher said, not unkindly. "You don't get to determine that, I don't either." He nodded toward the detective. "This is with the State now."

Finn broke his silence. "You have a warrant?"

"Not yet." Detective Clark shut her notebook and rose from her seat, carrying herself with the grace of royalty. "But we'll get one."

They hovered near Frankie, asking a few more basic questions, and she signed a statement. Detective Clark headed toward the front door, and the sergeant followed close behind. He scratched his head and eyed me, adjusting his coat. "Mr. Marshall, Roscoe, you'll need to come down to the station sooner than later, please."

He stepped outside and waited for Detective Clark, but she narrowed her eyes at me. "Bring identification with you."

"We'll be there." Finn loomed in the doorway as they drove away. He stepped outside, spinning his keys in his hand. "Frankie, stay inside, lock the doors, and call if anything happens. *Anything.*"

"She's not staying here alone," I said.

Finn grabbed his phone. "I'll call Dad to come out."

"Dad isn't coming to the rescue, I'll be fine." She held up the USB stick. "I've got a day, and I'm not wasting it."

"I'll have my phone and can be out here in twenty minutes." The rain shifted into a sudden downpour, and Finn hurried to his car.

"Come with me." I placed my hands on her arms, and she looked up at me. "Hang out at the station while they ask their questions."

"I'll be okay, really."

I had another gun stashed in the truck, and they'd take mine if I brought it into the station. Reaching into my waistband, I carefully pulled out my gun and handed it to her. "Take it."

"Are you sure? What about you?"

"I've got another one in the truck, and something tells me I won't need it for a few hours."

She took the gun, her fingers brushing against mine. "You trust me with your gun?"

I grabbed her face, kissing her, and she met my urgency right back. With my hands still on her face, I broke our kiss. "Frankie, I trust you with my fucking life."

"You punched Clay last night?"

"He disrespected you, he deserved it." I caressed her chin with my thumb.

She didn't pull away from me, holding the gun pointed down. "You can't just punch everyone who's disrespectful. He didn't deserve to die."

"I had nothing to do with Clay's death. I need you to believe that."

"I do, but I'm still mad."

"I know." Bending closer, I brushed my lips against hers, feeling her warm breath on my skin.

She held my face with one hand, her lips meeting mine in a rough, demanding kiss before she tore away, leaving me breathless. "Go before I don't let you leave," she said.

"Okay, hold that thought." I yanked my jacket on as I left her standing in the living room. "Lock the door."

"That's an order I'll follow, but don't push it." She shut the door, and I waited until the deadbolt clicked before rushing to my truck.

THIRTY
Frankie

Rain battered the window as I locked the front door. A chill lingered in the house, sending shivers through me. Flicking the button to turn the propane fireplace on, I sank into the chair, placing Rhett's gun on the side table. I trailed my fingers along the blanket's frayed edges and pulled it over myself. Rhett *had* me in this chair last night. I closed my eyes, remembering his warm mouth on my skin, and a flash of heat spread low in my stomach.

My eyes flew open. The orange glow from the fire flickered on the walls in the dimly lit living room.

Every warning flared inside me, whispering danger. Someone had murdered Clay, and suddenly, the memories plagued me, invading all other thoughts. I'd known Clay in high school, but we hadn't started dating until college. We'd lived together, sharing moments and empty promises built on lies.

Hot tears streamed down my cheeks as I buried my face in my shaking hands. I had once loved Clay Preston. I'd grown to despise him, wishing he'd disappear from my life and this town... But I'd never wished him *dead*. His family would suffer horrible, unending grief like mine, the same darkness that had trapped my father, making Mom, Finn, and me powerless to help him.

I cried until the pressure behind my eyes throbbed and my vision blurred. Staggering into the kitchen, I snatched a handful of tissues and blew my stuffed-up nose.

Get it together, Frankie.

I pulled the USB stick out of my pocket and held it at eye level. I didn't know how much information was stored on the tiny piece of equipment, but I needed to find out. Clay had wanted what the device held, either for himself, or for someone else. With my heart pounding in my chest, I bolted up the stairs and grabbed my laptop, carrying it into the spare room. I turned the light on and threw the lid off the plastic bin.

Perhaps Miles had written the password on something else and tucked it inside a book, or another picture frame. A frantic energy took over as I tore through the contents, checking the pockets of his clothes, and shaking his childhood trophies, listening for anything hidden inside. I flipped through albums again, laying everything on the floor until nothing remained in the bin.

I plugged in the USB, trying every possible password: sports teams, family names, birthdays, the dog we'd had as kids, Miles's name spelled backward... Access denied. With albums strewn across the floor amidst pieces of my brother's life, a weight sank in my chest. I opened the book where I'd tucked the photo of him with Clay. Holding it closer, I lifted my ass off the floor to grab my phone from my back pocket and turned the flashlight on, examining every detail under the bright light. Where were they, and what were they leaning against?

A pool table.

I recognized the logo on the napkin, The Eight & Out, a bar where Miles and I had played pool many times. When had my brother gone there with Clay? The background lacked focus, but someone's arm holding a pool cue, barely in the shot, caught my eye. The tattoo appeared higher on their arm, but it was identical to Rhett's. My eyes burned, and my pulse quickened to a rapid pace. I set the photo aside. That wasn't Rhett, it couldn't be, but one of the Morrigans had been there with my brother and Clay.

I tore through each album again, searching for more pictures or anyone resembling Clay, but found nothing else. Sitting back against the wall, I picked at the back of the framed photo where the memory stick had been, racking my brain for a damn password.

I searched the internet for how to break into password-protected USBs and called a local computer repair shop. They told me I could bring it in but made no promises, using technical words I didn't understand. Hanging up, I unplugged the small device from my laptop. So much for staying locked up in the house until Rhett came back. I'd deal with the photo later.

The directions from Ted, the computer repair guy, had led me to a brownstone in a neighborhood across town. A simple sign that read *Ted's Computer Repair*, with a hand-painted arrow, pointed to a side entrance. I parked along the curb and pushed a short iron gate, leaving it open behind me in case I needed a quick escape. No light shone from the elevated window at the front of the house, but two cars were parked in the driveway.

I knocked on the door, and a young man, who couldn't be much over twenty, peeked through the blinds as the knob turned. "You can come right in, no need to knock."

"You might want to add to your sign letting people know," I said. "Are you Ted?"

"Yes, yes, I sure am." He snorted as he laughed and held the door open as I walked inside. "You're not the first to say that about the sign, it's sound advice I need to listen to."

A woman of about the same age as Ted spun around in an office chair. She glanced up from the computer screen that reflected off the silver piercings lining her ears. "What can we do to help?" She looked up at me with intense amber eyes.

It could be bad for me if they accessed the information on the memory stick and witnessed something they shouldn't, but I failed to see alternatives other than handing it over to the police, and I wasn't ready to do that.

I exhaled and held up the device. "I forgot my password."

"Let me see it." The girl leaned over the desk with her hand out, and I dropped it in her palm.

She arched a thin, painted eyebrow. "This yours? Like, for real."

"It's mine," I said. "Can you reset the password or something? It's important."

"It usually is." Ted stood behind her with his hand on the back of her chair. Rings adorned each finger, including a gold band on his thumb. "Especially if you're here asking for our help."

"Yeah, well, I guess situations like these are good for business." I kept my tone light, but tension settled in my neck, adding to my headache.

The girl plugged the device into a computer, and her expression shifted as her eyebrows furrowed and relaxed repeatedly. "It's bricked."

"I'm sorry, what does that mean?" I stepped closer, looking over her shoulder at the screen, but nothing made sense to me.

"Encrypted, like you told me over the phone. The password's got it locked down." Ted dragged his teeth over his bottom lip and clicked his tongue. "If you forgot your password, the data may as well be gone at this point."

Desperation clawed at my chest. "There's something on that thing, I need to see it, there has to be a way—"

"If it's yours, wouldn't you know what's on it?" The woman folded her arms across her chest and played with the long braids dangling over her shoulders.

"Look, I'll pay you whatever you want, I just need to..." I choked on my words and cleared my throat. "I need to know."

"Uh huh." Her chest heaved as she faced the computer screen again. "There's no breaking through without the password." She pushed away from the computer, crossing her legs. "Recovering corrupted files like that requires skills we don't have here. We're not *hackers*, that's illegal."

"You wouldn't happen to know any? Hackers, I mean," I asked, and she regarded me, throwing a glance at Ted. Sweat clung to the back of my neck, and I wiped it away. They couldn't help me; I was on my own. "I'm just kidding. Thanks for trying, what do I owe you?"

The woman handed the memory stick back to me. "Not a thing."

Ted opened the door, stepping back to allow me to walk past him. "Sorry we can't be of more help—"

"You did great." I put my hand up before he could close the door. "Do me a favor? Don't mention this visit to anyone if someone ever asks." God, I sounded like a criminal.

"Never saw you, don't even know your name. *Literally*," he said with a nod. He paused in the doorway. "Words of endearment."

"Excuse me?"

"Often people choose words that mean something to them, you know? Something that they'll never forget, a moment, a place. Think back on something you might've used like that."

"Okay, thanks."

He shut the door, and I hurried to my Jeep, locking the doors as soon as I got in. I drove with a sense of isolation, suddenly fearful of trusting anyone. Checking my rearview mirror and confirming no one was tailing me, I pulled up to The Francesca Rose and stepped into the rain. Even if I couldn't tell Mom the gravity of my situation... I needed her.

A harsh rattle greeted me like someone shaking a can of nails when I walked in. "What the hell kind of bird is that one?"

Mom glanced up from decorating a festive wreath, the table beside the counter scattered with bright ribbons and pinecones. "A magpie, the bird that symbolizes both bad luck or good fortune, however you want to look at it, I guess."

"The bird that mates for life," I whispered, remembering Miles's words.

Mom held out her arms. "I'm sorry, honey." I collapsed against her, hugging her back as tightly as I could.

"I didn't even like him," I said through tears. "Why does it hurt so much?"

"Because you're a good person, and no matter how much of an ass the man was, what happened to him was tragic and horrific." Releasing me, Mom dabbed her eyes. "And way too close to home." She moved past me and locked the door, flipping the sign to closed.

"Closing early?" I glanced at my phone. Hours had passed since Rhett and Finn had left my place, and neither had messaged, only Lena, and she hadn't mentioned them, leaving me feeling uneasy. Would the police detain Rhett for hitting Clay? Would he be a *suspect*?

"It's my usual Saturday time, but it was slow today." Mom organized a shelf and locked the cash register. "I should've stayed home, that's what I wanted to do. It's like a dark cloud dropped over the town today. What are you doing downtown on your day off?"

"Just going for a drive, clearing my head... I don't know." Puddles splashed over the sidewalk as cars drove by, and the rain picked up, blowing sideways at the windows. "Mom, did that man ever come back?"

"What man?"

"The one who called and ordered flowers—"

"With the mother who was your patient, right? Never heard another word from him." She took her raincoat off a hook and put it on, grabbing an umbrella. "But something has been bugging me about that conversation I had with Clay since I found out what happened to him. Remember he was asking about Miles?"

The picture I'd found proved their involvement was deeper than I'd thought.

"I remember," I said. "Last Sunday at dinner."

"He wanted to know if we'd kept anything—"

My stomach knotted. "Like what?"

"Like old pictures, mementos. He brushed it off and looked so sad, telling me he was struggling lately, that's why he'd been spending more time at home... I felt *bad* for him. He treated you like shit, and bringing any of this up to you last Sunday was the last thing I wanted to do. But now he's been murdered, like Miles, what if it was the same person—" She exhaled slowly as her lips quivered. "I don't know Frankie, it just struck me as weird."

Had Miles and Clay worked together? Was that how Clay knew the USB existed in that frame? "Did you tell him I had Miles's stuff from the apartment?"

"I did, maybe I shouldn't have, but I told him to reach out to you, that you might have something." Tears trickled over her face, carrying mascara with them, and she wiped them away.

I couldn't bring myself to tell her he'd broken in and looked through Miles's things. He was dead now, and it would make her feel awful. "You were just trying to be nice to him. I think they kept in touch after we broke up, I don't know why." I needed a topic change to divert her away from the Clay situation surrounding me. She'd worry herself sick if she knew how bad it had gotten. "How's Dad? It's been too quiet, I worry."

"What can I tell you? Your father's okay, you know, not causing a scene in public. And I made him agree to call me if he gets stuck anywhere, not you, not Finn. It's progress, for now."

It's not enough. I want my dad back, I need him to be strong... because my own armor has cracked.

"He should... He needs..." I stuffed my hands in my jacket pockets and curled my fingers around the USB. I couldn't deal with my father's issues, not today. "Tell him I said hi and I'll come by for dinner soon."

"How about tomorrow?" Hair had fallen out of my ponytail, and Mom brushed the strands aside. "I'm making lasagna."

"I work until seven, but next time."

"Of course." She turned the lights off and draped her purse over her shoulder. "Are you going to be okay? Want to come back with me to the house? I'll make you something to eat—"

"No, I was downtown and wanted to see you, that's all."

"I'm here whenever you need me, got it?"

I hugged her again, wiping the tears as they fell so she wouldn't see. Stepping back, I avoided her concerned gaze. "You'll get through this, Francesca, just like always. Come on, I need to go home and park my freezing ass in front of the fire."

She ran to her car with a wave and shook the umbrella before she got in. I stood in the rain and watched her drive away before climbing into my Jeep. Her words resonated in my mind as I headed home. She was right. I was strong and had walked through everything life had thrown our way, dragging my family with me when I wasn't sure I could put one foot in front of the other. But I was tired. Not the physical kind of tired, but a deep emotional exhaustion that no amount of sleep could fix.

A notification buzzed on my phone from Rhett.

Tell me you're okay? I'm with Finn, won't be home for a bit unless you need me.

I'm fine.

Frankie, you gotta do better than fine this time.

I'm leaving Mom's shop

You're not home?

I'm going back now.

Text me as soon as you're safe inside, and don't leave again.

My fingers hovered over my phone, but I didn't respond with sarcasm about taking orders. I sat with the emptiness in my chest and took the long way home. Lena's car wasn't in the Magpie parking lot as I drove by, and police had the entrance barricaded. I called her, and her voice filled the car.

"Frankie! How are you? I can't believe he's dead."

"Me neither. You're not at the Magpie, are you?" Turning onto the road toward home, I stole a glance in my rearview mirror. "I just drove by, there's police everywhere."

"They've been there all day, I had to close the bar until they're done."

Silence filled the line, but having her there comforted me. "Have you talked to Finn?" I asked.

"Not since he left to see you this morning. He sent me a message a while ago, they're still at the station. Why?"

"I'm just concerned, do you know what's going on?"

"Other than Clay had more enemies that I thought, nope. You?"

Lena didn't know about the USB, and I hesitated to tell her. But she was my best friend... "Do you know much about encrypted memory sticks and how to get into one without a password?"

"Jesus, Frankie. What the hell have you gotten yourself into?"

"I found a USB stick on the back of a picture frame Miles had. If I can't get into it, I'll turn it over to the police."

"What? What do you think is on it?" she asked, hushed.

"That's what I need to find out. You knew Clay in college, was there anything... *off*?"

"That's a loaded question, my friend."

"I know, but any mention of... I don't know, side hustles among your mutual business contacts or Miles?" The rain streamed over the windshield, and I turned up the wiper speed as I rounded a turn. Dark cloud cover made the sky appear more like midnight than late afternoon.

"Nothing he'd ever tell me, and after you broke up, I didn't talk to him unless he was in the bar. Why don't you just come over and we'll talk, you don't sound like yourself."

"I'm pulling into my driveway." I stifled a yawn. A throbbing ache migrated to the top of my head, and I yanked the elastic out of my hair, relieving the pressure along my temples. I drove into the garage and sat in my Jeep as the door rolled down behind me. "It's just... you know that feeling when you're missing something or someone isn't telling you all the details?"

Lena's laugh carried over the phone as it transferred away from Bluetooth. "I'm with your brother, I know it all too well, but it's usually work stuff. I knew when I got involved with him there were things he couldn't talk about, and in fairness, back then, I had wealthy clients who'd sue my ass if I broke confidentiality. But you're not talking about Finn, you're talking about the sexy bartender I've got working for me. Don't think I haven't noticed how that man looks at you."

I put Lena on speakerphone as I walked inside the house and locked the door. "It can't go anywhere, Lena."

She gasped. "You had sex with him, didn't you?"

"Not exactly, I mean we... *fooled around*—"

"When?"

"I needed someone to get me out of my Fort Knox shirt you had me tied into." I smiled to myself, and heat rushed to my cheeks as I thought of Rhett's mouth on me. "He passed on sex because he thought I was drunk."

"You *were* drunk! But see? He's actually a good guy, Frankie. If there's something you want to know, just talk to him. I think he's just private about stuff, but he's into you."

She had no idea who Rhett really was. "For now." I draped my jacket over a chair and pulled the living room curtains shut, peeking through the gap. The street was quiet as the streetlights came on earlier than normal. Perhaps with Clay gone, everything would be okay.

"Still there?" Lena's voice pulled me back from my thoughts.

"Will you go to Clay's funeral?" I asked.

"Fuck, I think we might have to."

"I think so too. I'd never wish this on anyone," I said. "I couldn't stand the man, but I feel... I feel like what happened to Miles is coming back to haunt me, and it hurts."

"I'm here for you, sweetie, you're like my sister."

"Hey, maybe I will be someday."

"Christ, if your brother gets his shit together... Doesn't matter, you won't lose me."

"Back at you, Lena." I opened the fridge, rummaging for food, but settled on cheese and crackers, and made a pot of coffee. "I'm hanging up, but I'll talk to you later."

"Will I see you at your parents' for dinner tomorrow?"

"Maybe." I sat on a stool. "Depends on how crazy my shift is."

"Okay, well, I love you."

"Love you, too."

The phone line went quiet, and I glanced at Rhett's last message.

Did you make it home? Please answer me. I said please.

I had so much more I wanted to ask him about his family, the night my brother died, the photo... but kept my response simple. *I'm home safe.*

Dropping the USB stick on the counter, I traced the rips in my jeans as I drank my coffee. What good was an encrypted memory stick without access to the password?

Magpies mate for life.

My head snapped up.

"Oh my god."

Thirty-One

Frankie

Hunched over my laptop perched on the counter with the USB stick plugged in, and the photo of Miles and Clay propped against it, I typed a few versions of 'magpie'. When none of my attempts worked, I sat back and downed the rest of my coffee. I capitalized the first word, typing, Magpiesmateforlife.

I gasped, my hand flying to my mouth as countless folders suddenly filled the screen. The labels containing dates and names

I didn't recognize, financial and shipyard import ledgers, audio clips, images, all swam before my eyes as I scrolled. I paused at a folder named 'where the bodies are.'

Jesus Christ, Miles. What the fuck were you involved in?

I hesitated with the cursor hovering over the folder. I had seen dead people. I'd prepared them for the morgue, taking the utmost care to make sure that respect was carried out in their death. But these dead bodies could traumatize me, and did I need more trauma in my life?

I clicked the folder open.

A handful of murdered bodies populated small images, and ignoring the warning bells screaming in my head, I clicked them open. I viewed three images of distorted, bloodied bodies, their hollowed sockets where eyes should've been staring blankly ahead, their mouths gaping in silent screams, before my stomach lurched, and I closed them all.

With a heavy exhale, I opened the document at the bottom called 'map.' Arrows showed locations in Massachusetts, each bearing the names of the deceased and their murderers. I scanned the map, hunting for Everett Morrigan, Miles Roscoe, and Clay Preston, my breath catching in relief when I found none of their names.

I read through union contracts, some signed by a Noble, others by a Morrigan, financial documents and companies used to 'wash' money, authored by Clay Preston. The evidence Miles had on the memory stick incriminated a slew of people, including prestigious members in politics and dirty cops.

I scanned through the files, reading documents until my eyes burned with strain and my face ached, tight with focused concentration. I held my breath as I opened a 'kill list' document, but this time, two names gripped my chest.

Everett Morrigan. Miles Roscoe.

They'd gotten Miles, but would Rhett still be a target after two years? He'd mentioned returning to Boston tomorrow. I couldn't let that happen.

I slid off the stool and grabbed a can of ginger ale from the fridge to calm my anxious stomach. Clay must have known the USB existed. I resumed my perch on the stool and sorted through the audio files.

My heart skipped a beat when I clicked open the first folder.

For Francesca Roscoe only.

Miles had left me a message. Shaking, I turned up the volume on the laptop. My pulse thudded a heavy beat in my ears, and I couldn't breathe. Double-clicking the file, I stilled as static cut through the quiet in the kitchen.

His voice came through the speaker, and I choked on sobs ripping through my chest. "If you're listening to this... fuck, I can't believe I'm recording this," Miles said, his voice a low rumble through the laptop. I stopped breathing, holding the air in my lungs. "I'm sorry, Frankie, I didn't pull it off. If you're hearing me from the grave right now, I need you to know I love you, Finn, and Mom and Dad." His voice cracked, but he composed himself. "I know how hard you all tried to help, but my shitty decisions are mine, so if you're sitting there somewhere feeling sad because of me, *stop*. Do all the things you talked about, keep making music, and buy that grand piano you've always wanted. Oh, and if a man ever treats you like shit again, I'll haunt his ass," he chuckled, stopping himself, and I caught myself doing the same through a snotty nose and tears. "Fuck, I'm morbid. Okay, I'm wrapping this up before I'm a blubbering mess. I've got a job at the warehouse tonight and a really bad feeling things aren't gonna go down the way I want, but I need you to know this. Don't break Finn's balls too much, he's a pain in the ass sometimes, but he means well. He made a friend—I know, I didn't believe it either, but Everett is one of the few I trust in all this shit... So if he dies tonight too, and our brother is struggling, go easy on him. Your ex, Preston? A bigger dickhead than you know, I don't know why I trusted the son of a bitch, but I did, so he knows about this. I just hope I hide it well enough he doesn't find it before you do, and if he does? He'll never get into it. I knew you'd figure it out, magpies mate for life. I never found mine, but I sure as hell hope you find yours. Shit, I'm late. I gotta go. You're always cooler than me. I love you."

The message ended, the sudden deafening silence only broken by my ragged sobs.

A knock echoed from the patio door, and I jumped off the stool, my foot catching on its legs. Clutching Rhett's gun in my trembling hand, I hurried to the doors and yanked back the blinds, snapping the cords.

Rhett's muffled voice came through the door. "Open the door, Frankie." His hands gripped the handle as I unlocked it, and he slid the door open, rushing inside. "What happened?" He took the gun from my hand and placed it on the table as I broke down in tears.

Embracing me, he surveyed the kitchen, and his gaze fell on the open laptop as he walked toward the living room with me in his arms. "Are you alone?"

I nodded, burying my face in his chest. "Yes." I wrapped my arms around him, pulling him against me so tightly I could feel his heartbeat, letting myself fall apart.

"I've got you," he whispered, stroking my hair. "Can you tell me what's going on? What'd you see on that stick?"

I leaned back, craning my neck as I gazed up at him. "Everything. I heard Miles, he knew he might die that night."

"Jesus Christ." He kissed my forehead and enveloped me in a hug. "I'm sorry I'm so late, I should've gotten to you sooner. Tell me what I can do."

"Tell me *everything* and don't hold back. Don't just answer questions... *tell* me."

Lines deepened along his forehead as he scrutinized my face. "All of it, sure."

Sniffling, I choked back the tears, and stepped away from him, grabbing a handful of tissues. "If I'm going to trust you, really trust you, there can be no more secrets between us, none."

"I'm all yours," he said.

"Where have you been? It's been hours." Throwing the tissues in the trash, I picked up my ginger ale and sat on the stool in front of the laptop.

"The police had more questions than I expected, and Finn—"

"Where's he now?"

"As of right now, he should be home with Lena." I snatched the photo with the tattooed arm in the background before I lost my nerve and handed it to him. "What's this?"

"That man isn't you, is it?" I pointed to the tattooed arm holding a cue. "It's the same, but the position is different."

"No, it's not me."

I tugged at his jacket sleeve. "Take it off."

He slid his jacket off and lifted the sleeve of his sweater. The black nylon stitches stood out against the reddened skin; one had come undone as the wound had healed. They needed to be taken out, but I needed answers more.

"The man in that picture has the same tattoo."

Conflict raged behind his intense eyes, and his jawline twitched as he looked at me. "The first thing my father did when I graduated college was take me to get that fucking tattoo, so I would never forget where I came from. Back then, it meant I finally belonged somewhere. I was part of a family who had my back, no matter what. I failed to see the conditions attached."

My breathing slowed into a non-panicked rhythm. I knew he was telling the truth with a certainty that settled in my chest. "What does it mean now?"

"It's my daily fucking reminder I don't belong anywhere. It's nothing more than a branding to silence those who have it. If you work for him, you don't refuse it, but once you've got it, it's for life."

I took the photograph from his fingers. "If this isn't you, who is it?"

He didn't take his eyes off mine. "That man is my father or someone who works for him, but I promise you, it isn't me."

The relief sank into my bones, soothing my fears. It didn't matter how wrong he was for me, or what he'd done, I wanted to trust Rhett and didn't want to lose him. I wanted *him*. "Did you know Clay Preston before Willow Grove?"

"I met Clay Preston at the Magpie when I came to town, with no idea who the fuck he was other than I wouldn't trust him with a goddamn stick of wood." He hesitated for a moment before speaking again. "But I did know you before Willow Grove."

"How? We've never met—"

"No, we haven't. But I was at the hospital when you held Miles on that stretcher. I saw a woman in agonizing grief, and I walked away. That was the night I left everything behind. Frankie, I never thought I'd see you again, I sure as hell didn't think a day would come where we'd be,"—he stopped abruptly and cleared his throat—"where we'd meet."

He'd been there on the worst night of my life and never said a word. "And you couldn't tell me because god forbid I know the truth about Miles, or you and Finn. You should have said something to me, Rhett."

"You're right, I should've." He swiveled on the stool, shifting his legs so they were touching mine. "We wanted you safe, that's the only reason, Frankie." He looked at me with unguarded honesty. "I swear I'm telling the truth."

I waited for my anger to return like it had when he'd confessed the truth about Miles, but all I felt was aching sadness. I missed my brother, and nothing any of us did would bring him back.

"I was late coming home to you tonight because the police were busy informing me they know who I really am," Rhett said. "Finn got me out of that little mess, but now that I'm here, I'm not planning on leaving your side."

"Until you go to Boston."

"That depends on where Noble is, but if I go, I'll come back." His eyes darted from me to the laptop, and his brows furrowed. The audio clip box filled the laptop screen.

I held his face, turning him so he faced me. "Will you sit outside the hospital for twelve hours while I'm at work tomorrow too? Maybe this ends with Clay's death. I can't hide away and not live my life."

"It's not over." Taking my fingers in his hand, he held them against his chest, glancing at the laptop. "Baby, what did you find on that memory device? Can you fill me in on a few things too?"

I pivoted the laptop so he could see the screen and let him scroll through the contents on the USB stick. We sat next to each other in silence as he reviewed folders and documents.

He pointed to the 'where the bodies are' folder. "Did you look at these?"

"Just a few. I couldn't do it and not throw up."

Nodding, he shifted the screen out of my view. The light from the laptop cast a glow over his stern features as he looked through the photos. "Fuck me. There's enough evidence in just this folder to put some people away... the ones still alive anyway."

"I noticed your name isn't there."

"Of course it's not," he said.

I wasn't sure if that meant he hadn't killed anyone other than Noble's son, or if he'd just been more careful and didn't make Miles's list. I didn't ask. Right or wrong, I didn't want to know.

"What made you cry?" he said softly, his voice laced with concern.

I replayed Miles's message and left the counter, turning my back to him as I stared out of the patio door. Darkness had consumed the backyard, and the patter of rain tapped the glass. As my brother's voice filled the room again, the ache returned, starting in my chest and radiating toward the back of my neck. I couldn't control the tears, and the only way to relieve the lump in my throat was to let them fall.

Footsteps came closer as the recording stopped. Rhett wrapped his arms around me, taking my hands. He kissed my cheek, his lips lingering near my ear. "I'm so sorry, Frankie."

Turning in his arms, I guided his hands around my waist, my gaze locked on his face. I traced his jawline with my fingertips, drifting to touch his lips. "I believe you."

He kissed my fingers, and I pulled his mouth against mine, our lips moving in sync with each other. As his hands moved up my arms, I caught sight of his wound and pulled away, holding his arm. "Those stitches need to come out."

He eyed his arm and shrugged. "I'll rip them out later."

"*Rip?* You're not doing that, I'll do it."

"I don't need you—"

"It'll take five minutes." I headed into the main bathroom for my first aid kit and returned to the kitchen.

He folded his arms as I turned on the tap in the kitchen sink and washed the first-aid scissors with soap. I rubbed an alcohol wipe over the silver blades, his eyes on me the entire time. Heat crept up my back, settling into my neck. I suddenly longed for him to take me upstairs and kiss me until I couldn't breathe. I yearned for the weight of his body against mine.

As he moved closer, his cologne intensified. "You smell good," I said. "I'm going to need a little space if I'm to focus on taking those threads out of your skin instead of pressing my face against your shirt, inhaling like an idiot."

"Inhaling like an idiot sounds more fun. Is all that necessary?" As he leaned on the counter, his arm muscles tightened, making the tattooed cloaked figure on his forearm appear animated.

He doesn't feel like he belongs anywhere.

"If you want to avoid infection, yes."

With his face inches from mine, he eyed my hands as I washed and dried them with a paper towel. The heat between us could ignite a fire. Sweat pricked the back of my neck. "Want to sit down while I do this?" My breath caught in my throat.

"Here's fine." He rested his arm on the counter's surface. "Frankie—"

"Rhett." My fingers slipped as I opened the pack of gauze, and I nearly poked my finger through the gloves as I yanked them over my hand. I was never clumsy at work, *never*, but with emotions so raw they made me tremble, I was struggling. I worked fast, and my hand didn't betray me, holding steady enough as I used an antiseptic wipe over his healed wound.

"I have a question," he said.

"Go for it." If I lifted my head slightly, our lips would touch, and if I started kissing him again, I wouldn't be able to stop.

"How did you figure out Miles's password?"

I paused, lifting the wipe off his skin. "He named the bar when Lena bought it."

"The Magpie? Was that it?"

"Close... Magpies mate for life." I cleared my throat to keep the tears from building. "Miles thought they were cool, we thought it was hilarious, and that was how I unlocked his secrets."

His jaw twitched as his lips pursed, an attractive habit I'd noticed him do since we'd met, but only now understood this was Rhett's expression when he was deep in thought. "Good work, Frankie. What are you going to do with it?"

"I'm going to look through every single thing inside those files... except the dead bodies, maybe you can take those—"

"Sure, but why not just give it to Finn?"

I gripped his arm. "I need to make sure there's nothing on that thing that can incriminate you."

"I don't want you to do that for me," he said, furrowing his brows.

"I'm not asking permission. Miles trusted you, Finn trusts you. Even before I knew that I fucking trusted you." Stretching my neck from side to side, I positioned the scissors. "Ready?"

He spoke in a low tone. "I'm never not ready."

"I've gathered." Cutting the first knot against his skin, I worked my way along each stitch, tracing the area with a gloved finger, and dared to glance up at him. "Does it hurt?"

"Nope." His gaze fell to my lips, and I suppressed the need to reach behind my neck and wipe the perspiration away.

I averted my eyes to the first aid kit, searching for tweezers, but found none. "Shit."

"Something wrong?" he asked.

The stubborn thread slipped through my gloved fingers as I tried to pull it away, remaining intact in his skin. Heat from his arm radiated through the glove to my skin as our eyes met. "I need to take my glove off to pull the thread out—my hands are clean, it's just... I don't have tweezers and—"

"Do what you have to, I trust you."

"Good." I smiled and removed my glove. I plucked the last stitch from his arm and discarded the remnants in the trash. "All done, better than ripping them out yourself."

He straightened his posture as I curled my fingers around his arm and examined the reddened area. "It'll leave a scar."

"I can handle scars." He took a step closer. The simmering tension grew more intense than at any other time we'd kissed... or when he'd kissed *me* the night before.

"Scars are the easy part," I said. "They just mean you got through something painful." A shallow breath caught in my throat as I spoke, and my pulse was a frantic drum in my chest.

I gave in to the desire to grab his shirt and bridge the gap between us. Tilting my head back, I placed my hand on his chest, feeling the steady rhythm of his breathing. His hands moved down my back, intensifying the heat low in my belly as our bodies touched, steadying me against the counter.

I traced the dark silhouette on his arm and lingered on his scar. "You belong here with me," I whispered.

THIRTY-TWO

Frankie

R hett inched closer with a slow lick of his lips, his breath warm on my face, and I rose on my tiptoes, sliding my hand around the back of his neck. Grabbing my waist, he lifted me onto the counter.

I ran my fingers through his hair as a desperate need for his touch ignited over my skin. I craved him. *All of him*. "I want your hands on me again."

"Done." His hands trailed up my arms to my face, leaving a path of tingling warmth. He brushed his thumb over my bottom lip, and I held him tighter. I stared at his mouth, wanting it on mine. He caught my lip between his teeth and kissed me. Rough. Demanding. And I matched his pace.

He gripped the edge of the counter as I wrapped my legs around him. I ran my fingers over his tight stomach and chest, sliding his sweater up as high as I could. "Take it off," I breathed.

Tugging it over his head, he dropped it on the floor. Breathless, I held his face close to mine, my mouth greedy for more of him. I couldn't get close enough to this man. He tangled his fingers in my hair, tilting my head back to trail kisses along my neck and jaw until his mouth found mine again.

With a sharp inhale, he stopped and brushed strands of hair off my forehead. His closeness intoxicated me.

"I'm sober. You can take what you want," I said. There was nothing I wanted more.

"I don't have anything on me—"

"I do, upstairs in my drawer, and I'm on the pill."

His hands on me and the scent of his cologne mixed with rain would forever remain etched in my memory. I touched his jawline, letting my fingers linger. "Say fuck it and take me upstairs."

He kissed my hand, his familiar stubble tickling my skin. "Fuck it." His arms encircled me, the heat of his skin burning through my clothes like wildfire, and he carried me upstairs. The strong, reassuring strength of his arms made me feel *safe*.

A streetlight cast long shadows through the window across my bedroom, highlighting Rhett's unwavering gaze. He set me down and slid my shirt over my head. My hair crackled with static as it clung to my cheeks, mimicking every nerve in my body.

I kissed him, our tongues exploring and tasting, begging for more. His hands roamed my body before slowly making their way up to my breasts. "I don't want to let you go." His breath hitched between kisses.

"So don't." I gasped as his thumb traced circles over the lace of my bra. Safe in Rhett's arms, with the truth finally free, I gave in to what I wanted and let go of everything else. I unbuttoned his jeans, pushing them down with his boxers as he kissed my neck. Closing my hand around his hard length, I glanced up at him, demanding his attention with my eyes. "I need you naked with me tonight."

A low grunt escaped him, and he moved against my hand as I stroked him. "I'm all yours." His fingers trailed up my back, sending shivers through me as he unhooked my bra with one hand. "This needs to go, baby." As he slid the straps off my shoulders, his lips eagerly sought my breasts, and I moaned, releasing my hold on him.

His erection pressed against me as his arm tightened around my waist, lowering me to the bed. He braced himself with his hands on either side of my head. "Look at me." His eyes locked on mine as I lifted my gaze. "You are the most beautiful woman I've ever laid eyes on. I've wanted you since the day I met you in that fucking coffee shop."

I dragged my hands up the ridged muscles of his back. "I want you too, I can't seem to get enough of you."

His breath tickled my face as his mouth hovered close to mine, and I clung to his body. I ran my fingers along the curves in his muscles over his back and along his ass, feeling his chest rise and fall against my own. He took his time kissing me, letting his lips linger on mine. Unzipping my jeans, he slid them off my legs and parted my thighs, slowly running his fingers over my panties. I whimpered as he lowered himself on top of me. The weight of his body against mine sent a tormenting pressure of warmth through me. I traced his lips with my tongue, and a moan rumbled in his chest as he kissed me harder and my want turned into frenzied *need*.

His fingers trailed along my leg, and I arched against him, the rough texture of his hand a contrast to the smooth skin of my inner thigh. "Spread your legs more for me."

"Like this?" I whispered, letting my knees fall onto the bed.

"You're perfect." He slid my panties to the side and brushed his knuckles against my sensitive entrance.

I moaned, surrendering to his touch. "More Rhett... *please*." I throbbed as he dragged his fingers against me, rubbing in slow circles, and arousal pooled between my legs.

"I'll give you whatever you want." He hooked his fingers around the sides of my panties, tugging the silky fabric over my skin.

With my foot on his chest, his lips brushed along my calf, and I extended my arm toward the side table before I ended up too carried away to give a shit. "*Condom*," I said, breathless. I twisted to the side, and his hand kneaded my ass, moving down my thigh as I rummaged in the cluttered drawer. "Fuck, I know I've got them."

He shifted his weight, regaining his position on top of me, cupping my breasts, kissing and sucking each one. "Need help?" His voice was tight as the undeniable proof of his arousal pressed against my stomach.

Protection. That box better still be in there.

"No, don't you dare stop." My breath hitched as his hands moved down my stomach, touching me between my legs. I was losing focus as I searched for a damn condom.

He kissed along my thighs. "Oh, I fucking won't, I want to feel all of you." He dipped a finger inside me, and I cried out, a gasp of pleasure escaping my lips as another finger followed.

My eyes shut as my hand found the scattered packets in the back of the drawer. "Jesus." I released a shuddering exhale of pleasure. "Take this now." He pulled his fingers away, leaving me empty with a desperate urge to yell at him to hurry.

I needed him inside me. Close to me. I needed his body rocking against mine.

He tore the pack open with his teeth and rolled the condom down himself. "Come here," he groaned, pressing my thighs apart, settling between them.

My fingernails dragged up his back as I pulled him onto me, and his lips found mine with urgency. With a firm grip on my hips, he guided himself to my entrance, inching inside slowly as his body tensed against mine. "Fuck, baby."

"Keep going," I whispered. He hooked an arm under my knee, bending my leg against his side as he thrust deeper into me, releasing a moan. The sight of Rhett letting go of his usual control, with his body pressed close to mine, sent a wave of pleasure through me, pushing me toward the edge quicker than I'd ever thought possible.

I grabbed his ass, pressing myself closer to him. The sweat on our bodies created a sweet friction as we thrust in rhythm together. He fisted my hair, kissing a burning path along my jawline, and our eyes locked as our movements quickened.

"You feel so fucking good, Frankie."

"Don't stop." The words escaped in a furious rush as he stole my moans with his mouth.

"Come for me." The low groan rumbled in his chest between his panting breaths.

He had to know what he was doing to me. "Take me there."

Sliding a hand between us, he rubbed a finger over my sensitive clit, and leaned forward, thrusting into me deeper. "I've got you, let go."

The pulsing deep in my core overwhelmed me, and I breathed like I'd run a marathon. Arousal intensified into a tidal wave of an orgasm. Gripping the sheets with one hand and his arm with the other, I cried out his name. My legs trembled as I spasmed around him and tension left every muscle in my body.

He kissed each breast before claiming my mouth again. "Feel good?"

"So damn good." I wrapped my legs around him, holding him inside me. Arching against him, I exhaled. "But I'm not done. It's your turn. I want to see you let go for *me*."

His eyes glazed over, darkening with lust as they locked onto mine. "I think you already know I'll give you what you want."

"So you've said. Show me, Rhett."

He withdrew just a little and pushed inside me again. I moaned in his ear, and his eyelids fluttered shut as his breaths quickened. He thrust faster. Harder. And bracing his taut body against mine, he grunted and twitched as he came. "*Fuck me.*"

"Looks like I just did."

With a slow exhale, he slumped down next to me, holding me close as he kissed my forehead.

I wished the blissful stillness with him in my bed would last forever, but even mind-blowing sex couldn't make me delusional enough to believe that was possible. Moments like these always ended, but I held onto him tighter and kissed his face. I placed my hand on his chest as his fingers traced over my back, sending shivers along my skin.

He tugged a blanket over me. "Are you cold?"

"I have to go to the bathroom, but don't want to let my feet touch the floor yet."

"Why not?" His gaze fell on my eyes, and he brushed the damp strands of hair off my face.

"As soon as I do, this will be over, and despite everything happening right now, I had fun."

He squinted, furrowing his brow as he smiled, and I immediately regretted the use of the word *fun*. "What I meant to say is—"

"I had fun too." He tilted my chin up as he brought his lips to mine, his expression serious. "Despite everything that's happening, you keep me going. I'm not letting you go."

I wanted to believe he would stay, keeping his promise, but I couldn't see past this moment tangled in the sheets with the man I never wanted to leave.

Thirty-Three

Rhett

Frankie stirred in the bed beside me and turned on her side, facing me. Her hair fell over her beautiful face as she slept. The sun hadn't come up yet, but waking up next to this woman might turn into the first habit I'd never be able to quit.

Fuck.

Maybe I could start over and stick around in one place, have a life without looking over my shoulder every day. I just had a few problems to solve first, but the information on Miles's USB would help my family regain control, getting rid of barriers in our way. In the brief time I searched the folders, I hadn't found my name on any documents, but I trusted Miles would've kept that shit off the USB. If Bran had attended an event last night like Vivian had said, who'd murdered Preston? Clay never admitted he worked for the Nobles, but he'd been photographed with my family, with Miles, and if he had set his sights on that USB, what had he planned to do with it? Use it for blackmail and a way out?

As Frankie snored, I reached for my phone, dimming the screen. I still hadn't gotten a response from Vivian and had a heaviness in my gut that told me something was wrong.

Music blared from Frankie's phone on the side table, and she stretched an arm over her head. The light shone on her face, and she squinted her eyes against the glare. Last night, those same blue eyes looked into mine, craving every inch of me. She saw good in me I hadn't believed existed.

Frankie pressed a button, setting her phone face down on the table, and the music stopped. She flopped back on the bed and yanked the covers over her shoulders as she faced me. Her eyes blinked slowly, closing for a moment, and she snuggled against me. "Having you in my bed is making it hard to get up."

I wrapped my arms around her naked body, pulling her closer. "What time do you leave for work?"

"Six thirty," she said, yawning.

"Or you could just stay here, and we could have more... *fun*." I didn't wait for her to respond, and grabbed her face, kissing her.

Her soft skin rubbed against me as she shifted, melting into me. I was ready for round two.

She pulled away, a mischievous glint in her eyes as she smiled. "Trust me," she said, kissing me again as her fingers ran through my hair and down my neck. I traced my fingers over her back, feeling the goosebumps rise beneath my touch. "I would prefer to stay in bed with you for all the fun, but—"

"Work." I held her, inhaling the scent of shampoo lingering in her hair and whatever perfume she wore that still clung to her warm skin.

"Shower first, then work." Her lips moved against mine as she talked, and for a woman who never lost focus, I enjoyed being her distraction.

"You want breakfast? Coffee?"

"No time, I'll stop on the way." She eased herself out of my arms, sinking onto the pillows, and the sheet slid down, barely concealing her tits.

Frankie had gotten caught up in a world that she shouldn't have been a part of, and I wasn't letting her leave the house alone. Not until I knew without a doubt who killed Clay and where he was hiding. I sat up, and her hand touched my back as I reached for my shirt at the foot of the bed, yanking it over my head. "I'll drive you and pick you up, you're not going alone."

"I'll be fine—"

"That's the problem, fine isn't good enough." Standing, I grabbed my underwear and jeans from a pile on the floor and dressed like the room was on fire.

"Rhett, you can't just be my bodyguard, joined at my hip everywhere I go until they find out who murdered Clay. It's just from here to work and back home. The parking lot is gated, I use my ID card to get in."

Kneeling beside her, I brushed the hair from her face and took her hand in mine. "Baby, a gate won't keep them away from what they want, trust me."

She squeezed my fingers. "I'll text as soon as I get to work, and when I'm on my way home, but I'm driving myself."

"I don't like it." I had fallen for this woman. *Hard.* "If you're driving, I'm following you on my way to the bar."

"What about Boston?" The sheet fell down her body as she sat up and swung her legs over the side of the bed. She reached for the corner of a blanket to cover herself.

I kissed her. "I'll let you know if I go, but I'll be back in time to meet you at the hospital when you're off work."

Releasing the blanket, she got up and wrapped her arms around my waist. My hands instinctively cupped her ass, holding her against me.

"I'm going to be okay," she said. "Now let me go shower." Planting a kiss on my lips, she walked toward the bathroom, leaving me standing there, rock-hard in my jeans like an obsessed idiot. "I'll be quick," she called.

All I could think about was having my hands on her curves, her ass, wrapping her legs around my waist again, kissing every inch of her. Adjusting my hard-on, I headed downstairs into the kitchen.

Rain hammered the deck, blowing sideways on the windows, and dark clouds blocked out the rising sun.

I wandered into the living room where a picture of her brother sat on a corner bookshelf. I hadn't been able to protect him. What if I failed to keep *her* safe if they found me? Pushing the curtains aside, I surveyed the quiet street. A hairdryer hummed upstairs, breaking the silence as I moved into the kitchen. The gun lay on the table, and I tucked it into my waistband. I'd fucked up leaving the gun sitting out in the open, and the USB plugged into an open laptop on the counter, but last night with Frankie had knocked me off guard, and despite knowing better, I'd do it all over again.

She didn't have her laptop password protected, and I typed in 'Magpiesmateforlife,' picking up where I'd left off, scouring through documents and files. I'd run a tight business for my father, but there were documents exposing high-profile people and the depth of their involvement with the mob that even I hadn't realized.

I clicked the button to eject the memory stick, removing it from the laptop as the stairs creaked and handed it to Frankie as she approached. "Put it somewhere safe or give it to your brother."

Taking the device from my fingers, she opened the basket of the coffeemaker and dropped it inside. "I will make sure your name isn't anywhere on there—"

"I'm not, Frankie. I trusted Miles, and I looked. There's nothing to worry about, hand it over."

Sweeping her hair off her face, she secured it with an elastic, smoothing out the dark strands. "I need to see for myself."

She reached for her jacket, but I grabbed it first, holding it up. "You're being stubborn. I don't like that thing in your house—if anyone else knows it's here, nothing's stopping them from coming for it."

"I've got to go." Glancing around the kitchen, she approached the table. "Where's the gun?"

I lifted my jacket and pointed to the handle sticking out of my jeans, and she ran her fingers over it. She gripped my jacket, her hands bunching the fabric as she pulled herself up and kissed me. "Maybe you should leave it with me."

"Take it, keep it in the Jeep."

"I'm kidding," she laughed, straightening my jacket.

"I'm not." I followed her into the garage, and she locked the door behind me as I pressed the button to raise the garage door.

"I don't want a gun in my Jeep while I'm at work all day."

I held the driver's side door open for her, and she climbed in, bringing the engine to life. She backed out, closing the garage, and rolled her window down. "Wait for me," I said.

Rain pelted my face, soaking my clothes as I jogged to my place for my truck, pulling up behind her as she parked along the side of our street.

My phone rang after twenty minutes of keeping pace with her. *Her.*

"Miss me already?" I asked.

"Always. I'm going through our Danish shop drive-thru for coffee, take your turnoff for the Magpie, I'm good."

"Have a good shift, and don't leave until I get there."

"More orders?" she teased.

"Get good at them."

"Yeah, yeah, bye, Rhett."

"Please be safe, Frankie."

"I will."

The line went dead as she drove through a green light, and I turned right toward the bar. Frankie had me, and there wasn't a damn thing I could do to stop myself from wanting her, but she didn't belong in my world. I'd have to find a way to belong in hers.

Thirty-Four

Frankie

B etween the dark clouds swallowing daylight and the wipers losing their battle against the rain, my vision through the windshield was a useless blur. Only two other vehicles idled in front of me at Java Brew's drive-thru when I drove into the parking lot. Headlights glared in my rearview mirror as an SUV pulled up behind me, and I braked too hard, sending my purse flying off the passenger seat. I maneuvered closer to a van as they reached the speaker, unbuckling my seatbelt so I could gather the contents of my purse scattered on the floor.

Throwing my Jeep into park, I scooted over and leaned down. The driver's side door swung open, and a man shoved me face-down onto the passenger seat, slamming the door shut.

"What the hell!" I scrambled upright and screamed, but a massive hand clamped over my mouth, stifling the sound.

"Two choices, bitch," he grumbled. "Shut the fuck up or die." Wearing a black knit hat pulled over his brows, the man grabbed my hair and banged my head off the dash as the Jeep lurched forward. High-pitched ringing echoed in my ears, drowning out my thumping pulse as I fought to sit on the seat.

Think.

Driving out of the parking lot with one hand on the wheel, he reached across the console and smacked my face. I winced as pain throbbed along my cheek. "What do you want?"

He aimed a Glock at my chest, the barrel digging into my ribs. "If you speak or move, I will kill you." He spoke slowly with eerie calmness, and his eyes held a lethal gaze, darting from me to the windshield. Recognition sank into me.

Bran Noble. Trash flowers guy, son of my patient, mobster.

My mind spun out of control as I grappled with the stubborn door handle, but he hit me again, this time so hard the coppery taste of blood oozed from my lip into my mouth. Hot, relentless tears stung my eyes and ran down my cheeks. If this was the man who'd murdered Clay, I wasn't getting out of this alive. "I know you. Bran Noble, right? Where are you taking me?"

"Wrong choice." A chilling glint sparked in his eyes as he smiled. Steering the car with his knees, he reached for me again. I clawed at his arms, kicking and screaming, as his elbow connected with my temple.

He revved the engine, and the Jeep sped up, but the sound faded into a muffled hum as dizziness overwhelmed me, my vision tunneled into darkness.

Images of Rhett and me wrapped up in each other last night flashed in my mind as I struggled to take a deep breath, my lungs on fire. My body went numb, and I couldn't move, plunging into the black abyss of nothing. I'd witnessed humans survive horrible life-threatening shit... I just never imagined Death would come knocking on my door so soon.

Why didn't I let him drive me to work?

Gravel crunched under the Jeep's tires as it jerked and bounced over uneven ground. Radiating pain coursed through my head and into my chest, but I stayed still with my eyes shut. If that man hit me again, the force of the blow could be the end of me.

As the Jeep came to a halt, Noble opened the door, and a blast of cold air sent chills over my body. The rush of water surged from somewhere outside. Close to the river?

Seizing my legs, he dragged me out of the Jeep, dropping me in a pile on a gravel driveway. Coughing, I pushed myself up with my hands as blood trickled off my chin, mixing with the rain to paint the rocks crimson.

The SUV pulled up, and another, taller man got out. They both flanked my sides, and the tall guy rummaged through my purse.

Noble hoisted me to my feet with rough hands, forcing me toward a crumbling building. I glanced up at the smashed windows and lost my balance, slipping through his grasp to the ground. "I don't know anything—"

He jerked me up off the ground like I was a rag doll. He dug his fingers into my arms, and a wave of nausea sent bile creeping up my throat. My parents wouldn't survive a police officer arriving at their door again.

The taller man held the door open, and Noble shoved me inside the dark building, tearing my jacket off. He kicked my lower back, and a jolt of pain shot down my legs as I stumbled to the cement floor. Dim light filtered through shattered windows, casting shadows on the peeling walls. I couldn't let them kill me. Adrenaline shot through me, and I clambered to my feet, stumbling toward a rusted staircase in the corner. I clung to the cold metal railing, my heart pounding as hands snaked into my hair and pulled me back with surprising force.

Grinding my teeth, I punched behind me, elbowing him and connecting my feet with any part of his body that I could. A guttural scream tore from my throat, leaving me breathless and broken, dissolving into shuddering sobs. "Let me go you piece of shit fucker!"

He smacked me across the face, and warmth trickled along my chin, igniting a surge of determination to keep fighting. If I didn't do something, *anything*, I wouldn't survive. I raked his wrists with my fingernails, drawing blood, and he released my hair, tossing me to the floor.

I wiped my mouth as I sat up, leaning against an overturned garbage can. "Why are you doing this," I choked. "Killing Clay wasn't enough?"

The taller man held my phone in my face and grabbed my fingers, squeezing them until they hurt. "Unlock it."

Noble loomed over me, aiming his gun at my head. "Do what he says."

Tears stung the open wounds in my skin, mixing with blood. Dizziness came in waves as my vision faltered. I was sure I had a concussion and needed stitches... unless I left this rotting building in a body bag. My hand trembled as I held my thumb on the fingerprint scanner to unlock my phone. He made me do it again to remove my password. "What are you going to do with it?"

The gun remained pointed at my head as they looked at my phone, but I reached for the railing to stand. Noble crouched in front of me, and I flopped back down. The back of his hand stroked my face, and I recoiled, turning my cheek until it touched the cold floor.

He dragged the gun down my bare arm, and my breathing hitched through stifled sobs. I wasn't strong enough to save myself from whatever horrors they had planned for me. With the gun in his hand, he grabbed my scrub top, ripping the fabric as he pulled me to my feet.

The taller man advanced, flicking my bra strap so hard it stung my bare shoulder. "Fuck, you're a pretty one."

"You're fucking disgusting!" I squirmed, struggling against Noble's tight, painful grasp.

He handed me over to the taller man, and my eyes widened as a sinister smirk twisted his face. I screamed and punched at him, but he slapped my face and spun me around, pinning me against the wall. "I'll play rough if that's what you want," he said in my ear as he scraped my face along the brick and yanked my hands behind my back.

They're going to rape me.

"Please don't... don't do this, I'll tell you whatever you want to know, just please don't do this," I sobbed.

He tied rope around my wrists, pulling so hard it burned my skin raw. The cracking of knuckles sent a shiver through me, and the taller man grabbed my bound hands, turning me around. Light from my phone in Noble's hand illuminated iron steps leading down into a basement. No one would hear me scream if they got me down there...

My fingers twitched, aching to escape the taller man's crushing grip as he dragged me down the stairs. "What do you want from me!" I forced myself backward, leaning away, doing anything I could to stop him.

The man's knee collided with my back, and a searing pain ripped through me, forcing a grunt of agony from my chest. Water dripped somewhere, clanging off metal pipes, and the *smell*. The acrid stench of death, a sickeningly familiar smell of decay and blood, brought a fresh wave of nausea. My mouth flooded with saliva, and I couldn't breathe air into my burning lungs.

I was trapped. I was *nothing* against them, and they held all the cards. "Do you have families? Kids?" I pleaded. "Is there anyone you actually care about? Because I'm someone's daughter, I'm a nurse who helps people—"

Noble held a finger to his lips and winked. "*Shhh,*" he hushed.

I froze, glaring at him. Rhett's tattoo flashed in my mind.

Leading me to a pipe running from the floor to the ceiling, the taller man kicked the back of my knees, knocking me face down on the floor, and my teeth clattered together. Tiny lights flashed in my eyes as thudding pain ached behind my neck and along my scalp. He wrapped rope around my ankles, pulling it taut along my calves. I could feel myself slipping into unconsciousness, but I forced my eyes open and breathed through the pain.

"Which one is he?" Noble squatted in front of me, grabbing my hair and forcing my face toward him.

I gasped as excruciating sharp pain sliced through my broken body.

Holding my phone close to my face, he showed me a list of my most recent chats and spoke slowly. Or my brain had stopped functioning, and everything moved in slow motion, I didn't know anymore. "I'll be honest with you, Francesca," he said.

My arms prickled with pins and needles as the rope constricted blood flow to my hands. "You know me. I helped your mom," I slurred as my vision faded in and out.

"I don't give a fuck about you." He dragged a finger over my cheek and rubbed the blood between his fingers as though torture was a set of skills to be proud of. He smeared it on top of my exposed breasts under my ripped shirt. "I want whatever name your rat boyfriend is using. He killed my son."

Digging into his chest pocket, he pulled out his phone. The screen lit up the dark basement as he angled it toward me. He gripped my hair tightly and held my head in place as a silent video played on his phone. The grainy surveillance footage showed a warehouse crammed with armed men, and blinding flashes of light erupting across the screen.

"Miles?" I choked back a sob as I watched my brother's body jolt backward behind a large man attempting to shield him and fall to the floor. I'd know that man's silhouette anywhere. *Rhett*. Finn rushed into the frame and dropped to his side as another man advanced, leveling the barrel of a gun at my brother. "No—" I cried, trying to twist away. I shut my eyes, burning with tears.

Noble tightened his grip on my hair. "Do not look away," he seethed.

My eyes fluttered open as Rhett pulled the trigger multiple times and the shooter went down in a heap. The screen went dark.

Noble released my hair, and my head fell back against the floor, striking the cement. The taller man snatched my phone and read through the contacts. "Mom, Dad, Lena, Finn... *Him*."

Darkness pressed in on me as my eyes drifted shut. I wanted to give in, but a sharp sting exploded on my cheek, startling me back to face them as his hand connected with my face.

"Whose number do you want," I whispered.

He read the last few messages between me and Rhett. "The man in that video, what's his name?"

"He's no one." I couldn't stop the tears as they drowned out my words. If they found Rhett, they'd kill him.

My hands crunched underneath me as he flung me onto my back, and I wailed. Another slap to my face sprayed blood from my mouth. They were going to kill me.

"He'll find me," I slurred, trying to convince myself as much as them, but their amused expressions broke through my painful haze.

They're using me as bait.

"Sweetheart, we can keep this up all fucking day and night, but you're wasting time." Noble grabbed my bloody chin, forcing me to look at his disgusting face as his vacant eyes regarded me like a hunter's trophy. "I have a score to settle."

"Name." The taller man raised a gun from behind his back, aiming at me as he approached, taking the safety off.

Jesus Christ, they're going to kill me.

Noble flicked a knife open as the man with the gun kicked my stomach, knocking the air from my lungs. Lifting my shirt, he cut me, dragging the blade along my skin. I screamed through the searing pain, writhing away from him. Desperation suffocated the fight in me. They wanted Rhett, and if I didn't give them his name, I was a dead woman. My body's survival instincts won the battle against death. "Rhett Marshall."

I squinted as a flash of light flooded the dark room, and he typed on my phone.

"What will you do to him?"

"Shut the fuck up." A metallic click echoed close to my ringing ears as one of them held a gun to my head and the world went black.

Thirty-Five

Rhett

I lingered behind the bar at the Magpie and poured another cup of coffee. Turning on the music, I waited for a message from Frankie. The bar was empty this early in the morning, but Lena had texted saying she and Finn were on their way. She wanted to decorate the cabinets I'd made and clean up since the police had been through.

I checked the time again, comparing the wall clock with my phone. It had been half an hour since Frankie's shift had started. I called her again and hung up before her voicemail picked up. If she didn't call or send me something letting me know she was okay within *five minutes*, I was going to the hospital.

Muffled voices grew louder from the back room, and Lena and Finn emerged through the door.

"It's a mess back there, did they have to go through the office like that?" Lena placed a box of muffins from the coffee shop on the bar, and Finn grabbed one, engrossed on his phone.

Frankie was going for coffee before the hospital. I glanced out the window as rain streamed over the glass.

Where are you?

"What's wrong," Lena said. "I don't like that look at all."

"Have you heard from Frankie?" I asked.

Leaning against the bar next to me, Lena crossed her arms. "No, why? Should I have?"

"What's going on?" Finn glanced out the window.

"She was supposed to let me know when she got to work." I scrolled through my phone as it rang. "Frankie?"

"Not Frankie, your father." My father laughed and my eyes shot up to meet Finn's.

"Where's Vivian?"

"She's fine. We had a little chat about business and what's been going on behind my back."

"Put her on the phone." My jaw tightened, and every muscle in my body went rigid. The clock above the bar read almost eight.

Forty-five minutes and no word from Frankie.

Finn and Lena stared at me as my sister's voice replaced the shuffling over the phone line. "He didn't attend last night, no one knows where he is," she said in a quiet, breathless rush.

"Are you all right?"

"No. But I will be... they're working together," she whispered.

There was more shuffling on the other end, and I heard my father click his tongue with impatience through the phone. I *hated* that man. "That will be all," he said. "Get your fucking ass back here." He ended the call.

I looked at Finn. "My father's out. Noble isn't in Boston, and I haven't heard from Frankie. Something is fucking wrong." Coffee spilled over the cup as I set it down and grabbed my jacket off the back of a stool.

"What?" Lena's worried gaze shifted between us. "Where are you going?"

"To find Frankie." I headed for the door as Finn's phone rang, and I wheeled around.

His brows pulled together as he muttered short replies into his phone, and Lena perched on the stool next to him. He paced back and forth, his eyes darting toward me as he ended the phone call. "Frankie never showed up for work this morning."

Rage burned inside me. My past, here. In the present. All I could see was the worst happening to her because I'd fucked up.

"She probably just had an appointment or something." Lena eyed her watch. "It hasn't been that long."

"When was the last time you talked to her?" Finn asked Lena, shoving his phone in his back pocket.

"She called me on her way home yesterday, she had some computer stuff she wanted to take care of... You both have that look, like you know something I don't. Does this have to do with whoever killed Clay?"

Finn's eyes flickered from hers to mine. "Did you see her car leave the house this morning?"

"I was with her this morning. She left the house at six thirty, I stayed with her until she headed for the coffee shop near the hospital, and I turned to come here. I fucked up not staying with her, I'll find her."

I'd let my guard down, had gotten too comfortable, and stopped looking over my shoulder. And if anyone touched my girl, the Morrigan inside me would fucking kill them.

The anger in Finn's eyes almost matched mine, and I could feel the tension radiating off him. He made a phone call, rattling off Frankie's information—where she was last seen, height and build, her Jeep information... like she was a *victim*—slamming his hand on the bar as he hung up the phone. "Fuck!"

I hurried outside with Finn behind me, and got in the truck, starting the engine.

Lena chased him to the passenger side as the rain whipped at her hair, soaking her. "What the hell is going on? Talk to me, Finn. You put out a search for Frankie after only an hour?" Lena's pale face reddened as she gripped the open door, blocking him from getting in. "What the fuck is happening? Give me something!"

Finn hugged her tightly, his words an incoherent mess as he climbed into the passenger seat. I leaned forward, catching Lena's gaze. "I killed someone a long time ago, his father wants me dead, he probably murdered Clay and has been targeting Frankie. We're wasting time we don't have. That's all I got, don't make me drive away with that door hanging open." They weren't after her, they wanted me, and if I didn't find her, they'd fucking *use* her. My body shook with anger. "Lena, please—"

"Get her back," she said, and pushed Finn's leg inside the cab before slamming the door. I sped out of the parking lot as my phone buzzed, and my eyes darted from the road to my screen.

A new message with a photo displayed from *Her*.

Come alone or she dies.

Frankie stared back at me. The image of her lying on a basement floor, her hands and feet bound with rope, blood matted into her hair, her face a cut-up, swollen, bleeding mess. Raw anger and fear flared in my chest, constricting my throat as I forced myself to swallow. A location pin of an abandoned mill followed the horrific picture.

The fucker who did this to her will die.

Finn reached over and gripped the wheel, straightening the truck as it swerved. "Who is it?"

My fingers felt disconnected from my body as I texted *on my way* and handed him my phone.

"Jesus fucking Christ, *drive faster*," he said with his eyes fixed on my phone. I snatched it back, and he grabbed his, making a call.

"No cops, didn't you read the fucking message? I'll pull over and drop you, they're using her to get to me." I wanted to break his finger as he held it up, listening intently to whoever the hell was on the other end. He began launching into the location, and I smacked it away before he could finish. "What are you doing? They'll kill her."

"Listen to me, Rhett." He reached for his phone on the floor and talked fast. "They're already searching for her, it's too late. Staff at the coffee shop confirmed her Jeep showed up at the drive-thru, but she never ordered. Another vehicle was behind her in the camera footage headed west, too fucking dark to get a plate." Putting his phone against his ear, he gave the mill's location, leaning close to the window to distance himself from me.

"You fucked up letting her get close to you," Finn said, ending the call. "You didn't follow the rules! If she dies—"

"I won't let that happen." I passed cars on a solid line and ran a red light. Flashing red and blue lights appeared in the dark sky behind us, and distant sirens blared. I tuned out Finn's anger, and everything around me, focusing on Frankie... Remembering my father's training. Nothing else mattered but getting her back in my arms, safe.

I failed. I let her down, lost control. It can never happen again.

Finn's knee bounced, and he barely paused between his words as he talked, reliving the trauma of that night in the warehouse. This man differed from the cop I'd known years earlier. I didn't interrupt, just listened, keeping my thoughts on reaching Frankie so he wouldn't have to bury a sibling again, and so I wouldn't lose the woman... I *loved*.

"Why didn't you stay away from her?" Finn asked, desperate. "You got sloppy, fuck, we both did."

Her battered face stuck in my mind, and I gripped the wheel tighter. "We have to get there before the entire fucking police department arrives. They want me, not her." Rain covered the windshield, clearing briefly with each swipe of the wipers, and the truck hydroplaned as the tires hit patches of water.

The mill was another ten miles too far. I pressed down on the gas pedal, revving the engine harder, and navigated the winding road.

Finn rubbed his neck, shifting in his seat. "You think they'll just hand her over when you show up?"

"I'll make sure they do." I reached across him and opened the glove compartment, taking my gun from the holster.

"You can't go in there with that, give it to me—"

"No."

I checked my phone, but there were no new messages. Only that photo driving the rage in my chest. We were almost there.

"Don't make this more difficult, Rhett. Let us do our job, I'm not letting anything happen to my sister." Finn's voice cracked, and he cleared his throat.

But I didn't break my concentration as police cars turned off the main road. They kicked up a cloud of dust as they rushed toward the mill. "Too late for that."

Branches slapped my truck as I sped through the overgrown dirt path, passing police cars. The doors of Frankie's Jeep hung open, but there was no other vehicle. If they killed her to send me a message and fled... With my gun in hand, I charged toward the building.

"Jesus." Finn slammed the door and followed me, flashing his badge as an officer yelled and a tactical team surrounded the old building.

My heart pounded as I stormed through the door, searching the room. "Frankie!" I called to her, desperate to hear her voice.

Police swarmed inside. "You can't be in here!"

"He's with me," Finn said, falling behind me. "Where's EMS?"

"Get out of here, Roscoe, that's an order." A woman's voice boomed at the door, echoing off the walls as I held my gun alongside the light on my phone.

Finn's voice grew louder and frantic as he explained to her why we were here, but I blocked it out. All that mattered was locating Frankie *alive*.

In the back corner of the room, a pipe extended from the ceiling to the floor, and I brought up Frankie's tortured image on my phone, eyeing the pipe they had her tied to in a basement. There had to be stairs somewhere.

Shouts and threats of arrest echoed around me, but I aimed my light at a doorway with stairs leading down, running toward them. Switching off my light, I stepped down carefully, listening. Water tapped on metal, and sounds from rodents echoed below.

They left her down there, tied up with fucking *rats*.

I hurried, descending further as the muffled commands from upstairs reverberated. A small window offered light, revealing pipes flush with the ceiling and barrels lining the back wall. With my finger on the trigger, I strained to see, my rapid breathing pulsing in my ears.

"I'm here, say something, Frankie."

Gasping coughs cut through the large room. "Help me." Her voice was like a beacon, and my boots thudded on the metal stairs to the bottom.

I scanned the room, and my phone cast light on her crumpled body on the floor. "Jesus Christ."

She tried to lift her head, but it fell back to the floor, and I dropped to her side as officers arrived at the top of the stairs. With her cheek pressed to the cement, and her hands tied behind her back, she flinched, crying. "No more, please—"

"I'm here, baby." Tucking my gun into my waistband, I shrugged my jacket off and retrieved a pocketknife, cutting the rope from her hands and feet. Stuffing the rope in my jacket pocket, I gathered her into my arms as her hands fell limp at her sides.

Her eyes widened as she stared at me, and her head slumped against my chest. She started crying, and I had to strain to understand her.

"I told them your name..."

I gently placed my hand on her head as her body trembled. A fleeting moment of relief pushed the rage aside, but my mind shifted into action, planning my next move. I pulled my jacket over her shoulders, snapping the top button to keep it from falling off.

I took her hands and set them in her lap, running a finger along the bracelet I'd given her. She clutched my hand with a weak grip.

"I didn't think I'd see you again," she rasped. Blood crusted on her lips, and I cupped my hand over a wound gushing from her temple. I stood, lifting her with me.

Police surrounded us with flashlights and guns, but Finn shoved past them.

"Frankie!" His voice cracked. Finn placed his hand on her shoulder and kissed her bloodied forehead. "No one is ever going to hurt you again. I'm so sorry, this never should've happened to you. We'll find them."

I squeezed her hand, holding her close to me. It didn't matter if her brother blamed me. I wasn't going anywhere and wouldn't let her out of my sight until the man who did this was dead.

She blinked up at me slowly, and her hand rose to my face with blood-caked nails and cuts trailing along her arm. "Get me out of here."

Tears streamed down her face, getting trapped in gashes as they fell off her chin. Fuck, she was a mess. They'd broken her, and I wasn't around to stop them. If I had stayed a Morrigan, never joining forces with Finn, none of this would have happened. Frankie would never suffer at the hands of anyone ever again.

"An ambulance is waiting outside," an officer said.

"Don't need one, I'm taking her to the hospital." I headed for the stairs as Frankie curled her fingers around my jacket.

Finn trailed behind me. "She needs medics—"

Detective Clark approached, her heeled boots clicking on the cement. She scrutinized me as she reached over me, tucking the bottom of my jacket tighter around Frankie. "This woman needs to be in an ambulance, *now.*"

Frankie lifted her head off my chest, her hazy eyes darting from me to Finn. "It was Noble... and he had a friend." She winced, shutting her eyes as her trembling hand reached for her face.

Finn shifted his gaze back to the detective. "Let him take her out to EMS. I'll be responsible for him."

"You'll be responsible for no one, Roscoe." She eyed me again, her gaze falling to my waistband, revealing my gun. "Hand it over."

I walked away from her, and her voice echoed in the basement. "I could arrest you, Mr. Marshall, or should I call you Morrigan? Gun. Now."

Balancing Frankie in my arms, I leaned toward Finn. "Take it, but I'm not leaving her side."

He grabbed it from my waistband and held his hand out. "Keys too. One compromise, Rhett. If you can't take off, they'll let you carry her out. I'll go with you in your truck. They won't let you leave here without a police escort, and I'm not letting her out of my sight either."

"Quite the mess you've gotten this woman into." Detective Clark snapped her fingers, calling over two officers to make sure we followed the rules, not letting us leave the basement alone.

I carried Frankie up the stairs, passing officers whose radios crackled with static as they rolled out caution tape. Finn caught up to me as medics grabbed supplies, directing me to place her on a gurney, but I couldn't let her go, desperate to keep her safe.

"She'll be okay," Finn said. "You got her in time, let them help her."

Frankie's head flopped back as I laid her down, and the two medics rolled the gurney into the ambulance. They set to work poking her with a needle, hanging a bag of fluid, and placing a blanket over her shivering body. I stepped inside and crouched beside her, holding her hand in mine as they hooked her up to machines and placed an oxygen mask on her face.

"You have to go, sir."

I stood hovering over her and whispered in her ear. "I'm so sorry, Frankie."

Finn grabbed my arm, and I stepped out of the ambulance, letting them shut the double doors.

We'd gotten to her, but not in enough time to keep them from breaking her. The men who did this were still out there, and they'd come back until they had exactly what they wanted. I knew this life all too well. The words of my father echoed in my mind.

You're in this for life. There is no leaving unless it's six feet under.

Thirty-Six

Frankie

The rose dangled from my bracelet as I adjusted the IV tube attached to my arm. Staring out the rain-streaked hospital window, I held the delicate flower in my fingertips.

The Francesca rose. Beautiful, strong, and resilient. I'm never going to live up to my name.

A deeper gray settled over the sky as evening approached, but it had been a dark day. I couldn't tell what time it was or how long

I'd spent giving a statement, rehashing the violating abuse to my body no one should ever have to go through.

Every agonizing movement woke me from nightmares as I drifted in and out of sleep, reminding me of what they'd done. They hadn't raped me, and I'd survived. But within a matter of hours, those two men had victimized me, stripped away my strength, left me vulnerable and terrified, and stolen the sense of security I'd once had in my own skin.

It had been a whirlwind of chaos since arriving at the hospital on the receiving end of care for the first time since I could remember. I'd been stuck with needles, sent for X-rays and scans to rule out internal bleeding and life-threatening brain injuries, preventing me from having a chance to speak in private with Rhett and Finn.

The gruesome video of Miles's shooting tormented me like a real-life horror movie. And if Rhett hadn't stepped in and killed Noble's son, Finn would've died that night too.

I needed to know where the men who did this to me were hiding. They wouldn't stop until they got what they wanted—Rhett dead, which just wasn't an option I was willing to accept. I couldn't lose him.

Pooled tears spilled down my face, stinging the raw cuts and the tender stitches along my jawline. Uncontrollable shivers consumed my body, and I yanked at the thin blanket with a lingering scent of bleach, which was almost a comforting smell after the stench of that basement. Anything was better than the cold cement floor and the rats waiting to make me a meal.

I yanked the blanket again, desperate to be comforted, but the damn thing wouldn't budge, no matter how hard I tugged. I'd never make a bed this tightly if it meant someone couldn't cover themselves up.

Rhett entered the room holding a folded blanket. "I got this from a nurse." Heat enveloped my aching body as he draped it over me, his face inches from mine. He brushed his fingers along the side of my painfully swollen cheek and lifted an ice pack wrapped in cloth. He sat on the edge of the bed and gently held it against my hot skin.

I averted his gaze, blindsided by emotions I'd never had before and couldn't put into words. I'd always been independent, and needing someone to take care of me made me feel weak. The tears refused to stop. "I can hold it." I raised my hand, the IV tube catching on the bedrails, and I winced in pain as I twisted my body to the side to untangle it. "Fucking hell."

"Let me do it." Rhett held the ice pack to my face, and my hand dropped to my chest. The cold soothed my sore skin. "Can I do anything for you?"

I shut my eyes. "You're already doing it." A sharp pain sliced through my chest as I inhaled, and I flinched, opening my eyes. The fuckers hadn't broken my ribs, but they were bruised, and each breath hurt. The bed remote was just out of reach. "Help me sit up?"

He pressed the button, and my head lifted. "More?" he asked.

"That's good."

Our eyes locked, and mine filled with tears. *Again*. "My tear ducts are broken too, I can't make them stop leaking."

He took my hand and kissed my fingers. "Frankie, this is all my fault, I fucked up. I am so sorry they hurt you." His voice broke, rough with emotion.

"They showed me what you did," I whispered, conscious of the police and nurses hovering outside my door.

"What did they show you?"

"Warehouse footage from the night Miles was shot." I pulled his hand against my chest and covered his with mine. "I saw you kill Noble's son."

Rhett's jaw clenched. "They forced you to watch your brother dying?"

I could still feel that asshole's hands in my hair, and my fingers instinctively reached for the bloody strands. "I wish they were dead. Both of them." I glanced up at Rhett. "Does that make me a horrible person?"

"You could never be horrible. What they did to you was horrible, and they deserve to die." He said the words like a promise. It was one I wanted him to keep.

Finn walked into the room and stopped. "I can come back, just let me know when we can talk about a plan. And they're not laying charges against you, Rhett."

Rhett stood from the edge of my hospital bed, and I released his hand. He kissed my head and crossed his arms, studying Finn. "Of course they're not, Roscoe, I didn't do anything wrong. And we had a deal two years ago. I wore a wire and did what I signed up for. My name change is legal, and as far as anyone in this town is concerned, I'm an upstanding citizen who works in a local bar." Dragging a chair next to my bed, he sat with an ankle crossed over his knee. "You're not coming in here talking plans, give her space."

"She doesn't need space, she needs a plan for when she gets out of here." Finn paced the small room, squinting as he touched the bag of saline. "What is this?"

"It's just fluids." I reached for the ice pack. Rhett leaned forward, but I held a hand up. "I've got it."

As I held the icy block on my face, Finn sank into the only other chair in the room and raked his fingers through his hair. "What do you want me to do? I don't know how to make this right, if I'd lost you like we did Miles—"

"But you didn't, I'm going to be fine." I darted a look at Rhett, who raised his eyebrows at my word choice. I wasn't fine, not even close. The word had lost its meaning but would help me convince my brother to stop worrying. What terrified me the most was the gnawing fear that I'd never be okay or feel safe again. Uncertainty about what the future held for me and Rhett, or if we'd survive what would come next, consumed me.

I'm never going to be the same.

I ran my fingertips over my swollen lower lip, feeling the dried blood clinging to the cut. The taste on my tongue made me nauseous, and I took a deep breath. Rhett sat up, and the warmth from his hands spread through the blanket as he rested them on my legs, as though I would shatter at the slightest touch. "Finn, I'll be in here tonight, and after... I'll take it from there. No plans, okay? I can hardly get out of a hospital bed to go pee right now. Let me work on that first?"

Shoving the chair back, my brother stood and closed the door. He approached, looking me over, and for a fleeting moment, reminded me of Miles. "I'm sorry I push so hard, but it's because I love you." He faltered, glancing away before his eyes met mine.

"What is it?" Rhett asked before I could.

"They searched Clay's place and found a bunch of photos of Frankie at work and at the bar the night she picked Dad up... and he took pictures inside your house," Finn said.

I thought of the USB stick. "What exactly did he take pictures of inside my house?"

"Miles's stuff all over the floor upstairs, nothing stood out. But they have transcripts from a burner phone he was using, and they're looking for evidence that Miles kept. Clay knew about it and told the wrong person a couple months ago."

"He wanted out, didn't he?" I asked. There hadn't been a lot of information about Clay's involvement with the Nobles on that device, but there sure as hell was plenty to ruin the men he'd worked for.

"Looks that way," Finn said. "He moved millions from shell companies to an offshore account days before they killed him."

"He knew he was going to die." Rhett stood and headed toward the door, peeking through the narrow glass window beside it.

"Did you get my phone back? If they still have it, can't you somehow track them?"

Finn exchanged a look with Rhett. "Tried that already, didn't work."

"My purse was in the Jeep. Get the keys and go to my place, the USB is inside the filter basket of the coffeemaker. Rhett knows the password, he'll help you." I sat up and flinched as pain jolted through me like an electric shock.

Rhett reached for the door. "I'll get someone—"

"No need. Someone will come by, they always do, every hour at least. They're busy."

A look of shock hung on Finn's face. "What was on that device and how the hell did you get into it?"

I told him everything, including Miles's message from beyond the grave, and lost control in a fit of tears. Sitting on the bed, Finn embraced me like I would break.

Fuck, I might.

Wrapping my arms around him, the IV tube tugging with a sharp sting, I ignored the throbbing pain and hugged him back.

The door burst open with a sharp knock, fueling the relentless fight-or-flight response that wouldn't let me rest. A police officer stuck his head into the room, asking to speak with Finn, and as he left, one of my favorite nurses to work with entered.

"Sweet girl, what the hell have you gone through?" Darla approached, shaking her head. Rhett moved out of the way as she worked efficiently with gentle hands and took my vitals. Her butterfly scrubs and kind eyes contrasted the darkness inside me, and I'd hug her if my body could stand the pain of moving. "Am I to assume you two are together, or should he wait outside, Frankie?"

"We're together," Rhett said as I blurted, "he can stay if he wants."

I wanted him near me. I was afraid he'd walk out the door and never return.

Giving me a smile, Darla patted my shoulder. Despite her respectful and tender care, it was strange to have medical attention, and the poking and prodding of my body left me feeling exposed. I regretted letting Rhett stay the moment his disturbed gaze fell on the dark bruises and bloody cuts covering my chest and torso. A murderous glint flashed in his eyes as he faced the window, crossing his arms and running a hand over his jaw.

With another dose of pain medication pumping through the fluids in my IV, Darla adjusted the call bell and left us alone.

Rhett spoke in a low rumble, keeping his tone in perfect control as he glanced from his phone to the window. "I got too comfortable. I fucking promise you, no one's going to touch you again. I'll take care of them." He moved the IV pole aside and crouched beside the bed with his hand on the rail.

I knew what Rhett's hands were capable of, and as much as I wanted to crawl into a hole and hide, my body yearned for his careful touch. I needed his hands on me again, holding me tight to chase away the nightmarish brutality I'd endured at the hands of those two *monsters*.

A full bladder interrupted my thoughts, and I shoved the blankets aside. A numbing haze swept over me as the pain meds took effect. "I need to pee."

Clicking the rail down, Rhett extended his hands. "Just take them, Frankie."

I gripped his hands and let him guide me to my feet, holding me steady until I could balance on my own with the IV pole. "I hate that you're seeing me like this, battered, covered in bruises, swollen... I don't need help."

"Yes, you do," he said. Warmth from his arms around me tamed the chills. "Unless you want me to get someone in here, your choice. I'm not letting you fall."

I turned away from him, and cool air in the room brushed my exposed ass from the open hospital shirt. Pain shot through my chest as I reached behind me to grasp the ties, and I released the fabric, hunching over. "Didn't mean to give you a show."

"Baby, when I told you I'm not leaving you, I fucking meant it. Give me your worst, and I'll just meet you with my best." His fingers grazed my skin as he knotted the ties behind me. "Covered."

"Thanks," I muttered, holding onto his arms as I shifted around to face him. "I'm scared, Rhett. I..." *love you.* The thought came easily to mind, but I held it captive. "I care about you, and I'm just so scared someone's going to come back and hurt you."

He kissed my forehead. "I'm going to do whatever I have to so you feel safe again. Come on, let me help you." Towing the IV pole behind me, he kept me on my feet as I ambled inside the tiny bathroom. "Just yell when you're done or if you need help." He rolled the pole in with me and shut the door, leaving a small gap.

Lifting my stained hospital shirt, I lowered myself onto the toilet, clinging to the rail on the wall. Once finished, I washed my hands, turning the water pink as I scrubbed the caked blood from under my nails. I had clawed at his hands. That blood wasn't my own.

My gaze met the woman in the mirror, and I froze. She was without a doubt me, of course she was, and yet she wasn't *me* at all. The version of me in the mirror had broken blood vessels in her left eye, dried blood encrusted in gashes of varying degrees of nastiness on her face, and red bruises shifting into shades of a hideous purple. One side of her face had nearly swollen around the black thread holding a gash together, and her lower lip protruded... and not in a sexy way.

Fuck, I look like death.

I felt even worse. I shimmied the hospital gown up to my neck, revealing more battered flesh. Bruises crept from my chest to my torso, where cuts were sutured and bandaged, and when I moved to lean against the sink, pain burned through me, stealing my breath.

"Frankie? Are you okay?" Peering through the gap at the door, my mom's eyes widened. Her hand flew to her mouth as she looked me up and down.

Dropping the shirt around my knees, I grabbed the pole and pushed it ahead of me, trailing her as she stormed toward the door.

"What are they doing to find the men who did this?" She directed her questions at Finn and the officer outside the room. My dad's calm voice rose over the chatter and Mom's muffled tears. His words faded as he spoke in a hushed tone, pulling the door shut.

"What a shit show, I can't believe this is my life. How is this real?" I stood clutching myself, breathing through the pain that refused to ease. Rhett was at my side, wrapping an arm around my waist as he led me to the bed.

"I've got to walk around and get strong again." Lying down, I clung to my stomach. Every inhale was like blades in my chest.

"Give yourself time to heal first, I'll do the heavy lifting until you're ready." The bags of fluid swayed as Rhett rolled the IV pole closer.

"Is this as good as your best gets? Or do I have more of this side of Rhett in my future?" Fear snipped my daydream of a life with him short. "If we have one."

"You can have it all if you want it." He checked his phone, and deep creases etched on his forehead.

"What is it?"

He tucked blankets around me. "Just my sister again, it's okay."

"Are you sure?"

"Yeah, I'll call her back in a minute."

Something wasn't right. "Tell me what she says, after you talk to her?"

Hesitating, he distracted himself by putting the bedrail up. "Okay, sure... anything you need?"

"To go home, shower, and wash the blood off me, it's every-where." I grasped the neck of the hospital shirt, almost feeling their hands on me, tearing at my shirt and touching my bra, pinning me against the wall. My chest tightened and heart raced as Noble's face invaded my mind, smiling with his finger to his mouth. I couldn't breathe, couldn't move...

Rhett sat on the edge of the bed and carefully held my cheeks in his gentle hands. "Eyes on me."

Through ragged breaths, I met his gaze.

"Frankie, you are safe. They will pay for what they did to you."

"Promise?" I whispered through tears.

He placed a soft kiss on my battered cheek. "Promise."

For the first time in my life, I wanted death to win.

THIRTY-SEVEN

Rhett

I left Frankie in the care of her mother and Lena and headed into the hallway with my phone. I found a quiet corner in a seating area near the cafeteria and typed a message for Bran Noble to Frankie's phone. I threatened his mother's life and set up a meeting place at the hotel where he'd murdered Clay but stopped myself from hitting send. Meeting him would make it too easy for the asshole to finish what he'd started, and I wouldn't hurt his mother for fuck's sake.

I wanted him dead, but to carry out my plan, he couldn't know I was coming.

I stood near the window, scanning the ambulance bay below, and called Vivian. We had talked earlier, and I'd filled her in on what they'd done to Frankie. She'd promised to let me know as soon as she found out where Bran Noble and whoever he had with him were hiding.

As the phone rang, people holding umbrellas rushed from the parking lot, ducking inside the main entrance doors, but there were no signs of anyone lurking around.

"Hello?" Vivian's hesitant voice drifted through the phone.

"It's me."

"Jesus, Rhett, how is she?"

"Alive. Do you have a location yet?" I lowered my voice to a near whisper, shooting a glance over my shoulder as Frankie's father rounded the corner. He nodded at me and entered the cafeteria.

"You'll know soon," Vivian said. "Luca needs you to trust him with this."

"Never going to happen—"

"So trust *me*. You used to." She sighed. "I fucking need you to let him work with you... be ready, okay?"

"Why does Nash want me back?" I turned away from the window. I knew how my father worked. He had a plan for me, and it wasn't to rekindle a father-son business relationship. By showing what happened when someone betrayed him, he'd prove to both his allies and enemies that he had returned with a vengeance. And I couldn't leave Willow Grove until I took care of the men who dared fucking touch my girl.

"Don't do it, don't come back," Vivian said. "Dad's working with Bran again, but our father has to show him whose side he's on, and we both know the only way to do that is to deal with the man who killed Noble's son—*you*." Her voice rose as she spoke faster. "Nash Morrigan doesn't give a fuck about you, or anyone, Rhett. All he wants is his power back. I'll be fine, he thinks I hate you. Take her somewhere until we handle him or you'll be walking into fire, and not getting out this time."

My father wanted to kill his own son.

"Let me make a call and get you and Zach set up with documents, get you out—"

"Trust. Me." Vivian's words escaped through gritted teeth laced with a desperate plea. "I've never let you down, *never*. And I never will."

Frankie's dad approached, holding two cups of coffee. "I have to go," I said, ending the call.

Jared handed me one of the cups. "Milk and sugar? My daughter apparently knows how you take your coffee." He narrowed his eyes at me and sat in a chair against the wall. "Do me a favor and sit down."

I braced myself for a lecture on how I had ruined his daughter's life, advising me to stay the fuck away from her, with a sordid explanation of his disappointment that she'd chosen to spend her time with a low-life criminal, and how it had nearly gotten her killed. I wouldn't have a damn leg to stand on.

I sat, and Jared let me marinate in uncomfortable silence for a few minutes as he took the lid off his cup and blew on his coffee. I watched the steam rise and imagined what he was going to say to me. The faint smell of liquor hung between us, but he didn't appear intoxicated—a silent rage emanated from him. Shoving my phone in my jacket pocket, I clutched the rope. The rough fibers under my fingers were a horrific reminder of what Frankie had endured at the hands of men who walked free, still fucking *breathing*.

"Two men assaulted my daughter. They tore her clothes, had their hands on her, beat the shit out of her, and left her bleeding on the floor with the fucking rats." He drank from his cup as I gripped my own so tight that the lid popped off.

Anger graced me with clear focus and fueled my body with a dose of adrenaline. I snapped the lid back onto my cup. "If there is anything you need me to do, I'll do it."

What does a man say to his girlfriend's father who would murder or die for his daughter?

"That's what I thought." He looked straight ahead as someone in a lab coat pushed a squeaky-wheeled cart filled with vials. They swiped an ID card to open a locked door, pulled the cart inside, and disappeared.

I waited for him to continue, anticipating what would come next. Frankie's father, a retired cop, must have figured out more

SHATTERED SECRETS BETWEEN US

about my past and who I was than I'd realized. But nothing he could say would stop me from fulfilling my promise to her.

He pulled a set of keys out of his pocket. "She's getting out of here tomorrow, I'll need you to take her someplace safe until this shit is sorted out." He turned to me and dropped the keys into my hand. "I'll assume Finn has the number of your burner?"

"He does." I gripped my keys. I couldn't tell if he was guessing or if he was certain about my burner phone. I had no clue what his angle was.

"Our family cabin is remote enough, not too far, tucked in the woods. There's electricity and running water. I'll have him send you the location within the hour."

"You should know I have a few things to take care of before I can do that." I furrowed my brow, searching his unreadable face to figure out what else he wanted. "Can you stay with Frankie until I get back?"

"Of course I will." He rubbed a hand over his beard and shook his head. "I've fucked up, but when it comes to my family, I will never make a mistake again. Your new name threw me off, but I know you were with Miles that night. I am well aware of who and what you are."

"And you're okay with me taking your daughter away to a secluded cabin?" I asked.

Jared sat back in the chair and crossed his arms. "It's a second home to this family, and yes, I will be."

"What am I missing?"

377

"Alice Lane's been feeling lonely these days." He took a drink of his coffee. "So she called her son. Luca kindly informed me that his uncle is on his way."

He knows Luca Noble and is giving me Bran's location. Fuck me.

"Will he be bringing a friend?" I asked.

"He will."

"I see. Did Luca ask you to tell me this?"

"Finn isn't the only Roscoe with connections." He drank from his cup, stretching his legs.

Frankie's father had secrets too. "How are you connected to the Nobles sir?"

"Early in my career, a twenty-year-old punk kid was at one of the illegal poker games in Willow Grove," he said. "Same place as the Magpie, matter of fact, but nowhere near the bar it is now." Jared nodded to someone passing by and unbuttoned his jacket. "A fight broke out inside, but instead of waiting for back-up, I went in alone, outnumbered. Dumb move." He took a pack of cigarettes out of his pocket as he continued. "A man aimed a gun at my forehead and my entire life flashed by." Holding a cigarette between his fingers, he rubbed a hand over his weary face. The moment was like a damn confession, and I didn't dare interrupt. "Miles was a baby, Frankie was five, and Finn's tenth birthday was coming up that weekend... the kid in that bar spoke up and told my gunman I worked for his father, complete bullshit of course, but they let me go. That young man was Luca Noble."

"Jesus." I leaned forward with my elbows on my knees and faced him. "Why would he help you, a cop?"

"His father was an abusive asshole who made a habit of hitting his wife, landing her in the hospital. I got his son off assault charges when he stabbed his father to save his mother. The man died a year later, and Luca left town."

And now he was with my sister, and she wanted me to trust him. "You kept in touch?"

"Not until he reached out to inform me Miles was working for your father, but by then it was too late, and Finn was in too deep." Jared's eyes reflected the same torment Frankie had when she talked about her brother.

"And you asked him for help with Frankie."

"No, I'm asking for *your* help with Frankie," he said, shifting in the chair. "Not many I'd trust with my daughter, and he isn't one of them."

"But you trust his information."

"He hates his uncle almost as much as he hated his father."

Was Frankie's dad silently asking me to kill those two men? He didn't have to ask, and I didn't need permission, but I had to know who else would be waiting for me at Alice Lane's house. "Question," I said. "Why not just get your police connections on this?"

"Men like that have ways to avoid persecution, you know that as much as I do. If by some miracle they did end up behind bars, for how long? A year? Two? Not fucking long enough, and they'd send someone else to finish the job." Deep lines creased around Jared's eyes. "Let me ask *you* a question, Rhett Marshall. Do you care about my daughter?"

Without hesitation, I met his eyes. "I'd die for your daughter, and as long as I'm alive, no one will ever hurt her again." I hardly tasted my coffee as I drank the rest of it.

Rising from his seat, Jared patted my shoulder. "Good to hear. Finn will be in touch, and I'm going outside to smoke this cigarette before you leave."

I embodied everything that stood against Finn's principles, and he didn't approve of me with his sister, but there had been an understanding between us since we'd met. He trusted me, and if I was being honest with myself, I trusted him.

Thirty-Eight

Rhett

Leaving Frankie in that hospital bed was the hardest thing I'd done since meeting her. The *hardest*. And if I fucked this up, they'd get to her before I could, and no one would stop them from taking what they wanted from her.

Uncertainty and fear had replaced her usual curiosity in the way she'd looked at me when I told her I had to go. She'd made me promise to come back to her, and her request hit me harder than I expected. Frankie had paid the price for my mistake, losing a part of herself I could never heal. I wouldn't want to survive if I failed her again. Her beaten body and bruised face as I had walked out of her hospital room flashed in my mind, igniting the anger I needed to carry out my plan. If I let emotion take over, they'd have the upper hand.

Darkness had crept in like a warning. I'd parked a street away, and as I walked toward Alice Lane's house, the freezing, still air settled around me. Tucking my gun in my waistband, I cut through her backyard. The driveway and street in front of her house were empty, but if Luca Noble had given Frankie's father good information, they would arrive soon. Bags of raked leaves created a wall against the shed, and as I approached the front steps, the dead flower baskets were gone.

About fucking time.

I welcomed the familiar rush of adrenaline moving me forward.

Make the kill as efficiently as possible, in and out, leave no trace... Am I becoming my father?

I grabbed my leather gloves and tucked the coiled rope inside my jacket pocket, pulling out my bump key and a small hammer. There would be no gin and tonic fueled conversation with Alice this time. Concealed in the shadows behind the cedar, I turned the door handle, but it was locked as expected. As I made my way behind the house, a floodlight flickered on, and a loud buzzing filled the air. I checked the back door and tried each lower window. Nothing budged.

The faint sounds of the TV carried through the door as I inserted the bump key into the lock. With a slight rotation, I pulled it back a notch and gave it a sharp smack with the hammer. When no footsteps approached, I repeated the process, shoving the key in, rotating it against the metal, and yanking it back, using the hammer to drive it forward. On the fourth attempt, the key turned completely, unlocking the door, and I removed it, sticking it back in my pocket. It had been a long time since I'd used those skills, but they hadn't failed me yet.

Stepping inside the kitchen, a lemon aroma mixed with peppermint burned my eyes for a moment. The kitchen was spotless, with only a few dishes in the sink. I opened the fridge a crack, slipping my hand over the button to keep the light off. Three trays of ready-made meals rested on the wire shelves. Someone had finally been taking better care of Ms. Lane. Her son should be appalled at letting her go so long without help.

I shut the fridge and advanced, peeking around the corner toward the small living room. A show in black and white flickered on the TV in the darkness, the volume cranked, but Alice was nowhere. At the end of the narrow hallway, a red light flashed on a wall-mounted phone. I almost picked it up and dialed Frankie's cell number to see if Noble answered, but I held back.

If I didn't take care of the men who hurt Frankie, they would return to inflict more hell. Her father was right; jail time, if they served any, wouldn't be long, and someone else would come to finish their dirty work, taking me and Frankie with them. Headlights lit up the street, beaming through the living room window as a vehicle turned into the driveway.

Alice's son was going to die in her house tonight, and I would carry the weight of my actions, never speaking of them again.

The engine halted and boots crunched on gravel outside, thudding up the steps. I ducked into a small bathroom off the hallway. As the front door unlocked and swung open, I stepped into the tub. I slid the dark green shower curtain along a metal rod, but the blaring television drowned out the scraping sound. I curled my fingers around the rope they had used to tie Frankie's hands and feet, making her powerless to escape.

Wait in silence. Take the first opportunity.

"We should be lying low, not back here," a rough voice grumbled from the hallway. "I can hardly hear myself think with that fucking TV."

"Fuck you." Footsteps on the floor thumped outside the bathroom. "She likes her old shows, it's all she's got... Mom? What's going on, Luca said you needed my help."

A shadow darkened the bathroom wall, stretching to the ceiling. "She's not in the living room."

"Mom! Jesus Christ. She's got to be upstairs." The television went silent as footsteps echoed down the hall past the bathroom. "Stay here and watch out front. Message Nash, tell him we'll be there as soon as we get back."

My gut clenched at the mention of my father, confirming what Vivian had told me. They were working together.

"Sure boss, whatever you say," the man downstairs mumbled while heavy thuds resounded over my head.

Their separation sounded like an opportunity.

The rope dug into my palms as I readied to move, but his boots grew louder toward the bathroom door, and I braced myself against the tiled wall. Flipping the light on, he whistled and shut the door behind him. The toilet seat clapped against the tank as he pissed, and I remained still, hidden behind the dark fabric.

Quick. Efficient. Get in and out, no trace.

With the rope taut between my hands, I waited until he flushed. As the water echoed in the small room, I shoved the curtain aside and looped it around his neck like a noose. I shut the bathroom door with my hip as I yanked him off balance, pulling him down. His arms flailed. He reached for a gun stuck in his side holster, but I jerked on the rope, forcing him to look in the mirror as I shoved my knee into his back. "You touch her, you die."

Blood rushed to his face, turning it red, and he sputtered. "The fuck?" His lips paled, and his eyes widened, bulging in their sockets.

With ragged breaths and my heart pounding in my chest, I choked him harder. He kicked his feet as I dragged his slumping body to the floor. Within seconds, he stopped twitching, and his grip on the rope around his neck went limp. Muffled voices blended with the creaking floorboards overhead, and I tightened the rope over his carotid as the agonizingly slow minutes ticked by. A gunshot would be impossible if I wanted to keep Bran Noble unaware of my presence.

Footsteps and the steady thump of what I assumed was Alice's cane above me stole my attention, and I refocused, pulling the rope tighter. The man's chest stopped moving. His face transitioned to a deathly shade of gray, and his mouth gaped open.

Water rushed through the pipes from upstairs, and the thumps resumed over my head. I slackened the rope and removed a glove, pressing my fingers against his neck. His heart gave up beating, and I snatched a towel off the sink, wiping the skin where I'd touched him to avoid fingerprints. Noble argued with his mother. She denied calling for help, her voice barely audible, and he snapped at her, demanding to know where the credit card charges had come from. Would he hurt his own mother? Putting my glove back on, I released the rope from around the man's neck and tucked it back in my jacket pocket.

There was no time to second-guess or question myself. I concentrated on Frankie, picturing her face, and what they had done to her. I refused to let her live in fear that Noble would hurt her again. Grabbing the man's gun, I quietly left the bathroom.

With controlled movements, I made my way along the wall down the hallway, holding the gun steady in my hands. I pulled back the slide, finding the chamber loaded. Standing at the bottom of a walled-in staircase, my eyes darted from the door toward the voices coming from upstairs.

"What man? Did he tell you his name?" Noble spat the words, and his mother's voice cracked as she replied.

She mentioned the gin and tonic I'd made, and how kind I had been, but couldn't recall what I had looked like.

Me, kind?

"You need to tell me when these things happen." He slammed his fist into a wall and called for the man downstairs. "Get up here, we've got a problem."

Fuck.

How could I kill a man in front of his own mother? I didn't want to, but he'd broken Frankie. He'd broken her body and almost killed her because of who I was...

I hated how my father's words repeated in my head, as though he still owned my life. The words that had constricted around me, inescapable: *If anyone crosses the line and forgets who you are, or where you came from, stand behind the family name, son, and remind them.*

I'd never wanted this life, but Frankie had become part of it. I rushed up the stairs, slipping into an empty bedroom as footsteps and shouts echoed from a room further down the hall.

"You have become your father!" His mother's screams reverberated off the walls, and I froze.

I would never become my father.

"He built this place, you ungrateful woman!" Noble hollered. "Cal, let's go!" He stormed down the hallway toward the stairs.

"He's dead." I emerged from the room and stood behind him.

Noble spun around, matching my size as he filled the space leading down the stairs.

He reached for his gun. "I wouldn't do that," I said, racking the slide on mine first as I leveled it at his chest. I adjusted my stance, and he lifted his hands.

"Your father's looking for you, Everett," Noble spat. "If you stop running now, he might let you live, and with that gorgeous woman by your side,"—he laughed, a low, evil sound that made me want to shoot him right there—"well, she will be again, once her face heals. What was her name again? *Francesca*, like the roses."

"Keep her name out of your mouth." Rage clawed its way out of my chest, radiating off me, and I stepped closer.

He clenched his jaw so tight his face looked like it might split. "It's a shame, really," he said. "You brought in a lot of money for your dad, just to kill my son, you fucking rat."

"Bran? Who are you talking to, should I call the police?" His mother's terrified voice called out from the bedroom, but I maintained an unwavering focus. I'd already waited too long to shoot him.

"Close the door and make the call, Mother," he told her, not looking away from me. "You'd really murder a man with his mother in the next room? Just like Dad, aren't you?" His upper lip curled into a smirk. "You're not gonna kill me."

"You couldn't be more wrong." I controlled my rage and slid back into the Morrigan part of me I had buried. "Tell me. What would you do to someone if they fucked up your woman the way you did mine?"

"I'd put a bullet in their head. Seeing this disrespect from you makes it clear I was too kind to your *woman*. I should've fucked her." His throat bobbed as he swallowed.

The anger I'd held together shattered like glass, and I punched him, knocking him toward the stairs. He caught himself with a grip on the railing as blood poured from his nose, and an abrupt laugh escaped him as he smeared it with the back of his hand.

His mother's scream pierced through the hallway. Noble snatched his gun from a holster, but I raised mine to his head, and he froze. I should've pulled the trigger, but I wanted him to suffer and feel the torment first.

Blood ran along his lips and down his chin, saturating his white shirt. "You kill me, it's over," he said. "My family won't stop until they've *ruined* her, unless your father gets to you first."

"I guess it's over." I pulled the trigger, and the shot thundered in the hallway, hitting its mark on his forehead. Blood splattered behind him, coating the walls in a gruesome, viscous spray that turned my stomach. His eyes widened and mouth hung open as his lifeless body tumbled backward down the stairs.

His mother cried from beyond a closed door. I searched the floor, picking up the casing with a gloved hand. Descending the bloodied stairs, I stepped over Bran Noble's body and headed back to the bathroom. I dragged the dead guy's stiff fingers over his gun before slipping it into his holster and bolted from the house through the back door.

Branches snagged on my jacket as I ran through the trees toward my truck, avoiding streetlights. With sirens wailing in the distance, I yanked my gloves off and started the engine, checking my phone as I sped in the opposite direction toward my place to get rid of my clothes and shower.

I read the message Finn had left me ten minutes earlier.

I'll meet you at your house.

Not a good time, I wrote back.

Trust me, it's the perfect time.

I focused on the road and slowed to a reasonable speed, trying to look like a guy on his way home from work. My mind whirled. If I let myself dwell too long on what I'd done, I wouldn't be able to function.

I'd eliminated a threat, done what needed to be done, and I would deal with my father's wrath next. All I wanted was a life away from the weight of my family's name, free of debts and blood... out. This time for good.

THIRTY-NINE

Rhett

Rushing home before Finn arrived, I stripped my jacket and clothes off in the garage, bagging them with my gloves, and tossed the bag in the back of my truck. Inside the house, I clicked on the fireplace and waited for it to build up before dropping the rope. I watched it burn away until there was nothing left.

Shoving the twisted last expressions on the dead men's faces, I concentrated on getting back to Frankie and prepared to take her to the cabin. I showered, scrubbing harder than I needed to, and got dressed, filling a duffel bag with clothes and a stack of cash as the doorbell rang. Slinging the bag over my shoulder, I tucked my gun in my jeans and moved down the stairs toward the door.

Finn knocked as he stood in the pouring rain and peered through the window in the door. "Open up, Rhett."

"You alone?"

"Of course I am. I'm getting soaked, let me in."

I unlocked the door and let him inside. Scanning the room, his eyes landed on the fireplace. "I'm guessing that's not on because you're cold."

I ignored his question. "How is she? I need to get back to her."

"Dad's been with her, she's worried about you." Finn tapped my bag as he wandered around the living room and into the kitchen. Light from the porch outside streamed through the patio doors. He searched the wall and flipped a switch, turning the kitchen light on. "Do you have everything?"

I set the bag on the floor. He knew something. "What are you doing here, Finn?"

"Lena is meeting us at Frankie's, and I'll get the USB stick."

"Why is Lena coming? Someone could be watching Frankie's house, waiting for her to come home."

"Frankie needs some things and wanted Lena to be the one to get them."

"I could've handled it." I opened the cabinet and retrieved a bottle of Redbreast whiskey. "Want one?"

"No," Finn said.

Dropping ice into a glass, I opened the bottle and poured a small amount, enough to make the ice crack, but not too much to dull my senses. "Does Frankie know we're going to the cabin when they let her go?"

Finn hesitated, pacing the room. "Dad will break it to her. She won't want to go. It's a soft spot for my sister and will take convincing, but it's the safest place for her."

"I'll get her settled tomorrow night, but I'll need you to come out and stay with her so I can go back to Boston for a few hours." It was time to go back and face my father; I'd avoided him long enough.

Finn stopped pacing and gripped the edge of the counter. I watched as his eyes noticed my wet hair and my red-rubbed skin. He took a deep breath. "Were you careful?"

I swirled my whiskey and took a slow drink, letting it warm my chest. Finn knew what I'd done, but the words would have to come from him. If he thought I was wrong for his sister before, he'd barely stand me now—I could hardly stand myself. "What are you asking?"

"Rhett, you can trust me."

"Can I? Your sister is in the hospital because of me."

He shook his head. "Noble saw Miles and me on her phone in the hospital before she even met you. I should have told her the truth a long time ago. There's enough blame to go around, but the men who put her in that fucking bed don't deserve to live."

I raised my glass and finished my drink. "We agree on something."

Finn released his death grip on the counter and pointed to the gun on my waist. "Is that the weapon?"

Silence hung heavy between us. I wasn't going to prison, leaving Frankie vulnerable to another attack. I turned my back on him and set my glass in the sink. "Use your words, Roscoe, and string some sentences together so I know exactly what you're asking and what your intentions are."

"If I'm going to be your alibi, we can't have any holes in our story."

I faced him, crossing my arms. "My alibi," I repeated. "Do you have any idea what you're doing? That's the end of your career."

"If you hadn't done it, I would've."

"I don't believe you," I said.

"My career ended when Miles died, I just haven't been able to accept it until now." He ran his hands through his hair and glanced at his watch. "It's not me anymore. Everything's changed... how can I uphold the law I swore to protect and lie through my teeth?"

"Why lie at all? Why not tell them the truth and set yourself free, cut me out of your life for good?" My gray hoodie Frankie had worn was draped over a stool, and I shrugged it over my head. It still smelled of her perfume and shampoo.

Finn pursed his lips and surveyed the kitchen, opening a closet near the door to the garage. "I wouldn't be alive if it weren't for you." Grabbing a flashlight, he switched it on and off, handing it to me. He rummaged through the shelves and carried a box of protein bars and bottles of water to my duffel bag, unzipped it, and tossed them in. "You looked out for Miles—"

"I failed, and he died—"

"His problems started long before you," Finn interrupted. "We all tried and failed him. How do you help someone who doesn't think they need it? Frankie blames me, she always will, and I have to live with that."

"She doesn't blame you, you're the only brother she has. She loves you." I layered my jacket over my sweater and zipped the duffel bag. Flinging it over my shoulder, I adjusted to the weight. "We need to get out of here."

Finn stepped in front of the door. "Be the man she needs and get out."

"Time to go." I opened the door to the garage and pulled my keys from my pocket, hearing a metallic clang onto the cement floor.

Finn picked up the casing and held it in his fingers, inspecting it, before closing his fist. Shoving his hands in his pockets, he stood calmer than he'd been since his undercover days. "I'll ask you again. Did you use your gun?"

I shoved my boots on and opened the tailgate, sliding my bag inside the back of the truck. "You know I didn't."

"Where's the weapon now?"

"I choked his friend with the rope they used to tie up Frankie..." My jaw tensed, sending an ache through my head. The gashes on her face and dark bruises on her neck and body pierced my brain like a sharp knife. "I used his gun to take out Noble."

"Did you make sure he was dead after you choked him? It takes time—"

"He was dead." I pushed the button, sending the garage door rising.

"Gloves?" Finn asked lightly, like we were planning a fucking barbecue.

I sat in my truck and started the engine. "I'm not answering dumb questions."

"Witnesses? Reasonable question, Rhett."

"His mother." I slammed the door and backed out of the garage, rolling the window down as he followed, spinning his keys.

"His *mother*?"

"She didn't see my face and has no idea who I am." For whatever reason, my instincts told me Alice Lane was the least of my worries.

"You better fucking hope not," Finn said. "We'll end this together, I owe you—"

"*Nothing*. You owe me nothing." Using the remote in my truck, I lowered the garage door.

"Yeah, those days are over. They ended the second Frankie chose you." Finn tapped my window's door frame as Lena turned onto the street. "We'll go to her house, get what she needs and the memory stick. "You've been with me this whole time."

I stared at him in silence. How could he trust me when I'd put his sister in such a terrible situation? But Finn stared back, calmness in his eyes. I sighed and tipped my head against the headrest. "You better be sure, Roscoe."

He shook his head, the ghost of a smile on his face, and ran to his car, shouting over his shoulder, "It's already done!"

FORTY

Frankie

Dressed in leggings and a hoodie Lena had brought me, I maneuvered around the bed, waiting for Dr. Harper, eager to leave the hospital. Zoey had promised she'd be in at seven during rounds to clear me for discharge this evening. Rhett and Finn stood outside the door talking with Lena and a few police officers, peeking in every few minutes as they spoke in hushed voices.

Detective Clark had stopped by first thing in the morning to speak to me. A distraught woman had called the police last night, reporting that someone had murdered her son and his friend in her home. The men fit the description of my attackers, but she couldn't disclose their identities. But I already knew who they were.

Rhett had tracked them down—I'd seen it all over his face the moment he'd returned to my room—but we didn't dare speak of it, not here, not until we could be alone.

I didn't recognize myself anymore. Waiting for justice through the law to protect me wasn't an option, not with violent men who knew how to disappear. And perhaps I'd made excuses for the undeniable relief I had knowing they were dead. I hoped they had suffered at Rhett's hands, and that should sicken me, but the flashbacks of their hands on my body made me love that man more for what he'd done.

I had crossed a line I never imagined possible and wasn't sure I could ever turn back.

In the chaos of the past twenty-four hours, the tension that had always hung between Rhett and Finn was gone.

I ambled around the hospital bed as my father walked into the room holding a small white bag. "I picked up your prescription."

"Thanks," I said, taking the bag from him.

He looked out the window, glancing over his shoulder. "There are some things up in the air, honey. It's best you don't go home just yet."

"Don't do that... Don't talk to me like I'm a kid." I brushed my hair, wincing as I tugged at the matted blood. "Just tell me what things and stop beating around more fucking secrets." I glared toward the door, locking eyes with Rhett's concerned face. I surrendered to my tangled hair and dropped the brush on the floor. The attack replayed in my mind, each memory sharp and vivid. The impact of their fists against my face, kicking me, tearing at my clothes, blood soaking into my shirt and coursing down my face...

Sweat gathered at the back of my neck, and my fingers numbed as my chest tightened. Blood had never had this effect on me, and fear had never consumed me like this. I wasn't an anxious person, but panic coiled inside of me, and I wanted to run from this room—from this hospital. I wanted to lock myself in my bedroom and never come out.

I perched on the edge of the bed as Dad held out the brush. "Francesca?" He set the brush on the bed when I didn't take it from his hand and sat next to me.

"Huh?" I blinked, and tears crept along my tender cheeks as I wiped my sweaty hands on the soft fabric of my leggings.

"Should I go get someone?" he asked, rubbing my back as though I were a sick child. "Do you need medication? What can I do?"

"Nothing, I'm..." *Fine.* I had helped patients through panic attacks, I knew what to do logically, but the crushing weight inside me refused to listen. I inhaled slowly, holding my breath for five seconds, before exhaling, trying to ignore the pain slicing through my ribcage. I forced myself to focus on the objects surrounding me. The hairbrush, my dad's hand, a can of ginger ale on the tray... Rhett's broad shoulders in the doorway as he talked with my brother.

"I gave Rhett the keys to the cabin," Dad said. "That's where I want you to go until he deals with his father. That is part of *some things*. It's not my story to tell."

My head jerked toward him, and a dull ache pulsed along my temples. "You *know*?"

"When he came to town, I told Finn to keep him away from you, but he didn't listen. Never took advice well, then again, neither did Miles."

"All of this could've been avoided if you and Finn had told me the truth after Miles died. Maybe if I'd known what had happened, I would've been more careful when Noble asked me about that picture on my phone."

My father raised his eyebrows, and he rubbed a hand across his weary face. "I disagree. You would've fixated on it. You'd have been back in Boston, confronting people who would have killed you... Call me an asshole, but I have no regrets keeping secrets from you."

A flush of anger burned my sore face, the word "asshole" almost escaping my lips, but I couldn't bring myself to say it, not to my dad. "Don't do it again, no more secrets."

He rose from the bed and stood in front of me, looking at me with his intense blue eyes that reflected my own. "I want you to do what you hate most and follow orders, just for a bit."

"I don't want to go back there, Dad, I can't." Fidgeting with the brush, I pulled at the stubborn tangles again. "As soon as I can walk without doubling over in pain, work needs me—"

"I need you not to die, and so do your mother and Finn." He gestured with a thumb over his shoulder toward Rhett, who glanced up at me. "And as much as I hate saying this, so does he."

The police officers who had gathered outside my room darted curious glances between my father and me, and Rhett shifted, closing the door to keep prying eyes away. I needed *him* not to die.

"I'll come out and stay with you when he goes to Boston, make sure you're safe—"

"He won't survive his father, he can't go, not alone..." I stood up too fast and burning pain throbbed in my chest, radiating into my head. Dad reached for me, but I stepped back. "And when was the last time you shot a gun? You're out of practice and drunk most of the time, you struggle to keep yourself safe." The moment the words left my lips, the familiar sorrowful expression he'd worn for months after Miles had died crossed his face. "I'm sorry, I didn't mean it."

"Yeah, you did, and it's warranted."

"No, it isn't, I'm just... so tired."

"Francesca, you're my daughter, and I love you. You've been through hell like I can't even begin to imagine, but I will protect my family, and right now I can offer a safe place. Go to the cabin, it's got running water, heat, and it's off the grid far enough you can rest and heal. Give it a week." He kissed the top of my head and left, holding the door open for Lena.

Our family cabin held years of laughter and tears, and the thought of returning intensified the persistent ache in my chest. The once peaceful log home had become nothing more than a painful reminder of everything we'd lost. If the threat on my life had been eliminated, why couldn't I go home?

Lena dropped my large, very unused gym bag on the bed. "Don't hate me for agreeing with them, but you can't go home yet, and you know that place is a haven in the middle of nowhere. I think I've got you covered, we had to be fast. I packed a bunch of clothes, underwear, shampoo, soap, a toothbrush..." She glanced at me, and her eyes scanned my face. "Are you hanging in there?"

"They're not giving me much choice, I don't like it."

"They're whisking you away into the night like a fugitive, sweetie. Just for a few days."

I placed my hands on the window ledge, staring into the dark sky. The rain had stopped, and the sliver of a moon struggled to peek through the clouds. "Who's coming with me?"

Sidling up beside me, Lena wrapped an arm around my waist. "Rhett is. There were talks of a police guard, but since the threat appears to be... *eliminated*." She dropped her arm and met my eyes as I looked up at her. "Well, let's just say, stay tuned on the guard situation, but Finn has already been out with Rhett and checked the property. Made sure it's free of bad guys."

I tried to wrap my mind around returning to our family cabin. It had once been like a second home for me, and my parents still went often. Dad had made the cabin his project over the years, having solar panels and a generator installed, insulating the well for running water, and keeping a stack of wood ready in the shed for the stove.

"Did they tell you what's been going on?" I whispered, glancing over my shoulder. The gathering outside my door had thinned, leaving Rhett, Finn, and my parents talking in low voices.

"I gave your brother an ultimatum, something I swore I'd never do."

"What sort of ultimatum?"

"A no more secrets one. He brought Rhett into my bar without telling me who the man really was." She tilted her blonde head to the side. "Don't get me wrong, I can see what you see in him, but Finn lied to me."

I shuffled back to the bed and sat down. If Lena were with any other man, I'd tell her to leave him and that she deserved better. But I was only beginning to understand what it meant to love a man shaped by a past he couldn't share. Knowing the difference between deceit and withholding truths hinged on the intentions behind them. What felt like betrayal had never been about hurting me or Lena. Rhett and Finn believed that the safety of the ones near them depended on keeping secrets buried.

Sudden clarity pierced my medication-induced haze as I snapped out of my thoughts. "You did what felt right, Lena, you always have. Neither of them meant to hurt us, but I don't want to be with someone who feels the need to keep me in the dark like I'm too fragile to handle the truth anymore than you do. Relationships like that can't survive."

Lena's eyes filled with tears. The only time I'd ever seen her cry was at Miles's funeral. "If I ever leave him, promise me we'll find a way to always be friends."

"I promise."

Crouching down, Lean cradled my cheeks. "You're gonna be okay, Frankie. You're a survivor, my beautiful friend."

"I love you," I said.

"Love you too." Lena embraced me, and I winced through a jab of pain. "Sorry." She released me with a grimace.

The stitches along my jaw felt tight and itchy, and I brushed my fingertips over the threads and swollen curve of my lip. Lifting my arm as far as the pain would allow, I smelled myself, tracing dried patches of blood along my arms. "I've never been so desperate for a shower in my life."

Rhett knocked at the open door and stepped into the room. "You've got company," he said, moving behind me as I stood.

I could *feel* his presence fill the room like a bodyguard ready to strike at any sign of threat. I was in danger because of him, but he was the reason a sense of safety washed over me. An overwhelming urge to reach behind me and feel his fingers laced with mine struck me, but I clung to the strings dangling from my hoodie instead.

FORTY-ONE

Frankie

Detective Clark strode into my hospital room followed by two police officers. "Francesca Roscoe. We haven't been successful in tracking your phone. The last place was near the mill, but it's been dead since."

"What does that mean? Someone else has it?" I asked.

"Maybe, or it's been destroyed. I wish I had a better answer," she said.

I hugged myself to keep my body from trembling as every muscle holding me upright protested in agony. "Anything more on what happened at that woman's house last night?" I wanted to inquire about the investigation into who they thought had killed them, but I'd do whatever it took to keep suspicion away from Rhett.

"Shut the door," Detective Clark ordered. An officer with her hair pulled into a bun so tight I wasn't sure how she could blink closed the door as the other man stood with his thumbs tucked in his vest.

"This may come as a shock to you," Detective Clark said, her eyes roaming over each person in the crowded room before fixating back on me, "but the woman who called the police had been a patient of yours recently. Alice Lane. I've been told her son sent you flowers after she was released, and the local police checked on his whereabouts after the break-in at your house." Hesitating, she scanned the room again. "Her son was among the victims in her house. Unfortunately, while she did see the intruder, she never saw the man's face. The only name she could give us that was out of the ordinary for her day-to-day contacts was Clay Preston. As we all know, unless he came back from the dead, he was not in her home last night." She smoothed her gray hair and crossed her arms. "A relative of the woman has been in contact with her recently, and we've reached out to him to see if he has any information. That is all we can tell you at this time. We *are*, however, reopening a case that has been closed for some time now, given that Mr. Marshall is out of hiding, and Mr. Roscoe has cooperated and turned over a device belonging to your deceased brother." Her abrupt words softened as she addressed me. "Can you confirm this had been located in your home, Ms. Roscoe?"

Out of the corner of my eye, I saw Finn shift uncomfortably; Lena slid her hand down his arm, intertwining her fingers with his. I maintained eye contact with the detective. "I can confirm that I found it the day before I was attacked and didn't have a chance to do much about it." I bent the truth without hesitation.

"But you did have a chance to review the contents on the device?" she asked with a raised eyebrow.

"The device was encrypted, impossible to unlock without a password." I reached for the bedrail to steady myself. "Without me, you'd never be able to get into it, isn't that right?"

She gave me a curt smile. "You've done some research."

"I didn't look through everything my brother had on that thing, but enough to know that because of my family, you have a fucking massive amount of evidence, Detective Clark. And there is one audio file I would like returned to me, it has my name on it, and I'll be very upset if I don't get it back." A sudden high-pitched ringing resounded in my ears as I recalled Miles's voice message. I ran my fingers along the suffocating fabric at my neck; the collar of my sweater felt like a noose. The metallic smell of blood in my hair and clinging to my skin made my empty stomach lurch. I took a deep breath, recoiling at the stabbing pain in my chest.

The warmth of Rhett's body radiated next to me as he stepped closer, placing a comforting hand on my back.

"You have my word I will get the audio file back to you." The detective dropped her hands to her hips. "If you need a police escort home, we can do that—"

"We've got it from here." Rhett stepped forward, extending his hand, and she shook it, narrowing her steely eyes at him.

"Thank you Detective Clark," I said.

Zoey opened the door and scanned the room with a casual smile, carrying a paper bag. "Can I have a few minutes with this patient?" The tension in the air released like a deflated balloon.

Her bright white doctor's coat was like a beacon of relief. If my aching body allowed me, I'd run and hug her for the interruption.

"We're leaving," Detective Clark said. "We'll be in touch." She trailed the officers out of the room.

Lena let go of Finn's hand. "We can give you some privacy."

"She's just here to release me, I'm ready to go... to the cabin," I muttered. "No privacy needed."

"Discharge is signed; I grabbed you some antiseptic and bandages..." Zoey said. "Your dad gave you the prescription?"

"Got it." I took the bag from her and stuffed it into the duffel bag. "I still haven't talked to staffing about my shifts." I felt an unfamiliar dread at the edge in my chest, tightening with overwhelming anxiety.

"It's handled, Frankie." She embraced me, careful not to squeeze too tight. "Get out of here and let your body heal, don't worry about work. It'll still be here when you're ready, trust me." Giving Lena a quick hug, she eyed Rhett with a piercing gaze. "Just..."

With hands pressed to her chest, she turned back to me. "Please be safe?"

"She will be," Rhett said.

Zoey muttered over her shoulder as she left the room. "She better."

Swallowing down the emotion building in my throat, I made to follow her, but Rhett held his jacket over my shoulders. "It's cold out," he said. I reached for the bag, but he grabbed it first, slinging it over his shoulder. I wanted to argue—I could still do things for myself—but I was just too tired.

Finn had a small smile on his face, as if he knew what I was thinking. "We'll walk you down to the truck, Rhett's going to stay with you tonight, and I'll be there tomorrow." He handed me a cell phone. "Take this."

"Thanks." I held the phone and flipped the bottom open and shut. "What is this?"

"Keeps things untraceable and simple." Rhett held his jacket over my shoulders.

My mind struggled to catch up, like my life wasn't my own anymore, and I was a bystander watching someone else go through the motions. With an uncontrollable, pained grunt, I slid my arms into the sleeves, each movement sending pain through my chest. Rhett zipped it up, and heat enveloped me, soothing my body. "Thank you," I said.

His dark eyes blazed with fierce determination as they locked with mine, intensely studying my face. "We'll take it slow, and if it's too much, don't be stubborn and let me know. I'll grab a wheelchair or carry you."

"It'll be fine," I said as Finn held the door open and we filtered out of the room. I wanted to pull a hood over my head to hide myself from the curious onlookers in the busy hallway. I could imagine the gossip behind closed doors as we walked toward the elevator, my face bruised and stitched.

My body protested with each step, but I gritted my teeth, hiding the pain behind a mask of composure, and stepped inside the elevator. The four of us stared at the digital numbers in silence until the low hum faded. The doors slid open, and we made our way to the parking lot. A burst of frigid air surrounded me as we stepped outside, where Rhett's truck waited next to Finn's car.

Rhett opened the passenger-side door, but climbing into the truck looked more like scaling Mount Everest. "Hang on, Frankie." He handed the duffle bag to Finn as Lena grabbed two shopping bags from the trunk of Finn's car.

I can do this myself, I have to do something for myself.

I gripped the door, stepping onto the edge of the doorframe. My shallow breaths fogged in the cold as I hoisted myself up, shivering underneath Rhett's oversized jacket. I winced and tears stung my eyes, but his arms caught me, supporting my weight as he placed me on the seat. With his face inches from mine, he tugged the seatbelt across my chest, snapping it into the buckle beside me. "Not everything is an order, baby." His voice was gentle, and he kissed my forehead before stepping down and shutting the door.

Settling into the driver's seat, he started the truck, rolling down my window for Lena and Finn, waiting on the other side. My brother's features softened as he leaned on the door frame, taking me back to when we were kids and Mom made him play board games with me at the kitchen table while she made dinner. She'd left him in charge of Miles and me often, and he'd never complained about it.

"Promise me you'll be careful, don't leave the cabin. I'll need you to say it—"

"Jesus, what are we, twelve?" Tears trickled down my cheek, and I wiped them with the back of my hand. "Sure, promise."

He raised his eyebrows, the line between them fading. "I'll see you tomorrow." Reaching into the truck, he squeezed my hand, pulling away so Lena could say goodbye before Rhett rolled the window up. The parking attendant opened the gate for us, and we drove away, leaving Willow Grove behind.

The truck thumped over bumps as we veered onto rural roads, and I hugged myself as the motion sent pain through my chest.

"Sorry, I'll try to be careful." Rhett's gaze flickered from me to the road.

"It's not your fault." I looked out the window as a blur of trees whipped by.

He clasped my hand in his, and his fingers interlocked with mine against my thigh. "This is *all* my fault. I let them get to you."

I tightened my fingers around his. "You stopped them from coming back. It was us or them."

Gripping the steering wheel, he locked his eyes on the dark road ahead. "I'm not proud of myself, but I can't say I'm sorry for what I've done either." He pulled his hand from my grasp, resting it on his leg. "I know I don't belong with you. I'm just not sure I can leave you when this is over. Doing the right thing isn't in my DNA."

The more I saw beyond Rhett's world and understood the complex man he was, the more I couldn't imagine a life without him. "What if I want you to be mine, and leaving me is the wrong thing?" Shifting in my seat, I extended my hand and curled my fingers around his. "If you go, I'll just have to order you right back." My swollen lip throbbed with pain as my smile stretched it, and I touched my mouth to suppress it.

"You're breaking me with these orders, Frankie." He brought my fingers to his mouth and kissed them.

The trouble with wanting a man who had killed for me without hesitation meant entering a world of danger that I knew nothing about, with the chilling awareness we could both die. Rhett blamed himself for getting too close, but I had allowed him in, and even after everything that had happened... I didn't regret *him*.

FORTY-TWO

Frankie

Rhett steered off the main road onto a familiar hidden pathway, the truck's headlights leading the way through the darkness. Gravel crunched under the tires, and pine trees closed in on the windows as he eased the truck along the narrow road.

The road back in time.

"I can't believe I'm back here." My eyes strained to see past the road to where the trees cleared and our cabin waited.

"Thanks for taking orders and letting me do this." He leaned over, keeping his eyes on the road, and opened the glove box, pulling out two guns.

"I think you've hit your orders limit." The endless road wound toward the clearing, and Rhett drove up to our log cabin.

The moon offered little light through the dense trees, but frost covered the overgrown yard, triggering memories. Miles and I had climbed those trees, competing for who could reach the highest branch. I could still hear my mother's panicked shrieks for us to come down before ordering Finn to get us. And after two years of staying away, I had returned, making the cabin a hideout instead of a place for family gatherings.

Rhett tucked a gun in his waistband and pulled out a flashlight. He opened the door and climbed out, handing me the other. "This is for you. Wait here until I get you."

He shut the door and headed toward the cabin, leaving me alone with my hand still on the door. My breath was the only sound in the truck's cab. This place was part of my home, my family... mine.

I hated the paralyzing grip of fear as I tracked Rhett's shadow in the beam of his flashlight. Placing the gun on the dash, I shifted in my seat and strained to look over my shoulder, but darkness shrouded the path behind me. I flinched and faced forward, opening the door as Rhett moved around the front of the cabin and ducked inside. Light bounced off the walls through the cabin's windows, and stabbing pain hit me as I stepped down from the passenger seat and tumbled to the ground.

"Fuck," I groaned, bracing myself on the footrest as I stood, brushing dirt off my leggings.

The front door opened, and light danced over the truck as Rhett hurried toward me. I shut the door, facing him. "Don't ask, I don't know why I didn't wait, it was stuffy in there."

"Stuffy?"

Gravel crunched under my feet as I trudged toward the back of his truck. "I can carry something."

"I have no doubt." He gave me the flashlight. "Hold this please?"

"I can handle more than the flashlight, Rhett." I took the light and held it over the back of the truck as he reached in and grabbed our bags, draping both over his shoulder. "What about those two?" I pointed to the two shopping bags that Lena had stowed away, but he took them and shut the tailgate.

He glanced down at me, stepping closer. "Take the keys from my pocket and lock the truck."

"Any more orders for tonight? Because I'm tired." I reached into the pocket of his jeans, letting my fingers linger as I met his eyes.

"Wrong pocket. But I like your hands on me."

"I gathered that." With one hand nestled in his pocket, I set the light on the bed of the truck and plunged my other hand into the opposite one. I fished out the keys, removing my hands with a swift motion. "They're warm, and I'm freezing."

"Let's go inside. Grab that gun off the dash." He adjusted the bags as he hovered near me.

Turning away from him, I retrieved the gun from the cab of the truck and snatched the flashlight. Angling the light ahead of us, I led the way through the dense underbrush toward the cabin. I cursed under my breath as my battered body screamed in agony, begging me to lie down and rest.

The front porch greeted me with a creak. Rhett held back until I entered the spacious living room first, placing the bags on the kitchen table. He locked the door and pulled the curtains closed as I set the gun down and gripped the back of a rocking chair, silently taking in the cabin.

Family photos decorated the walls, and the quilt my grand-mother had made covered the worn, plush sectional. Mom's rose wallpaper border, a relic from the early 90s, had faded to a muted blush, yet stubbornly clung to the kitchen wall. Holding onto my aching stomach, I wandered around the room. I ran my fingers over the knots in the log walls. "Nothing has changed."

I sank onto the antique rocking chair. The ticking of a bear-shaped clock matched the constant throbbing of my swollen face. It was almost midnight, and every inch of me burned with a deep, relentless ache.

Rhett bent down in front of me and held onto the armrests. "Tell me what you need, and I'll do it. I don't care what it is."

"I wish it were that easy, baby." I placed my hand on his face. The stubble had grown along his jawline, and his hair had gotten a bit longer. He appeared as exhausted as I felt. "What do you need, Rhett?"

"For you to be okay. I'll start a fire and get you pain pills."

"I can't take more for another hour." I shoved my hands into the pockets of his jacket I wore as he opened the woodstove.

He arranged kindling and paper, using my father's lighter to start a fire, and the scent of woodsmoke drifted in the room, reminding me of campfire days. "It's not as hard as I thought it'd be, being here. I feel like he's still around or something. I know that's weird."

"How you feel isn't weird." He placed logs on the growing fire and shut the door as the flames danced behind the glass.

Leaning forward, I kicked my shoes off, holding my breath to stifle the pain. Moments of the attack haunted my mind. A rough touch against my throat. Cruel fingers in my hair. The impact of their hands across my face. "Rhett? I need to wash the blood off myself. Can you just help me get into the shower? If you run the water and stick me in there, I can do the rest."

Rummaging through my gym bag, he grabbed the soap and shampoo that Lena had packed. "I can do better than that. Hold on to me." He held out his arm.

"I can walk—"

"I know, just let me help make it easier."

Linking my arm with his, I shuffled down the short hallway into the bathroom. Mom had redecorated it after Miles had died, making it the only place in the cabin untouched by nostalgia. I unzipped Rhett's jacket, and he set the bottles down, taking it from me.

He eyed the plastic thermostat on the wall. "Are you cold? I can see if the heat works in here."

"I'm okay," I said as he yanked the shower curtain aside and ran the water. The bears adorning the bottom of the curtain weren't my mother's choice. Dad despised all the flowers and had requested that this be the one place he could have a say in the decorating.

"Is the water warm enough?" Rhett's eyes swept over my face, and he gently touched the bandage over my stitched cheek. "Should you take that off?"

I peeled the bandage off, and he took it from my fingers, tossing it in the garbage can. Gripping his arm, I held my hand under the stream of water. I let go of him and reached the other hand in, scraping blood from underneath my nails as tears blurred my vision. "It's perfect."

"I'll find a towel," he said, leaving the bathroom.

"There's a closet at the end of the hall." A desperate need to scrub away the lingering touch the two monsters had left behind consumed me. Pulling my wet hands back, I steadied myself against the wall and pushed my leggings to my knees. I had no bra or panties on underneath, but it wasn't as though he hadn't seen me naked before. I longed to submerge my body under the water, let it soak into my hair, and scrub my skin until it was raw, but I flinched when I tried to pull my sweater over my head.

Rhett returned and placed two towels on the small vanity. He tugged my leggings down my legs to my ankles. "Put your hand on my shoulder and lift your foot." I lifted one and then the other, and he shoved them aside, standing to face me. "Let me help. I promise to be careful, I'll make sure you're comfortable, and you can tell me to leave anytime. You can trust me."

I nodded through tears. "Okay." I raised my arms, gritting my teeth, and he gently pulled off my sweater, leaving me naked and shivering.

Rhett's fingers traced the bandage high on my stomach where Noble had sliced me with his knife. "Should I take this off too?" He shuddered as he spoke, his jaw twitching.

"I'll do it." I picked at the edge of the tape, flinching as I ripped it off my skin. The stinging sensation gave me a strange sense of relief from the constant pain in my chest.

He helped me step over the side of the tub into the shower and pulled the curtain, cocooning me in the warmth. I let the water cascade over my head, running down my body, carrying blood down the drain. A whimper escaped me as I tried to reach up and wash my hair.

Rhett's silhouette moved to the other side of the curtain. "Frankie, can I come in with you? I'll just wash your hair and get you out faster."

I wanted to curl up in a ball and sob at how helpless I felt. "You can come in."

The curtain slid open at the opposite end, and he stepped into the tub with me, holding a shampoo bottle. His naked body filled the space with a comforting warmth.

"You want the water?" I said through chattering teeth.

"Don't worry about me." His gaze dropped from my face, lingering on my chest and torso. The desire and need from our night together were gone, replaced by a darkening expression filled with sorrow and a palpable, vibrating rage. "I'm so fucking sorry for what they did to you."

"Kiss me. I'd do it myself, but I can't reach your face."

Leaning over me, he touched the cut on my lip before capturing my mouth with his in a soft kiss and pulled back.

My eyes locked with his. I needed more of his touch, more of *Him.* "Wash the blood off me."

He squeezed a tiny amount of shampoo into his palm, and I touched his hand with a smile. "I've got more hair than you." I looked up at his hair. "Like a lot more."

"Got it," he smiled back and squeezed a little more out of the bottle. "Better?"

"That'll do it."

As he stepped closer, the water ran over me and down his broad chest. His arm muscles tensed as he reached for my head, lightly massaging the shampoo into my scalp with his fingers. The suds turned pink as he washed the blood from the long strands. Our bodies pressed together, the water cascading between us. He rinsed the soap from my hair, and I wrapped my arms around him, placing my hands on his back to calm my uncontrollable shivering. "You're good at this."

His length twitched against my leg as I held him close, and he leaned back, taking my face in his hands. "Clearly I could do better. He's got a fucking mind of his own, ignore him."

"He's okay, I'm flattered he likes me so much."

A laugh escaped him. He soaked a facecloth and gently dabbed at the blood on my face and arms, rinsing the crimson from the cloth. His hands on my body chased away the vicious attack, if only for a short time. He added soap and washed my back with tender hands, handing it to me so I could wash my intimate areas.

I dropped the cloth in the tub, and he wrapped his arms around me and kissed my shoulder. "Did I miss anything," he said against my ear.

"If my body didn't hurt so bad—"

"This isn't about sex. This is about making you feel safe and as okay as you can be right now." He turned off the water and reached for a towel. Drying me off, he wrapped it around me so I could hold it together.

"Thank you," I whispered.

"Don't thank me for taking care of you." He ran a hand through his messy wet hair and secured a towel around his waist, opening the bathroom door.

Cool air sent goosebumps prickling over my skin—I couldn't stop shaking. He glanced in the room with the bunk beds and cot before leading me to the opposite room, helping me sit on the queen-sized bed.

"My parents refuse to get rid of the bunk beds." I smiled, remembering. "They always kept a lock on the closet in that room because there's a crawlspace in it with a door that leads outside."

"They thought you'd take off?"

"They *knew* we'd take off."

Rhett pulled the sweater he'd worn over my head. His scent clung to the fabric, and I inhaled, immediately regretting it as my chest heaved in pain. He'd brought my gym bag into the room and rummaged through it. "Lena packed a brush, underwear... which ones?" He looked puzzled as he handed me the brush and held up two pairs of lace-trimmed panties.

I brushed the ends of my wet strands, unable to get the tangles out. "At least they're pretty. The pink ones, I guess. Do they go with the shades of red and purple covering my body?" I froze. "I don't know why I said that."

"You can say whatever you want, I would." Adjusting himself beneath the towel, he crouched in front of me, holding the pink underwear so I could put my feet in. "Hold on," he said, and I obliged with my hands around his neck. He stood, pulling me with him, and my towel fell to the floor as he slid the panties up over my damp skin.

Setting me back on the edge of the bed, he looked me over, concern etched all over his face. "What's next?"

"Is there a hairdryer in the bathroom cabinet? I just can't seem to get warm."

Yanking a pair of boxer-briefs on, he discarded his towel and headed for the bathroom. Rhett had no idea how much he'd altered my perception of what it meant to take care of someone. He cared for me the way no man ever had, instinctively and without hesitation, like it was the most natural thing in the world.

I think I'm in love with this man.

He returned with a small hairdryer and plugged it in beside the bed. "Your father made sure there was enough gas in the generator if the solar doesn't work."

"He's good like that. My father is probably at home drinking now that I'm out of the hospital... You don't have to dry my hair."

Rhett sat on the bed behind me with his legs on either side of mine. "I want to." He kissed my shoulder softly. "He'll get help, Frankie. This will change him."

"Nothing will change him."

"Don't give up on him." He turned on the hairdryer. Aiming the hot air over my head, he ran his fingers through my hair.

The heat warmed my neck and shoulders through his sweater. We sat in silence as his fingers carefully brushed through my wet strands and he dried my hair.

The humming dryer stopped, and he placed it on the nightstand. "It's still damp, I can keep going."

"It's clean, that's all I wanted." I rested my back against his chest and ran my hands along his thighs. "I'm happy you're here, Rhett."

He got off the bed and crouched in front of me, encircling my waist. I cupped his face and tilted his head so his hazel eyes met mine. He didn't turn away or say anything, but an unfamiliar seriousness hung in the silence between us. "What is it?" I asked.

Taking my hands, he held them to his bare chest. "I love you, Frankie."

He uttered the words that had been in my mind for days. "I love you too." I leaned forward, ignoring my body's protest, and fell into his arms. He rubbed my back, kissing my face, my lips, lifting me as he stood. A bond had formed between us, and I never wanted it to break. He was mine, but I was all his.

He kissed my forehead and dressed in a pair of worn jeans and a T-shirt. As we headed into the living room, Rhett turned off the lights. "Let's keep it as dark as possible."

I settled on the couch with the quilt, and he handed me the paper bag, my prescription, and a water bottle. I popped a pill and took out the bandages Zoey had packed. He sat next to me as I touched the stitched gash along my cheek and lifted the baggy sweater to inspect the cuts on my stomach. "This will all scar, I'm sure of it."

"You're beautiful and strong, Frankie. I'll never see scars, just you." He opened an antiseptic wipe, tilting my face up, and I grabbed his wrist.

"I can do it—"

"You did it for me." He dabbed at the stitched gash. "Does it hurt?"

"It all hurts, but I'll heal."

"You will, baby." He placed a small bandage on my cheek and worked quickly to take care of the gashes on my stomach. His fingers brushed along my swollen cheek. "I'll get ice."

I shook my head, dull pain ricocheting around my face. "I don't need ice right now, I'm not sure what I need." I needed to crawl out of my skin for a while, away from the pain, but settled for the comfort of Rhett's sweater and pulled the quilt over my legs.

He rummaged through the bags, placing coffee, eggs, bread, and a box of protein bars on the table. "Are you hungry?"

Usually composed and steady, Rhett was restless, unable to be still. I'd never seen him so shaken and uneasy before, like something had come undone inside him. "Come sit with me for a minute."

"I can't—"

"Please." I moved the quilt aside and patted the couch. "Five minutes and then you can go back to whatever it is you need to do."

He sat next to me, and I moved closer. "What do we do next?" I whispered.

"*We* don't do anything, Frankie, *I* will take care of what happens next."

"We're a 'we' now, you're not in this alone anymore."

He rose from the couch, running a hand through his disheveled, damp hair. His gun was in his waistband again. "They could've killed you. When I saw you on the floor in that fucking basement..." His brows knitted together, forming a deep line between them. "I put a target on your back, and I won't forgive myself for it. I sure as hell won't let it happen again."

The springs in the couch shifted as I moved, and a twinge of pain radiated in my chest. I exhaled slowly. "I was a target the day Bran Noble saw that picture on my phone, before I met you. This isn't your fault, Rhett. It's no one's *fault*." I wanted him to hold me until we both stopped hurting. "I feel broken, way too vulnerable, and for the first time I can't stand on my own two feet... *literally*." Wiping my eyes, I fought back tears.

He braced himself with his arms on either side of me. "Then you use my arms to hold you until you're back."

I traced the tattoo on his forearm. "I trust you. I can't turn off these feelings, and I don't want to, but I'm scared of losing you."

He leaned closer, his face inches from mine. "I don't want you to be scared of anything."

I ran my hands up his arms, placing them on his chest, feeling his heartbeat against my palm. "You got caught up in a life because of who your father is, but it doesn't mean you're a bad man. I don't want you to run anymore."

"I meant it when I said I love you." He lowered his lips to mine. "But I'd die if you got hurt again because of me. I can't let that happen, I won't."

"I love you." Tears ran down the sides of my face, and he wiped them before I could. The pain subsided as the pill took effect, and my eyelids grew heavy.

Taking my hands, Rhett pulled me to my feet and swept me into his arms. He carried me to the bedroom and set me on the bed. "Stay with me?" I asked.

He tucked the blankets around my body and crawled into bed next to me, pulling me against his chest. I turned my head to face him, and his face grew blurry as my eyes blinked slowly, sleep overtaking me. His fingers laced with mine, and his thumb rubbed back and forth over my hand.

Moving closer, his warm breath caressed my skin as he kissed my cheek. "Get some sleep."

Sleep won, dragging me into a restless nightmare. I relived the horrors in the basement and screamed for help, but no sound came out.

FORTY-THREE

Rhett

I shoved the curtains aside, surveying the trees surrounding the property. A small amount of moonlight through the clouds reflected off the thick frost covering the truck. Soft snow drifted down, blanketing the empty road leading to the cabin. My phone buzzed as I added wood to the fire. Finn's hourly check-in. He couldn't have slept, but neither had I, not really. It was just past three, and Frankie had tossed and turned for hours, her soft cries filling the room as she slept, but I couldn't bring myself to wake her up. I'd told her I loved her. The words had come out of my mouth without a thought, like they'd been waiting for her, and only her.

I had to finish what I'd started two years ago. I messaged Vivian. *I'm coming tomorrow, don't tell him. I want to see him on my terms.*

She surprised me when she wrote back. *Meet me at my place and I'll make sure he's here. We'll back you up, please trust me.*

I had no other choice, and if I didn't go to him, he would hunt me down and punish me for not obeying his order. I wanted Frankie nowhere near his fucking rage. *Luca?* I replied.

Yes, he's with us.

Tell him I got his message.

Locking the phone, I stretched out on the couch with my gun digging into my waist and folded my arms across my chest. Fuck, I was tired. I'd never been so goddamn exhausted. I shut my eyes for a few minutes. Frankie was safe, and the men who had hurt her were dead. If anyone dared touch a Morrigan's woman, they'd find out the consequences pretty fucking quick. She was everything good, a woman who would do anything for someone she loved, and deserve it or not, she loved me.

"Rhett?" Frankie's voice cut through a haze, and I jolted awake, sitting up with my hand on my gun. Her face was damp with sweat, and her hair stuck to her forehead. She sat next to me on the couch, her breaths shallow.

"I'm here, baby, what's wrong?" I held her face in my hands, gently turning her toward me, and her blue eyes found mine. She took a deep, shaky breath, wrapping her arms around herself. "There you are, keep breathing," I said. "I'm not going anywhere."

She gripped my wrists and pulled my arms around her as she straddled me. "It was a nightmare, that's all."

I held her, sliding my hands underneath my sweater she wore. "You're safe."

Sitting back, she moved her hand to my face. "I want you to chase it all away." She reached between us, rubbing me over my jeans. Taking my gun, she placed it with care on the coffee table.

She wanted to have sex with me, but I didn't want to hurt her, and condoms were the last thing I'd thought to bring with us after what happened. "I don't have a condom—"

"I don't care. I want to feel like my body is mine again. I want to feel something other than this fucking pain." Tears glistened in her eyes. "Can you help me... with that?"

"I can do whatever you want."

The way she flinched when she took off the sweater killed me, but I let her do what she wanted, holding back until I was sure I could touch her. She grabbed my shirt at the bottom and lifted it up with a quick tug. "Take your shirt off," she demanded, and I removed my shirt for her.

Her hands grasped my face, and my cock hardened as she moved against me in her pink lace panties. "Please don't see the bruises, see me like you did before."

"*You* are all I see." With my hands on her hips, I pulled her closer and gently sucked her lower lip.

Frankie kissed me, her tongue tracing my lips, coaxing them apart. I rubbed her back, kissing her harder, the sounds of our mingled gasps filling the room. She undid my jeans, her warm hand sliding inside to grip me tightly. I moaned, and she smiled against my mouth. "Take off your pants," she breathed, and I tried to ignore the slight gasp that sounded more like pain than lust.

Gripping her ass, I lifted her, moving her aside, and did as I was told. I dropped my jeans and boxers on the floor. "What do you want, Frankie?"

"Sit back down... please." Desire filled her eyes, her chest heaving with each ragged breath.

"I need to hear you say you're okay," I said.

"I'm okay, Rhett. I promise."

Kneeling on the couch, I kissed her lips, moving down to her chest, and she sat back, letting her arms fall to her sides. I dragged my tongue around each nipple, tasting her sweet skin as they hardened. Hooking the sides of her panties with her thumbs, she moved them down her legs. "Help me."

"Anything," I rasped, as I slid them off her feet.

Frankie pushed me backward, and her eyes blazed with intensity. "I want to be on top of you, I want to feel you inside me."

I wasn't sure I'd be able to go as gently as she needed, but I settled against the couch and helped her climb over me again.

Frankie was on her knees, gripping my cock against her wet pussy, and I had to restrain myself from thrusting into her.

She closed her eyes with a faint wince, and I wrapped my arms around her, *aching* to bury myself inside her. "You're sore, baby, we can't do this, I don't want to hurt you."

"You won't, trust me. Can I?" Her eyes widened, and slowly, she edged herself down on my tip.

"*Fuck me*," I groaned.

"I'm trying to." She kissed me, and my fingers dug into her hips, guiding her down, feeling the warmth of her body molding against mine.

"*More.*" Her head fell back as she sat all the way down, and her hands slid up her body, pinching her nipples. "You feel so good."

"So do you." I let go of worrying I'd hurt her and matched her rhythm as she released her nipples and clasped her fingers around my neck. Lifting her ass, she came back down on me, eliciting a desperate groan from my throat. "Keep going."

I moved her body up and down, feeling her grind against me. She called my name between moans, nearly making me come. Dragging my other hand up her back, I tangled my fingers in her hair, tugging her head closer to mine.

"Let yourself go, Frankie."

Her mouth met mine, demanding and needy, moaning against my lips. She shivered, and her pussy spasmed around me in waves as she came, surprising me as her pace suddenly quickened. "Your turn," she breathed against my ear.

My release came, pulsing inside of her, and she collapsed on my chest. I stroked her back, pulling the quilt over her, holding her like I could shield her from the world. "Please tell me I didn't hurt you."

Lifting her head to face me, she kissed my cheek with tears in her eyes. I panicked, sitting up as I held her. "Oh, fuck, what is it? I'm so sorry—"

"No, you were perfect. I feel like I can breathe."

"Are you sore?"

"It's worth it." She swung her legs over the couch, struggling to stand, and I wrapped an arm around her, guiding her to the bathroom.

I helped her clean up and get dressed in a T-shirt and sweatpants that I found in her gym bag. "Do you want to go to bed or the couch?" I asked, handing her a pain pill and a glass of water.

Tossing it back, she wiped her mouth with the back of her hand. "By the fire would be great."

I grabbed pillows and blankets off the bed and settled her onto the couch with me. Her dark hair fell over her shoulders onto my chest, and I held her close. The sun hadn't risen yet, and the only light in the cabin was the orange glow from the fire.

"How'd you do it? Kill those men?" she asked.

I stilled. That was a question I never wanted to answer or talk about. "Frankie, I'm not answering that."

She tilted her face up at me. "I want to know, and I think I deserve to know."

The swelling had subsided, and the bruises faded from red to a dark blue, but even when they disappeared, I'd never forget how she looked, injured and beaten. I couldn't afford to risk slipping up and putting her in danger again.

"You deserve everything, but not this part of me."

Tracing her fingers along my jaw, she kissed me. "I figured you had to kill the first one quietly not to draw attention, and maybe you shot the other? I heard them talking at the hospital, I know shots were fired in that house. What I want to know is how you killed him without a sound?"

Jesus. If she stayed with me, she was going to know all of me. "I choked him in the bathroom with the rope they used to tie you up."

Her hand dropped from my face to my chest, and I braced for anger, fear, or a distant look in her eyes, but she rubbed my chest as she spoke. "Sounds like a good use for that fucking rope."

I swallowed hard. "I don't scare you?"

"You make me feel safe. But I feel like we're running out of time. Like this is all going to blow up in our faces and it'll be over... We're only just getting started together."

I had finally met a woman I couldn't live without, who made me feel alive, and I wasn't letting her go, but I felt the same way. "I really hope not, Frankie."

"You don't do reassuring well." She smiled, but her eyes glazed over as her pain pill kicked in.

I caressed her head and neck, hoping to ease her pain. "I'll get it right, I promise."

"Promises are no good if we can't follow through."

"I'll follow through." I kissed her forehead, my lips lingering on her skin. I'd never get enough of kissing her or simply being near her.

Killing my father was the only way I could be free to build a life with Frankie. I just had to get to him before he stole everything from me.

FORTY-FOUR

Frankie

F inn sat at the kitchen table as the snow drifted outside the window. I'd kept the fire going all afternoon and turned on a table lamp Mom had made of recycled glass years ago. Waves of nostalgia surrounded me everywhere I looked in the cabin. I assumed my parents had left so much unchanged for fear of erasing the memories of us when we were kids.

Opening a bottle of red wine I found in the cabinet, I filled a wineglass and sat across from Finn. As I sipped the wine, sweeter than I was used to, a drop ran down the stem of the glass, soaking into the sleeve of my white sweater. My eyes settled into a blank stare, and I didn't rush to scrub the stain. I toyed with the rose charm on my wrist as the burgundy spread into an abstract blot in the fabric... like blood. Releasing the bracelet from my grasp, I blinked a few times, clearing my eyes, and ran my fingers over the dents in the wood. Years of use had worn down the table, leaving it smooth and scarred.

I'll never forget the memories here. None of us would.

Rhett had left for Boston a few hours earlier and hadn't returned my messages. A sick feeling had settled in my stomach. What if he never came back to me? The man's soul was stained like my sweater. He'd killed people and might be on the run for the rest of his life, but I *loved* him.

"I think Lena might leave me," Finn said into our shared silence.

He glanced up at me with a pained look in his eyes. I wasn't used to Finn sharing his life with me, but I wanted him to talk. "She loves you, but you can't keep hiding things from her. If she loses trust, she might."

"So she told me."

"So listen to her. Lena isn't complicated, Finn. She's the most straightforward woman I know, and not afraid to speak her mind or be alone. She chose you when you met, and she keeps choosing to be with you, don't fuck that up."

"I can't. I won't." He rubbed his face and shoved his hands in his pockets. "I thought she lost her mind when she bought the bar. My Lena, the alpha businesswoman, headed for massive success... and she left it all behind to live in my town to buy some forgotten dive bar? But she decided, and that was the end of it."

"That's Lena." I laughed, remembering the Magpie in its dive-bar days. She'd moved in with Finn, and he'd traveled for work in Boston, often staying in the city for days at a time. "That road to *massive success* made her miserable."

"Now it's just me making her miserable."

"Bullshit. She'd be gone if that were true." I set my glass on the table, checking my phone again. Still nothing from Rhett. Holding my chest through the stabbing pain, I got up and stood in front of the window as the sun set over the trees.

"After all this is done," Finn said, "I'm leaving the force."

He sat in the chair, motionless, without his usual nervous knee bouncing or fidgeting. I approached him and touched his shoulder. "What will you do?"

"Work for—*with* Lena at the bar, if she'll have me. Didn't see myself trading police work for making beer, but it relaxes me, and nothing else fucking does that."

"Lena will love nothing more than to be your boss." Ruffling his hair, I gave him a hug, standing upright when the motion sent another wave of pain through me.

His narrowed gaze swept over me. "How are you?"

"Been better." I sat in the rocking chair, pushing it with my foot. "I'm worried about him."

"He knows what he's doing—"

"Does he, Finn? You really think he knows what he's walking into?"

He leaned forward, running his fingers along a dent in the table. "It's not the first time he's dealt with family drama."

"He killed a mob *kingpin*... boss, whatever you call it. I've seen enough movies to know what that means."

"This isn't the movies, Frankie. He's got this. His sister and Luca are proving to be trustworthy so far..."

"What about his father?"

Hesitating, Finn averted his eyes. "If you're asking me—"

"That's exactly what I'm doing."

"None of them can be trusted, not really."

"Not even Rhett?" My chest ached. I knew him, and he didn't want this life.

Finn clasped his fingers together on the table, giving me that familiar look he used to have when our parents had left him in charge, and he got to scold Miles and me. "I trust Rhett with my life as much as I trust him with yours. I'd never let him work for Lena or be anywhere near my family if I didn't."

"But you warned me to stay away." I matched his pose, linking my fingers together. The stain on my sweater had dried into the fabric. I'd never get that stain out.

"And you didn't listen," he said, fighting a smile. "Neither did he, but you know everything now and you're choosing him, regardless."

"You don't approve." I didn't need my brother's approval, but for some reason, it bothered me when he showed disappointment in me. "Do you hate him for who he is... or do you hate me because I love him?" I whispered.

His chest heaved as he exhaled. "Frankie," he said, and his expression softened. "I hate myself."

"For what?"

He dropped his hands to his lap. "For getting in too deep, not getting Miles out, allowing my past to find me..." His lip quivered, and he bent forward again with his elbows on the table. He dragged a hand across his mouth, and his voice shook when he spoke again. "I hate myself for not telling you the truth. I keep thinking if you'd known, they never would've gotten to you. If you died that night, I'm not so sure I'd be here either."

I'd never seen him so vulnerable. *Never.*

The ache in my chest navigated into a lump in my throat, and I sniffed back tears. "That's the most real you've been with me in a long time."

"I promise to do better for you, Mom and Dad, Lena."

I held the armrest and rose from the chair. "Stand up and hug me." Tears fell over my cheeks, stinging the stitched cut, and Finn stood and embraced me.

"I'm sorry," he said.

"I know, Finn." I hugged him back too hard, and pain shot through my chest, making me wince.

Keeping his arms around me, he muttered under his breath, "He did the world a favor killing those disgusting excuses for men."

I gave him another squeeze, ignoring my sore body. "Tell me he's coming back, and everything will be all right."

"Rhett's good at leaving." Finn released me. "He can disappear so that no one finds him unless he wants to be found. It's how he's survived for two years without them knowing where he was."

I reached for my wine, taking a slow, deliberate sip, and set it back down.

Finn hesitated before he spoke. "He'll come back for *you*. He's got to fix things, it's what he does, and protect his sister's family from the fallout."

"Killing those men made everything worse, didn't it?" He'd taken care of them to protect me, but no one would be there to keep *him* safe from the fallout.

"He had to send a message the way the law wouldn't be able to. If they were caught and went to jail, and that's a big if, Frankie, it wouldn't be for long enough. Rhett will die to keep you safe, hell, I'd do the same."

"Is that why you agreed to cover for him?"

"I couldn't let him go to prison for taking care of what I didn't have the balls to do myself. I just hate that you're a part of his world now." Finn opened the door to the woodstove and tossed in another log, prodding it with an iron poker. "It's late, did he message you?"

"No." I checked the burner phone he'd given me, bringing up my contact for Rhett—*Him*—and sent him another message.

Where are you?

An undelivered notice popped up, and I opened the door, holding my phone outside. "Why can't I get service?" The wind rustled tree branches, tossing huge snowflakes along the porch.

"It's the phone," Finn's voice carried outside. "I'll try... *Shit*, we gotta go."

I ducked inside, shutting the door. "What is it?"

"Lena." He held the phone to his ear. "Are they still there?" Finn's jaw tensed as he paced the room, glancing outside. "Send the staff home and close... No way, you need to get out of there." With an exasperated sigh, he glanced at me as he spoke to Lena, gripping the phone. "I'm sorry, I know, please close the damn bar. I'm fucking begging you." He turned with his back facing me. "I love you." Grabbing his jacket, he stuffed his phone in the pocket. "We're going back to town."

"What happened?"

"Three men came into the bar asking questions about Everett Morrigan, showing a picture. Lena told them he moved away a week ago, but they're looking for him."

"Who's *they*?"

He held up his phone, displaying an image I recognized from the photos on Miles's USB. My pulse raced, thumping madly in my ears. "Rhett's father is in Willow Grove. I'm not leaving, what if he comes back and we're gone, and he doesn't know?"

"I'll keep trying his cell—"

I ran my fingers through my tangled hair and folded my arms across me as I moved close to the window. "What if something happened to him? I'm staying."

Finn's knuckles paled as he gripped the back of the chair, pushing it with a creak against the table. "I'm not leaving you here."

I rushed to the bedroom, returning with the gun Rhett had given me. "I'll be okay, no one knows I'm here, it's the middle of nowhere. Get Lena and bring her here, you'll be gone a couple of hours at most? I'm not leaving."

"Fucking hell." Finn shoved his arms into the sleeves of his coat. "I'll get Dad to come out here."

"He won't be able to drive, and I don't want Mom dragged into this."

Opening the door, Finn scanned the yard. "Lock the door behind me, keep the place dark, shut those curtains, and don't answer for anyone. I'll be right back."

"Go, trust me. I know what I'm doing."

Hesitating, Finn eyed the gun in my hand. "I sure as hell hope you don't have to use that, but if something happens, don't forget what I taught you." He rushed to his car, the slam of his door echoing behind him.

His headlights faded as he backed up and turned around, heading down the snow-covered path toward the main road. My heart thudded in my chest, mimicking the pain along my ribcage. I locked the door and yanked the curtains shut. The chain on the lamp stuck, so I unplugged it from the wall, plunging the room into an orange glow as the fire burned.

I was alone and isolated, without a vehicle or a way of knowing if Rhett was okay, and I couldn't shake the fear that had settled in my stomach. Placing the gun safely on the kitchen table, I sat on the couch. I tried to reach him again, but the message failed to send, and the call refused to connect.

My head throbbed with a dull ache, and I sank against the back of the couch. The minutes slipped away with every tick of the clock on the wall. A haze clouded my mind as my eyes drifted shut, and the ticking faded. Silence fell around me. Bran Noble flashed into my mind, smiling as he held a knife...

I jolted upright and cried out as a searing agony sliced through me. Tears stung my eyes, and I rose from the couch slowly, peering through the window. Nothing. No Rhett. No Finn. Not a damn signal on my phone.

Grabbing a flashlight, I used the bathroom and made my way into the bedroom we'd shared as kids. Miles's Boston Bruins comforter was folded on the bottom bunk, and I wrapped it around myself. We'd had a deal growing up. My brothers would come to my piano recitals wearing dress shirts and ties, and I wouldn't complain when hockey dominated the TV.

The crushing grief of missing him swept over me, and I angled the light away from the bunk beds, shining it around the room. The storage closet was slightly ajar, but my father had always locked the exterior door inside. Pain overwhelmed me as I ducked into the crawlspace, and I collapsed onto the dirty cement floor.

A flashback to the mill struck without warning, leaving me breathless, as though someone had wound a tight rope around my midsection. I sat against the cold wall, shaking uncontrollably, and a ringing pierced my ears. The memory of the rope digging into my wrists and ankles brought a fiery sensation into my chest. I rubbed my wrists and reached beside me, clawing my nails over the wall, anchoring myself in place. I was inside my family's cabin—the place I'd visited many times growing up. The place that had always been safe.

They're dead, they can't hurt me again.

Tears streaked my cheeks, and I wiped my face. I stood on unsteady legs, and bent my head down, making my way toward the end of the short tunnel where the narrow door led outside. The deadlock was secure. No one could get in from the outside.

An engine rumbled, and a door slammed. Heavy boots thudded up the stairs on the front porch, and a bang echoed. With my heart pounding, I scrambled back through the crawlspace into the bedroom and grabbed the gun as I hurried to the front door. "Who's there?"

"Frankie, it's me, let me in."*Rhett.*

My hands trembled as I turned the deadbolt and opened the door, flinging myself into his arms. He lifted me, carrying me inside. "I was worried something happened, and you weren't coming back," I said.

Setting me down, he shut the door, locking it, and took my face in his hands. "The only thing that'll keep me away from you is death." My fingers tightened on the worn shoulders of his jacket, pulling him into an urgent kiss. He slowed it down, breaking away. "You're not safe here anymore. My father was gone when I got there, and Finn messaged. We need to go now. Where's your brother?"

"Finn's with Lena, there's no way your father will know to come here. —"

"My father is in Willow Grove, he needs to settle a score." He typed a message on his phone.

"You're his son—"

"I'm nothing." Rhett glanced over his shoulder toward the window as beams of light cast shadows through the curtains. "It's too fucking late." He handed me his keys and phone, his sad eyes locking with mine as he reached for the revolver on the table. With a quick, metallic flick, he opened and shut the cylinder, extending the gun toward me, grip side out with the barrel pointed to the ground. "It's loaded, safety's on." His gaze snapped to the window again as car doors slammed in quick succession. One, two... three. Rhett took off his jacket and draped it over my shoulders. "Get into the crawl space, open the back door, and *run*. I texted Finn, call him and tell him where you are—""I'm not leaving you to face them alone—"

His grip on my arm was tight as he pulled me toward the back room. The hinges of the closet door groaned when he opened it. With his fingers on my chin, he kissed me one last time. "I love you, but get your ass in there, and let me take care of this."

Heavy knocking rattled the walls. "I know you're in there, son. Open up or I'll break it down." The man on the other side of the door projected a commanding presence that sent terror through me.

"Go. *Now*." Rhett walked away from me, turning as he shut the door. "Frankie, so help me. I need you to take an order without arguing, this one time."

"I love you too," I whispered as he left me alone, but he couldn't have heard me as he shut the door. I tucked the gun in my waistband and shoved my arms in the sleeves of Rhett's jacket, inhaling him as his scent surrounded me.

As I crawled through the cramped closet, I shone the flashlight's beam and moved toward the beckoning door leading outside. My shallow breaths fogged in front of me, and shivers wracked my aching body. I turned the deadlock carefully to avoid noise, but I froze when footsteps shook dust off the walls around me.

The floorboards creaked as heavy boots stormed the cabin in chaotic movements, and a chair screeched across the floor. "Sit. Find his gun," someone said, and a thud followed as the voice continued. "I assume you understand why I'm here."

"I've got a general idea," Rhett's muffled voice resonated through the walls.

The calmness in his voice hurt my heart. There was nothing he could do to protect himself from those men. My hand fell away from the doorknob, and I turned around, scooting back through the closet. Stepping into the bedroom, I approached the door.

Sorry, Rhett. I'm not taking orders this time.

FORTY-FIVE

Rhett

I rose from the kitchen chair, but Vivian's bodyguard, Darius, the man who'd always had my back, stepped away from my father and slammed me back into it. He racked the slide of his gun and aimed the barrel at my head, forcing my hands in front of me. I stared at him, willing him to make eye contact, but he moved behind me. My father's right-hand man, Remy—everyone called him Remington—secured my wrists with duct tape and moved on to my ankles.

Vivian lied. I'm fucked.

Taking his coat off, my father casually undid his cufflinks and rolled up his shirt sleeves. He smoothed his dark hair and stood over me, pointing to his matching tattoo. "Does this mean nothing to you? We are *family*. You betrayed me, forcing my hand. A father should never have to decide who should take his own son's life."

"So you are here to kill me." I'd always known that this would be my end, I just never imagined it'd be my father doing it. I moved my hands back and forth, but the tape wouldn't loosen. Without a weapon to defend myself, I was a dead man sitting, and all that mattered was that Frankie had escaped unharmed.

Her wine glass on the table caught my eye. If they found out she was here, they'd hunt her down and kill her.

"You never touch a boss, it's suicide. You knew this." My father patronized me like he'd caught a toddler eating crayons.

"Had to be done," I said. "They threatened me."

"And you killed his son. What the fuck did you expect to happen?" He held the same revolver he had carried for decades. Opening the cylinder, he tilted his head as he checked the chamber, shutting it with expert hands. "You started a war over a woman who is *nothing*. A man attacks your wife, we can talk, but some whore you pick up on the run like a pathetic coward? Unacceptable, Everett." He held the barrel down with his hands crossed at his waist, and strands of his hair fell over his forehead.

I hated him. "Fuck you, you know nothing—"

"I know enough," he said.

"Is that how you felt about my mother?"

"Feelings had nothing to do with it, son. I had a wife, she was second—"

"And they both left you."

"Your disrespect will make this easier than I expected. You were the mistake I had high hopes for after she died, but all you've done since you walked into my life was prove to me you do not live up to your namesake."

My body went rigid, and I clenched my teeth. "I don't want your name." My mother had shielded me from him, leaving me missing out on a dad for years until I found out the harsh reality of his life, and it was about to cost me my own. "I just want out. Let me go, you'll never see me again."

"Out? There is no fucking *out*." He stepped forward, swinging his gun across my head with a sickening thud, and a high-pitched ringing echoed in my ears. "I never once heard you complain, Everett. You used your talent, following in my footsteps. You were the man who got things done, *handled* things. Now you disgust me."

Blinking the blood from my eye, I cleared my vision, refusing to allow myself to flinch as the pain throbbed across my face. Darius moved in front of me, and Remy held his stance at my back.

My father paced the living room, grabbing the iron poker from the brick hearth. "Because of you, I went to prison. You bailed on your sister, the business." Opening the woodstove, he stuck the iron in the hot coals.

This is going to hurt.

As he stepped toward me, his polished boots caught the glow from the poker. "You are a disappointment. I can barely stand to call you my son."

Remy's footsteps scuffed the floor behind me. "Are you a wine drinker, Morrigan?"

I listened for movement in the back of the cabin but heard nothing. She'd better have taken orders and disappeared outside somewhere. "Just red," I said.

"Raise his sleeve, left arm," my father ordered. His dark eyes darted from the wineglass to my face, and Remy shoved my sweater up my arm. My father hit me with the poker, the heavy iron branding my tattooed arm, and I gritted my teeth as searing pain exploded into my chest.

"Fuck!" The acrid smell of burned flesh choked me, and I almost threw up.

"My son drinks whiskey. Search the bedrooms, closets, bathroom, fucking underneath the sink. She's here."

I couldn't let them get to her. Finn had to be on his way with an entire team of cops. I spoke louder as a warning to Frankie, hoping she wasn't still tucked away in the crawlspace. "There's no one here but me."

Dropping the iron, he stormed to the table behind me and brought the wine glass toward my face. "Where. Is. She." He threw the glass across the floor, shattering it against the brick and spilling wine across the floor.

The two men scoured the cabin, kicking down doors and tearing apart closets. My father tapped his gun on my shoulder. "What was your plan exactly? Take out Bran Noble and go running back to Vivian like you didn't just start a damn war? She doesn't want *rats* near her son. I will be teaching him the business, you lost that privilege." Shaking his head, he pulled a phone from his pocket. *Frankie's* phone. He held it up, displaying old photos taken inside the cabin. One photo captured a young Frankie and her family laughing while playing board games, and the next was a screenshot of a map with the cabin's fucking location. "You sure know how to pick them, at least she's pretty." He paced back and forth slowly, not taking his eyes off me. "Bran proved his loyalty the minute he gave me her phone, informing me of where you've been spending your precious time while I was behind bars. His family is waiting on me to take care of this problem, or our alliance is over, and that would be bad for business."

I had to do something. I'd never been so fucking helpless in my life. The tape dug into my ankles as I used my bound feet to inch forward, moving the chair. I had nothing to lose, and my father didn't plan on leaving me alive.

"Sit the fuck back down." Remy put me in a chokehold and hauled me back. "If she was here, she's not anymore, sir."

My chest heaved, and eyes darted to the window. Still no sign of Finn. I had to believe Frankie had gotten a hold of him and made it to the main road. Maybe he'd picked her up, and they were already driving far, far away from here.

"If you're gonna kill me, *Dad*, just do it. Nothing I say will make one fucking bit of difference." Another punch landed, this time a brutal blow to my jaw, and I pressed my fists to my throbbing face, tasting blood.

"You give me no other choice." With the revolver in his hand, he rubbed his head. "I gave you everything!" His yell reverberated off the walls.

"You gave me a life I never asked for."

A sinister laugh escaped the man who shared blood and DNA with me. I'd killed for him, *because* of him. I'd become someone no better than him, deluding myself into thinking I could have a better life with a woman like Francesca Roscoe.

"And yet, you had no problem taking money. Power. Respect and *loyalty*. How do you pay your father—*flesh and blood*—back? I expect rats, but never my own fucking son. You burned down what I built, ruined alliances that I must step up and fix. You make me sick." As he raised his gun to my chest, I shut my eyes and focused on Frankie. I could picture her piercing blue-eyed gaze fixed on mine, holding a silent secret. I was all hers. I could almost feel the warmth of her body underneath mine, kissing her mouth, tasting *her*. The gentleness in her laugh could light up the darkest part of me.

Remy yelled behind me. "What the fuck—"

My eyes snapped open as a deafening blast echoed off the cabin walls like a bomb detonating, and Remy collapsed to the floor, convulsing as blood sprayed from his neck.

With a nod, Darius flashed me a quick glance and turned the gun on my father. "I'm keeping a promise to your daughter, I won't let you do this."

Tilting in the chair, I fell on the floor and rolled to the side as my father took aim at him. Darius had waited too long to take the shot. His hesitation would be his end. "Put that fucking gun down," my father seethed, "you son of a bitch piece of shit."

"No sir..."

Darius's words died in his throat as my father's bullet slammed into his head, sending him reeling backward. His pulverized face hit the counter before he crashed to the floor in a bloody mess.

My father loomed over me. The potent smell of burning metal, like a live wire, filled the air between us as he leveled the gun toward me.

It was my turn.

Forty-Six

Frankie

My hand gripped the doorknob, ready to burst into the living room and do something... *anything* to save Rhett from his father's rage, but I couldn't let them find me first. I'd almost confronted the man who charged through the bedroom, tearing the door off its hinges, but I'd run instead. I had slipped free of the cabin through the back door, out into the snow. If I remained hidden from them, maybe I still had a chance to save him.

How long had it been since Finn had left? I checked my phone—still no service—but Rhett's phone had a message from my brother.

On my way. Don't do anything stupid.

I sent him a text, typing frantically, and turned the ringer on silent.

There are at least two men inside, maybe three... They're going to kill him, I'm outside... Don't come here alone. Bring medics.

A gunshot exploded from inside the cabin, and I hurried from behind the woodpile to the back door, suppressing a cry, but the handle wouldn't budge. The asshole must've locked it.

Please don't be Rhett, please...

Shivering, I zipped Rhett's jacket and ran through the snow toward the front porch, tripping and scrambling to my feet. Muffled voices crept through the log cabin walls, and a sliver of light streamed like a pathway to the dense forest, but I couldn't run away. I refused to abandon him. I had to see him again, I would not let him die.

Adrenaline coursed through me, numbing my aching body, leaving one option. I had to take them by surprise and rush inside the cabin. I needed to know Rhett was still alive, and I hadn't lost him.

My body begged me to stop, and pain split my chest with every inhale, but I pushed on, taking my boots off as I went up the stairs. The curtains obscured my view as a thud echoed, and men yelled.

The sharp crack from a second gunshot echoed from inside, and movement jutted behind the living room curtains. Panic seized me like a vise, threatening to suffocate me as my vision blurred. Choking back tears through ragged breaths, I swallowed and held the gun steady with my hand on the door handle.

Rhett's muffled voice carried through the door, burned into my memory like a jazz song. He was inside, alive.

My thumb rested on the grip of the gun, remembering each step from target practice as Finn's authoritative instructions relayed in my mind. I let the weight settle in my hands like it belonged there, an extension of myself. I nudged the front door open enough to get a glimpse inside. A man lay dead on the floor, his vacant eyes wide, staring at nothing as blood pooled around his head.

Steadying my breath, I took the safety off with my thumb and pushed the door open further. Nash Morrigan had his back to me, pinning Rhett down, blood streaming from a gash on the side of his head where his father pressed his foot down on his face.

This was Nash Morrigan. Mob boss, someone not to trifle with. "Not the mess I had planned on," he said.

I glanced to the right, and another dead man had crumpled forward in a gruesome display of brain matter and blood. His face was... *gone.*

Saliva flooded my mouth, and I tasted bile as nausea gripped my stomach. I couldn't throw up, not now. Tightening my grip, I stepped forward, my foot steady on the threshold of the door, ready to enter.

Soften your knees and lock your elbows.

Repeating Finn's lessons quieted the fear, allowing me to focus on my target as I adjusted my thumb, supporting my trigger hand. Unseen, I still had an advantage. It was me against him... a skilled killer.

If I don't do this, he dies.

Rhett grunted as his father kicked his back. "It's over, they're dead," he coughed out. "Let me live, and go, and no one will know, you have my word."

I froze, locking my aim through the gap in the door on the man hovering over Rhett. He crouched near his son's face and spoke in a cold, even tone.

"If I don't take care of you, they will take care of me and everything I worked for, the years of growing a business, my network, will all be gone. *Your* word means nothing. *You* are worthless. You are not my son. Your death will give me my life back."

I pushed the door wider, and Rhett's eyes met mine, widening as his lips parted to speak. I held my finger to my mouth to silence him.

His father released his foot from his back, and Rhett rolled over. Nash aimed the gun at his son and fired as Rhett darted to the side, but he was too late. His breathing hitched, and a cough rattled in his throat. Pain flashed across Rhett's face, and something inside of me shattered.

I raised my gun, a scream catching in my throat, and stormed toward his father as he stepped over Rhett's bleeding body, taking aim at his head. "Don't you fucking *dare*. Step away."

Rhett's father spun around, his mouth agape and eyebrows raised as he regarded me.

"Frankie run... *run!*" Rhett coughed, and blood gushed through his shirt, surrounding him on the floor in a dark pool of crimson.

Hot tears streamed down my face, and I took a step closer. "Get away from him!"

"You're not going to shoot me, sweetheart," Nash said. "Put the gun down." A smile crossed his face, and he pointed his gun at me, extending his other hand toward mine.

I backed up. "Don't touch me or—"

"Or what? You and I both know you won't pull that trigger. You're a nurse, I hear, is that right?" He matched my steps backward as Rhett pushed himself toward the wall with his feet, leaving a trail of blood.

"I am. He needs medical attention, or he'll die," I said, unable to hide the urgent begging from my voice.

Pursing his lips, Nash gestured over his shoulder, not taking his dark eyes off my gun. "Take that fucking weapon away from my face, or you'll join him." His fingers twitched on the trigger as he lifted his gun. Each slow movement was a deliberate threat; he was going to kill us no matter what I did.

"Get out of here..." Rhett blinked slowly, choking out his words.

His father's ominous smile stretched wider, taunting me as he inched closer, but I blocked him out. I tracked the jagged movement of his hand on the gun, counting in my mind.

Three.

"Hell, the whole Roscoe family can join him. One young man already has," Nash said. "Miles. Such promise, gone too soon."

Two.

His hand jerked up, and I pulled the trigger.

One asshole.

His hand flew to his stomach, the other still clutching the gun. Blood saturated his dress shirt, soaking into his tie. He took aim at me again, his finger searching for the trigger as blood ran along the tattoo on his arm. Staggering, he glared at me. "You're the whore who started a war."

I fired a second shot, square in his chest, and he dropped face down on the floor.

FORTY-SEVEN

Frankie

Dropping to Rhett's side, I yanked his shirt up, moving his bound hands aside. He blinked slowly, and his breathing was shallow and raspy. Pink froth mixed with flowing bright red blood had burst through a dark hole the size of my fingertip, just underneath his collarbone. "Stay with me, baby," I said.

A smile touched his lips, but his words came through shallow breaths. "You keep calling me that..."

"Because I love you." I sniffed back tears as I shrugged off my jacket and grabbed the phone he'd given me, dialing 911.

I answered the dispatcher's questions as I navigated around blood and broken bodies on the floor. Bolting down the hallway, I gathered towels strewn across the floor, and a kitchen knife on my way back to him. I ended the call despite the dispatcher's pleas to remain on the line and sliced the tape from his hands and ankles. Rolling up a towel, I pressed it down on his wound with my body weight against him.

He reached for my face, his clammy hands touching my cheek, and I bent toward him. Tears fell off my chin, soaking into his shirt. "You killed him," he breathed in a ragged whisper. "I want your gun."

"And I want to save your life. I need to roll you to your side." I planted a fleeting kiss on his lips and pulled back, moving him to the side to look for an exit wound. Dark, thick blood oozed from a larger hole, and the edges curled outward, but the hissing sound only came from the entry wound. I'd had enough experience treating bullet wounds working in Boston to know the bullet had gone clean through, but the damage left behind was going to kill him if help didn't arrive soon.

I helped him lie flat on his back.

"I can't... breathe." He shivered uncontrollably, and I yanked the quilt from the couch and covered him.

"Yes, you can," I snapped. "I'm going to fix it so you can."

With a weak hand, Rhett reached for me as I pressed the blood-soaked towel against his chest.

I squeezed his hand and moved away from him. "I'm getting something to help you breathe—"

He gasped for air as he spoke. "I'm dying, baby."

I rushed back to him, cupping his battered, bleeding face in my hands. "No! I won't let that happen! Fight back, you stubborn man. You owe me a Danish, remember?"

"I don't deserve you... no bullshit excuses... truth." His skin paled, and his eyelids drooped. "If I die, you'll be free."

A sob caught in my throat. "Eyes on me, *now*."

He snapped his eyelids open. "*Orders...*"

"Yes, *orders*, take them once in a damn while. We deserve each other because I fucking want you, I love you, and I'm not letting you give up." I released him and hurried toward the kitchen cabinets, rummaging through drawers, grabbing a roll of plastic wrap and... *duct tape*. The roll of tape lay on the floor near the fridge, and I scooped it up. The bullet had damaged his lung, and I needed to relieve the pressure so he could breathe.

I charged back to Rhett, slipping in the blood of his dead father, but couldn't look at the man I had killed. All that mattered was saving Rhett.

A high-pitched wail sliced through the open door. Sirens, far off but growing closer. "Hear that? Help's coming." I straddled Rhett and absorbed blood from the wound so the duct tape would stick to his skin. Placing a piece of plastic wrap over the bleeding wound, I used the knife to slice three pieces of tape, sealing the entry wound, except on one side.

Release the pressure in his lungs, help him inhale and exhale.

"Talk to me... You still with me? Rhett—"

He grunted. "I hear you." His breath hitched, and I placed my fingers on his carotid, finding a weak pulse.

"What's the first thing you want to do when this shitshow is over?" My eyes darted from his glazed eyes to the gunshot wound.

His breathing slowed, and he dragged a hand slowly over his body. I held the saturated towel against his gushing wound as he curled his blood-slicked fingers over mine, his grip weak. "Make love to you."

"Survive and you got a deal."

Blue and red lights flashed through the curtains, and beams of light shone through the open door as car doors slammed.

Rhett glanced toward the door and back at me. "Give me your gun, I'm confessing to this." His breathing shifted into the restless shallow inhales again, and I lifted the towel. Fresh blood coursed underneath the plastic, and it slid off. The tape wasn't holding.

Pressing my weight back on the towel, I bent over him. "It was self-defense, and I'd do it again." His hand found the back of my head, and he pulled me toward him. His chest heaved, each shallow breath a rasp against my ear, his skin deathly cold against my face as his lips met mine. "I don't want to lose you," I whispered. My hands slipped, and I sat upright, applying pressure to his chest. "They won't let me stay with you."

The police burst into the cabin, weapons drawn, their commanding voices sharp as they fanned out, searching rooms, and assessing the bodies scattered on the floor.

Two officers approached with guns raised. "Hands where I can see them."

I didn't move, but tilted back, offering them an unobstructed view of my hands. "He's been shot—if I move my hands, he'll bleed out. Get EMS first."

"She didn't do this," Rhett choked.

"Don't move." One of them stood over me and gave the all-clear over his radio for EMS to come in, holding his attention on me.

Police officers near the door stepped inside, making way for two medics. They rushed toward Rhett and me.

Making eye contact with the woman who approached me first, I immediately gave her Rhett's name and rattled off all the information I could before the police would inevitably drag me away. "He's got a chest-sucking wound. I sealed it with plastic and tape, but it's not holding."

The other medic started an IV and cut Rhett's shirt off, taking his vitals and asking him questions. But Rhett gave short answers through his gasps, observing me in quiet stillness. Creases lined his forehead as he furrowed his brows in the deep-thinking expression I adored. Except now, the brightness in his gaze had dimmed as he fell unconscious underneath my hands.

My composure fell apart, and the floodgates burst open. Tears stung my cheeks, and I stifled sobs as the medic placed her gloved hands over mine.

"Please don't let him die," I said. "*Please.*"

"You kept him alive this far, I'll take it from here. Are you ready?" She didn't rush me, maintaining a steady presence next to me amidst the chaos as I caught the silver glint of handcuffs in the officer's hands behind me.

"I'm ready." I removed my hands from Rhett's body, and the medic took control.

The woman moved in swift motions, pulling a flat packet from her first aid kit as her colleague gave Rhett oxygen. Tearing the square packet open, she peeled out a plastic seal and placed it on the entry wound. "Sealed. Let's move him."

They slid Rhett onto a stretcher, and officers flanked me, each donning medical gloves. The pressure of their hands on my arms tightened as they hauled me up, closing handcuffs around my wrists.

Blood was caked under my fingernails like it had in the mill. A pattern of blood splatter soaked into my white sweater, and the entire cabin carried a nasty metallic scent mixed with the distinct smell of death.

"Frankie!" Finn halted in the doorway, his mouth dropping open as he scanned the room. "Jesus fucking Christ." His hands flew to the top of his head as he watched EMS move Rhett out of the cabin before he focused back on me, eyes darting to the cuffs. Finn stepped backward as the two cops walked me toward the door. "You're cuffing her? It's clearly self-defense, look around! Do you know who they are? You think she did this?"

One of them held a hand up, keeping my brother away. "Following protocol, Roscoe."

Finn argued with the officers as they led me onto the porch, but I kept silent, inhaling deeply to settle my hyperventilating sobs, and taking slow steps toward the stairs. Someone slammed the ambulance doors shut, and the siren blared as it sped away with Rhett inside, taking him farther away from me.

Blood from my socked feet left a trail of pink in the pristine snow. I glanced over my shoulder inside the cabin. Nash Morrigan stared up at me from his position on the floor, his mouth hanging open, and hollow, unseeing eyes frozen in a mask of hatred.

I'd killed a man to save another, and something inside me changed, but I wasn't sure what it was. A dark sorrow consumed me as Rhett's dying face etched in my mind and wouldn't let go.

I couldn't lose him.

Forty-Eight

Frankie

The snow's relentless chill soaked into my clothes, mixing with the blood clinging to my clothes as the police officer led me into the station.

"Get her a blanket, for fuck's sake." My father hurried toward me, pulling me into his arms, and fresh tears erupted as I cried against his jacket. "And as far as I know, she's not under arrest, so take the cuffs off."

Officer Bennett, the man who had escorted me in the silent car ride back to town, remained at my side. "It's not up to me, sir."

"Can someone please give me a status report on Rhett?" I asked. "Is he in surgery?" I pulled away from my father, shifting my arms from side to side as the cuffs dug into my wrists.

Finn stood behind a glass window of an office, red-faced with his hands on a desk as he talked to an officer in a chair. The man rose and walked toward the door. As he opened it, their voices carried, and I caught the tail end of the conversation.

"...she *ended* this," Finn said as he followed the man.

I stumbled as I stepped back, but my dad steadied me. Finn paced with his arms folded, rubbing his chin, and the flush in his skin subsided.

"Finn, I need to know if he's okay, please tell me something." I shivered and my teeth chattered as I spoke through sobs. Police bustled around, ignoring my pleas. My stomach tightened with anger about to boil over. "Is Rhett alive!" I hollered, stomping my feet like I was having a tantrum. But this was my life, and the man I *loved,* who had no one else.

"Lena's at the hospital now, she'll call as soon as he's out of surgery." Finn opened a closet in the corner and brought over a blanket, draping it across my shoulders and pulling it tight around me. He glared at the man from the office. "She's being held under investigative detention, why is she still in cuffs?"

The man approached, carrying a file folder and clicking a pen. "Roscoe, stay in your lane." He wore jeans and a sweater instead of a uniform and had a gun holstered at his hip. "Francesca Roscoe,

I'm Detective Robinson." He exhaled, darting a look from Finn to me. "You're not under arrest, but we are holding you to ask you some questions, do you understand?"

"I'm staying with her," my father said.

"No, you are not. Ms. Roscoe, do you understand what's happening here, and why we need to talk to you about the events at your family cabin tonight?"

"I do," I said. "How long will you keep me here?"

Turning his back to me, he walked away with the folder at his side. "Until we're done. Uncuff her and bring her to room one." He poured coffee from a full pot into a paper cup. "Finn, go to the locker room and see what you can find—sweatpants, a clean shirt, socks. Ms. Roscoe, how do you take your coffee?"

"Just black." My voice cracked as I called after Finn. "Let me know as soon as Lena tells you what's going on."

"I promise you I will. I'll drive you over there when you're free." He shot another glare at Detective Robinson on his way out.

The handcuffs released from my wrists, and I rubbed each, tugging the blanket around my shivering body. Officer Bennett gestured toward a hallway, following me as I walked toward the first room on the left and sat down in a metal chair.

A shiver ran through me, and the bare walls seemed to close in on me as I shifted in my seat. The ticking clock on the wall reminded me of each passing moment that meant life or death for Rhett, and my helpless distance from him.

Detective Robinson strolled in and set the coffee in front of me, followed by Officer Bennett.

Bennett handed me a pile of folded clothes with a pair of socks placed on top. "There's a bathroom just outside the door, I'll wait for you to change and escort you back in when you're done."

"I'm not a flight risk if that's what you're worried about, I just want this over with so I can get to the hospital." I took the clothes from him and entered the bathroom. Standing in front of the mirror, I brushed my hair off my face. Dried blood covered the bruises on my cheeks, and my white sweater looked like I'd come from a slaughterhouse.

An ache slammed into my chest, and my jaw tightened as a lump in my throat choked me. I couldn't stop the tears flowing from a bottomless emotional pit of despair. He could be dead right now. Finn had better not let me sit in that room without telling me, not after everything that had happened.

I already missed him. I missed the warmth of his touch, his mouth on mine, his arms around me... I wanted him in my life. The good, the bad... *all of it.*

Stripping off my clothes, I scrubbed the blood from my hands and face with paper towels. A knock sounded at the door and Officer Bennett's muffled voice followed. "Everything all right in there?"

Fuck off and leave me alone.

"Just great." I yanked on the navy sweatpants and matching sweater with Willow Grove Police embroidered on the left breast. My socks stuck to my feet as I pried them away from my skin, but the dry pair warmed them. I blew my nose and gathered my clothes. I had to stop crying and get myself together. Opening the bathroom door, I held my filthy clothes. "Should I throw these in the garbage?"

Donning a pair of gloves, he fanned open a bag, holding it away from himself so the clothes wouldn't touch him. "Drop them in here."

"You come prepared," I said, walking back to the interrogation room, and he shut the door behind me.

I sat back in my chair, wrapping my hands around the hot cup of coffee, and took a deep, shaky breath. "What do you want to know, sir? I won't go anywhere, won't leave town. Whatever it is you need me to do so that I can get out of here and go to the hospital."

"This interview is being recorded, Ms. Roscoe. As I said earlier, you're not under arrest, but are being detained for questioning. Do you understand?" He put on a pair of glasses and shuffled papers.

"Yes," I said. The relentless ticking clock begged for my attention. I'd already been here for half an hour. Could all this unravel, leaving me locked up in prison for murder?

Is that what I am now, a murderer?

Rhett and I would both be dead if I hadn't shot that man.

The detective's lightning round of questioning was straightforward, starting with the attack, and police awareness that I'd fled to my family's cabin, remaining in place when the two men who'd beaten me were found dead. He asked what I knew about the men who'd attacked me, Clay Preston's murder, and about Everett Morrigan, including his previous criminal activity, and involvement with the Morrigans.

An endless stream of questions persisted as the clock's hands moved with its taunting ticking, signaling the passage of precious time. This needed to end.

I weighed my responses when he inquired about the gun I'd had in my possession, and what I'd heard before walking into the cabin. I gave him the most honest and complete information possible.

"It's my understanding that Rhett... *Everett Morrigan* risked everything two years ago," I said. "He was never charged with any crime and befriended my brother, an undercover cop at the time." Emotion burned in my chest, but I stifled the tears. Detective Robinson pushed a tissue box toward me, but I ignored it as I continued talking. "Those men attacked Rhett to kill him tonight, his own father wanted him dead. If I hadn't walked into that cabin..."

His pen scratched over paper as he jotted down notes. "Take me through exactly what happened when you walked inside the cabin, please, Ms. Roscoe."

Nash Morrigan's smirk flashed in my mind, and I blinked my eyes to suppress the fear building inside me, glancing over my shoulder toward the door. "There were two bodies..." My stomach churned, and I swallowed, locking away emotions as I clung to the clinical part of my brain that knew how to compartmentalize. I described the bloodbath on the floor in my family's cabin as I met the detective's surprisingly kind eyes. "I'm a trauma nurse, but I've never seen so much blood." Saliva gathered in my mouth, and I leaned back, shoving my coffee aside.

"Can you keep going? It's important we know as much detail as we can." He stuck the arm of his glasses in his mouth.

"I didn't murder that man, I survived him. It was self-defense."

"Did he say anything?"

My heart pounded, radiating a terrifying mix of anger, fear, and the numbing weight of devastation through my body.

The fucking asshole had the nerve to taunt me, calling me sweetheart... whore, questioning if I had the guts to take the shot.

The detective dropped his glasses onto the table. He clicked his pen, matching the ticking clock as he studied me with a quiet resolve. *Waiting.* I licked my dry lips, tasting the salt from my tears. "He told Rhett that he was worthless and not his son. He shot him in the chest, and I screamed. That's when he turned around and saw me."

"And then what?" Detective Robinson spoke slowly.

"I told him Rhett needed medical attention, or he'd die, and he smiled at me. He fucking *smiled.* He aimed his gun at me, I took the shot before he did, and you know the rest. Can I please go to the hospital? If Rhett dies..." My tears won the battle, and I snatched a handful of tissues, dabbing at my eyes.

I sat upright and clenched my hands together in my lap. "Rhett was unarmed, bleeding on the floor, attacked on my property. I help save people for a living, no matter how shitty a human they are sometimes. I'd never kill someone in cold blood, *never.* This was self-defense, and that is the truth. Now can I please leave and go see my boyfriend in the hospital?"

Hours had passed, and I wanted to scream, or pull my hair out, or both. I needed to see him to know if he had made it out of surgery, if he was alive. Bouncing my leg, I tapped my fingers on the table, agitated. Surgery would take hours, assuming he'd even made it to surgery. My breathing shifted, and I couldn't get enough air. Gripping the table, I shoved my chair back, hanging my head between my legs.

My face felt too tight, and my heartbeat pounded in my ears. A choking sob escaped me, and my hands dropped from the table to cover my face as I surrendered to convulsive sobs.

The door swung open. "We're releasing you to your brother—" Detective Robinson stopped as I lifted my head from my hands and met his gaze.

Finn walked past him, holding a pair of black boots, and crouched in front of me. "He's out of surgery, he's alive. Lena's going to try to see him, and Mom and Dad are on their way there to meet us." He embraced me and rubbed my back as I cried, relief coursing through me.

I wiped my face as Finn released me and handed me the boots. "Not sure if they'll fit, it's the best I could do."

Rhett was alive, and I needed to see him like a drowning person who needed air. I shoved my feet into the boots and wiggled my toes. "They're perfect, thanks."

Detective Robinson stood in the doorway as I trailed Finn out of the room. "Stay in town until we finish our investigation. We'll be in touch."

"I'll be at Willow Grove Hospital," I said, passing him.

"And Ms. Roscoe?"

I stopped at the door, turning to face him.

He rubbed his forehead and dropped his hands to his sides. "I am sorry for what happened to you. Take care of yourself."

"That's the plan, detective."

No one would hurt me or my family again.

Forty-Nine

Rhett

The beeping of a heart monitor and the distinct smell of clinical disinfectant told me I was in the hospital before I opened my eyes. My chest burned like a lit match inside of me, and each breath brought a sharp, needle-like pain slicing through my lungs.

I remembered gunshots and Frankie's wine glass shattering on the floor, but mostly I could still see the look on her face when

476

she walked into the cabin. I knew she was terrified, but she'd taken control, exuding power at the same time. With a desperate need to know what had happened to her, I lifted my head, but it felt like lead. Dropping back onto the pillow, a wave of dizziness made me sick to my stomach. Something tugged inside my chest, and I reached across my body, glancing down. A tube hung from the left side of my chest, draining reddish liquid.

"That tube is there to help your lung heal, we can usually take it out after twenty-four to forty-eight hours." A man in scrubs hung a bag of clear fluid on an IV pole and pressed buttons. I'd met this man at the Magpie during Frankie's birthday. "The surgery went well, much less damage than we thought."

My voice came out hoarse. "I can't be here for days."

"The alternative would've been worse. You're lucky." He asked questions about pain, and took vitals, looking at the numbers on a screen as he wrote on a piece of paper.

"Where's Frankie?" My throat clenched with a raw sting. Grabbing the bed rails, I pushed myself up. "I need to know she's okay." I raised the head of the bed, gritting my teeth as the pain kept me from moving.

He depressed a syringe into the IV tube. "This will help. Get some rest, and you'll be able to move around faster than you think, okay?" Pushing his glasses up on his nose, he bent forward. "Look, Frankie's not here, last I heard, cops took her in for questioning. Lena is in the waiting room—"

"Get her." I coughed. "Please... Logan, right?"

"Yes," he said. "I'm sorry, only family is allowed in here."

"Can you make an exception?"

He glanced at the busy hallway as staff rushed past, and machines beeped. "If you lay back and rest, I'll bring Lena in. But you've got to promise you will chill."

"You and Frankie are good friends, right?" I asked.

"I adore that woman."

"So do I."

"Well, look at that, we've got something in common." He adjusted a pillow underneath my head and tucked a blanket around me. "I'll see what I can do, just be still?"

My head fogged as whatever he gave me kicked in, and I struggled to keep my eyes open. I hated being this fucking powerless, exposed and an easy target. Doctors and nurses came and went as hands on a wall clock ticked too slow, but too fast, and all I could think of was Frankie covered in blood in a jail cell.

"Jesus, Rhett, you look like death." Lena approached the bed with a quick glance behind her.

"It could be worse." Sitting up was useless, so I settled for letting my head flop to the side. "Where is she?"

"With Finn, they're on their way. There are cops waiting to talk to you." Lena stood over me, her expression unreadable as she eyed the tubes connected to me. "I don't know what to say, I'm just happy you're both alive. Logan's giving me five minutes, I'm not supposed to be here unless I'm family."

"I don't have family."

"Frankie would disagree." She smiled at me and blinked tears from her eyes, wiping them quickly. Lena was almost as good at hiding emotions as I was. "Fuck, I disagree with you, and so would Finn."

"She almost died because of me."

Lena held onto the bedrail. "Frankie is stronger than you think, don't you dare bail on her."

"I'll never bail on her, Lena." My eyelids drooped, and I fought to keep them open. "In case you haven't noticed, my track record for keeping her safe hasn't been so good."

She placed a hand on my cheek, cold against my hot skin. "But you used to have an excellent track record, or so Finn has told me. She loves you."

"I was a different man."

"Stop denying that part of yourself, Rhett, and bring him back. He's still part of you, she's seen it, so have I." Standing, Lena tapped her fingernails on the rails. "If it helps, when you get the hell out of here, your job will still be waiting, if you want it."

"Between us, I'm not sure I'll pass the criminal check." My lips cracked as I smiled, and my mouth was so dry I struggled to get the words out, but Logan's syringe had taken the edge off the pain.

"You intimidate the assholes, and between us? You're Finn's only friend."

"Fuck, I knew it."

Logan peeked into the room. "I'm sorry, Lena, but time's up."

"Yeah, yeah, I'm out." She squeezed my hand. "As soon as she gets here, I'll get her in."

I ached to hold her. "*Please,*" I said, fading out of consciousness.

My father's voice echoed in my head, taking me right back into the cabin, calling Frankie a whore.

You are nothing.

My only regret was not killing him myself so she wouldn't have to carry the weight of taking someone's life.

The warmth of fingers laced with mine spread through my hand, and I forced my eyes open. Frankie sat in a chair pulled close to me, her tears running along my skin as she held my hand against her cheek.

"It's good to see you, baby," I said.

She bent over me, her lips soft as she kissed mine and pulled away. "I thought I lost you." Her gaze fell on the monitor and back on me. She tilted my hand down, her touch gentle on the sore spot where the IV tube stuck out of my skin.

"Did they arrest you?" I asked, clasping her hand in mine.

"No, there's no charges. I don't see how there could be."

She had a heartbroken expression that I'd seen when she talked about Miles. My girl had killed a man, saving me, and I owed her my life. If I couldn't grab her and pull her into my arms, I'd improvise. Ignoring the burning pain, I made room on the bed. "Come here."

"I'm not getting in bed with you—"

"Give me one good reason."

"I'll give you two, that tube needs to stay in place, and you're in a world of hurt."

I took her hand again, searching for the right words to tell her how sorry I was for everything she'd been through.

I opened my mouth to speak, but she beat me to it. "He was your father. He has a daughter who I've never met, and I... I'm scared everything's going to change because of what I've done, but I'd do it all over again. What does that make me?"

"A strong woman who protected herself. Who loved someone else enough to protect them. No one's ever done anything like that for me before. Part of me wishes you'd just left me there, but fuck, Frankie. You saved me, you keep saving me in ways I can't thank you for." Every move I made sent pain through me, but I needed her closer. "What do I have to do to hold you?"

She held my face in her hands, and I curled my fingers around her wrist. "Get better and come back to me," she said close to my ear and kissed my forehead.

The doctor friend of Frankie's walked into the room, adjusting a stethoscope around her neck. Her shoulders relaxed when she looked at Frankie. "I'm about to get real unprofessional, but I can't look at your sad face and not hug you." She didn't wait for a response and approached Frankie, pulling her into a tight hug.

"Mr. Marshall, if you're not comfortable with me examining you given the situation, let me know and I'll have someone else—"

"Do what you have to so I can get out of here."

"You're stuck with us for a while yet," she said. Her name was Zoey, if I remembered right.

Frankie glanced at me with curiosity in her eyes. "Am I allowed to know your private medical stuff?"

"Share whatever she wants to know," I grunted, moving wrong and pulling the chest tube too hard.

The doctor explained the surgeon's repair of a small laceration on my lung grazed by the bullet, using clinical terms like blood vessel cauterization, and stitches that my body would eventually absorb, but it all came down to the same word.

Lucky.

I sure as hell didn't feel lucky. Grateful, sure. But never lucky.

"I'll be back," Frankie said and walked out of the room, pausing in the doorway as a security guard peeked in.

"Rhett Marshall?"

Frankie folded her arms across her chest. "That's him."

"A woman named Vivian Morrigan is here claiming to be immediate family. She's pretty adamant about seeing you."

"She's my sister," I said.

Frankie raised her eyebrows. "Looks like I'm about to meet your family."

Vivian had hated our father, but I had no idea how she'd react when she met the woman who killed him.

FIFTY

Frankie

I left Rhett's room and headed into the waiting area as a hushed conversation between police officers and the nurses triggered an immediate protective response toward him. If they were waiting to talk to him, they'd be here a while. But he had survived his father, and the threat was gone... for now.

My mother handed cups of coffee to my father and a woman sitting next to him. The woman crossed her legs, and black heels peeked out from her pinstriped dress pants. She unbuttoned her suit jacket and settled against the back of the chair with flawless posture.

She had to be Vivian Morrigan.

Dad gave me a nod, his eyes flickering between Rhett's sister and a hulking man standing a few feet away, clasping his hands at his waist like a bodyguard.

Mom rushed toward me, embracing me in tears. She pulled away, brushing hair out of my eyes. "Finn and Lena went to find something to eat." She lowered her voice, giving me a concerned look. "Rhett's sister just arrived."

Rising from her seat, Vivian set her coffee down and approached me. She tousled her fiery auburn hair, quickly finger-combing her bangs. And she embraced me in a hug.

She's hugging me? I killed her father, she should hate me.

My body tensed, but I hugged her back.

Releasing me, she smoothed out a crease in her jacket. "I'm Rhett's sister, Vivian Morrigan. I want to see my brother, and I'm told you know where I can find him."

I cleared my throat, not sure how to respond. "The doctor's in with him—"

"I really don't care." She lifted her wrist, revealing a gold watch, and lowered her hand, allowing the sleeve of her jacket to fall back down over it. "It is after 3 o'clock in the morning, he's all the family my son and I have, and I haven't seen him in two fucking years."

I could feel my mother's eyes boring into me but held Vivian's smoky-eyed gaze. "Follow me," I said, and the man trailed her as I led the way toward the recovery room. "I doubt they'll let him in with you."

She patted him on the chest. "This man goes where I go. That's what he's paid to do." He followed her as she snatched her coffee and took a gulp before dropping it in the trash can. Grabbing the door handle, she pulled, but it didn't budge.

"The door needs a key card," I said. "They keep it locked so people can't walk through when patients need to rest."

"Well, I'm not people. I want to see my brother."

"Give me a minute." I hurried to the nurses' station and explained the situation. Someone came out of the locked doors advising that Rhett was resting and would be transferred from recovery to another room in half an hour.

"But she's immediate family." I rubbed the back of my neck. "Can't she have five minutes with him?"

Vivian spoke in a voice that challenged attention, "She's family, too." My head snapped toward her, speechless. She didn't hate me. Rhett's sister continued before I could think of anything to say. "You know what? Forget it. We'll be back in half an hour and you can direct us to his room." She spun around, glancing over her shoulder. "Is there somewhere private we can talk? You work here, right?"

"There's a quiet room down the hall." I pushed past her and her bodyguard. She gave him orders to wait outside the room, and I shut the door behind us. My legs ached. My entire body ached, and I sat on a couch lining the wall. "I'm Frankie, by the way. I should've introduced myself back there."

"Short for... *Francesca*?" She said my name like a melody.

"You got it."

She ran her fingers over an abstract painting in the room. "You'd think they'd make this place more inviting or at least paint the walls something other than white." She stepped closer and crouched in front of me, balancing her elbows on bent knees. She squinted, examining me as though I were an ancient relic that had been unearthed from a tomb. Touching my face, she brushed her fingers along the stitches from low on my cheek to my jawline, and I let her. "Who the fuck did this to you?"

"They're dead now."

"I would imagine. They hurt a Morrigan's woman." She slid onto the couch next to me, surveying the room. "I had ordered someone I trusted to stay with my father and stop him from hurting Rhett. He didn't tell me they were here until it was too late. I tried to warn my brother." Her nostrils flared as she drew a sharp breath, and something cold flashed in her eyes. "That man was like family, and he failed me. No one fails me. Who knew a fucking nurse would have better skills at killing someone than a hired hitman?"

I wasn't sure what to think of her. She came across as tough as nails and untouchable, but as she sat up and leaned forward, she wiped her eyes before looking at me. "As much as this pains me to say, I'm indebted to you for saving my brother's life. Try not to worry about retaliation, I have my finger on the pulse and a plan—had to after Bran Noble fucked us in the ass and my father joined him again."

This was an unfamiliar world, but I was getting one hell of a crash course. "Retaliation?"

"Darlin', two bosses are dead. We are in damage control as I sit my Pilates ass here on this seat. But I do have an ace in my back pocket."

"What sort of *ace* are you talking about?" I asked, mesmerized. I couldn't even *begin* to imagine what she meant.

She tapped her long fingernails on her lips, making the 'shhh' gesture, and I cringed. "Can't talk about that just yet."

I could almost see the strategy happening behind her dark eyes, but her lips held a small smile. I didn't know whether I should be terrified or fascinated. "Aren't you pissed off? Your father is dead because of me."

"Oh, I'm pissed, no, I'm *mad*. Everett helped put our father in jail. In our world, he's a traitor, a rat." She used air quotes.

"What makes you different, Vivian?"

"Excuse me?" She tucked her hair behind her ears, straightening her back.

"If it's your world as you say, shouldn't you hate Rhett for what he did too?"

She clasped her manicured hands between her knees. "I once loved my father, he always treated me like a fucking princess, but once I saw him for who he really was, I hated him. He uses people, *women*." Stretching her neck from side to side, she furrowed her brows. "He destroyed my mother. She left, threatening to take what she knew to the authorities."

"What happened to her?"

Vivian's eyes glistened with tears that didn't fall. "She was found murdered one day later. *One day* was all it took for him to have her killed. Everything, everyone he touches, dies. I had papers, fake IDs for me and my infant son."

"Why didn't you go?"

"Everett moved into that fucking big, empty house without an ounce of love between the walls, and suddenly my father became obsessed with power and molding Ev... *Rhett*, into what he wanted him to be. Nash Morrigan used his son, took advantage of Rhett's grief. He was seventeen, just lost his mom... It all looks glamorous when you've got nothing else, no family, no one. Nothing I did could tear Rhett away from that life, that sense of belonging, but I tried to keep his mother's legacy close to him. She spent her life keeping her son away from the Morrigans, and he still found his way to us."

Rhett had been lost. Seventeen, impressionable, without his mother keeping him safe, it was no wonder he'd fallen into a life that promised a place to belong.

"Did your father know you wanted out?"

"Fuck no. Rhett got wise to all of it, and wanted out too, but there is no way out when you're in that deep. I'd die to protect my son and Rhett. I felt like his mother, you know? Playing the role of doting daughter was the only way I could keep our father off Rhett's radar the past two years. Until it finally came crashing down."

My mind struggled to process Rhett's life through his sister's words, leaving me speechless.

Vivian glanced at her watch. "You did what I've wanted to do since the day my mother died, but it would've meant leaving my son without his mom." She got up, extending her hand to me. "Let's go, I need to see him." She held the door open for me and buttoned her jacket. "I'm going to need a place to stay for what's left of the night and tomorrow, any recommendations in this town that won't make my skin crawl?"

"You can have my place, I haven't been home in days, so I have no idea what kind of shape it's in. Rhett's is next door, but I don't have a key."

"Yours will do, thank you, Frankie." She glanced at the two officers hanging around and ran a finger over the police embroidery on my sweater. "They here for you or Rhett?"

"Rhett. They released me not long ago. My brother drove me here." I gestured to Finn, who stood near them, talking. "That's him."

"He's a cop too?"

I hesitated about how much to tell her, but she narrowed her gaze, observing them. "My brother worked with yours, didn't he?" It wasn't a real question, so I didn't answer. "Did they charge you with anything?"

"No. Not yet, anyway."

"Don't bother hiring a lawyer. I'll take care of you." She waved a hand toward the police officers. "I'll handle things for both of you. When are you planning to go home?"

It didn't matter to me that Rhett's sister was here. Now that I had him back, I wasn't leaving his side. "I'm not going anywhere until I know he's okay." My pace quickened as I walked down the hallway back to the waiting room. Vivian's clacking heels echoed in the hallway, matching my pace.

Finn glanced at me as I approached, and Lena sat next to my father. "I'll be out here with my family so you can have time with him, let me know the room number, and I'll go in next."

Vivian's mouth fell open as she maintained unwavering eye contact. "You're in love with him."

She can read me better than I thought.

"I'm not sorry I killed your father," I said. Shivering with exhaustion, I wrapped my arms around myself. Lena and my father chatted with serious expressions, and Mom darted her eyes from me to her phone. "I'd do it again to save my family, and he's just as much a part of that as they are." Holding her intense gaze, I told her my absolute truth. "I am very much in love with your brother, Vivian."

"I didn't expect to like you so fucking much, Francesca Roscoe." She brushed strands of hair out of my eyes. Shaking her head, she gestured to her bodyguard to wait and strutted toward the nurses' station. Her voice carried as she demanded Rhett's room number and his status.

Within minutes, someone directed her to the elevator, and she disappeared with a wave behind the doors. I collapsed into a chair between Mom and Dad, taking a coffee from Lena's outstretched hand.

"She's something, isn't she?" Dad flipped through a home improvement magazine. He hadn't built or fixed anything around the house in years.

"She's a Morrigan," I said. "Planning home improvements when all this is over, Dad?"

"Something like that, honey." He wrapped an arm around me, and I rested my head against him. He didn't smell of alcohol or cigarettes, and that brought tears of relief to my eyes.

I didn't want to get my hopes up, but I had a glimpse of my father, the way he used to be. Maybe Rhett had been right, and this had changed him.

FIFTY-ONE

Rhett

Saturday night was busy at the Magpie, but a hockey game was on, leaving Frankie and me alone in the billiards room. I'd spent three days in the hospital, and two at home. Lena refused to let me come back to work until I healed, but asked us to come out, and despite Frankie begging me to rest, I wanted us to do something that felt... *normal*. Even if only for a couple of hours.

My mind wasn't with her, not fully, but I wanted it to be. I was caught between my old life with Vivian and her son's future, my father's funeral on Tuesday, and this unknown new life with the woman I never wanted to be away from. And I couldn't help but have doubts in my mind about where I would fit in, and how our worlds could meet somewhere in the middle. I had to go to Boston and stand next to my sister to prove we were a united front, and I hadn't told Frankie.

Frankie took a drink of her beer and set it down, hovering over the pool table as she lined up her next shot. Her bruises had faded, and movement had become easier for her. I still couldn't get enough of being near her.

I strained as I bent forward, my face inches from Frankie's, trying to distract her from her pool shot; she smelled like vanilla and flowers. I gave her a sly smile. "You're kicking my ass."

"And your charm isn't working on me." She extended the cue along her positioned fingers.

"I've lost my touch." Pain coursed through me as I inhaled, and I instinctively gripped my chest.

Walking around the table, she patted my chest, and I grabbed her hand before she could pull it away. "Sit down so you don't hurt yourself," she said.

"I've been sitting for days, Frankie." I released her hand, and she eyed the table.

"We can sit for as many as you need."

I fucking loved this woman and the way she loved me back.

The remaining balls spread across the table like a battlefield. Frankie surveyed the six-ball, pulling back on the cue. "Six, corner pocket," she muttered, her focused expression sexy as hell.

The crack echoed in the room, and the green ball spun, sinking into the bottom corner. I strolled around the table as she chalked her cue. I tried to hide the relentless ache in my chest, but she stared at me, her blue eyes sweeping over my body.

"You know what?" she said. "I think we should just call it and go home, you're doing too much too soon."

"And let you win? No way. If you're winning, it's got to be fair."

"Or... hear me out." Stalking behind me, she dragged her hand up my arm, rubbing the back of my neck as she kissed me. She could be very convincing when she needed to be. "We just go and no one wins, no one loses," she said.

"You're good." I leaned forward, almost dropping the cue as I clutched my chest, and my movement didn't go unnoticed.

Frankie wrapped her arms around my waist. "I'm not kidding anymore, let me take you home. Please?"

"I'm gonna be fine." I kissed the top of her head, and she held me tighter.

"Someone once told me that's an overused word to hide how you really feel."

"Sounds like someone doesn't know what they're talking about." I laughed, but a gasp escaped, and she glared at me.

"I need you to be more than fine."

I rubbed her back, and she tilted her head back to look up at me. "What?" she asked.

"*Fine* is a promise to stay by your side for as long as you want me."

"Maybe I'll be the first habit you can't quit."

"You're not a habit, you're a choice... Best decision I've ever made." I shifted, trying to find a comfortable stance, but nothing was comfortable anymore.

Frankie placed her soft hand on my face, and I kissed her palm. "Rhett Marshall, I think you did it."

"What did I do?"

"Gave up the ridiculous notion that your life is too fucked up to deserve love... To deserve *me*. After everything that's happened, I don't regret us."

Holding the back of her head, I tangled my fingers in her hair. I would never let her go. "I love you." I teased her lower lip with my tongue, and she parted her lips for me as we kissed. Clasping my fingers around her waist, I gazed down at her face. "Being here with you feels good. Let's finish the game. I'm just sore, I'll rest later."

"Promise?"

I released her and bent over the table. "Promise." Scanning the pool table, I took aim, holding the cue stick positioned between the 'v' of my thumb and finger. "Ten-ball, side pocket."

She scrunched her face. "Your aim is way off, Rhett. Let me help you." Running her hand over my ass and up my back, she stood behind me, slightly on my left side. She trailed her fingers down my arm, matching them to mine on the pool cue.

Her touch distracted me from the pain, and I watched her closely, eager for her next move. I tilted my head to the side so that our faces were close and lowered my voice. "What are you doing?"

"Helping."

"I don't need help," I said as her fingers guided mine. I linked my thumb with hers, and she pulled away, smiling.

"Try hitting the ball to the right..." She repositioned my fingers, angling the cue to meet the ball. "Here." Holding her stance so her body was flush against mine, she locked her eyes on mine. "Eyes on the ball, baby," she said.

"I like this view better."

"Perfect, I win. Let's go home."

With a jerk of my head, I pulled back on the cue, striking the ball where she told me. It spun, sending the ten-ball toward the rail, dropping in the side pocket.

She laughed and finished her beer. "Good shot," she said.

"That was all you."

Snow covered the ground, and the smell of smoke from the Magpie's chimney hung in the cold air as we climbed into the truck.

"I'm freezing," Frankie said, cranking the heat as we drove away. "My place or yours tonight? I don't go back to work for a few more days, and I want to pretend real life doesn't exist for a little bit longer."

I had to tell her about the funeral. "Whatever you want... Frankie, I'm going to Boston tomorrow."

She stared straight ahead, her profile going in and out of darkness as we passed under the streetlights. "For his funeral. Are you sure that's a good idea?"

"No, but people are watching, and Vivian's right. We need to be there, they need to know we stand by each other. I'll go tomorrow and stay for a few days with her, make sure things are taken care of." I glanced over at her, and she looked at me. "I know it doesn't make sense—"

"Want me to go with you?"

"Fuck no. I mean, this has nothing to do with you, but baby, if the wrong people see you, knowing you put him in that coffin..." I shook my head. "It's too risky."

"Is it always going to be risky?"

I hesitated. The truth was yes. "It could be, but this is new for me, and Vivian. Two families fell apart almost overnight... I have no fucking idea, but all I know is risk." My eyes darted from the road to her. I couldn't lose her, not now. Not after everything. "I won't lie to you, I just don't know what's next. But I can't let Vivian do this alone."

I braced myself for the end. Frankie had been violated and broken, and I still hadn't found a way to offer her stability. She reached a hand across the truck and squeezed my leg. "Okay, Rhett. Do what you have to do, I just ask one thing."

"Anything," I said.

"Promise me you'll come back in one piece. And if something changes and you don't want this life with me anymore, tell me right away. Don't ever leave me hanging or waiting on you. Either you're in or you're out, but I need honesty, always."

I took her hand in mine and kissed each of her fingers. "I promise you. I'm yours, I'll always come back to you."

Frankie showed me how good life could be if I allowed myself to live without a constant need for escape. She made me feel like I belonged somewhere, without strings attached. That was what my mother had always wanted for me. Loyalty that grew from love, not obligation.

FIFTY-TWO

Frankie

I walked into the Magpie, shaking snow from my boots, and spotted my parents at a table near the fireplace. They shared an order of tacos from the food truck outside, and each had a beer in front of them, but Dad appeared steady in the chair. Taking my hat off, I ran my fingers through my hair and made my way toward them, cutting through a few tables bustling with conversation.

499

Lena waved to me from behind the bar, but neither of my parents noticed me. Dad's hand reached across the table, holding Mom's, and she smiled, tilting her head as he talked to her. I'd never seen them look so enamored with each other.

"Francesca!" Mom stood and embraced me as I approached, pulling out a chair. "Sit with us."

"You guys enjoy, I'm here to see Finn." I couldn't tear my eyes away as my father drank his beer. Nothing had changed, and the longer he sat there, the more someone would have to assist him to the car.

"It's my last one," he said, locking eyes with me.

"No, it isn't, Dad."

My mother sat back in her chair. "He's serious."

Shrugging my coat off, I sat closest to the fire, letting the heat warm me up. "You're going to rehab—"

"Absolutely not, I'm doing this my way."

The chair grated against the floor as I stood, mimicking my high hopes crashing. "Okay, enjoy the rest of your Sunday."

Dad grabbed my arm. "I've signed up for AA, my first meeting is tomorrow."

I flopped down in the seat, shock staggering me. Dad had never been to AA before. My hopes soared, and I braced myself for the crash. "The holidays are coming, what if it's too much?" We all struggled with Miles's loss the most through the holidays, and alcohol was my father's crutch this time of year.

"I won't let you down, Frankie," he said. "I need your support."

"You have it, you've always had it. I just can't fix it again when things fall apart, it hurts too much." My words had stolen their moment of peace, and I regretted them. Maybe this time really was different, and I would finally get my father back. "Of course I'll support you, we'll make it work."

This has to work.

My mother placed her hand on my face, touching the scar along my jawline where the stitches had been. "Are you doing okay?" With a worried frown, she dropped her hand. "Finn told me Rhett left for Boston this morning."

"His family needs him right now," I said, draping my coat across my lap. Moving forward with Rhett and navigating our separate worlds would take time and patience if our relationship had a chance of survival.

"Did you see the arrests they made because of that thing Miles had?" My father beamed, his eyes crinkling at the corners. "His life meant something, he really left his mark after all the fucked-up shit."

I had always seen the end of Miles's life as a tragedy, overshadowed by crime and addiction. I'd never considered the risk he had taken in his own way, bringing light to his dark world. The evidence he'd gathered had shattered years of unsolved investigations.

"I heard about them," I said, my thoughts drifting to the night in the cabin. Sleepless nights haunted me, and for the first time, I relied on anxiety medication. I had my first appointment scheduled with a therapist to unpack the gnawing trauma—I wasn't looking forward to it, but I needed to regain control of myself.

"Are you selling the cabin?" I asked.

My father picked up a taco, pulling the takeout box closer to catch the lettuce falling from the shell. "Hell no. Insurance is paying for the cleanup crew. I left the windows open to air out the bleach for four days after they left. I'm ripping up floors and walls, your mother's working with a contractor to do the renovations."

"We're revamping the place, but we are not selling, honey," Mom said. "No one will run us out of a home we spent years making memories in."

If I struggled with the cabin before, I sure as hell had no interest in returning now. Holding my coat and damp knit hat, I rose from the table. "I'm gonna go see Finn."

"Dinner tonight?" Mom asked. "Your father wants to cook, don't put me through that alone."

"You can't fuck up pizza," he said.

"Sure, why not." I bent down and gave her a quick hug, turning my attention to my father. "Cheers to your last drink, Dad." Walking away, I kept my gaze forward, not wanting to see his reaction. I also didn't believe for one minute that beer would be his last drink.

I pushed through the swinging gate and went behind the bar, passing Lena. "Please tell me you're going to my parents' for pizza tonight?"

She laughed as she spoke, pouring beer into a glass with the Magpie logo. "I'll be there."

Venturing out back, I found my brother talking with a staff member near pipes and tanks. He left them when he saw me, and we sat in the office.

"That looks interesting," I said. "There are more of those keg things."

"I'm trying a porter, adding to the pale ale and IPA." He stacked invoices into a pile. "The funeral is Tuesday?"

"Yeah." I took the seat against the wall, glancing out of the office door.

"You're anxious," he said.

"Is it that obvious?"

"To me it is."

I got up and shut the door, facing him. "It's just... he is going to a funeral for his father, and people will be there staring at a coffin holding the dead body of someone I killed, and I can't get past it."

"Would you rather the coffin hold the dead body of Rhett or you?"

"Jesus, Finn, of course not."

"When you can't let go of those thoughts, remind yourself of the alternative, that's all I'm saying." The chair creaked as he leaned back, tapping his thumbs on the armrest.

I paced the small room and sat back down.

"He'll be back for you, I know he will, but I'm not so sure he'll be able to walk away from everything like he thinks, Frankie."

Somehow, Finn could read me, speaking my deepest fears out loud. "I'm not so sure I can walk away from him if he doesn't," I muttered. "I'm not sure of anything right now—"

"Except you love him and he loves you."

His expression held the same deep concern as Mom's had a few moments ago. "That's right," I said, forcing myself to stop thinking. "Did you give your notice?"

"On Friday. I'll work until Christmas and be done. What about you? When do you go back to work?"

"Tomorrow." Work was the one thing I still had that remained part of who I was. "I need the distraction."

"Just don't bury yourself in it again, trust me. It changes you after a while."

"Look at you being all introspective. I like this side of you."

He glanced through the window beside the door. "I'm trying."

"Me too, Finn." I shifted in my seat as the staff person waved to him.

"I'm training Ash, they came in on a Sunday for this, so I gotta go, but I want to show you something first." Standing, he opened a safe inside the closet, retrieving a black velvet box and handed it to me. "Open it."

I lifted the lid to see a sparkling ring tucked in a satin cushion. A sudden giddiness took over as I tilted the box under the light. "You're actually going to do it? I am so proud of you." Flecks of black and white glittered inside the diamond, catching the light. "It's so unique and beautiful, it's bold and totally Lena." Carefully shutting the lid, I handed it back and hugged him. "She's going to love it, Finn. When are you proposing?"

"I rented a spot on the water in Rhode Island next weekend. I'm going to do the romantic thing, I'll figure it out."

"I know you will. Congratulations, I'm happy for you."

"She hasn't said yes, Frankie. Hold that thought." He tucked the ring away, locking the safe, and opened the office door. "Everything with Rhett will work out, and if it doesn't for whatever reason, I'll be here."

"I know you will."

A change had taken place over the past month, and the weight of having to fix everything had lifted off my shoulders. Maybe taking control of myself wasn't what I needed at all. Perhaps getting too close to death and taking a life had altered me in ways I could never undo, and what I really needed was to learn to live as the woman I'd become.

I left the bar, but instead of driving home, I parked near the grave-yard where Miles was buried. I didn't have flowers or anything to leave behind, and I'd never had the urge to return to my brother's grave, but something had shifted inside me when my father mentioned the risk Miles had taken.

Clouds hid the afternoon sun, and the frigid air chilled me through my coat. I pulled my hood over my hat, tucking my hair inside to keep the wind from whipping it around my face.

My footprints disturbed the snow-covered path as I trudged through the gate, reading the names and dates of death etched on a variety of stones. A crow perched on a tree branch next to Miles's grave. It cawed as it flew away, shaking snow from the tree in a flurry. I crouched in front of my brother's stone.

Brushing snow away, I traced his name, letting my numb fingers fall to the words we'd chosen for him.

If love could have saved you, you would've lived forever.

I swallowed past the dull ache of grief as it rose to my neck, settling along my jaw.

"I miss you," I whispered. "Not sure if you're still around or can hear me somehow, but I wanted you to know that." Tears rolled down my cold cheeks, melting into the snow as they fell. "I found the picture, thank you for trusting me... and excellent choice on the password by the way." A laugh escaped through my choked sobs. Kissing my palm, I sank my hand into the snow on the ground. "I'm sorry I didn't do more for you, Miles. I'll love you forever."

I stood still for a moment, my eyes closed, picturing his smile and hearing his laugh.

I had told my brother goodbye for the last time.

FIFTY-THREE

Rhett

I stood in the spacious living room of our father's brownstone in Beacon Hill. Vivian had taken over the house after he'd gone to jail. It had been in our family for decades and would be worth a damn fortune now. She had agreed to cater a fucking reception for our father with the stipulation that we hired extra security. Getting inside was like an airport search. The designer suit that Vivian had ready for me when I'd arrived yesterday was a trap disguised as luxury, tailored to fit, and *stuffy*. She'd been right about one thing. Standing together with a network of new allies, including Luca Noble, all knowing that a Morrigan's woman had taken Nash Morrigan out, had people on edge. The entire funeral and reception had *me* on edge.

Keeping my back to the wall and my gun hidden in a holster underneath my shirt, I loosened my tie and sipped whiskey. With his usual confident swagger, Luca strode toward me. The man was smaller than both me and Vivian's bodyguards, but he was *skilled*. Underestimating him had gotten people killed.

He fidgeted with his cufflinks, surveying the room. "Thanks for being here," he said.

I considered my words. He had made bold, calculated moves to gain my trust, but I still had my guard up around him. "I'm leaving as soon as this is done."

"Vivian needs you here at least until the end of the week."

Narrowing my gaze at him, I took another drink. "Then my sister can speak to me on her own."

He smoothed the sculpted lines of his mustache and goatee, covering his mouth as he talked. "You can change your name and leave town, but you can't run from who you are. You're a Morrigan, always have been, always will be." Dropping his hand, he toyed with the thick gold ring on his finger with another glance around the room. "You are needed, Rhett. The families are scattered, watching to see what your next move is. My uncle died at your hands, you're untouchable. Talk to Viv, she'll explain. Without you, the money stops, and trust me, no one wants that."

I'd suspected Vivian was holding back from telling me something, but our focus the past couple days had been on securing the shipyard and the house. "I'm keeping Frankie away, she doesn't belong here."

"She does now." Luca folded his arms across his chest as he faced me. "She's no longer the daughter of a cop family, she's a Morrigan's woman. They know who she is and what she did. No one will touch her again. That's a promise."

"We agree on one thing, Luca," I lowered my voice as two men I didn't recognize passed by the hallway. "No one will ever touch her again."

Nodding, he walked away. The Morrigan name would never belong to me again; I didn't want it. Downing the whiskey, I set my glass on the mantel and headed outside into the private backyard as people left through the front doors.

Zach smoked a joint near the fence, bundled in a winter coat. He glanced at me as I walked toward him, extending the joint. "Want some?"

"No, does your mother know about that?"

"She's cool with it."

Vivian had set the bar at an unreachable level for Zach, and I doubted that included any drugs or alcohol in her son's life. "Everything okay?" I asked.

He laughed, shivering. "Sure, everything's fine."

"*Fine*, right." I needed to get home to Frankie.

"Mom said you got a new tattoo yesterday. Can I see it?"

The new tattoo on my forearm blended seamlessly with the old one better than I had imagined possible. "Hold this." I handed Zach my suit jacket, and uncuffed the link freeing my wrist. Rolling my shirt sleeve, I gradually revealed a skull surrounded with roses intertwined together through the clear tape.

Zach leaned over my arm, scrutinizing the tattoo. "It's really gone." He straightened his back, his height matching mine. "What does it mean?"

"Freedom." I slid my sleeve back down. The skull symbolized the end of my old life, and the roses represented her—my future. I wanted to be Frankie's safe place.

He exhaled smoke from his lungs, filling the air with the pungent smell of weed. "Are you coming back?" he asked, putting out the joint against a stone light. "I'm going to Suffolk, taking business. I want to take over my grandfather's shipyard someday, but I won't run it like a fucking criminal."

"Why not do something for you, away from all this?"

"No way, look at that place, Rhett. You made a lot of money before you left, I want that too." He squinted the same way his mother did when she was determined to get what she wanted. "I think I can run it legally, no guns, drugs... *women*."

I snapped my head toward him. "How much do you know?"

"I asked Luca, and he told me the truth. Mom was pissed at him, but whatever."

"I told you not to smoke that shit." Vivian stepped outside with her arms crossed. Her bangs hung over her eyes, and she blew them out of her face. "It's freezing out here, coming in?"

Zach turned and headed for the door, pausing to look at me. "The tattoo is better, maybe I'll get one too."

If we weren't careful, Zach Morrigan would find himself on the same road I'd been on. "He's a good kid," I said as he went inside and shut the door.

"For now." My sister rubbed her arms, glancing around the yard. "I'm sure I've fucked him up somewhere along the way. College keeps him out of trouble. He's smart, like you."

"Don't let him have the business, Viv."

Her heels sank into the snow as she stepped onto the buried cobblestone. "Fuck, why are we out here?"

"It's better than in there."

She ran her hand over my suit jacket draped over my arm. "You're ruining this suit."

"I'll pay for it."

"Jesus, Rhett, I missed you. Luca said you're planning to go back tomorrow, but I need to tell you something that might change your mind."

"Nothing will change my mind, I'm going home."

She swept her bangs out of her eyes with her fingers. "This used to be your home."

I slipped my arms into my jacket. "A lot has changed."

"Dad neglected to update his will. The shipyard and the North End bar are yours."

"He'd never leave anything to me—"

"He'd have no choice if prison and death kept him from changing it." A sly smile crossed her face. "I'm not fighting the will, and you're not signing anything over to me or my son. This is your legacy. You built it just as much as he did, if not more." She grabbed the sides of my jacket, smoothing them out with a tug. "This is an opportunity that you should have. Build a life with that gorgeous woman of yours. Live in Willow Grove, it's close enough, but come back home and work your goddamn magic, Rhett. We'll keep you safe."

"What about Frankie? I can't bring her anywhere near this place."

Vivian stepped back, pursing her lips. "Make it known she's yours and no one will come near her." She patted my chest. "Fucking marry her and make her your wife if it makes you feel better."

I raked a hand through my hair. The only woman I wanted by my side was Francesca Roscoe, but she wouldn't want this life. Unless I rebuilt the business into something we could be proud of. I could protect our future, perhaps one day leave everything to my own kids—if I ever had them. Boston wasn't that far; I could make changes here and live a quiet life in Willow Grove.

A quiet life.

I'd spent the past week signing paperwork and settling the businesses left to me by my father. He'd probably haunt my ass from hell somewhere for his fuck-up. Frankie and I had messaged daily, but her replies had come slower, and she seemed distant. Something was wrong, and I needed to get back to her. I sped across town for one last stop before driving the hour back to Willow Grove.

It'd been almost three years since I had last visited the graveyard where Mom was buried. I was desperate to find a calm place for a few moments that could still my racing thoughts before facing Frankie again. I had to reassure myself that I wasn't a horrible, worthless asshole whose bad karma was about to catch up to him.

I parked the truck and walked through the iron gates. Being surrounded by the dead should've made me feel uneasy, but it didn't. The silence of the graveyard allowed me to think. I passed the rows of headstones with worn names engraved, focusing on the tallest monument beside the elm tree. That's where my mother had been laid to rest.

Standing on the small piece of land where her body remained deep beneath me, I bent down and placed my hand on the cold stone. I ran my fingers over her name, Beth Marshall, silently reading the inscription she'd chosen herself.

The song has ended, but my melody will forever linger.

"Hey, Mom." I looked around, pulling the hood of my sweater over my head as a gust of wind blew. "I met a woman, she's amazing. I wish you could've known her. She plays the piano like an angel—I'm gonna buy her one—and I think she might like jazz as much as I do." *Fuck.* What was I doing? I exhaled. "I didn't turn out like you hoped I would, but I'll do better. I have to for *her*. I'm going home now."

I stood and wiped my eyes as they filled with tears. Jesus Christ, I had a hard time with emotions. I shoved my hands in my pockets and grabbed my keys. "I love you, Mom."

As I walked away, I took a shaky breath. My lungs filled with cold air, soothing the lingering burn from the bullet. I was starting over and wouldn't be alone anymore. I had her and would do whatever she needed to earn her trust and build a life together.

FIFTY-FOUR

Frankie

S now drifted softly, but I carried my jacket, welcoming the cold night air on my sweaty skin as I walked to my Jeep. The past thirteen hours had been a marathon in the ER, and the chill numbed my frazzled nerves. I couldn't handle domestic cases like I used to, not anymore. Anxiety had moved in and crawled its way to the surface at the first sign of a battered woman. Zoey had tried to convince me to take more sick leave, and I'd resisted, but the past week back at work had been a struggle.

Checking the backseat and the parked cars surrounding me, I got in my Jeep and locked the doors. Goosebumps replaced the pleasant chill, and I cranked the heat and switched on a jazz playlist. Rhett's promises to return had stretched from two days, to four, to over a week, with no end to his absence in sight. Maybe he'd changed his mind and would never come back. He hadn't said those words, but my expectations for our new life together dwindled by the day. Anger and hurt battled for dominance in my emotional chaos, and heartbreak patiently waited to step in.

Breathe. Stop creating drama when nothing's happened. Rhett loves me, that hasn't changed...or has it?

I drove home on autopilot, and a weight settled in my chest as I pulled into the garage and stole a quick glance at Rhett's darkened, quiet house next door. I went inside, turning all the lights on—a new routine I'd adapted—and headed upstairs to shower and climb into the softest pajamas I owned.

I caught my reflection in the mirror while I was blow-drying my hair and shut it off, running my fingers through the damp strands as I looked at myself. The bruises had all but disappeared, leaving behind areas of faded yellow and brown. Lifting my shirt, I inspected the thick red scars along my chest and torso where the knife had broken my skin. Those scars might fade to silver but would forever be a part of my body.

But I survived, and so did he.

With a sigh, I padded downstairs and poured a glass of wine. The snow fell heavier, sliding down the window. I plugged in the strand of holiday lights I'd hung outside, and the vibrant colors against the snow gave me a glimmer of happiness. I shoved my feet into a pair of rubber-soled slippers, and stepped outside, inhaling the smell of winter.

As I stood under the overhang, jazz music drifted from next door, and my heart raced. I sipped my wine, savoring the sweet warmth, and checked my phone. Rhett had returned home but hadn't told me?

Boots echoed on the steps next door, followed by the scraping of a shovel. I peered through the lattice as Rhett cleared a path leading to my place. I wanted to run and throw myself into his arms, but the need to know if he was still *with* me was stronger.

He shoveled snow off my bottom step and glanced up. "Hi, baby." The yearning and warmth on his face melted me, and by some miracle I didn't give in to the desperate need pulling me toward him.

"When did you get back?"

"Not long ago." Setting the shovel against the railing, he took a few steps closer, but I held my stance.

I refused to let him make me look like a fool if he'd come back to Willow Grove to break the news he wasn't staying. "Are you here to say goodbye?" I narrowed my eyes, my fingers tightening around the glass.

He hurried up the stairs, meeting me under the overhang as snow swirled around us, and held my face in his hands. "I'm here to ask you to join me at my place. I missed you."

A smile I had no control over tugged at my lips. "Your hands are *freezing*."

"I shoveled, forgot my gloves."

"You don't forget things." I covered his hand with mine, almost spilling my wine.

"Not the important things. Will you come with me?"

Practicality emerged out of nowhere, warning me not to let him break my heart. "How long are you in town, Rhett?"

"For good." His brow furrowed as his gaze swept over me. "Do you need a coat? Boots? Or should I just carry you to my place?"

"Carry me? Really."

He held out his arms. "*Really*. I need to talk to you, Frankie. I want to make plans with you."

"You're sticking around long enough to do that?" Heat rushed to my cheeks. I wanted him in my arms so badly I could hardly stand being apart from him.

"I found a place I want to stick around." His forehead creased as he ran a hand through his hair. "My father didn't change his will, and the shipyard is mine. His business is in my name, my hands." He started pacing on the small deck, glancing at me as I collected my thoughts.

Finn had told me he didn't think Rhett could walk away, and perhaps my brother had been right. But I never wanted Rhett to give up who he was or where he'd come from for me. Right or wrong, those were the things that made him the man I'd fallen in love with. "I don't understand. How can you stay here?"

"I'll figure it out, travel when I need to, but I don't want to do this unless you're with me. If that isn't something you can do, I'm going to give it all to Vivian."

"No! I would never ask you to do that. I don't do ultimatums, Rhett. It's yours, you've earned this." He couldn't give up what he'd sacrificed *himself* for. "I never expected to feel like this for someone, and I was worried you might not come back to me. I thought if I could just go back to my life before I met you, maybe it wouldn't hurt so much, but that's impossible." I set my wine on the table and brushed snow from his hair. "I've done things, we both have, and everything's changed, including me. Maybe I should be miserable about it, but I'm not. Whatever your life is, I want to be in it."

He reached up and rubbed my arms as I wrapped them around his neck. "For so long I believed the only way to survive was to disappear... to be alone. I didn't plan on *you*. You see me, all the darkness, the fucking mess, and you make me feel alive without trying. So, yeah, baby. I can stick around. I just hope you still want me even half as much as I *need you*."

I held him closer, my mouth claiming his. I needed him, all of him. His hand found the back of my neck, and he embraced me, his mouth owning mine right back. Pulling away, he looked at my lips, lingering for a moment before his eyes met mine. He traced the spot on my lip that had been tender and swollen. "Was I too rough? Does it still hurt?"

"It's much better. My body is better, it's just..." I pointed at my head. "I'm working through some things."

He kissed my head. "Come home with me, please."

"Did you put the heat on over there?" I teased, shaking snow out of my hair.

"It's warm, I promise."

"All right, I'm coming." I brought my glass inside and grabbed my coat and boots. Stepping outside, I blinked away the snow as it fell on my lashes. "I didn't plan on you either, but somehow you get me. You make it hard to walk away."

"Good, happy to hear it." He smiled and a familiar warmth spread through me. But it wasn't just Rhett's charm like the day we'd met in the coffee shop. That initial spark between us had shifted into promises I trusted he would keep.

We trudged through the snow together and settled inside his place. I draped my coat on the back of a chair, grabbing his arm as he took off his jacket. He had a new tattoo. I ran my fingers over the ink on his forearm. "It's scabbed, how long ago did you get this done?"

"It was the first thing I did when I got back to Boston."

Tilting his arm at an angle underneath the light, I traced the lines of the skull and detailed roses. "There's nothing left of the man that was there."

"It's still in there somewhere, just different."

"What does it mean?" I asked,

"The end of my old life, the beginning of a new one... something beautiful, not so dark." His fingers brushed against mine as he touched the roses on his arm. "They're supposed to be Francesca roses. They might not be exact, but that's what this is to me."

He'd gotten a tattoo that symbolized *us*. Tears filled my eyes, and I hugged him as tightly as my arms allowed.

He cradled the back of my head. "I love you, Frankie. I don't want a life without you in it, I just don't know what that's gonna look like."

"Maybe we're not supposed to know yet." But the doubt I'd clung to earlier was gone, replaced with certainty. We were in this *together*.

Rhett caressed my lower back as we kissed, sliding his hands down my hips to squeeze my ass. "I've got a promise to make good on."

"Yes please." I craved his touch, and the anticipation of making love to him unraveled every nerve in my body.

He led me upstairs toward his bedroom, but we stopped in the doorway, kissing like we needed each other's air. Rhett's tongue found mine, and our gasps mingled into one breath. I clung to his shirt, tugging the fabric, desperate to bring him closer. In this moment, nothing else mattered, nothing existed except Rhett and me.

Wrapping an arm around my waist, he pressed himself against me, and I clasped my hands together at the back of his neck. He moved his hand slowly along my stomach, slipping underneath my sweater. My breath caught in my throat as he grasped my breasts. "I want you to be mine tonight," he murmured against my ear.

"Not just tonight."

Reaching behind his head, he took hold of my wrists and pinned them above my head. Our eyes locked, and he rubbed circles on my hand with his thumb. His grip slackened, but he tensed against me. "Is this okay?"

I could *feel* the profound worry radiating from him, and curled my fingers over his. "More than okay." My chest heaved with ragged breaths. I wanted more of his touch. It was gentle and safe, nothing like the trauma I'd gone through. "I trust you, Rhett."

His other hand traveled down my body, and arousal pulsed between my thighs. I whimpered as his mouth collided with mine. Loosening the ties of my pajama pants, he dragged his fingers along my waistband and stopped.

"What's wrong?" I broke our kiss, tilting my head back.

"No panties? You are sexy, Frankie." He was hard against my leg, but I'd surrendered to him. And as much as I wanted to, I couldn't touch him.

Spreading my legs, I spoke in gasps. "Touch me."

He slid his hand down my pants, massaging the top of my leg as he braced me against the wall. Trailing his fingers along the inside of my thigh, he grazed them between my legs, and I moaned. No longer able to think, my body moved against him instinctively.

"Do you have any idea what you do to me?" His lips skimmed along my throat, meeting mine, and he kissed me slower this time.

"Do you have any idea what you're doing to *me*?" I breathed against his mouth.

He pushed my pants down my thighs, and they dropped to the floor. My head fell back against the wall as he plunged two fingers inside me, eliciting another uncontrollable moan. "I do now," he said, releasing my hands. He tilted my chin up. "Look at me, baby."

I stared into his intense, dark gaze as he slowly pulled his fingers away from me. "I *missed* you," he said. "I need you. *Now*." He picked me up in his arms, and I wrapped my legs around his waist.

"It's about time." I cupped his face in my hands. "I've missed you, this... *us*."

Stepping away from the wall, he carried me to his bed. As he lifted my sweater over my head, his touch lingered on my skin, triggering a wave of shivers through me. I followed his gaze down my naked body. Light from the hallway gleamed on the jagged scars marring my chest and torso. A cold sweat broke out on the back of my neck, and my heart pounded. I was painfully aware of the damage to my body and mind that would never leave me. "These will never go away," I whispered, folding my arms across myself.

Tugging his shirt off, Rhett slid his jeans and boxers down, kicking them to the side. Faded bruises covered his body in patches, and he ran a hand over the scars on his chest. "They just mean you got through something painful, Frankie." He laced his fingers with mine, gently prying my arms apart. "I wish you could see yourself the way I do. You're perfect, all I see is *you*."

I kissed the scars on his chest, drifting over the bumpy texture left by the bullet. I had almost lost the love of my life, but he was here in my arms, adoring every part of me. My lips found their way to his. "I love you."

He lowered me onto the bed and pulled a blanket over us. "I love you too." His lips swept along my skin as he kissed each of my scars.

I held him closer as he settled himself between my legs, and his fingers wound in my hair as he kissed me. Unhurried, tender. All-consuming in the most desirable, can't-live-without-each-other way.

As he lifted his head, our eyes connected like an unseen tether bonding us together. "Make love to me, Rhett."

He smiled, his nose brushing mine. "I would love nothing more." A strained groan that matched mine escaped him as he pushed inside me.

I anchored myself to him with my legs, coaxing him deeper. We moved slowly at first, holding each other, building faster, matching each other's pace... Until we *let go* together.

I snuggled into the crook of his arm after we finished, and he kissed me. "Are you hungry?" he asked.

"*Starving.*"

"Good. I got something for you."

I sat on a stool at Rhett's counter wearing his sweater as he made me tea. He grabbed a large platter from the fridge and placed it in front of me.

"Charcuterie board?" I asked.

"I wish I could say I put all this together, but I bought it."

"Local place near our coffee shop?"

"That's the one."

A spread of cheese, crackers, deli meats, grapes, olives and jams adorned the plate. "It's too pretty to eat," I said.

He popped a piece of cheese and a pepperoni in his mouth. "Nope, have some. And for dessert..."

"There's dessert?" I sipped the tea, savoring the warmth as he opened a box and angled it toward me.

Two flaky Danishes sat inside, one blueberry and the other raspberry. I plucked the raspberry pastry from the box and handed it to him, and he gave me the blueberry one.

"Cheers," I said raising my Danish.

"Cheers, baby." He tapped his against mine, and we each took a bite.

Rhett and I lay in bed talking for hours about music, food, growing up in such different worlds, and the conversation shifted to his father's business... *Rhett's* business.

With my head against his chest, I looked up at him. "Do you think you'll be able to let go of the illegal stuff? Serious question."

"Serious answer... I don't know. My plan is to run the business the same way I had Vivian take care of things while I was gone, but—"

"There it is. *But.*"

His fingers traced along my back. "She made deals I need to look at."

"Do you want to get out of the dark side of your father's business, or not? The *truth*, Rhett."

He kissed my forehead. "I want out. That's the truth. I'm just not sure how to do that—all I've ever heard was there is *no way out*. But I promise you I'm going to make it work."

"Maybe I can help?"

He lifted his head, and his forehead creased. "No way, I can't let you get involved—"

"You told me you only wanted this if I was with you, well, this is me, *with* you. That's all I'm saying."

"Frankie, I promise to let you do whatever you want, but the second someone threatens you, I'm stepping in." His head rested back on the pillow. "That's all *I'm* saying."

"It's a good thing I'm a Morrigan's woman." The words tumbled out of my mouth naturally, easily. *Too easily.*

There was no tension between us, no lies... There were no secrets between us anymore. We'd shattered those.

Rhett's Tattoo

"The skull symbolized the end of my old life, and the roses represented her—my future."

Artist: Whitney Law of New Ink
Book Services

Acknowledgments

The first person I want to mention is Brenda Pickering. Not only is she one of the best trauma nurses I know, she's also a long-time friend. Thank you for letting me ask all my many graphic medical questions, and for never holding back. Your experienced nursing perspective helped me bring authenticity to Frankie's scenes in a way that no research could've done.

My Beta Reader Group—Barb, Suzi, Cyndi, Nishell, Kamy, and my lovely PA, Nina. Thank you for letting me trust you with my book before anyone else laid eyes on it, and for taking the time to read this manuscript in its early stage. Your valuable feedback means the world to me.

I had debated bringing together an official street team for a while, but truthfully, I wondered if I'd find people willing to jump into my author world. I couldn't have been more wrong. To the supportive group of readers on my author Street Team, I appreciate each one of you more than I have words, and I love wording! Your enthusiasm for ARC reading, sharing and creating content for my books is a dream come true. *Thank you* isn't a big enough statement, but please always know how appreciated you are.

I'm grateful to my family for still loving me (and making me sandwiches) when I lock myself away, sometimes shutting them out for hours... *days* to meet a deadline. When I started brainstorming this book, one person listened to me constantly ramble about my characters, the town of Willow Grove, and helped me give depth to the bad guys. He literally got out a notepad and wrote ideas, even drawing a map to help me narrow down specific details I couldn't see clearly in my mind. Roman, my own six-foot-six, bearded, tattooed man, thanks for letting me consume your time with this story. Get ready for book two...

Tess Watters, you're a talented author without question, but your friendship in this wild business has kept me going. Thanks for being a sounding board for all things life, writing and crafting those spicy scenes. I swear your encouragement keeps me sane through the writing process. Thank you for always cheering me on and proofreading the final manuscript. So grateful for you!

Writing five books has taught me a lot about the editing process, but I couldn't have gotten this far without Kayla Ramoutar, my editor, who challenges me to elevate my writing more every time we work together. The way you teach through your editor's notes, along with your suggestions, have helped me give this story my absolute best. *Thank you.*

I'm a visual person who sees the story unfold in my mind as I write, like a movie. Working with real bookish artists to bring those images to life feels like *breathing*. I have been so unbelievably fortunate to work with amazing artists, one of which drew the character art displayed at the end of the book of Frankie & Rhett.

This was my third time working with Anastasia (@mirolubova_art on Instagram), but stay-tuned for future art from this talented artist, I'm definitely a tad obsessed.

I wanted a book cover that displayed a few symbols from the story, adding to the mystery with "easter eggs", and Gigi of @heygigicreatives delivered. Gigi, you are so patient, kind, and I'm looking forward to what you bring to book two in this series!

I'll always return to Whitney Law (@newinkbookservices on Instagram) for chapter headers, but she was the first artist I turned to when I knew a Magpie logo and Rhett's new tattoo at the end of the book required its very own art. I am so grateful for you.

It's fascinating that I can write a whole book, and yet, those 160-ish words capturing the essence of the story on the back feels just about impossible. A special nod to Jessie Cunniffe (@bookblubmagic on Instagram) for your book blurb assistance and audits. I adored collaborating with you. I wanted to sharpen those skills, and you helped me learn, as well as offer advice I will take with me for the next book.

Writing is solitary, it really is, but when I need to be reminded that I'm not failing when I feel like I am, or that the stories I dream up really are worth sharing, the bookish community shows up, sometimes when I'm not expecting it, but need them so much. I've connected with readers and authors, other writers... people who understand how important art and storytelling will forever be. My passion keeps me moving forward in this author gig, but you lift me up when I feel low.

What I really want to say is *thank you* for being here and turning these pages filled with the dark and light, danger, intrigue, romance, love, sexy time, and everything in between. I sure hope you stick around for the next book in the Willow Grove series...

Your author friend,

Angela

Also by Angela van Liempt

Launch into an upper young adult paranormal mystery, the Atlas Cliffs series.
Ghosts, witchy magic, found family, and romance.

And an Atlas Cliffs series prequel:

Angela van Liempt is a small-town girl with big dreams. Music inspires her and she creates a playlist for every book she writes. Romance, yearning, and love will always be woven into her stories, and after completing a young adult paranormal mystery series, she's excited to embrace a new genre.

The Willow Grove series will begin her journey into spicy romantic suspense, and she can't wait to share more of this dark, contemporary world.

A lover of the ocean, full moons, and sunsets, she'd choose to be barefoot on a beach any day over big city life. Escaping into fictional coastal towns with characters who feel like real people is one of her favorite pastimes.

Follow for writing updates, book playlists and more!
https://www.dawn-publishing.com/
https://linktr.ee/angeladvl

www.ingramcontent.com/pod-product-compliance
Lightning Source LLC
Chambersburg PA
CBHW020239120726
47904CB00001B/24